INVERCLYDE LIBRARIES

By Adam Nevill

Banquet for the Damned

Apartment 16

The Ritual

Last Days

House of Small Shadows

ADAM NEVILL

Banquet for the Damned

First published 2004 by PS Publishing Ltd

This edition published 2014 by Pan Books
an imprint of Pan Macmillan, a division of Macmillan Publishers Limited
Pan Macmillan, 20 New Wharf Road, London N1 9RR
Basingstoke and Oxford
Associated companies throughout the world
www.panmacmillan.com

ISBN 978-1-4472-4092-1

1 3 5 7 9 8 6 4 2

A CIP catalogue record for this book is available from the British Library.

Typeset by Ellipsis Digital Limited, Glasgow
Printed and bound by CPI Group (UK) Ltd, Croydon, CR0 4YY

Visit www.panmacmillan.com to read more about all our books
and to buy them. You will also find features, author interviews and
news of any author events, and you can sign up for e-newsletters
so that you're always first to hear about our new releases.

For Clive Nevill

From castles built of bones comes unknown music.
Arthur Rimbaud

ONE

It is a night empty of cloud and as still as space.

Alone, a young man walks across a deserted beach. His eyes are vacant and his mouth is loose. The steps of his unlaced boots in the sand are slow, as if they are taken under duress, or as if he is being led.

Guided away from the jagged skyline of St Andrews town, he moves west toward the Eden Estuary and the Tentsmuir Forest beyond, until the distant streetlights become nothing more than specks winking at his back. As if beckoned, he then moves to the base of the dunes, where the shadows are long and the sand cold.

Suddenly, he stops walking and makes the sound of a man surprised by the touch of a hand from behind, or by the appearance of a figure at his side. He loses balance on his trawling legs, staggers backward and drops to a sitting position.

He dips his head and then raises its weight on a neck made weak by sleep. Reaching his hands out, he fists the sand. It feels wet against his dry palms. Blinking sticky eyelids, he sucks all the air he can into his lungs. Acids churn in his empty stomach and his heart starts to thump. Slowly, he lifts his face to the sky. His eyes widen. A dark but clear canopy of night comes into focus and a fuller awakening hits and spreads throughout his body. Some of the numbness in his walk-warmed muscles goes right away, some of it stays, like in his gums and in his tongue, where the air has come in through parted lips.

Glancing about, he sees small waves from the North Sea lap and fizz against the shoreline. To his left stand the sand dunes, shadowy humps with sparse grasses growing upon their round summits, through which the lights of a hotel flicker yellow and orange in the distant hills.

Confused and alarmed, his mind peels itself from the final wrappings of sleep. Standing up, he struggles to keep his feet and looks down to discover that dressing has been hurried and incomplete. Beneath the padded jacket his naked skin slides against the coat's lining. Under his jeans there is no underwear and his naked toes wiggle inside a big and empty space until they touch smooth hide. No socks.

Shivers prickle his skin, though they are not caused by the midnight chill at sea level, and fear tightens his scrotum. Through the mess of his mind comes the memory of his mother's hands reaching down to collect him from the floor outside of an airing cupboard. She'd often recount the story to guests at Christmas: how her little boy would sleepwalk and be found mumbling about the crows. Relief dares to enter the young man's mind. He's not been sleepwalking for years, but that's all it is. A sleepwalk, so there is no need to panic, it's nothing.

Deep breaths are taken. His heart feels fit to burst. His voice is weak but talking aloud to himself adds something real to this undefined night. 'Walter, relax. Take it easy. Just relax.'

The idea of dressing and walking a mile from the Andrew Melville Hall of Residence to the West Sands is difficult for him to understand. It is such a distance and no one stopped him. A frost sews across his stomach lining at the thought of wandering across all of the roads and passing the deep waters of a high tide to reach these far sands.

Trapped in the dark, somewhere between late evening and the lightening of dawn, he looks for the time. His wrist is bare. But as he raises his hand and swats away a quilted sleeve, desperate to see the luminous digits and hands of his watch, he becomes aware of something on the lapel of his jacket and he begins to sniff. It is perfume. But he has no recollection of the pale arms that touched him there.

Standing still, Walter rewinds his memory back to the last time he was awake. Anxiety about a deadline on his *King Lear* thesis bustles inside him. That's right: he'd been working late in his room, well past twelve. Did he turn the computer off? He can't remember. But as he worked past midnight, his eyelids grew heavier and his head nodded over the desk until, without choice, his exhausted body took him to bed. Sleep had arrived quickly. And so had the dream.

The dream.

A vague dream where something appeared in his room close to the bed. His recall is hazy, but the experience seems familiar. At first the figure would just watch him. Then it would whisper something he could never understand. Finally, it would reach out and paw, more than touch, the lump of his body under the bedclothes. But was the dream a singular experience, and did it only now seem to have recurred over successive nights? He doesn't know, but stress makes sleep go bad, and there seem to have been so many nightmares lately, in tune, perhaps, with his worrying about the thesis.

'Walter.'

3

He starts and then turns to the dunes. Nothing to see, nothing moving up there, just the black humps of sand and the spikes of grass outlined against the star-dotted sky.

'Walter.'

Again, there it is. Quieter this time, as if the speaker is moving away from him with a note of insistence to her tone. It's a woman's voice, mature but soft, and makes him think of a mother who has called her child to dinner. Thinking of the perfume, Walter says, 'Who's there?'

No one answers.

'Walter.' A voice at his back. This time it's younger, but still female, and it swoops at him from above and behind. Quickly, Walter turns and raises a hand to fend off something he's sure is speeding towards him.

But there is no one on the expanse of moon-white sand. Down to the harbour wall, at the foot of the town, he sees acres of beach where the shallows scrape, white-topped, and withdraw back to the sea. The water looks inky and the horizon is lost against the sky. He can smell brine, fishy foams and the fresh slap of spray. But he sees no one.

He hears a tremor in his own voice. 'Who are you?'

Amidst the roar and swish of the surf, a far-off bell clangs on a buoy, but no voice will answer him. Sucking more of the salty air into his lungs, he takes a nervous step away from the dunes and looks, anxiously, toward the town. Returning to the flat to drink coffee, and to light a fag, and to tell someone – anyone – in the morning, is all he can think of now. But then, from a third location, close but lost to his eyes, a third woman cries, 'Walter!'

'Shit,' he whispers, and wants to push the voice back into the mouth it left. It was a command. It insisted on his attention and it was not polite. His jeans cling to weightless legs and his strength drains through his shoes and into the cold sand.

Could be a hoax. Some pranksters could be hiding in the dunes right now, who have seen him sleepwalking and have decided to give him a fright. Enough is enough.

'Cut it out!' he shouts.

Silence.

'Who's there?' he says in a voice that falters, and then he jogs away from the dunes, wanting to be in the middle of the beach where there is more light. And as he does this, there is only the melody of the waves and the distant sound of a car to accompany him. And he envies the driver, far off, as he glides between the houses, under the streetlights and past the shopfronts.

'Walter, he's here for you,' the first voice, the mother's voice, whispers through the dune grass. 'Won't be long now, sweetheart. He's here just for you.'

Not wanting to understand what she says, Walter turns and then runs across his own smeared footprints, that he could not remember taking, back toward town. But his legs refuse to pump quickly enough inside leaden jeans, and the rest of his body feels bulky and useless and slow. A glance over his shoulder cannot be resisted.

There's movement in the sand dunes. He stops running and a cry dies before it leaves his throat. It's there for only a moment. A long shape, twice the height of a man. The head is covered but cranes forward as if to probe at the air. Then, the raggedy thing folds away into shadow.

He shakes his head and in his mouth he can taste rust and phlegm. Instantly he knows any attempt at escape would be

5

pure moon-lit slow motion. A cold wind picks up a strand of hair from his fringe. 'Please,' he says, and begins to stagger backward while his eyes scour the dunes for the silhouette that has slowed the blood inside him.

A quick and sudden motion, further down the beach, of something moving fast across the sand on all fours, catches his eye and he yanks his head around to look. But it's gone so quickly, as if it were nothing more than a shimmer at the edge of his sight. The movement occurred up in the dunes, parallel to a point on the beach he would have reached had he kept on running. It was cutting him off. Sweat turns to shivers.

How had it moved so quickly – from behind him to so far down the beach? But there's always an explanation for every strange sight. Could it be nothing more than the shadow of Venus, or the movement of matter in the eyeball's aqueous humour? 'Christ, this is not happening to me.'

'Walter. Walter. Walter.' Three voices form a chorus behind the dunes, their cries led by the younger woman who screams his name into the sky. And before the cold starry heavens, something thin rises again from the dunes to stand upright and look down at him.

Walter turns and runs for the sea.

Instinctively, he thinks it won't follow and that the long blanket of bitter water will offer a haven if only he can reach it. Now his heart is up between his ears, and there is a pain in one lung, and his knees knock together as if the cross-country race on a winter's morning has just begun. From behind he hears sharp feet flit down the side of the dunes to take up a quick and purposeful stride across the flat sand.

And the flapping of whatever cloth is twisted about its length grows louder as the distance between them is closed.

Walter runs for all he is worth, losing a boot but never able to look behind again. And soon his feet skitter through the thin watery ice the sea has left after the waves retreat back into the liquid universe of splashes and sparkles and white foamy tips, and where the air is cold enough to make his ears ache inside. And he plunges through the shallows and slides to the deeps, lurching forward, until the cut of the freeze rises above his knees and into his thighs.

As he is poised to scream, the temperature of the water steals his breath and froths with quicksand tugs about his heavy hips. His arms sweep about and clutch for balance. His spine twists. Deafened by the noise of his explosive path, he wrenches his legs high but not clear of the surface, and then plunges them down, deeper, onward, out there, further into the sea.

Something ploughs through his wake. Is it the sea-spray or does it hiss? He feels its presence, its proximity, in the tips of his ears and at the ends of his hair. And before he can decide to face it and to steady his feet for the grapple, it looms up, then down, and he is covered in a heartbeat. He seems to dance with it for a second – two shadows in a drunken piggyback ride – before he plunges through the icy surface of the sea with it all about him.

TWO

'You're going to miss this place, mate,' Tom shouts over the judders and roar of the speeding Land Rover.

'Yeah, like toothache,' Dante replies, his concentration split between driving, thinking, and now Tom's jabber. He wants to dwell, uninterrupted, on the city where he's spent most of his adult life, the city he feels he is leaving with few regrets, besides taking his best friend along.

Birmingham dwindles behind him in the rear-view mirror and he feels it was never a city indifferent or unkind to him. They were comfortable in their squalid life. But the city of their birth and childhood and teens and early twenties wants them to remain with the other musicians, bums and losers of the rock scene, floundering in the shallows of a tide long gone out. Too late for a second start, his instincts suggest. The groaning activity in his stomach, caused by his doubts about driving four hundred miles to depend on an old man he's never met, reinforces this suspicion.

And the statistics are not good. Every other band and musician they know who attempted to leave the Midlands returned home in anything between a month and a year to scratch around again. Some came back with babies and girls with strong accents, some with suntans and new tattoos, and some even returned with short hair. But no one seemed to escape the lifestyle it was so easy to slip into at eighteen and impossible to leave once you passed twenty-five. Or perhaps this insecurity is just the result of waking early, fleeing a house you owe rent on, and then staring at your entire collection of earthly things in plastic bin liners strewn across the chipped and dusty floor of an old Land Rover. It is hard to tell.

Out the side of his eye, Dante can see Tom fidgeting. His seat belt remains unfastened, cassette cases are littered around his footwell, and his scuffed boots are planted on the dashboard where the green paint is worn down to brown metal. 'God ran out of everything but horseshit when he gave you brains,' Dante says, without turning his head.

Tom frowns and pushes his head forward, over the gearstick, with a familiar what-did-you-say? expression on his face. Dante says nothing. He checks the rear-view mirror, and then glances at the fuel gauge beside the broken speedometer, making sure his eyes only leave the road for a second. In a 1969 Lightweight Land Rover with no midships, anything beyond a second's distraction can be fatal. A white van, with a ladder tied loose on the roof, overtakes them on the inside lane before cutting across the Land Rover's square nose. Dante brakes and then listens to their luggage begin an uneasy slide behind his seat.

'Do your bloody belt up. Jesus!' he shouts, and gives Tom his best look of disapproval.

Tom grins. 'When you left home you forgot something.' He raises two fingers. 'You left these!'

Dante sweeps the de-mister sponge off the steering column, which is heavy with dew, and throws it against the side of Tom's head. There is a wet slap from the chamois leather as it blasts off the side of Tom's face. Dante roars with laughter at the success of his shot. Tom's arm, tight in biker leather, rises to deliver the retaliation. 'Don't!' Dante shouts, but his cries become laughter. Should have known better. The sponge hits his left ear. It feels like a cow has kissed the side of his head. 'Stupid bastard!' he screams through his laughter, and begins a fight to control the Land Rover as it swerves on the approach to Spaghetti Junction.

'For fuck's sake!' Tom yells, his voice slipping into laughter. 'We're only five miles from Northfield and you've nearly crashed the War Wagon. Should have let me drive the first leg.'

'Should've left you behind! Look at this bloody mess. You've got cassettes out of their cases, ash all over the friggin' luggage, and you've eaten half the fucking food. And close that bloody window! It's cold enough in here without you freezing my nads off.'

'Who are you, my mother?'

'Damn right. Mother, father, priest, analyst.'

'You're just pissed because I get the chicks.'

'That's right, hundreds of screaming chicks who knock on the door at midnight, crying. Or phone every twenty minutes. I can do without that, mate. This is a new start, I've told you. Any of that crap and you're on the first train home.'

Music begins to drown him out. Guitar sounds crunch from four speakers and drum rhythms thunder around the cabin. It feels like the hits on the snare drum are interfering with his breathing. Tom lights another Marlboro and winks at him through the smoke. Then he fidgets on his seat and shakes his mane loose from neck to waist. On only one occasion in their long friendship has he seen Tom get serious enough not to fool around. It takes a death to rattle Tom.

He's about to say *You're not going to ruin this*. But he stops himself, remembering a vow against dwelling on Tom's philandering. It'll get him nowhere. Just accept it and let it go. Remember your purpose and focus on it, that's what Eliot Coldwell says – his mentor, his second chance, a man he would drive to the ends of the earth to meet. But whenever Tom so much as hints at his sexual history, his recollection stubbornly winds back to Imogen, Tom's most recent girlfriend. And the thought of her freezes Dante's stomach, and his notion of loyalty and brotherhood is challenged.

He shakes his head and whispers, 'Fuck it.' To think Tom's success with women used to make him a little proud. But now it only makes him think of Imogen – the woman he'd waited his whole life to meet, who fell in love with Tom. It was instant and obligatory.

In the Land Rover cabin, the music begins to die. One of Tom's tanned hands, the fingers heavy with silver rings, swivels the volume dial down. 'I love the summer!' he shouts, and frees his camera from a leather case. 'So much light. Look at this, 5 a.m., and I can take a picture of Birmingham. Something to remind you of home.' He winks and reaches across the handbrake to slap Dante's thigh. Clambering to his knees and then shuffling about-face, he photographs the apricot light that smoulders behind the black chimneys, lonesome spires and cuboid flats as Birmingham fades behind them, all set to a shimmer by the rattle of the Land Rover's passage across the tarmac.

Dante hits the stereo EJECT button and flips the Metal

Church cassette onto the floor: too early for speed. That could keep him awake later. After searching for an alternative, he pulls one of the few remaining cassettes out of the rack and holds it before the big steering wheel to read the label.

AC/DC: *Highway to Hell*.

'Perfect,' he whispers, and slots the cassette into the stereo.

Dante stops at the Preston services at 9 a.m. His vision shakes, his buttocks burn, and his jaw is frozen. The War Wagon has no consideration for passengers. It is a piece of machinery craving short bursts on muddy fields, but they have given it four hundred miles of motorway to rattle across. They try to counteract the engine noise with music, and that only deafens them.

A shaky wheelbearing is checked on the forecourt of the petrol station with a kick to the tyre. It seems secure, but the oil level in the reconditioned engine is right down. Dante pours two litres in and crosses himself. Something is steaming under the raised bonnet too, even though the water level is fine. Back pressure: not good. Or so he's been told by weary AA men in yellow jackets who often rescue him and Tom. But the War Wagon only has to get them to Scotland. After that, it can maroon them both for all he cares. He's never going back.

Staring at the cashier's booth, he watches a small Asian man inside restock a tiered rack with mints and gum. In front of the attendant he sees his own reflection on the glass, a lean and rangy spectre standing between sacks of barbecue fuel and pumps that dispense unleaded petrol. A lonesome crow, a black crow, a big-nosed Rolling Stone, a threadbare scarecrow, a stoned Ramone. Who is he at twenty-six? A joke or a rock'n'roller?

'Where are we?' Tom asks. His face, drowsy from sleep, peeks from the side window.

Tired, Dante sighs. 'Lancashire.'

'How long have I been asleep?'

'Three hours. Remember what I said about a second pair of eyes?'

'Yeah, yeah. Sorry, mate.'

At midday they stop again, this time at Penrith, and eat fish and chips in a truckers' cafe. 'I stink of petrol, man,' Tom complains, trying to fluff some life into his sleek hair before he gives up and pulls it away from his angular face, tying it into a ponytail. Two large hoop earrings shake gently against his cheekbones. With a yawn, Tom lights another cigarette and his topaz eyes drift across the tables. *No girls in here.* Dante smiles.

'Now, when we get there, everything will be square with Eliot?' Tom asks.

'Mr Coldwell,' Dante corrects him and raises an eyebrow. 'We pay the deposit and one month's rent in advance. It's a good deal. Less than what we were paying back home.'

'Yeah, but what if it's a shit-hole? I could not take another house without heating. I swear.'

'St Andrews doesn't have shit-holes.'

'You've never been there. I've heard Scotland is rough. They have these posters in pubs about carrying knives. And they're for the chicks.'

'That's Glasgow. St Andrews is different. It's a jewel. Eliot . . . Mr Coldwell has told me all about it. There'll be no more scallies trying to nick our guitars up there, mate. You should be grateful. Imagine just turning up and looking for a room stinking of the War Wagon with frizzy hair. They'd drop us right back on the border.'

Tom starts to laugh. It is the same conversation that has replayed throughout the last month. Shaky supports holding the escape tunnel open. 'Sure, sure,' Tom says. 'But why couldn't we just stay at his house?'

'Who would want to live with us, man? Come on, get real. He has enough work to do: the academic stuff and his second book.'

'Do you think he will let us read it?'

'I don't know. I mean, I'll ask.'

Tom gazes past Dante to the carpark outside. 'I tell you, buddy, the other thing that's weird, is him and his bird liking our album. I mean he's an old guy. A philosopher.'

'So? He's flattered. His book was written fifteen years before we were born and we want to do a concept album on it.'

'Yeah, but it's rock music. Does he even know who the Stones are?'

'That's irrelevant. He knows we have a goal. A need to transcend all of this. That's what *Banquet for the Damned* is about. Our record will show it's still valid. Timeless. It can appeal to a man in his twenties today, or someone born in Eliot's generation.'

Tom nods. 'Yeah, and I'll tell you something. When the second record is released, if the critics write us off again, I'm off to London with a pistol in my belt. They fuckin' killed us.'

'They killed him too.'

*

'Did we waste our time?' he asks Tom at a motorway service station near Carlisle. Because now it's his turn for doubt. The closer they get to Scotland the more ludicrous the whole expedition begins to feel. It's choking and he can't keep it down.

Tom fiddles with the zip of his jeans, having just returned from the gents'. 'With what?'

'With the band.'

'Where did that come from?'

'Driving in the slow lane at fifty miles an hour, where the caravans overtake you. Gives a man a lot of time to think.'

'How's the wagon doing?'

'OK. Seventeen to the gallon and the bearing is holding out.'

Tom taps a cigarette into his hand from the red and white packet he keeps tucked under the sleeve of his T-shirt. He flicks the cigarette into the air with his thumb and then catches it between his teeth on the way down. He rolls it between his incisors before embracing the filter with his lips. 'Materially, it was a joke. Blowing our own money like that. Personally, it was a huge achievement. We're just ahead of our time.'

Dante smiles. After shuffling further up the Land Rover's bonnet, he gazes about the carpark, takes a long drag on his Marlboro and points at the surroundings. 'Doesn't this just get to you, though? I'm twenty-six and still in fancy dress. I don't have a pot to piss in. Look over there at that couple in the BMW. They're what, our age? She probably got that tan in the Maldives. Just look at them. Plenty of disposable income. Great jobs. Fucking home owners. Mate, we've got one mobile phone between us and it's been out of credit for two months.'

Tom shakes his head for the entire time Dante speaks. 'Man, I hate it when you talk like this.'

'But what if we never get anywhere, if this Scotland thing is a mistake, if the second album dies a death? We have nothing, we're nobody, we're mediocre, exactly what we've been trying to avoid.'

'Buddy, if that guy over there with the Beamer took one peek into our lives, he'd trade places in a flash.'

'Piss off,' Dante says and grins, secretly adoring the fact that he's kick-started Tom along the familiar path of reassurance he can't do without.

'Sure he would. Think of the girls. And the gigs. We're fuckin' rock stars. What about that darling in the red dress at the Rock Café? That one night you had with her is worth any BMW.'

Dante grins.

Tom slaps his thighs. 'We're on the road, baby! Shooting up to Scotland with a bag of pot, two guitars and a prayer. We've got edge. More edge than you can shake a stick at. Have we ever gone hungry, not had a smoke, or good company, and a few cool tunes?'

Laughing, Dante looks through the grimy Land Rover windscreen at the plastic bags containing everything they own in the world. 'It's a mockery, man.'

Tom laughs. 'Now you mention it, let's just end it right here. Who in their right mind would drive this piece-of-shit four hundred miles to hang out with some old bloke they've never met? It's one long explosion from start to finish.'

'But it always sounds so rock'n'roll when you say it.'

*

16

'M90, M9, who gives a . . .'

'Tom, we've put about fifty miles on the clock, and that's about a grand's worth of fuel in this shitbox. All you had to do was say "right" back there before Edinburgh.'

'Oh come on, there were like six different lanes, and fifty signs with arrows going all over the place. My compass is all screwed up.'

'You're fucking useless.'

'Gimme a break. It's this bloody tank. My arse cannot take another minute of it.'

'You're a waste of fucking space.'

'And the stink of petrol is giving me a headache. Man, we're getting poisoned. That battery should have a cover. It gives off explosive fumes or something.'

Dante watches Tom flick his Zippo lighter open to spark up another cigarette. He begins to laugh.

'What you laughing at?'

Ignoring Tom, he leans forward across the steering wheel to gaze at the sky. 'It's beautiful. Look at that sky. Don't you feel we're getting somewhere?'

'Sure, never doubted it for a minute. It's you I worry about.'

'I was only thinking out loud.'

'Yeah, well no more of it. We are going to be in St Andrews. Man, that's in another country. In a different dimension. Just think of the ocean and the beach. There's a ruined castle, and all those cute student chicks. It's going to be so cool.'

Dante nods his head in approval and opens a packet of chocolate buttons while gripping the steering wheel with his knees. They pass a can of Cherry Coke between them and

Tom lights another cigarette before leaning across to place it on Dante's bottom lip. 'Cheers,' Dante says, and relaxes into his seat, daring to steer the Wagon with one hand. 'There's something I'm curious about, Tom.'

'Oh shit. What are you, a homo?'

'No,' he replies, smiling, and flicks his fringe out of his eyes. 'But don't knock it until you've tried it.' Tom's mirth hisses between his teeth and stabs through the cigarette smoke that gathers around his face. Killing his smile, Dante says, 'We tell each other everything, right?'

'Right,' Tom says, frowning.

'Well, there's one thing that doesn't sit right with me. We've been incurable romantics since school. Always looking for the Muse.'

'Fussy means less and settling is forbidden, or so we used to say.'

'You used to say. I never had the bone structure to be so arrogant.'

Tom chuckles.

'But you had her,' Dante says.

'Who?'

'Don't give me that *who* crap. You had Imogen. You should have dropped me like a hot coal and lived happily ever after.'

'You're so sweet on her. You should have gone out with her,' Tom says, quietly. He looks away and out of the window and Dante cannot see his face.

He grips the steering wheel tighter than he needs to. He clears his throat. 'I'm being objective. Come on, I have some integrity. I would never have fooled around with her.'

'That was low.'

Dante changes gear down to third to round a tight corner. The face of Punky, their last and best drummer, enters both minds. Tom split the band apart by sleeping with Punky's girlfriend – and it was the best line-up they'd ever managed to assemble. 'Tom, I'm not having a go, believe me, but Imogen is a doll. So why are you sitting next to me in the War Wagon, driving four hundred miles away from perfection?'

'Long story. I really don't feel up to talking about it.'

'Come on. She loved you, man. You had the greatest times. I always envied you her. I admit it.' Dante clears his throat again. This is further than he's ever gone toward the mystery of Tom leaving Imogen. Their umbilical bond, their empathy, seems to have frozen somewhere by the handbrake.

'Drop it, Dante,' Tom says after a long silence. 'Just accept that it wasn't right and I should be on the road with you. You'd be lost without me.' He feels the knuckles in Tom's hand press against his shoulder, providing a friendly nudge.

For over an hour, no one speaks.

When Dante next checks his watch it has gone four in the afternoon and the sun shows no signs of abating. It flows into the Land Rover cabin, warms his face and glints off the dusty instrument panel. Inside, he feels his muscles relax and even the engine, humming in fourth gear, seems to mellow in sympathy with him. They rumble through villages built out of stone, and thread between the small hills, the name of St Andrews now appearing on every directional board they pass. And for a moment, just before Tom turns the stereo on to play The Black Crowes, Dante senses something grow inside him. It is the same sensation he experiences when the right combination of chords for a song flows through his fingers, and the hair stands up on the back of his neck. It makes him a little dizzy. This is why he is going to St Andrews: to unleash this inspiration, and to pay homage to the man who awoke it.

'The sea! Straight to the sea! See that, it says "West Sands". Let's go.'

'Sure,' Dante says, steering the Land Rover around a small traffic island as he tries to adjust to the sudden vision of old buildings, the rows of trees, and the swept streets.

Above the town the sun smoulders towards dusk. Beyond the spires the sky is purple, tangerine, lemon, and rippled with sparse dark clouds. Mediaeval and Victorian buildings, all neatly aligned, huddle on the hills and cliffs above the green expanse of golf course, the winter-blue of infinite sea, and the wide sands that divide them.

'Beautiful.'

'End of the rainbow.'

Dante steers the Land Rover down a narrow street toward the golf links. On their right, a long wall of distinguished hotels snakes up a hill; to the left, small shopfronts peek between more of the stately hotels. Straight ahead, over the grimy bonnet, the sea is as flat as a mill pond and stretches down the coast until the West Sands become a yellow ribbon leading to a conifer forest.

Dante pulls the Land Rover around the bends in the road, his eyes wide with excitement and wonder. He hits two sets of speed bumps and spreads a landslide of luggage toward the War Wagon's rear doors.

'Careful, buddy,' Tom warns. 'The guitars.'

'Sorry.'

'Those doors will hold, won't they?' Tom asks, reluctantly taking his eyes from the view.

Dante grins. 'Hope so. If they don't, we'll look like a Hercules dropping aid boxes over Rwanda.'

Tom laughs. 'Imagine that, picking leather jackets and guitars off the road. What would the locals think?'

'That hell had come to St Andrews.'

They chuckle and punch each other's fists.

Slowly, Dante eases the hot Land Rover into a carpark between the Old Course and the sand dunes. Tom rapidly chews his aniseed gum. 'Look at the place. Fucking look at it. It's magic. Our album will be so cool. I can feel it.'

They clamber down from the wagon and stretch their cramped bodies; kick their legs out and then rub stiff knees. Tom stares at the sky and groans, digging his open palms into the small of his back, attempting to massage some feeling into his lower vertebrae. He squints at the horizon. 'To the sea.'

Hobbling together out of the carpark, they cross a small road parallel to the dunes. They stumble down to the sand and suck draughts of salty air into their lungs. Tom sparks up the last two cigarettes. He slides his Zippo flame across the shorn ends, until they glow red and release the scent of toasted tobacco to mingle with the briny air. A jog revives their limbs and carries them across the flat sand to the shoreline where they stand and marvel at the water that froths around their weathered biker boots.

'What's that?' Tom asks, breaking Dante's trance, and he points down the beach. A solitary police car is parked on the sand and two officers, stripped to their white shirts, stumble about in the distance. Patrol car lights flare an electric-blue, piercing the hues of summer twilight like an acetylene flame.

'Let's go look.'

As they move down the beach toward the commotion, they hear someone crying. A woman. An elderly woman in a tweed skirt and brown pullover, who pulls at the leash of her yapping Jack Russell terrier to keep him away from the policemen. Other people stand back, exchanging glances. Their faces are pallid with shock. Behind Dante and Tom, the urgent wail of an ambulance splinters the air. They turn their heads and see an emergency vehicle drive down a stone jetty and begin to rumble and shake across the sand.

'Someone's drowned,' Tom suggests, his face stiffening with concern.

'Maybe,' Dante replies, squinting through his contact lenses as he searches for the macabre details he doesn't want to see, but cannot stop looking for.

They come to a standstill, about twenty feet from the commotion, wincing at the sound of the distressed woman. One of the officers opens the rear door of the patrol car and helps the woman and her dog inside. Then he walks back to the red thing on the sand.

'What is it?' Dante asks.

'Shit,' Tom replies, wiping his hand across his eyes.

'What? I can't see. These damn lenses are useless.' The ambulance passes, its tyres sinking through the damp sand. Its siren deafens them. Tom shouts something, but Dante doesn't hear him. 'What is it?' he repeats, just as the ambulance kills the siren.

'An arm!' Tom yells, his voice bringing a fresh surge of woe from the woman in the police car.

'It's an arm,' Tom repeats, his voice subdued. 'A human arm.'

Two paramedics slip past the policemen and cover the red thing on the beach with a rubber sheet.

THREE

Thin unseen hands paw her body. Just like the night before. Until long fingers grip her shoulders and yank her upright in bed. Then her face is touched by something sharp before her limp shape is thrown down to the mattress, so *it* can clamber upon her. Rustling, as if spidery limbs are being drawn in, it perches upon her chest. Before lowering its face. To whisper.

Punched from sleep, Kerry's long blue eyes open. Pebbles of sweat cool on her forehead.

Only *the* dream. She exhales. It's over now, it's gone.

Should have gone to sleep on my front. I'm sure I went to sleep on my front. But understands the bad dream came back to turn her over.

Out of dream-time, Kerry glances around her dark room, cocooned within the sturdy walls of St Salvator's Hall of Residence. Moonlight filters through the thin curtains and transforms her quiet chamber into smudges and silhouettes. She swallows to calm her staccato breaths, and the waking moment brings tears to her eyes and a shudder beneath her ribs, as if she's just climbed out of cold water to seek a towel. There is an urge to cry, to call Sarah in from next door so she can cling to her neighbour's gown in these first moments of waking. But beside the window she sees the outline of a

Sheryl Crow poster and above her desk Brad Pitt hides in shadow, with his shirt off, square jaw clenched and strong hands still. Familiar things kill her desire to cry. This is Kerry's real world in real time, and safe from nightmare.

Smiling through her tears, she hears the little ticks from the Homer Simpson alarm clock. At nine in the morning he'll shout 'Doh!' and she'll phone home. Her thesis is nearly finished and she's ready for her dad's comfy arms and her mom's raised eyebrow. Back to Kent, back home and away from the nightmares. Relief makes it possible for Kerry to almost smell dad's pipe-smoke, to hear her little sister's piano, Jasper barking in the conservatory, and her grandmother cackling before the television. She can even hear . . .

Something moving.

No God, please.

A sniff and then a rustle out there in her room.

Please, please, please, no more. She's awake. It can't continue.

The sounds are coming from the dark annexe by the en-suite bathroom. Something is on all fours as it pads through the murk of night. She can hear it feeling its way about the floor, as if blind but intent on being close to her.

Kerry tries to move her head and sit up. No use. A familiar tingling, a paralysis, fastens her down beneath disturbed sheets still damp with sweat. Her legs and arms are immobile, useless. Not wanting to see, Kerry closes her eyes. Muscles twitch in her face and then crease. Panic surges through her body and she wants to beg, plead, and then scream, to bring the world to her door.

But maybe if she doesn't struggle and stays quiet it won't find her.

A lump gathers in her throat. A swollen clot of fear, because she can sense it emerging from around the corner to turn its face toward her. She holds her breath, her stiff body shivers and a deep silence engulfs space and time. There is no sound or movement for a moment, just the dark room and the waiting she must endure inside it.

And then the touch. It has reached out.

Something dry and sharp presses into her cheek. A spider web of icy tingles spreads up from her shoulders and sparks inside her neck. Hair follicles prickle on her scalp and her blonde hair stiffens against the pillow. It's freezing now and the sheets feel like tissue paper. Stillness roars. She gasps. Keeping her eyes shut tight, she tries to scream but everything swirls inside, voiceless and adrift. A sudden thought demands annihilation to end the delay. The sharp thing then scratches down and across her face and pushes at her lips. A bitter taste seeps into her mouth and spreads to her sinuses, leaving a taint of blackened antiquity. There is a sudden hiss and a gust of air teases the feathery hair around her ear. A presence hovers above her face. It has risen to stare.

Suddenly, her throat feels naked and exposed, and she tries to push her chin down to protect the soft cartilage and intricate pipes in her neck – the flesh she imagines being smashed flat or squeezed until it cracks – but lowering her jaw is impossible.

Little pin-pricks of red light flash beneath her eyelids. She thinks she will faint. Or is this shock?

A weight spreads across her chest, and her small breasts are flattened. Long frozen fingers clench around her biceps and pin her to the bed. A face she cannot see nears, to hover no more than an inch from her own. The image of a thing old and bestial and terribly thin bores through her failing mind. The salvation of darkness claims her.

The cold that numbs her feet and spears her ankle bones wakes Kerry. She's outside and it's still night. There is a sound of water, swelling and lapping around stone. Peering down, she sees her long white feet, oddly luminous against a black surround. Before her stands a small tower with an iron ladder clinging to it. To her right she hears the power of the sea, rushing in to froth around the pier.

The pier. I'm on the pier. And right down at the end, so far from the shore, with her arms wrapped around her chest. It's freezing and her skin shivers beneath the thin T-shirt and underwear she wears to bed. Stepping from one foot to the other, she tries to make sense of her situation and turns around to see the lights glimmer in the harbour and around the cathedral walls that loom upward to craggy demolished towers and holed façades.

Am I drunk? Am I mad?

And just as she remembers the thing in her room, sitting on her chest, something scrabbles across the wall by the little black tower. She staggers backward, her foot slips and the night sky whirls above her. The sound of the inky sea, heaving down below, becomes deafening.

She shrieks, regains her balance and then hops forward, away from the edge. She looks to the pier wall on the other side, more than a metre thick and raised four feet off the promenade. A memory of edging along it on her first day at university, four years before as a fresher, spills into her mind. She sees herself hugging the wall with friends who giggle, terrified of the unprotected edge so close to her with the sea below it. It had been a dizzy, spinning fear back then, that secretly demanded she hurl herself off and down to the clashing waves.

Must be a dog, she tries to convince herself. A big dog and it's gone away now. Go home, run home, get Sarah. But something is still moving up there. It crawls forward on its front, indistinct but for its length, pressed into the stone.

Kerry begins to sob. She remembers the smell and movements of the thing that groped around her bed and paralysed her muscles. Instinctively, her hands fly up and cover her nose and mouth. It was there in her room, and now it has brought her down to the pier. She will die. It will take her to the edge of the pier and bite her, throw her off, leap after her and hold her head under the cold water. Already, she can feel her lungs screaming, the briny freeze in her mouth, and the long fingers capping her skull and ready to push down.

Kerry screams. In her mind, she can see her own face: a wrinkled tomato-face. What Dad used to call it whenever she had a tantrum as a child. Now she has it again, on her own, down on the pier. Instinct tells her to fall to the floor, to grip the polished stone, worn by pilgrims' sandals, to hold on with all her might and save herself from the edge and the waves that will smash. If it kills her on the pier, she won't have to go over the side and see it follow.

The thing hisses. It scuttles like a crab. The head is dark but something glints inside the oval of its coverings. Images of yellowed ivory and black lips flash through Kerry's mind. Running away is impossible. She knows she lacks the strength, and it's so fast up there, skittering about, before it tenses and makes ready to leap.

'No! Leave me alone. Please!' Kerry screams. Her voice breaks into sobs. She falls to her knees, where the hard stones thump her bones and freeze her thighs. It will get her, swing around her neck, and take her over the side. Raising itself upright on the wall, it hisses with delight.

'Hey!' someone shouts from the shore.

'What the fuck's going on?' another voice bellows, words slurred by drink, the accent local. At the base of the pier, she sees two silhouettes, that run and then bump against each other; the soles of their feet slap in a frenzy, sounding a welcome urgency. On the wall, the thing raises itself to nudge at the air with its mercifully obscured face. Then it glances at Kerry before settling down to its haunches. Rage trembles through it.

The men draw closer, out of breath, intent on reaching the frightened girl, all sunken and witless on the pier. With a sound of dry cerements dragged across stone, the ragged shape disappears over the side of the pier. One of the drunken men has seen it and leans over the wall, ten feet away from where Kerry sits. 'Oi!' he shouts, craning further forward over the edge.

Kerry hears a distant splash, far away and below.

'What . . . ?' The man on the wall queries, and squints into the moving darkness below.

'You OK luv?' the other asks, and squats down, wide-eyed with shock. His breath reeks of beer. Kerry sobs – it's the most wonderful thing she can remember smelling.

On shore, away from Kerry and her two saviours, a car engine erupts into life on the road that runs alongside the masts of small fishing boats bobbing and grinding together in the stone-walled dock. Lights flash on, tyres ripple over tarmac, and a sleek black vehicle speeds away towards the Pens archway.

FOUR

'It still seems like an omen.'

'Cut it out, Tom,' Dante says, dropping his head to stare at the sea so far below, rushing in with a foamy roar to crash and then drag itself back across the black rocks and reef. They stand on the coastal path, outside of their new flat at the end of the long and leafy road known as the East Scores, that ambles from the ruined castle to the long pier, the latter built from the consecrated stone of cathedral rubble. Despite the early-morning excitement of waking up in strange beds, in a house somewhere other than Birmingham, they fail in their attempts to ignore a growing sense of unease.

'But within the first ten minutes of us getting here, Johnny Law pulls an arm out of the sea,' Tom continues, his face tense and committed to his point. 'Things like that just don't happen up here. I mean, look around you, Dante. It's beautiful. I bet the place hasn't changed in centuries.'

'Must have been a shark attack. Or some fisherman who fell under the rotor blades of his engine,' Dante says, gazing into the middle distance, the familiar focus of the preoccupied. 'It probably didn't even happen here. You know, just got washed in from the sea.'

Tom follows Dante's stare and looks at the horizon, to

find what his friend is searching for. 'And I was looking forward to a swim down there,' he adds quietly, to himself.

Dante looks at his friend's face, at the strong bones and even features, framed by a fringe of silky hair. Tom's lips are pursed and he blinks his eyes quickly as he tries to make sense of things in his own way: not often given to protracted thought or tiring anxiety like Dante, who begins to laugh at himself, and at Tom.

'What?' Tom says. His mouth twitches with the notion of laughter.

'You thought of going for a swim.'

'You're sick. But I do need two arms to play a guitar.'

Dante laughs until he wheezes.

Tom slaps his shoulder. 'Man, why did I let you talk me into this? There's shark-infested waters, no totty, and to top it off our flat is probably haunted.'

'Enough,' Dante says. He wipes his eyes. 'You never cease to amaze me. You have seen some poor bastard's arm on the sand and already your prime concern is pulling.'

Tom grins, relieved their camaraderie has returned. 'I have to do something when you're yakking to Eliot. Which reminds me, you still haven't phoned him, have you?'

Dante's stomach tightens. 'There's time.'

Narrowing his eyes accusingly, Tom says, 'You're scared. You're crapping yourself. Aren't you?'

'Come off it. There was no time last night and I don't have his home number.'

Lighting a cigarette and smiling to himself, Tom turns his body and leans against the iron rail separating the path from an awful drop that does something to the nerves in Dante's rectum whenever he looks down. 'What was wrong with this morning? His study is, like, thirty feet from our pad and right behind us.'

'I'm not scared. I just want to familiarise myself with the town first.'

Tom squints through the cloud of smoke that drifts over his face. 'Familiarise yourself. Of course.'

Dante can often fool himself, but fooling Tom is impossible. A mutual intuition has existed between them since the day they met at school, aged fourteen. And the very thought of meeting Eliot Coldwell saps the strength from his limbs. He's always fantasising about what it would be like to meet someone famous, like Axl Rose. What would you say to someone like Axl, someone you admire but also fear? What if they are vile? What if they ignore you, or even smack you down because you're just another dumb fan crowding their space? Guns'n'Roses ignited a renaissance in his musical tastes. After hearing *Appetite for Destruction* for the first time, it was as if his destiny paused and then turned in another direction to kindle the awakening of his interest in music, and to create Sister Morphine. And then an album that led him to choose part-time work after graduation and the threadbare rock'n'roll lifestyle it barely supported.

But he knows Eliot Coldwell's influence goes far beyond his musical infatuations. *Banquet for the Damned* offers not just an escape but a confirmation of everything he wants to be. As a teenager he read the book continuously in a darkened room festooned with Mötley Crüe and Ratt posters, warmed by a glow of wonder under his skin. Some kind of epiphany had begun inside him, a strange blend of awakening, inspiration, and comfort. Telling anyone how he feels about the book now, other than Tom, is difficult. Difficult to find the words and difficult not to sound like a fool. It seems like such a cliché – a book changing your life – but it is as if *Banquet for the Damned* exerted a strange influence on the choices he's made. Suddenly, after the first read in his mid-teens, the acquisition of experience became his goal. Tasting every aspect of life became his aim. The search for fulfilment had to be endless, no time could be wasted with routine, nothing ordinary settled for, mediocrity became the devil. Eliot Coldwell's motives and desires became his own. And now he is going to meet the forgotten author. To sit before a man he considers great. A man who writes of riches lurking behind the everyday world, and waiting to be found.

'In at the deep end, buddy. It's the only way,' Tom says.

Dante's face pales. Cigarette tar curdles in his stomach and he becomes light-headed. 'What if I make a tit of myself? Start gabbling and saying stupid things. We're talking about research work. I'm not a scholar. I write lyrics for heavy metal songs. Who am I kidding?'

'Bullshit,' Tom says. He stares at the side of Dante's head. 'I have seen you sing in front of three hundred drunken bikers in shit-kickers' heaven and you never let us down. Even when we were the support act and people just wanted to throw shit, you came through. You always won the punters over, getting them all clapping and freaking out. You did it. There's nothing to worry about. You can do anything. And Eliot's just a man. An old man. OK, a clever one, but flesh and blood all the same. Problem is, you've spent too much time reading his book by candlelight, elevating him into a god or something. I mean, you even reckon he's a saint.'

Tom's words resound inside Dante. His tide suddenly turns. He feels gregarious and confident. He remembers the haggle with sullen bar owners over the band's fee and he sees himself crooning above a mesmerised audience; he recalls the girls after a gig, gathering around them, and the strangers that always wanted to shake his hand. Why should he falter now? It was Eliot that spoke for leaps of faith, discovering purpose, heightening the mind and taking a glimpse behind the screens. Dante turns around and smiles at Tom. 'Find me a phone box.'

Eliot Coldwell is waiting and will see him right away.

Something hot and strong pulses through Dante's entire body. After barging out of the phone box on Market Street he offers his hand to Tom, who gives it a firm two-handed clasp. 'See, I told you,' Tom says, pleased with the smile on his friend's face. 'Nothing to worry about. He can't wait to meet you. What did he sound like?'

'Don't know. It was his secretary. She was really sharp though.'

'Well, the sun is out. Who wants to be stuck in some divinity office on a day like this?'

'Sure, maybe. Jesus, what shall I say? Should I change?'

'The day you sell out, buddy, is the last day you see me.'

Laughing, Dante strokes his fingers through his hair, breaking the little fringe knots before tying it back. Tom dances on the spot. 'Just waltz in and get chatting. Get me on the guest list for dinner at his place.'

'What're you going to do? It might take hours.'

'Don't worry, fella. I'm going to check out the castle and wander around the town. Just kick back and get some food for the flat too.'

'Good call,' Dante whispers, only hearing the end of Tom's answer.

They punch each other's fists before separating. Tom disappears up Bell Street toward South Street, leaving Dante on his own amongst the morning shoppers on Market Street. Taking deep breaths and trying to compose opening lines, he makes slow progress back to the School of Divinity on the Scores, muttering. 'Mr Coldwell, it's an honour.' Dante shakes his head in disgust. 'Mr Coldwell, you don't know how much this means to me after all I've been through.' He swears under his breath. Nothing but pitiful clichés roll through the fog in his head. It just isn't coming, he is too highly strung, too excited and scared. Will his throat clog up? Will his eyebrow start to twitch the way it did at the first Sister Morphine gig? Will sweat drench his back while something dizzy runs around his skull, throwing the first piece of crap that shoots through his brain straight onto his tongue? 'Just be cool. Just be yourself. Be honest,' he whispers, as his boots roll across the cobbles at the top of Market Street by the monument. After turning left down South Castle Street, he feels the shadows from the surrounding stone walls cool on his face.

Dante crosses North Street. Tall flat-faced houses stand in shadow on one side of the street. Most of the homes are shades of grey or brown in colour, Victorian terraces embellished by an incongruously pink or yellow front. Across the wide road, the sun transforms the chapels, towers and faculty fortresses into a mediaeval city of gold. After what seems like a limbo in the industrial purgatory of the West Midlands, he begins to wonder if he'll ever become accustomed to the new aesthetics of space, antiquity and grace in St Andrews.

Retracing his footsteps, he finds North Castle Street at the easterly end of town, just before the perimeter wall of the ruined cathedral, and wanders down the narrow street, between the shadowy Episcopal Church and the small stone houses with deep-set windows offering glimpses of exclusive interiors; all wood, pottery, and tiled floors. Comfortable homes promising silent nights.

It makes him think of all his unchecked hours in a comfortless house, endured for the last two years, reading anything that reinforced his alienation and the sense of purpose that he hoped would arise from it. *Banquet* saved him. There is no doubt in his mind. *Banquet* added a direction to a young life embalmed in endless retrospection and dreaminess. Everything he read in the book about Eliot's adventures, optimism and willpower allowed some kind of warmth into his cold room, or into the lock-up on the industrial estate they spent hours inside, freezing while they rehearsed and made endless eight-track recordings of what was to be their first album. Despite the poverty, at times the hunger too when they waited for Giro day, he only had to think of *Banquet* – of the creased cover and broken spine of his paperback copy beside the mattress and overflowing ashtray in his room – and he would know the struggle was necessary, forgivable, justified.

Reaching the foot of North Castle Street, where the lane joins the Scores, he is confronted with the view of the ruined castle once again. Overlooking the harbour, its broken walls stand across the road from the tree-fronted School of Divinity where Eliot works.

'God give me strength,' Dante mutters.

Two years before the trip to Scotland, he'd written to the last publisher of *Banquet* seeking confirmation that Eliot was still alive. In his letter, he detailed plans for the band to write and record their second record as a concept album on Eliot's book. Nearly one year later, when Eliot finally responded, Dante read the letter over and over again, slowly analysing each line until he knew them by heart. And he learned that Eliot taught at St Andrews University, in the School of Divinity, following a bout of ill health in North Africa which ended his travels. Other letters followed and a correspondence ensued, forcing him to rise to the occasion, writing to his hero with every ounce of passion and honesty inside him.

Turning the corner of North Castle Street, he wanders along the Scores and watches the grey majesty of the School of Divinity rise from between cottages on the left and Franklin House on its right. Standing at the foot of the gravel drive, he pauses to stare at the school's austere buttressed and turreted shape. Its three storeys of solid stone seem to hum like some vast reactor from the power of the minds within.

St Andrews University, School of Divinity: a strange place for Eliot to work. Dante frowns. By his own admission, Eliot is a mystic and born in the wrong century. He recorded his dabbling with occult science and pagan ritual in *Banquet*, while deriding Western religion for its severance of the bond with nature. Won't Eliot's interpretations of Christian thought be heretical? Maybe they study the Hindus too, Dante muses, lifting his face to the Gothic structure and feeling like a tattooed barbarian blinking awe-stricken eyes at the splendour of Ancient Rome. Above the chimneys, slate roof and skeletal fire escapes, the deep-blue sky engorges his chest with the one value he cherishes above all – hope.

Eliot has given him a vocation. Is he strong enough for it?

Dante walks up the smooth, dipped centre of the stone steps. At the top, he turns the front-door handle, hesitates, wipes his feet on the bristly mat, and then takes a step inside.

Like a powerful acid, the fragrance of academia dissolves his brief spell of confidence. It is as if a giant book has been snapped shut beneath his nose, wafting an intimidating scent-cloud of dusty spines, laminated plastic and varnished wood into his head.

Standing still inside the door, he looks at the glass-panelled bookcase fixed to a wall and filled with scholarly hardbacks written by the lecturing staff. Reminders of knowledge he does not have turn his stomach over. Dipping his head to steady his breathing, Dante catches sight of his scuffed biker boots and faded jeans and feels his legs go immediately numb.

On his left, beside an oaken honeycomb of pigeonhole post boxes, he sees a white door marked SECRETARY, and hears the judder and clatter of a keyboard from within. For a moment, the idea of running back to Tom and loading up the Land Rover glows in his thoughts.

'All change serves a purpose,' Eliot had written in words he could understand. 'Change and progress are not acciden-tal; they come through the unchaining of an imagination. And behind them, faith and the will must power the sails.'

Dante forces himself toward the door and gives it a firm knock. Through the wood, he hears a long sigh and then a shrill female voice says, 'Yes.' Through the small gap he's made between the door and the frame, he pokes his head inside before following it with an arm. A woman, frowning but handsome, sits straight-backed behind a desk and computer.

Dante smiles. Her face doesn't move. He swallows. She raises an eyebrow above her glasses, perched halfway down her thin nose and fastened around her neck with a gold chain. 'Yes?' she asks, unable to conceal her annoyance. When her slender hands reluctantly leave the keyboard they create a red flash of long and immaculate fingernail. When he opens his mouth, a rasp dislodges from the back of his throat.

'Do you speak?' she asks.

'Yes,' he whispers before clearing his throat. 'I –'

'Will you come in? I can't hear you.'

Dante shuffles through the door and crowds his body into the corner, as far away from the woman's stare as possible. 'I'm here for an appointment with Mr Coldwell.'

The woman studies him. 'Dante Shaw,' she says to herself. 'What an appropriate name.'

'Sorry?'

'Nothing,' she replies, and leaps from behind her desk with an alacrity he doesn't expect from a secretary who works in a School of Divinity. High heels cage her feet and an elegant tight-fitting dress – sleeveless and cut above the knee – turns her slender shape into neat lines and hard curves. With an expert's ease on pencil-thin stilettos, the glamour-puss and guardian walks across to him, her pale legs flashing like a strobe, luring his eyes down. 'My name is Janice Summers. I am the senior administrator. Do you mind me inquiring about the nature of your appointment?'

'I'm here to assist Mr Coldwell with his research,' he

announces in a voice controlled enough to submerge his Brummy accent.

She places her hands on her hips and a mocking smile spreads across her mouth. 'Research, you say. An investigation of Scotch whisky, no doubt?'

Dante flushes with annoyance. 'Research for his second book, actually.' His face reddens further, as he suddenly feels foolish about his use of the word 'actually'.

But, for a moment, whatever he said introduces a fleeting spectre of vulnerability to the woman's hard face. 'Book?' Her voice is little more than a whisper.

Dante nods his head, rejoicing inside from something that feels like an unexpected victory. She takes a deep breath and smiles, weakly. 'I had no idea Eliot was considering another book. I mean who would . . .' She stops herself, and reaches for the door handle behind him. Shuffling to one side, he lets her open the door. In a voice softer than her opening salvo, she asks him to follow.

Beside the administration office is a door marked STAIR-WELL. As she moves down the stairs, he catches sight of her profile and notices the inquisitive, bird-like face has become preoccupied again. Eager to break the uncomfortable silence, he says, 'I've never met Mr Coldwell. We've not even spoken on the phone. I hope he isn't too busy.'

She frowns at him as if he has said something imbecilic. Dante averts his eyes and decides it will be better to stay silent around Janice Summers, who continues, with a puzzled expression on her face, to teeter down the stairs to a door marked BASEMENT.

Taking what he feels are reluctant steps, she then walks along the narrow basement corridor between walls covered with a patchwork of flyers, lists, scholarship details and emergency evacuation procedures. The corridor is lit by two overhead strip lights, and a glimmer of natural light seeps through a dirty window in the top of the fire escape, situated at the far end of the passage.

Pausing before an unmarked door on the right, just before the fire exit, she then hesitates, and appears to be summoning the courage required to knock. Her face set with a grim concentration, she finally raps on the door.

In preparation for meeting his mentor, Dante brushes at his shirt, tightens his ponytail, and clears his throat.

A muffled sound rises from the unseen depths behind the door. As if repelled, Janice immediately steps back. 'Go on in,' she says, quietly, and it becomes apparent to Dante that she is not prepared to open the door and introduce him to Eliot. Instead, she hurries past him, back along the corridor toward the stairs. Dante places his hand on the door handle. A final glance down the corridor reveals Janice hovering in the mouth of the stairwell, still watching him, as if he is a menace. Eager to evade her eyes, he turns the door handle and enters.

A thick, smoky gloom confronts his eyes, all green-grey as if he is underwater. There is a strange spice in the air too, reminiscent of the cupboards in his gran's house, and thousands of book spines are crammed into every inch of ceiling-high shelfspace, or littered across the tables and chairs. Closing the door, he turns to face a desk anchored heavily into one corner, beneath closed curtains faded to a shade of discoloured brass.

At first, the seated figure behind the desk is indistinct. In the dusk of the study, only an outline of Eliot's thin shoulders and lank hair can be seen. As he takes a puff on his cigarette, however, the little orange flare of burning tobacco briefly illumines the suggestion of a long nose and wide mouth. Between small hillocks of paperwork and pyramids of hardback books, Dante can see the shirt of the sunken silhouette. It may have been white, and there is a dark tie running down the front to broaden out between two barely visible arms. A weak band of light falls across the figure's slender hands, at rest beside a large overflowing ashtray.

'Hello Dante.' The shape speaks with a quiet, sonorous voice. 'I've been looking forward to meeting you for some time.'

'Me too,' Dante says, before immediately trying to analyse the connotations of his first words to Eliot Coldwell.

'Please come in and take a seat. I'm sure you'll find one before my desk.' All his words seem to have been weighed, in precise copper scales, before dropping through the air.

'Thanks.' Swinging his jacket off, Dante steals a glimpse at the great man's face now that he is closer. Dark eyes watch him beneath a broad and flat brow. Cheekbones are pointed and the jaw is square below hollow cheeks. Taut skin has weathered to a mahogany brown on his face and is salt-sprinkled with whiskers, but the neck is wizened. The distinguished face suggests wisdom, and time endured beneath foreign suns. A good face to end up and slow down with. Tom would look like that; he has that sort of skin.

'Is your accommodation satisfactory?' Eliot asks, his teeth stained and his breath tainted by alcohol.

'Yeah. Great. Thanks for –'

'Good. It provides a grand view of the sea, at any time of year.'

'We love it, Tom and I. Really it was very –' he has to remember to say good instead of cool '– good of you to sort us out. The place we were living in before, I think I told you –'

'In Birmingham,' the voice interrupts again.

Dante nods. He wants to offer his opinion of Birmingham, but checks himself, trying to find the right gear in his mind and an appropriate vocabulary with which to survive the very beginning of this journey. Eliot speaks again, his words softened by a constant wheeze. 'I went to Birmingham. In the fifties. The city suffered in the war. But the people have spirit, no doubt? All working-class cities have spirit, at least.'

'I guess so.'

'And your journey?'

'Ecstatic. I think escapes are.'

Eliot smiles. 'Yes, quite. Would you like a cigarette?'

'Cheers.' He reaches forward to accept the cigarette from Eliot. It is long and bound in black paper. Their fingertips touch and Dante tenses, before Eliot's hand withdraws to rest beside the ashtray. For a moment he admires the small gold hoop around the cigarette's filter before slipping it between his teeth.

'They are Russian. Black Russian cigarettes,' Eliot says, his stare making Dante glad of the dark.

'Cool.'

'I would offer coffee, Turkish coffee, of which I am fond, but Janice is frightened.'

Dante lights his cigarette, glad of the distraction between his lips, and he feigns a smoke-in-the-eyes frown to conceal his unease. 'Frightened?' he asks, amplifying his voice to conceal the squeak that is ready in his throat.

'Yes. Never comes down anymore, if she can help it. It's a shame. I miss her scent down here and her legs. She has good legs, wouldn't you say?' Dante sniffs and offers a grin that immediately begins to ache on his face. 'And what a mouth,' Eliot adds, slurring his words. 'Would a young man like to taste that mouth?' The skin stiffens across the bones on Dante's face and his mouth dries out. A wry smile forms on Eliot's thin lips. 'Don't be shy,' he says, but an awkward silence begins and Dante looks away, unable to bear Eliot's stare any longer. Was it mocking?

'Every researcher I've had, Dante, has swum in murky water.'

A quickening sense of importance pulses through him. 'Yeah, I'm really excited about the work.'

Eliot nods and considers the end of his cigarette. 'And you have much to read. Before we can begin the real work.'

'Read?'

'You read a great deal?'

'Yes. I know *Banquet* inside out. In fact I've lost count of how many times I've read it.'

'Thank you. But we must go beyond *Banquet*. Much further, into times and places I've discovered since that enthusiastic apprenticeship was written. I have quite a collection of, shall I say, rare material. I know it will interest you and it's necessary to complete the canvas. The oils may be a little dark at first, but the final portrait, I'm sure, will astonish you. *Banquet* has moments, but is rather innocent. Wouldn't you agree?'

He feels trapped. The gloom presses against him, shrinking his body and making his head feel heavy, while Eliot's eyes eat at every twitch that disturbs his face. 'I, I don't know about that. I mean, of course I will read anything you suggest. I'd like that. But I find it hard to fault anything in *Banquet*.'

'Your loyalty is touching in an age of fads, but it was written in the early fifties, Dante. Much has happened since. And it has been a long walk before nightfall.' Eliot finishes with a smile he seems uncomfortable with. 'A Long Walk Before Nightfall' was the last chapter – the tragic chapter – in *Banquet*.

When Eliot rises from behind his desk, Dante notices his shoulders are hunched and his limbs seem especially thin beneath the crumpled shirt and grubby trousers. He extends his hand toward Dante, as if a trial has been passed – a grin stretching his broad mouth, tensing the little knots of muscle at the sides of his jaw.

Standing up, Dante accepts the hand and is surprised by the strength in Eliot's grip and the dry texture of his palm. 'Thank you, Mr Coldwell,' he says, suddenly relieved and unable to conceal his pent-up emotions any longer. 'Thank you for, for everything.'

Eliot nods, but looks past Dante, in such a way as to acknowledge thanks but prohibit further praise. 'Call me Eliot. I think formality is a hindrance.' He moves from behind his desk and coughs. 'Some fresh air. I feel a stroll to the pier is in order.'

They leave the office and walk through the basement corridor to climb the steep and narrow staircase to the foyer. Remaining quiet, Dante is content to study Eliot and think on what he should say. He wants his conversation to be careful and measured, like Eliot's, who now pauses by the secretary's door and listens to the sounds of her keyboard clatter with something approaching sly amusement on his face.

In the sunlight that passes through the reception windows, Dante then notices, with a slight shock, the abrasions on Eliot's skin. There are scores of white nicks interwoven within the seasoned grain of his face. His treacle-coloured forearms are also marred with pink slits of scar tissue, and around either wrist he spots what looks like a ring of tender flesh. As if sensing his scrutiny, Eliot tucks his hands inside his trouser pockets. And watching him walk to the front door, Dante reflects that there is none of the leisurely elegance he remembers about his grandfather's walk, rather something tired in the way Eliot moves. Maybe it's nerves, he thinks. He's pissed and nervous. But in and around his pale-blue eyes, set wide apart in the leathered face, with pupils ringed by burnished gold, he senses a hard quality too; something reminiscent of the cruelty in his Maths teacher's eyes.

They leave the foyer in silence, saunter down the stone steps and cross the gravel drive. In the mouth of the open gate, Dante turns his head to follow a quick movement behind the first-floor office window, and sees the stiff shape of Janice Summers fold away from sight. Immediately, an odd smile appears on Eliot's mouth, as if he knows she is on lookout, but the smile is not warm. Instead, it seems full of delight; a revelling in something unpleasant. 'Don't worry about her, Dante,' Eliot says, looking across the road at the ruined castle. 'She is a silly and vain creature, if not a beautiful one.'

Eliot moves to the other side of the road, neglecting to watch for approaching cars. Something reminiscent of Tom: the careless assurance that a higher force has blessed him at birth and will endeavour to preserve him, forever. Eliot then peers through the spiked fence, encircling the landlocked side of the castle, and surveys the battered stone with its gaping rends and stubborn peaks.

'Great castle,' Dante mutters.

While flicking a finger across the bars of the fence, Eliot cuts him short. 'Not a castle, Dante. A bishop's palace and the home of many an atrocity. The good Christians hanged and burned each other here over pitiful interpretations of the scriptures. It was Catholic to begin with before a Protestant infestation.'

'You're not keen on Christians then.'

Eliot snorts. 'Interesting rituals, but full of weeds. The whole faith. Hypocrisy and superstition, ceremony and apparatus. What use are they?' Unsure whether he should answer, Dante stays quiet, suspecting his silence interests Eliot more than his opinions. 'You shall find out more about true mystics,' Eliot adds, and bows his head away from Dante's eager eyes.

'Like the Moslem Sufis,' he ventures. 'Brahmins, Taoists and Buddhists. I especially like that part in *Banquet*. And what you said about higher magic.'

With his back to Dante, Eliot speaks over his shoulder. 'What an apostle you would have made. Be patient, though. There will be time enough for talk on these matters.'

'Sure,' Dante replies, crestfallen and hoping to crack the code on when to talk and when to listen.

'Have you been on the pier yet?' Eliot asks, turning his tired face to the sea.

'Yes, this morning.'

'Fair in summer, Dante. But you should see it in the wet season.' Dante nods, trying to assume a serious posture. What was the 'wet season'? Winter? He did not entirely like the way Eliot had emphasised those words, widening his mouth to issue them, with the first flicker of anything resembling real emotion on his face. 'The wet season?' he probes, fishing a Marlboro packet out of his jacket pocket, which Eliot refuses with a leisurely waft of a hand.

'This little picturesque town can become quite dramatic in the wet season. You should come here at night, when the sea is enraged. I often used to. I felt close to something powerful.' This is more like it, more in line with what he enjoyed in *Banquet* about the godlike and visionary quality inside man. The 'wet season'. He begins to like the sound of it; a song title maybe.

As they stroll down the empty pier, Eliot squints up at the sun, and begins to rub his cheeks and the contours of his weathered face. He looks like he hasn't been sleeping well, and Dante realises it will take time to accustom himself to the man's enigma. Thinkers can be strange creatures after all, he decides, and a man like Eliot, who has done and seen so much out of the ordinary, is bound to be a little weird.

He wanders to the end of the pier, in silence beside Eliot, and stands before the small tower and ladder that rise from the wall to overlook the harbour. 'Beautiful day,' he says finally, to break another long silence, but Eliot doesn't reply and remains preoccupied. Dante sits down and fishes for another cigarette.

'Don't be alarmed by me,' Eliot eventually says, staring at the sky. 'By my moods. I am quite a chameleon they say.' He turns and looks down at Dante, who tries to smile. 'What an expressive face you have.'

'Heart on my sleeve.'

'A virtue. The last remnant of innocence. The unclean like that.'

'What?'

Eliot shakes his head, as if the remark is of no importance. 'Your colleague, Beth, will want to see you right away.'

Dante nods. 'Yeah, you mentioned her in your letters.'

'And?'

'She sounds great.'

'She's unique,' Eliot murmurs, his thoughts wandering again until, by a conscious effort, he forces his mind to recall their conversation. 'Beth. Yes. She wants to meet you on Friday. There is an orientation. It will be suitable. Bring your friend too. She is so excited about meeting both of you. I'm very busy at the moment and Beth will have to guide you through our work. To which your presence is vital.' For the first time that day, Eliot looks relieved, and suddenly keen to have Dante sitting at the end of the pier.

'What exactly will I be researching?'

Eliot looks away and mumbles something he doesn't hear.

'Pardon?' Dante asks.

'She'll show you. Beth has all the answers,' Eliot replies, with a hint of bitterness, perhaps, but Dante can't be sure.

'The Orientation you mentioned. What is it? Do we bring wine?' Eliot totters on the spot, utterly self-absorbed again, leaving Dante to suspect his questions are distracting the man from an important train of thought. Already, he is annoying his idol.

'No,' Eliot eventually says, with a dismissive sigh. 'It's

nothing more than a gaggle of faculty members and staff in Younger Hall. You will find it in the Quad, where the guests will be discussing the coming academic year. Which they all look forward to. You will see a few fools, I warrant.'

'Right,' Dante says, feeling the first signs of fatigue in Eliot's company, manifesting as a crease of pain behind his eyes.

'It is important we form a certain understanding, Dante.'

'About the work?'

Eliot nods. 'I'm tied up most of the day with the new book and what have you and, although I am not insensitive to your need for information, I must beg a small favour.'

'Sure.'

'For the moment I would like you to become familiar with Beth. She knows how things stand. But you must not come to the school unless I call you, and I am afraid my home must remain strictly private.' He looks at Dante, but can't meet his eye for long. 'You know what it's like. It must be the same with your music. A man needs solitude to contemplate. His own space. I do not, I cannot, tolerate disturbances from anyone.'

'Of course. I wouldn't dream of interrupting your work. I have the luxury of time, and there's the reading list. Just give me a shout when you're ready.'

Eliot smiles with relief. Feeling deflated, Dante presumes Eliot is wary about the hell-raising reputation of rock musicians. St Andrews is a conservative place; he makes a mental note to keep an eye on Tom.

'Can I ask you a frank question, Dante?'

'Yeah.'

Now Eliot is agitated and speaks more quickly. 'What are your thoughts on sacrifice?'

He thinks about the question. It confuses him. 'In what context?'

'Let's say, to rid yourself of sentimentality to explore . . . No, to satisfy. Yes, to satisfy an extreme appetite.'

'Well, in a way I have already experienced that. I put my music before anything.'

'So you are saying you would give yourself to a higher purpose?'

'I don't know about that. I just hope our music will come to something, eventually. That it'll mean something to a lot of people. We've pretty much sacrificed everything for the band.'

'Admirable,' Eliot says, impatient, dissatisfied. 'But I sense a reluctance.'

'For what?'

'Real sacrifice. What if someone stood between you and . . .' Eliot stops. He looks at Dante with what appears to be sympathy. What is he talking about? And does he feel sorry for him? Does he think him stupid and unable to understand a philosophical question? Feeling out of his depth, Dante looks at his boots.

'I only ask because I need to understand how you will feel about me. There have been victims in my life, Dante. There are things you don't know. Some say I am responsible for the deaths of several people during my travels. Did I have the right to push companions beyond their tolerance? Is that right? Using people on the mere and improbable chance that I could find my own enlightenment?' But Eliot seems dispirited as he says this, losing his enthusiasm like a man reciting old platitudes that once served him well, but in which he no longer believes.

Dante looks up, eager for the chance to make his hero feel good. 'I think everyone is guilty of manipulation to some degree, Eliot. And the men who died in the last chapter of *Banquet* wanted to be there. Before the ceremony, you warned them about what they might see after taking the drug. Surely their deaths were reactions to the hallucinogens.' Dante grins, unsure of himself. What has he just said? He doesn't want Eliot to think him callous, but can't think of anything else to say. The man confuses him, intimidates him. And all he wants is to be liked by Eliot, who now regards him: thoughtful, impressed perhaps, even grateful, or is it just pity in the old man's blue eyes?

Eliot smiles. 'Maybe you have already excused me.'

Whistling and suddenly more animated, as if he has arrived at an important decision, Eliot paces about near the edge of the pier. He pauses by the little tower, looks into the sky and quotes a verse of something unfamiliar to Dante, in a tone of voice that sounds like a mocking, triumphant affront to the beautiful view of St Andrews harbour. It is the same tone Eliot used back by the castle when he was disparaging Christians. But there is something in the man's voice that penetrates Dante, to stir a dark melody inside him, something disquieting but seductive:

> *'Dead loves are woven in his ghastly robe;*
> *Bewildered wills and faiths grown old and rotten*
> *And deeds undared his sceptre, sword, and globe,*
> *Keep us, O Mary Maid,*
> *What time the King Ghost goes arrayed.'*

After the brief performance, Eliot places a hand, gently, on Dante's shoulder. 'These are difficult times we have. Strange times. And you've come a long way, I know. Because you knew I needed help. I thank you.' And as Eliot turns and begins the walk back to the shore, Dante stands behind him, baffled, and thinks he hears the great man say, 'Forgive me,' but he isn't sure.

FIVE

Visiting Doctor of Anthropology seeks students suffering from nightmares, disturbed sleep patterns, night terrors. Completely confidential analysis. Contact Hart Miller.

Africa's red dust has finally cleared from his eyes, nose, and thick brown beard. The sight of naked children playing in unsanitary water has disappeared too, along with the grease on his skin and the flies that were attracted to it. Milling below his window in the cooler and thinner air, cleansed by the sea, the people of St Andrews have replaced the familiar sight of African tribesmen wrapped in their damask robes, swatting at mosquitoes with lazy arcs of their peroxide palms in the sweltering sun. Smells of roasted goat, crushed ginger and his own sweat are also swept away by the tang of salty breezes and the aroma of stones bleached by the sun. And there are no crippled beggars in Fife singing for their food. Shouting mothers, laughing students and rumbling car engines have changed the soundtrack for Hart Miller. Following six months of fieldwork in Nigeria, he has spent several hours of each day gazing from the window of his flat on Market Street, watching and adjusting to the new world.

Occasionally a passing tradesman or shopper will glance

up and meet his brown eyes, small behind the round spectacles that he repeatedly pushes up his stubby nose. And only when the time approaches for his first interview with a student does he move away from the bright sunlight and rub his face in an attempt to massage some feeling back into his hairy cheeks, and into his small, bullet-shaped forehead. 'Time I started work on some professorial eyebrows,' he says, and begins wheezing and giggling to himself, while padding across the lounge on his hairy feet to reach for the bottle of whisky on the coffee table. A bottle of Laphroaig has been his first purchase in St Andrews. During the headaches and fatigue on the flight to Edinburgh, he dreamed of the Scottish spirit and its distinctive peaty taste. It was earthy. A local product with a smattering of anthropological information on the label: enough professional justification to put a spin on things. Hart tugs on the bottle, sucking the nectar through his dense facial hair. After a gasp he wipes his mouth and begins checking the living room that will double as a study during his stay in Scotland.

Everything is set up: the couch, with an Ecuadorian throw-rug draped across it; a tape recorder positioned on the coffee table; his books, papers, and a laptop computer, amassed on the desk.

Exhaling loudly, he checks the diver's watch on his freckly wrist and thinks of the approaching interview. Talking to an English girl about her nightmares should be routine. Pressures of late adolescence and the stresses of a student lifestyle can create any number of recurring nightmares in a young mind. And perhaps there will be no connection between the reports his e-mail service in Nairobi was receiving from St Andrews, and what he's been studying in Africa, Asia and

North America. It could be a waste of time: another one. But he has to be sure.

When his friend, Adolpho, first sent him an e-mail from the Anthropology Department at St Andrews, two months earlier, the news had been tragic. A fourth-year student, Ben Carter, had committed an unusual suicide. The history undergraduate had burned himself to death in the car given to him by his parents on his twenty-first birthday. According to Adolpho, who knew Carter personally, the undergraduate had been sleeping poorly for months, had become increasingly withdrawn throughout his final year, and failed to show for his exams. More importantly, prior to his death, Ben Carter had become terrified of the night and the vivid terrors that came with it. And, according to rumour, he was not alone.

With the offer of Adolpho's flat, rent-free for a month, Hart booked airline tickets immediately. Although his sponsorship grant and the publisher's advance for his book on dream culture in primitive society had nearly run dry, Adolpho's e-mail message had excited him enough to make him head for the airport the minute his work in Africa concluded. This new territory was special. Of all places, a night-terror phenomenon could be occurring in Scotland. That would cover Northern Europe and the last ground in Hart's rarely studied global puzzle.

After spending his first two days in bed, or on the toilet, recovering from jetlag, a hangover, and a recurring bout of amoebic dysentery, he began posting his flyers at strategic locations around the town, invariably popular with students at any university: the library by necessity, the Student Union complex on Market Street, and the Union diner on North

Street. And within an hour of the first poster going up, a message from a young student called Kerry Sewell had been left on his answering machine:

'Hello, Mr Miller. I'd like to see you urgently. I'm a student here. Art History. And when I saw the flyer in the library . . . It's so odd, it's as if you knew. I really need to see you soon. About the night terror thing. The sooner the better. It is confidential, isn't it?'

Hart had called her straight back and arranged the first interview. Now, in an attempt to relax before the girl arrives, he turns on his small portable stereo and plays *American Beauty* by the Grateful Dead, an album full of summer memories from his youth in Chicago. And while he nods his head to the lonesome and mellow harmonies, he continues to pull on the Laphroaig bottle and to enjoy the throatburn and stomach-glow. But right before the first chorus of 'Friend of the Devil', the front doorbell emits a single solemn chime.

Hart leaps up from the rug, staggers forward, bangs his shins on the corner of the coffee table and shouts, 'Shit!' Hurriedly, he wipes his mouth and runs back and forth with the bottle before he finds a place to hide it, behind a stack of tomes on the dining table. After rinsing Listerine through his cheeks and over his teeth, he then siphons it through his lips into the kitchen sink. Smoothing out the front of his red flannel shirt with the moist palms of his hands, he trots down the narrow staircase to the ground-floor reception.

Through the glass in the top portion of the front door, he sees the profile of a tall girl. Stylish tortoiseshell sunglasses conceal her eyes. Shoulder-length hair, ice-blonde in colour, is tied at the back of her head with a black velvet band, which gives the effect of sharpening her already striking cheekbones. But her young face, that in any circumstance is arresting, seems distracted. Although she gazes down Market Street, so bright with sunlight, toward the large and modern Student Union building, it is as if she sees nothing. 'Jeez,' Hart mutters. She is nearly a foot taller than him and he can already smell money.

When he opens the door, she turns to face him. Her tight lips part and there is a pause – a fathoming – before she says, 'Hi.'

'Hey now,' Hart replies, nodding his head to some inner rhythm and raising both hands as if he has just met an old friend unexpectedly, and wants to do nothing more than spend time with them. 'Let me guess. I'm not what you were expecting,' he says.

Kerry pushes her sunglasses up and into her hair. 'No.' She slinks through the doorway, blinking her pale-blue eyes quickly as she scans the walls. Sensing distress, Hart manages to sustain his characteristic warmth and endearing smile, in an attempt to put her at ease. 'Up there?' she says, and points toward the open doorway at the top of the staircase.

'Yeah, yeah, go on up, honey.'

With his eyes fixed on her wrap-around skirt, which is long and falls to the top of her leather boots, he follows her up the stairs to the lounge. As the stairs groan and creak beneath them, he becomes conscious of inhaling her fragrance across his copper-wire moustache. After Africa, and Guatemala before that, it is a sudden but refreshing opportunity to share time and space with all the things he enjoys about Western women: perfume, shaven legs, and painted lips. He briefly entertains an image of Kerry, naked, in his mind, but then dismisses it, feeling ashamed. After so long in the wilderness he suddenly worries about blowing his first lead with an inappropriate leer.

'So, Kerry, you saw the flyer in the library,' he says with a chuckle when they reach the lounge. 'I've been pasting those things all over town.'

She stays quiet. Hart loses his grin, fast. 'Sit down, honey. Umm, let me get you a drink. I haven't had time to go to the store, but I have some coffee. It was in the cupboard when I arrived. Guess I inherited it.'

Kerry approaches the couch. 'That would be nice.'

As he gets busy in the kitchen, he hears Kerry sit down in the lounge. When she crosses her long legs, the little whisper created by the innocent gesture runs a prickle down the nape of his neck. Shake it off, he tells himself. This ain't a date. Don't start with some Woody Allen routine. Ensconced in the kitchen, out of sight, he also looks at his hands and sees shakes. Christ, I'm an anthropologist. What if she needs a doctor?

'Will you be taping this?' Kerry asks, and he thinks her voice sounds even more feminine with the cultured English accent. It drifts through the arched white portal, separating the lounge and kitchen. 'Sure,' he says. 'But don't worry about a thing. If it fits my study, I'd like to use it for my book. With your permission of course, and I can always change the names.' Holding two cups of black coffee that steam in his chubby paws, Hart reappears in the lounge. 'Like it black?'

Kerry nods. Hart blushes. 'Just as well, there's no milk.' With the cups placed on the table between them, he pulls a wooden chair around to host his bulbous hips.

'It's OK about taping me,' she says. 'I'm just a little delicate at the moment. I've not been sleeping.'

'Go on.'

'Well it's very strange. I . . . I think I could be losing my mind.' The skin across the thin bones of her face blanches, losing its honey-coloured sheen, and after she speaks there follows a nervous and apologetic giggle before she dips her head. A long silence follows and Hart begins to fiddle with his beard. Finally, he smacks his lips, and rubs his hands down the front of his weathered combat trousers. 'Don't be ashamed of anything, Kerry. Just feel free to let go. I got two good ears here and a lot of experience in this field. It doesn't matter how wacky you think your dreams are, I want to hear everything you can remember about them.'

Taking careful sips from her coffee, Kerry stares across the room and beyond the far wall, her eyes unfocused, looking inward. 'Is it nightmares you study?' she says, breaking from the daze, suddenly uncomfortable with letting herself drift in front of a stranger.

'Yes, that's a significant part of the whole deal. I'm an anthropologist and I've been studying occult beliefs in primitive or isolated societies – from what we call an ethnographic perspective. I study people and why they believe in the supernatural. Not whether magic works or not, but why some communities still maintain occult practices. This took me down the avenue of primal fears in a wide range of cultures and night terrors became a by-product of my original thesis. Something I picked up along the way. It interested me and I saw my chance for original work.'

'Tell me about the nightmares,' she says, staring right at him now.

'Well, when a locale has a long tradition of superstition, and if the roots of that history are deeply entrenched in the occult, sleepers often suffer the same nightmares for generations.' He feels himself light up inside and, despite his reticence at becoming an academic bore with such a pretty girl, his enthusiasm carries him along. 'You know, the bad dreams last for years, even centuries, like a kind of echo. I've travelled to Newfoundland, South America and Africa chasing this pattern for my book. I want to collect data reflecting how, inexplicably, a haunted past can become locked, like an energy, in a specific area, and affect the sleep of even those people who are otherwise oblivious to the history of the place in which they live.'

'How do these night terrors affect people?' Kerry asks, her voice sharper.

'Well, some of the good people who have confided in me have had the same dreams since they were kids, and want to know why they go to the same place every time they close their eyes. Others are too afraid to sleep, or find their dreams affect the way they behave. In some extreme cases, well, folks do unusual things. They become volatile, or unreasonable. They can sleepwalk too.'

The girl's eyes widen and her body stiffens.

'But it's usually just the sleeping consciousness, and night terrors are a universal phenomenon. There is no need to –'

'Sleepwalk, you say,' Kerry interrupts. 'How extreme does sleepwalking get?'

'Well, it varies, from strolling around the house to incidents of amnesia. In extreme cases –' he pauses '– well, it seems to be the start of something more complicated.'

Kerry closes her eyes and covers them with a slim hand,

pressing her varnished nails into her cheek, just below an inflamed scratch. He hears her say 'Shit' under her breath.

'Kerry, I'm sorry. I don't want to frighten you. Girl, that is a very unlikely scenario.'

When she removes the hand from her face her eyes shine with tears. Hart swallows. 'Listen, Kerry, I think we should start. Just lie back there on the couch and relax. If you want another drink or a smoke just holler. That's it, get comfy. Don't worry about your boots, just relax. I'm going to ask you a few questions and I want you to be as candid as you are able. I'm not an analyst, but I believe talking about it, to someone who knows what's going down, will take the world off your shoulders. Clean off, honey, where it hadn't ought to be.'

She reclines on the couch and sinks into the cushions and throw-rug. She dabs at her eyes with a white tissue she has kept tucked up her sleeve. Hart stretches his arm across to the tape recorder and indents the RECORD button as quietly as possible. 'This is Doctor Hart Miller on August 25 at 11:00 a.m., speaking with Kerry Sewell, a fourth-year student on the Art History honours degree programme, at St Andrews University. Kerry, I would like to ask you a few frank questions about your general wellbeing and state of health.'

'OK.'

'Are you taking any medication, or have you been over the course of your troubled sleep?'

'No. Wait a minute. Yes. Some hay-fever tablets. And I had a really bad flu. Like a forty-eight-hour thing. I took anti-biotics.'

'Have you suffered unduly from stress or depression?'

'I'm not depressed, but I have been working hard. I had final exams and still have my thesis to finish.'

'So you often work late?'

'I would say so.'

'How much do you drink a week, on average, in terms of units of alcohol?'

'Umm, I don't know. Wine sometimes with a meal, or in the evening, and at the weekend I go out with friends, but I rarely get drunk.'

'OK. Is there a family history of mental illness? Schizophrenia, to be precise?'

'No. Grandma's a bit scatty, but she is nearly eighty.'

'Right. Have you ever had any psychological problems?'

Kerry looks away.

'Kerry, I am not asking for specific details, but generally have –'

'I saw a psychiatrist during my A-Levels.'

'A-Levels? What are those?'

'Exams you take before university.'

'Oh, right. So you needed counselling for something?'

'Yes. I had a few problems in my teens. Nothing major.'

'That's all right, honey, I –'

'Sorry, but it was very painful. Can we talk about the dreams now?'

'Sure, sure. I was just establishing a bit of background.'

'And you think I'm a nut already, because I saw a psychiatrist?' Her words come quickly and her face hardens with annoyance.

Still smiling and keeping his voice steady, Hart says, 'Kerry, there is no taboo in counselling. I think everybody should have an analyst. I spent most of my youth on a couch talking about my mother to some dude in a check jacket and brogues.'

Anger changes to relief, and her face softens with a smile. 'I'm sorry . . . for snapping. But everything is difficult for me at the moment. I'm not sleeping and I think I should leave St Andrews.'

'Kerry, I hear you, but I think you should start at the beginning. You mentioned your nightmares on the phone. Just give me what you can remember about when and how they began.'

She folds her arms across her chest, as if for warmth, clasping the top of each arm with a hand. 'It started about two months ago, when a student called Ben Carter killed himself. At first I thought it was a reaction, like delayed shock. I didn't know him that well, but when someone your own age dies, it's terrible. You just don't expect things like that to happen.'

Hart nods his head. 'It was awful. Did you and Ben take the same courses?'

'No. Ben and I were part of a group. I knew him from there.'

'What kind of group?'

'Umm, a paranormal society, run by a lecturer in the divinity department. Eliot Coldwell. Lots of people went, but it was all quite harmless.'

Hart frowns.

'Most of the people there went out of curiosity. Mr Coldwell has quite a reputation for being weird. Bit of a giggle, really. That's why my friend Maria and I went along.'

'So this lecturer, what did he do?'

'Oh, gave talks and things. Like the stuff you see on those

Arthur C Clarke's Mysterious World programmes. I heard he conducted experiments with some people who thought they were psychic as well. But I dropped out early. I had too much work to do.'

Hart squints and tries to remember where he's heard the name before. 'Eliot Coldwell. The name rings a bell.'

'He wrote a book. Some of the boys in the group kept asking questions about it. Because of the drugs in it.'

'Yeah. Can't remember the title.'

'*Banquet for the Damned*.'

'That's right. I've read about it. Started a few cults in Britain and some of those heavy metal bands went for it in a big way. Led Zep, I think. Maybe Sabbath too. He was into the whole Eastern thing. Kind of like a minor-league Crowley or Huxley.'

Kerry nods. 'It's in the library. I never read much of it. Found it a bit heavy going.'

'Did these group meetings start your nightmares?'

'No. That was all finished before the summer. People say the university stopped it. There was a lot of fuss about a group like that here. It's a very quiet place and I think Mr Coldwell was told to stop the group. It was nothing really, though. Just discussions and some meditation. It helped me to relax and he had a beautiful voice. Like Anthony Hopkins.'

'What about your friend, Maria? Did she have nightmares?'

'I don't know. We fell out. A while ago. Over a stupid man.'

Hart nods. 'Most of them are. I can say that because I don't count. With this much hair I gotta be the missing link.'

Kerry giggles.

'Did this lecturer stop his group?' he asks.

'I think so, but there was talk about it going underground.'

Hart frowns. 'Ben Carter was a member too. I didn't know that. My buddy Adolpho went back to Brazil after Ben's death to do his fieldwork. He only mentioned the kid's nightmares.'

'Ben was into it more than most people. I think he was Mr Coldwell's research assistant.'

Hart nods some more, deep in thought, before turning his attention back to Kerry. 'Your nightmares. Tell me about your disturbed sleep. I'm sorry for digressing, but this is all new to me. I was in Nigeria last week.'

'You don't look very brown.'

'Too many insects on me. The sun never had a chance.'

Kerry laughs again and then looks toward the ceiling to concentrate her recall. 'These dreams were different to anything I've experienced before. They're so real.'

'Go on. How are they vivid?'

'I could swear I'm awake. In the beginning, something terrible would happen in a dream and I would wake up, suddenly. And be really frightened. Even in tears. And my bed sheets would be all strewn about the room. And things would have been moved around my bed.'

'Can you remember the dreams?'

'No. Not really. Not in full. I would just wake up with a horrible taste in my mouth and my arms and legs . . . and things, would hurt, as if I'd been attacked. Sometimes there were bruises, but I thought I had done them to myself. Then recently, these dreams came back every other night, and I began to remember bits. There is always someone in my room. Trying to find me. To get at me.' She sniffs again.

'So Kerry, let's concentrate on the waking moment. You said that things in your immediate physical environment had changed. How so?'

After clearing her throat and dabbing the now crumpled tissue at the corner of both eyes, she continues in a quivery voice. 'I used to leave my bedside light on. It sounds silly, I know, but after it all began I just couldn't bear to sleep in the dark. And when I woke up, the light would have been turned off and I could hear someone in my room.'

'You're sure you were awake? This wasn't the residue from a dream?'

'I didn't really know at first. My whole body would be like tingling and I couldn't move. It was terrifying. I was paralysed and tried to scream for my neighbour, Sarah. But I couldn't make a sound.'

'Aphasia,' Hart mumbles, nodding his head and staring toward the window.

'What?'

'Just a technical term for the inability to speak when paralysed. It's more common than you think.'

'Really,' she says, her eyes widening and something approaching relief entering her tone of voice.

'Sure, but anyway Kerry, please go on. You said there was someone in your room.'

'Yes. Someone's by my bed, in my room. Sort of sniffing. Like a dog, but not in a dog way. Not friendly. It's slower. And I can't move but I can hear it moving about, and reaching for things. Like . . . Like it's looking for me.'

'Did it vanish quickly when you woke up fully?'

'Yes, to start with, but as the dreams became much worse, it would linger. A couple of weeks back, I saw it for the first time, just as I woke up. I saw what looked like a long arm reach across my bedside cabinet to touch the light, which went off. And it just sat there, huddled over in the dark, making these sounds.'

'The breathing and so forth?'

'Yes, and more. It was . . . It's hard to describe, it seemed to be whispering to me too, but I didn't recognise the language. It just sounded very old and unpleasant, with bits of English breaking through, but I could never fully understand the words. And it would hiss, like . . . like it was excited.' Kerry pauses to dab her nose. She turns her face away from Hart but he can see her jaw trembling as she tries not to cry.

He feels terrible for pushing her even further, but he has to. 'The intensity of the visitations, I will call them, increased as time went on. The nightmares became more vivid and the presence stayed a little longer each night.'

'Exactly,' Kerry continues, her voice breaking around the edges. 'There was this one time when I'd woken up and it was still there. There was some light coming through a gap in the curtains, so I got a better look at it. A dark shape over by the window. Very tall. It went right up to the ceiling but still had to bend over. My heart nearly stopped. And it was trying to show itself to me. Leaning right over toward my bed. But its hands were covering its face.'

Hart leans forward in his chair, resting both hands on the edge of the coffee table.

'And I remember feeling so cold at that moment and I heard it whispering to me. Through its fingers. It was there for a moment and then it moved very quickly to the side of my bed. I could smell it. It was horrible. I closed my eyes. I couldn't bear it for a moment longer, but I did see it move. It wasn't like a normal walk. Not natural. It was more of a glide. But very quick. I remember it was very thin and then it was making a sniffing noise. Right by me.' Kerry's face is pleading for an explanation.

He clears his throat. 'And it would stay beside you and watch you?'

'Yes, but it was agitated. It sounded fierce and I was just so frightened with it hovering by me, waiting for something.'

'Kerry, it was only a dream. A very vivid dream.'

The girl's face crumples and reddens. She covers it with her hands and sobs. Her chest heaves, and Hart hears her final stand. 'It's trying to kill me. The nightmares have always been leading to something, that gets stronger and more real every time, until the thing in my dream attacked me. Last night it nearly killed me.'

He stands and flits across to the couch in alarm, but only manages to dither beside her and look at the ceiling in exasperation. What can he do? What has he forced her to remember? He isn't trained as a psychiatrist and the girl seems manic. It could be more than his theory about night terrors. For a moment he wishes he'd never come to St Andrews. Maybe the girl has been raped, repressed the memory and been too scared to tell the police or her parents.

Maybe there is a stalker on the campus.

Forcing composure, he sits back down on the corner of the couch. It is important he doesn't touch her and he feels like a louse for all of the desperate and hungry thoughts he entertained earlier. 'Kerry, listen to me. I know this has been painful, but draw some comfort from what I am going to say. You're not the first young woman to suffer from dreams like this. I've heard about this more times than I've wanted to. You're not crazy. But I think you should go home, to your parents, or a friend's or something. Can you do that?'

Kerry nods.

'Just get out of here for a while. Maybe see a counsellor.'

Kerry sits up suddenly, and removes her hands from her tear-stained cheeks. 'I'm not mad! I know what you're thinking. That I'm some stupid little girl who's been raped and can't face the truth. You're wrong. These dreams are real. There was something in my room. It took me to the pier, Mr Miller. It took me to the pier and tried to kill me. It wanted me to die. Like Ben Carter. That's why he burned. It made him do it! I know it!'

The violence in her voice forces Hart away from the couch. His hands hover at the same level as her shoulders but fail to narrow the distance. 'OK, honey,' he says, his voice no more than a whisper. 'But did you hear me? Go home. Leave today and put some distance between yourself and this town.' Just in case, he wants to add. Just in case you're right and everything I've been studying is true.

The girl continues to sob.

Kerry walks through Market Street in a daze after confessing so much to a stranger. These night-time experiences are more than bad dreams and Hart Miller knows it. She could tell by his face. Other girls have suffered the same thing, he said so. That's why he is in town, looking for the thing that came for her at night. It sniffed around her when she slept and attempted to consummate its final wish down on the pier. She can't spend another night in St Andrews and doesn't need Doctor Miller to tell her so. She's only stuck it out because of her work. Four years of study can't be just thrown away. She needs the degree for the job promised her by a management consultancy in London. But last night changed everything.

Pausing at the newsagents at the top of Market Street, Kerry decides to top-up her phone. She'll call home and ask her dad to come and fetch her. Most of her work in the library is done and the last bit of the thesis can be finished at home. She'll post it up to the university.

Before she enters the shop Kerry turns around and glances at the town made dark by her shades. A place she's lived in for four years and loved, but now the very sight of the monuments and old churches makes her feel different. During the day, she is more frightened than she ever was as a child alone in a room at night, not knowing any better. There is something here that has killed her hope and even her most simple joys – something unholy.

After progressing no more than a few steps inside the shop, she suddenly stops and closes her eyes for a moment. Her composure unravels. It is right there, the confirmation of her fears in black and white, on the front page of the *Herald*:

POLICE FIND MYSTERY REMAINS ON WEST SANDS

In a young life inexplicably filled with terror, there is no such thing as coincidence. Every screech from a hungry gull is a reminder of the dreams; every placard commemorating the death of a Protestant martyr is a sign; every newspaper's report of a death is connected. Kerry pulls the paper off the bottom shelf and hurries up to the counter. She slaps a pound coin down and races out of the shop. The girl behind the counter raises a quizzical face. As she drifts back into the sunlight, Kerry's eyes race across the opening paragraph on the rustling newspaper:

> *Police officers responded to an emergency call from the West Sands yesterday. A local woman, Beatrice Hay, found part of a human body washed up on the shoreline. 'I have been walking on that beach for thirty years but I've never seen anything like it before. This was awful, a terrible thing to see.'*
>
> *A police spokesman issued a statement late last night, indicating a belief that the grisly body-part – still unspecified as to which limb or organ – had been washed ashore from the channel. 'It could have come from the sea,' Sergeant Lindsay declared. 'But we are not ruling out suspicious circumstances.'*

Suddenly remembering the strength of the night terror and the power in its hard fingers, Kerry feels Doctor Miller's shaky assurances vaporise. Breaking into a run, she bumps into a couple of men with long hair. She knocks them apart and rushes away, unable to apologise, thinking only of a phone call, a suitcase, and the safety of home.

Thin trails of perfume, left behind by Kerry, make Hart melancholy. After a long shake of his grizzled head, he takes another slug from the second fifth of Laphroaig. He's been sitting alone and still for a long time after Kerry's departure, drinking and going through every possible angle and explanation he knows of to explain away her story, until coherence has begun to fragment and his theories have become jumbled. But instinct tells him her confession and reaction are genuine.

In a way, he should be elated. If what she has just recounted is true, and he can think of few reasons to disbelieve her story, then his work could continue in St Andrews in dramatic style. Night terrors might just be the beginning – the first telltale ripples before the contagion spreads. Everything he's studied so far has always been after the fact – hearsay, folklore, the incoherent ramblings of witnesses. But today, in the Kingdom of Fife, it is possible he's landed in the thick of something extraordinary.

It is ironic. He should be whooping with delight at the find. But when something creates so much anguish in a young and faultless girl, when her sanity and perhaps even her life are in danger, he cannot rejoice. Staring at the tape recorder, he moistens his lips and begins to mutter to himself. 'You're afraid, buddy. No wonder you swallow so much wine. Maybe you looked too hard.'

Waiting for the slight judder to vanish from his vision, Hart forces himself to stand up and to remove the image of Kerry's tear-stained face from his mind. Sweeping up his Dictaphone, he checks the battery light and begins pacing about the lounge, murmuring his initial observations into the tiny microphone:

'My first interviewee has experienced a classic night-terror situation. Is it metachoric? Is her visual field hallucinatory on waking when there is such defined evidence of a physical manifestation in her immediate environment? It is still unclear, however, why the apparition has begun to appear in her room. A previous adolescent trauma suggests a reactive vision, but there is much evidence to the contrary. She is struck dumb with aphasia upon waking and also confesses to acute paralysis. This state lasts too long for the conditions of a false awakening.

'The manifestation is particularly profound, as recorded in a number of case studies. She engages in a tactile, auditory, and visual experience. Temperature, smell, touch, hearing and sight are all affected during the visitation. I would like to observe her further and carry out REM tests, but, as I have advised, it is best she desert the locale and reintegrate herself into a familiar environment. If these experiences fit my research and are more than just bad dreams, I can only hope she takes my advice.'

Hart stops the recording, places the Dictaphone on the coffee table and presses REWIND. Wearily, he slumps across the couch. No sooner has he made himself comfortable than Kerry's scent, and the troubled air she left behind, surrounds him again. The tape stops rewinding with a loud clunk, which makes him flinch, and he upends the bottle of Laphroaig. But, before he is able to gulp his way any further into the whisky, the phone rings. He crosses the room, unsteady on his feet, and raises the receiver. 'Hey now, Hart Miller speaking.'

'Hello, Dr Miller. My name is Mike Bowen. I saw your flyer this morning concerning nightmares and think I have something for you. Can I arrange an appointment?'

'Sure. Are you having the nightmares?'

'Afraid so.'

'Is tomorrow good for you?'

'Yes. I'd appreciate your thoughts. I need to get this thing resolved.'

Hart clears his throat and shakes some clarity back into his fuddled mind. 'Let's say after one.'

'That's great,' Mike replies.

Hart hangs up and mutters, 'This is crazy.' He'd expected one or two calls stretched over a month, but two on the first day following the posting of his flyer is incredible. Night terrors are usually isolated to one individual before the remote chance of a gradual spread.

After he's pushed a sandwich around his plate for half an hour, the phone rings again. A girl, who introduces herself as Maria, wants advice and an interview. Does she know someone called Kerry? he asks. Yes, she answers, and he can tell immediately the girl is doing her best to maintain a steady voice and not crack up. Hart books her in for an interview after Mike Bowen, hangs up, and then drifts back to his favourite window overlooking Market Street. It is almost too much too soon. And he only has a month to gather his data. He needs to think and process the information, authenticate the stories, check out this Coldwell character, and find out how a beautiful Scottish university town can be afflicted with night terrors. But what he needs more than anything else is another drink. So he has one.

SIX

They form a triangle, divided by a heavy silence in a room made red by the ox-blood leather of the furniture they sit upon, and by the crimson velvet curtains that droop, half closed, over large windows facing inland. Smoke from a cigarette hangs in skeins above their heads, where a myriad of dust particles falls through a beam of sunlight shining through the partition in the drapes.

'Eliot must go.' The long and frustrating silence is broken by Harry Wilson, the University Proctor. Seated behind his orderly desk, with his protruding jaw set fast on a thin face that looks increasingly worn as each week of the summer passes, Harry pronounces sentence on the friend he's known for thirty years. Slowly, his grey eyes move from one guest to another, to assess their reactions.

In the antique chairs, usually occupied by doctoral students with thesis propositions or problems, Arthur Spencer, Hebdomidar, adjusts his position in his chair when it requires no adjustment, and Janice Summers, Administrative Supervisor, Divinity, lights another cigarette. 'Harry . . .' Arthur begins and then stops. His smooth pink face tightens. One of his plump hands rises from the armrest of his chair and hovers before descending again to paw at the wood.

The Proctor has the air of a man about to enjoy closure,

but who remains tense due to the possibility of disagreement. 'This issue has consumed a great deal of my time,' he says. 'I've assessed the situation from every angle, thought of every possible scenario, agonised over Eliot's predicament, but there can be no more chances. I fought hard to get him here in the first place and have deflected criticism from the moment he arrived. The patience of others is at an end too. My petition to the Principal has been drafted, and he and I will meet before the week is out to finalise Eliot's end of contract. He should be gone before the Martinmas term begins.'

Arthur manages a nervous smile. 'And Eliot's reaction? I mean, what of the repercussions?'

Looking toward the large window of his study that oversees the East Scores, the Proctor becomes impatient with his friend's continuing vacillation. A spring uncoils inside him. 'If his drink problem is not sufficient reason for dismissal, then I don't know what is. There is also the matter of substance use. Regardless of the threat of repercussions, he must go.'

Arthur lowers his eyes and begins to chew at the inside of his mouth, as if forced to remember something distasteful. Harry clears his throat and reddens slightly, uncomfortable with the words that have left his mouth. Janice seems content to watch both men. 'Then we can take into account his abuse of trust,' Harry continues, determined to maintain momentum. 'His negative influence over certain students, and his incompetence in academic matters. And is it a coincidence, Arthur, mere chance that a student – his research assistant no less – is now dead? We may have been excited by his rituals when we were younger, my friend, but well you know, he went too far up here. Both Ben Carter and Beth . . .' Pausing, the Proctor clears his throat. When he speaks again it is apparent to his guests that although his words are chosen carefully, they are spoken with difficulty. 'In our hearts we all know his influence had an unfortunate effect on at least two students. If word of this were ever to reach the wrong ears . . .' The Proctor lets the suggestion hang in the air.

'The welfare of the student body is my concern,' Arthur says, quietly. 'And neither of you had to speak to Carter's parents. I did. No one feels the impact of that tragedy more than I, but to force Eliot out at such a sensitive time by exposing the sensational nature of our suspicions . . . Well, will we not be connecting events previously unconnected in the minds of others, and therefore be opening ourselves to inquiry with such a move? Until now, Harry, we've managed to keep things under wraps, wouldn't you say? But a drama would only serve to encourage unwelcome attention.'

The Proctor dips his face in exasperation. 'We've been through it over and over. We've dithered and delayed. A decision has to be made and you'll find, I'm sure, a great deal of peace once the action has been carried out.'

'Too late,' Janice says, raising an immaculate eyebrow. 'Should have thought about the students a long time ago, before you tried reliving your days at Oxford by inviting him up here. Think of the grief you'd have spared us all.'

Harry glares at her, but she remains indifferent – her face as pale as alabaster, smooth save for a few fine lines, and haughty as a sculpture beneath her shiny hair, restrained in a sleek bun on the rear of her small head. Arthur glances across at her, warily, but his body is unwilling to turn and follow the head's lead. 'He's not stupid,' she says, glad of their attention.

'In fact he is far smarter than we three. I know, I sit above the bastard every day. I listen and I watch, as instructed by you, Harry, and he won't go quietly or willingly, of that I can assure you. What does he have? No family and no money, from what I can remember. He's trapped in that wretched house, supplied through your misplaced charity, with nowhere to go and only that slut, Beth, for company.'

Arthur winces. 'Janice, really.'

'You saw the signs well over a year ago, but you wouldn't listen,' Janice continues, ignoring Arthur and oblivious to Harry, whose lips have thinned and whose complexion has paled with anger. 'And I'm not just talking about his drinking. He's far more devious and manipulative when sober. It's a blessing when he's pissed. At least he has the sense to lock himself away. It's just unfortunate he never drank himself to death like you secretly hoped he might.'

'Now really,' Arthur cries out.

'Well, I'm right and you know it. How much abuse can a man of his age take, you thought to yourselves. But Eliot's more durable than you imagine. A lifetime of abuse has preserved him, not destroyed him. Some people can survive anything and he's one of them. He's insensible both to decay and the feelings of others. And only now, when some long-haired hooligan arrives and announces the continuation of his work, are you prepared to act. You make me sick. It's too late, boys. Threaten what little he has left and he'll start to sing, and those who invited him to lecture here, and protected him when he left the rails, will have a lot of explaining to do. Am I right? Isn't that why we're here, to save reputations and all that? When that nonsense started with Beth, I warned you.'

'What an appalling thing to think of us,' Arthur says, his bald head now gleaming in places with droplets of sweat, as he begins to rise from his chair. 'We're compassionate men who endeavoured to help an old friend in need. We had no way of predicting the outcome of Eliot's time with us. And what you're suggesting, Janice, is callous to an extreme, and downright libellous. I will have nothing further to do with this stupidity. We're doing nothing beside scaremongering and adding credence to the man's ludicrous and, dare I say, unwholesome interests.'

The Proctor holds out two hands, one for each guest, palm outward, to silence them. 'Sit down, Arthur,' he says in a quiet but loaded voice, as if his words are the steam escaping from a pressure soon destined to explode if he is not understood, and quickly. 'Do you need it waved in front of your bloody face, man? Remember May? You were there. You saw the results of his sordid experiments on the students. I too would like to wipe it from my memory, but I can't. Whether you believe anything extraordinary happened or not, Eliot was convinced his little conjuring tricks had begun to work and so was Ben Carter. He was in on it from the start, way deeper than any of us imagined, and now he's dead. Something happened to that boy, whether it was all in his mind or not. And Eliot was directly responsible. It's a deplorable thought, but he may even have twisted the boy's mind with –' Harry pauses, the words too difficult '– with chemical assistance.' He looks to his companions, each in turn, his glare steady. 'And that goes no further.' Then he relaxes, exhaling and adjusting the papers on his already immaculate desk top. 'As long as Eliot remains here, other young people are at risk.'

He turns his face to Janice. 'And Janice. Not for a moment have I acted in my own interest. We all have positions of considerable responsibility, and we have a duty to maintain the standards and reputation of this university. In my book that comes before self-preservation. Can you imagine what the papers would do to this place if there was any suggestion of drugs and black magic? It'd be ruined.'

Arthur sinks back into his chair. Harry continues to glare at Janice, leaning across his desk to reinforce the reprimand. 'This "I told you so" attitude has worn thin, my dear. And as for this bloody sarcasm, we can all play that game. We warned you to stay clear of the man from the start. But he was so charming, so well travelled, so cultivated, so distinguished. And such a bastard into the bargain as you soon found out. Now I can't differentiate between your sour grapes and common sense. And I wonder if you can either.'

The silence returns but has a tension it lacked before. Arthur stares at his feet. Janice stiffens. 'In the hierarchy of academic administration,' the Proctor continues, 'I command the highest authority among us. It is within my brief to protect the academic integrity of this university and I will do so. Arthur's endorsement will add weight, with or without your testimony, Janice. Eliot may have been one of my closest friends, but he's an embarrassment, a liability, and he's dangerous. He goes.'

Janice recrosses her legs quickly, and begins bouncing one foot up and down with annoyance. 'A bloody iceberg for our little Titanic. Take him down by force and we all drown. Eliot won't slip away with that mad bitch without a fight. He'll go with his mouth wide open. You'll dance to a differ-

ent tune then, Harry. I know all about your high-jinks at
Oxford.'

'Your language, Janice. I must insist,' Arthur cries out.

Arthur is ignored. 'What do you suggest, Janice?' The
Proctor raises his voice. 'That we go along with it? Turn a
blind eye?'

Her voice rises in challenge, 'Exactly. We leave him to it
and avoid him. We ignore him. When he makes another
mess, it's a matter for the police. Let him sink himself. You
weren't to know he'd pull those pranks, and I wasn't aware
of just how far he'd push his luck behind the smokescreen of
"consenting adults".'

Rising to his feet, Arthur begins to shake his head. Again,
the Proctor waves him down. 'He won't desist. There's been
a brief respite following the aftermath of Ben's passing, but
it's started again. This Dante is proof enough. He actually
asked that character up here in order to carry on dabbling
with his occult nonsense. Other students could become involved again. I won't take that risk. You had strange tastes,
Janice. I remember them well. Perhaps you are unable to
let go.'

'You bastard,' she says in a low voice, and then stabs her
cigarette out in the ashtray beside her chair.

'Harry. Janice,' Arthur says, and begins looking to his
companions with a succession of imploring glances. The neat
privet of hair that rings the back of his head suddenly
appears whiter between the pink of his scalp and the red of
his neck. But Janice is out of her chair and marching across
the polished floorboards toward the office door.

'Janice, please,' Arthur cries out, turning in his chair to
watch her leave. The door slams behind her and both men

listen to the fading echoes of her heels in the corridor and then the stairwell outside. 'Why did you have to mention that?' Arthur says, his stern face directed at the Proctor.

'I don't trust her motives.' The Proctor stands behind his desk, and then moves to the bay windows. The leafy Scores, lit with afternoon sunlight, greets his tired eyes. How beautiful this view used to be, back when he could see through the shadow Eliot has cast on his every thought. He opens the window and takes a deep breath. Two students cycle past, clad in shorts, with rucksacks on their backs, their faces full of laughter as some joke is tossed back and forth, lost in the breeze before he can hear it. Fourth years, no doubt, remaining over the summer to finish their work. Just like Ben Carter. Was he once that carefree, cycling through the alleys and cobbled lanes of St Andrews, before the change in behaviour his friends attested to at the coroner's inquest? The cyclists carry on along the cliff-exposed East Scores toward the coastal path, passing the yellow-stone immensity of St Salvator's College. And although the road is mercifully unlittered with cars at this time of year, that will soon change, when the main body of students returns for the new year. Order will have to be restored before then.

Harry speaks without looking at his friend, moving back from the open window but still gazing out. 'When Eliot first came back to us, Arthur, he'd changed. I thought it was that wretched mescaline, but I should have known the problem went deeper. Perhaps I did. But my intentions to rehabilitate him were honest.' He can still see Eliot, five years earlier, half-starved and blackened by foreign suns, reappearing with the drama of any prodigal. Glancing down at the road, but no longer seeing it, Harry thinks of Stevenson, and what he wrote about Englishmen becoming depraved in the South Seas.

'I know,' Arthur says. 'But Janice is right in a way. We allowed it to go on for too long. Perhaps I am more to blame.'

'We weren't to know. No one has any idea what that fool did,' the Proctor says. 'What he'd been crawling about in, out in Haiti and God knows where. But do you know why I asked him back, Arthur? Because I missed him. His company, the eccentric discussions, and crazy stories, and all the experience that came to me second-hand because I never allowed myself to throw caution to the wind. Not once. I wanted to see him again, posturing like Crowley, and making those ridiculous claims. It was the camaraderie I missed more than anything. It's something even your own family can never match. That connection with your peers from way back. The sort of friends you made at that time in your life. Are we not all guilty of trying to engineer a continuance of our days as students?'

'No. You're not alone in that respect, my friend,' Arthur says.

'But we grew up and left the excesses behind, in youth where they belong. Eliot never did. A man of his age and education still messing about with some theory about the "unseen world". It's absurd. But can we be blamed that it led to this? I thought we could help him, Arthur. Maybe we owed him something. Think how we used to laugh together.' Arthur relaxes his shoulders and chuckles to himself.

'But were we ever able to really trust him? Was our regard ever returned? Did we deserve this?' Harry says, peering into the sky. 'Could you trust anyone who was that good at chess?'

'And cricket, and rowing, and climbing. At anything he put his mind to.'

'We both know, he bears little resemblance to the man we knew at Oxford.'

Arthur nods.

'We owe him nothing.' A car passes. Sunlight blesses the street in summer; snow distinguishes it in winter. This is a home for learning built from old stones, with an elegance to its arches and courts, and a mystery endowed by its shadows and legends. But the aesthetics have shifted: he can feel it. Something has arrived to disturb the calm, to wind back time and reinstall a grimmer place where thinkers burned for heresy and darkness brought dread to small grey towns.

SEVEN

'Hey now. You must be Mike.' Hart's vision is starting to swim and something beats against his temples from the inside. Before he knew it, the one shot of scotch he needed for Dutch courage, an hour before Mike Bowen was scheduled to arrive, grew swiftly to four generous measures.

'Hello,' the stiff figure answers, and embellishes the greeting with a single nod from a slender head. There is something graceful about the tall, thin-faced figure's movements as he steps, cautiously, into the flat's reception area, and Hart wonders if his heart beats at half-speed. Only the student's grey eyes are quick and animate, but whenever they flit toward Hart they take in his beard and then glance away to peer at the wall or floor.

'Just go up the stairs,' Hart says. His guest begins a slow climb. 'What you studying, Mike?'

'Classics.'

'Liberal arts, God bless 'em. All set to be an academic?'

Mike nods. 'I hope so.'

'Where you from?'

'Boston, originally.'

Hart recognises the type: single, old money, with a manner as straight-backed as a Puritan's church bench. Takes himself seriously and only adopts the little silver earring to fit in, which only serves to make him look more incongruous.

In the lounge, Mike begins to shuffle about on his sensible shoes before coming to a standstill. 'What exactly are you studying?' he asks, and raises himself onto his toes.

Hart smiles. Kid with an attitude. Someone like Mike would only come to him through desperation, and would never tell a soul afterward. He gives Mike a run down of his credentials and the book he is writing.

'Interesting,' Mike says, sincerely. 'I've specialised in Ancient Greek religion.'

'Great,' Hart says, and slips a blank cassette into his tape recorder. 'Do you speak Greek?'

'Ancient Greek, Latin, and a little Pictish for amusement.'

When Hart wafts his hand, palm outward, at the couch, Mike looks uncomfortable and is eyeing the recorder. Nodding toward it, Hart says, 'Don't worry. I'd only use your interview with permission and I always change the names.'

The student sits stiffly on the couch. There is little point asking him to relax. 'Let me guess,' Hart says to clear the air. 'You wouldn't usually associate with anything resembling my work, but you're fascinated.' He says 'fascinated' slowly and hopes the whisky hasn't added a sarcastic tinge to his voice. There is another gentle nod of Mike's narrow head and a sideward sweep of the eyes. 'Absolutely.'

'You've never had a history of vivid, perhaps hallucinatory dreams?'

'That is correct.'

'But recently your world turned upside down?'

Mike adjusts his position on the couch.

Hart grins. 'Seems to be happening a lot in this town. Makes you wonder.'

Mike angles his head toward Hart. 'Really?'

'Oh yeah. You're not the first.'

'Lifestyle or atmospheric conditions perhaps. A suscepti-bility to the baroque ambience of the town.'

Hart smiles. 'Maybe.'

'Will you let me know of your results?'

'Sure. When I've collected enough data, which doesn't seem to be in short supply, I'll let you all know.'

Mike removes his coat and stretches out his corduroy-clad legs. Sitting opposite, Hart runs through his spiel and open-ing questions about medication and alcohol consumption, which Mike answers candidly; he confesses to treatment for depression. Hart nods in sympathy, but swiftly moves on, remembering Kerry's aversion to his prying. 'So, Mike. What I'd like you to do now is tell me about your dreams, in your own time.'

Mike clears his throat. 'Well, about a month ago I began suffering from a series of recurrent nightmares. I was recov-ering from a particularly bad flu. I couldn't remember the exact subject matter, but became convinced it was more or less the same dream each night. You see, the situation was always the same after I awoke. And the dreams increased in frequency to the point when . . .' Mike pauses until Hart gives him a friendly nod. 'There was little point in even attempting to sleep. I never sleep for more than five hours and after a nightmare, I was too –' Mike hesitates '– wary about returning to sleep.'

'Anything in your room move?'

Mike licks his top lip and Hart notices his white knuckles

– both of his hands have balled into fists. 'My bed linen had been seriously disturbed. As were some of my books and papers.'

'Pulled off shelves and things?'

'On the contrary. Turned around and upside down, and then placed back on the shelves. I must have done it in my sleep.'

'Been sleepwalking?'

Mike nods. 'I live in Dean's Court and have found myself in the castle grounds twice after midnight.' Hart tries to keep his face deadpan. 'Should I see a doctor?' Mike asks.

'Why haven't you so far?'

'I don't think it's a physiological matter. I work hard and eat well. My health is good. There's only been the pills for depression.'

'Yeah, you mentioned that. Which drug?'

'Prozac. I consulted a physician's desk guide and couldn't find anything about this medication having a connection to sleepwalking. My actions while asleep are quite deliberate.'

'What makes you say that?'

'Well, after every episode, I find a copy of *Caesarious* open on my desk, at the same page. Didn't notice it the first two times. And what's most odd is the fact I seem to highlight a certain phrase with . . .'

Hart frowns. 'Go on.'

'With my own blood.'

There is a perceptible tightening of Hart's scalp and something catches at the back of his throat.

'Alarming, isn't it?' Mike says, raising both eyebrows. 'I make a small incision somewhere on my body and select the same passage. Three times now.'

Hart clears his throat. 'What passage?'

'*Sit tibi terra levis*. Roughly translated it reads, may the earth rest lightly on you.'

This is new, but Hart says nothing.

'It's as if,' Mike continues, 'I'm taking an interest in resurrection – in the Jungian sense, and then wandering into the castle. I'm getting quite alarmed. There are cliffs nearby.'

'And you're still in town?' Hart asks, incredulous at the young scholar's calm.

'My work is at a crucial stage.'

Hart begins to rub his beard, and feels like he could use a drink. 'Do you see or hear anything when you wake up?'

'In my room, no. But in the library, yes.'

'The library?' Hart raises his voice, before apologising.

'Quite all right,' Mike replies. 'No one is more shocked than I. It happened as I worked late one evening, on a difficult translation, on the top floor of the university library. I always select the same spot. There's too much talking on the stairs and by the computer terminals, so I hide in a corner when I need to work. I must have fallen asleep because when I awoke, someone was touching me.'

'What time was this?'

'About nine in the evening. It stays open late for final-year students and postgrads in the summer.'

'Did you see who was touching you?'

'No. I would have turned had I been able, but I was completely paralysed. I couldn't move so much as a finger.'

'But you were able to see?'

'Oh yes, I was fully awake. I was able to move my eyes but not my head. I could see the coloured spines of the books to my right, the strip lights above, and my notebook on the desk below. Everything the same as before I fell asleep. As I explained earlier, I had not been sleeping well at night.'

'How would you describe the touch?'

'Like fingers. Pawing me.'

'How did you feel? I mean it was unpleasant, wasn't it?'

The grey eyes are roaming again and his little tongue flicks between his taut lips. 'Mr Miller, I was terrified. Unable to call for help, I just sat there incapable of anything besides a feeble whimper. It was talking to me, very quietly. In old English and broken Latin, I think.'

'It?'

'Yes. Not like a man's voice. Not quite. And not a pleasant voice either.'

'What was it saying?'

'To tell the truth, I was too frightened to concentrate and there was this appalling smell. But I understood one phrase. Although, in hindsight, it may have been my imagination, I think I heard, "*Dies Irae*". Latin again. It means day of wrath.'

'Day of wrath,' Hart mutters.

'Insane, isn't it? Do you believe me?'

'Thousands wouldn't, but do you see me laughing?'

Mike begins to fidget. 'My imagination has never been so active. I enjoy science fiction, but this is all new for me.'

'I bet it is.'

'Well, Mr Miller. What's my problem?'

'Please, Mike, call me Hart, and as to what's wrong with you, I don't know. I could speculate, but it'd sound crazy. I'm used to studying undeveloped communities ridden with superstition and elaborate belief systems, where apparitions are never questioned, but in Scotland? I don't think any of you are ready for what I think.'

Mike smiles. 'I would certainly not entertain any thought of a supernatural cause. I was hoping for something a little more concrete. A passing malady for instance, caused by stress or overwork.'

'Can't tell you what you want to hear. I think this goes way beyond mental strain or illness.'

Mike smiles and rises to his feet. 'Think I better consult a physician. I've been worried sick about a tumour.'

'Do what you think is best. But if you want my advice, I'd leave town.'

'Not possible,' Mike answers, and then removes his glasses to pick at a lens. 'I think I'll ride this one out with sleeping tablets. Of the strongest variety. Here's my number. Please keep in touch.'

'I will. And look after yourself, buddy.'

As Mike descends the stairs, Hart has a hunch there is one more question he'd like to hear an answer to. 'Hey Mike, one more thing.'

Mike turns on the stair.

'It's a long shot, but did you go to any of the paranormal group's meetings? With Eliot Coldwell?'

Immediately, Mike blushes. Hart nods, smiling. 'I know, you were fascinated.'

Mike grins. 'Coldwell is an interesting man. I enjoyed his book immensely.'

'Did he hypnotise you?'

'No. I merely attended a few talks and watched a meditation session. It's amazing what a man of his age believes.'

'Like?'

Laughing, he continues down the stairs. 'Perhaps, like yourself, Mr Miller, Eliot Coldwell is convinced of the existence of an unseen world. Rumour has it he communes with the dead.'

Hart follows him. 'Don't you think there could be a connection?'

'Gave it some thought, but found it too improbable. I'm even sure he was unable to suggest anything to me subliminally. One session involved a Mantra and some exercises in concentration. Some took fasts, they say, but I hardly think we were at risk. Goodbye.'

Rubbing his face, Hart walks back upstairs. He rewinds the tape. Thinking of a drink, he ambles to the fridge, deciding against Scotch. It could knock him out and he still has Maria to interview in less than an hour. Instead, he plunders a four-pack of Budweiser. Drinking steadily, he drifts around the lounge, excited by the information but feeling something else too: like a diminishing sense of control, after being suddenly dropped into a small stone prison to rub shoulders with something unpleasant he's chased for years and never expected to run into.

Finding a chair by his favourite window, Hart sits down and enjoys the effect of the cold beer. After a while his thoughts roam across the garret flats, hotels and placid cottages of St Andrews, and he considers the young men and women who live here. They are protected from bacteria with bleach, nursed through colds with doctor's prescriptions, and coddled through broken hearts by parental cheques and union beer. But what of the night, and those who walk while others sleep? 'If it's all coming on down,' he mutters, 'breaking through, these people have no defence.'

He begins to feel out of his league. He does the market research. It isn't his role to provide the sale, the cure, or the answers. He scurries around the back corners of the world on all fours with a tape recorder interviewing witnesses and collecting hearsay. He isn't an exorcist, only an observer. He arrives after the stage has been cleared and only the stragglers are left behind chattering about something resembling a dangerous animal.

This is everything he's been working toward and studying, but overnight his objective distance has closed. As an anthropologist, he's always studied the social and cultural aspects of folklore and traditional sorcery: why people feel a need to weave magic and the supernatural into their beliefs and lives. Tales of nocturnal pests used to be no more than passing distractions, a little extra colour to enliven the sawdust and sweat of hard academic work. But while he trudged across North America and Canada for his Masters degree, he first heard of the night terror. In Newfoundland, the Old Hag tradition connected directly with the witchcraft existing at the time of the Pilgrim Fathers initiated his preliminary interest. He interviewed farmers, bank clerks, students and doctors, and found a recurring pattern: terrifying nocturnal disturbances experienced by his subjects. Nearly every research candidate, besides the inevitable cranks who responded to his adverts in the small newspapers of rural communities, had been struck by paralysis and aphasia while asleep, and all within the same locale. Against their wills they'd entertained the whispers and touches of something they couldn't see or were reluctant to address. Some candidates were even plagued by a sense of something sitting on their chests after being awoken in the middle of the night.

Those brave enough to seek medical advice had found doctors dismissive, and their troubles were passed off as the side effects of stress, or medication, or even the menopause. But Hart was unconvinced. The experiences in men and women, young and old, were too similar, and shared a historical connection, dating back to the early European colonisation of North America.

By the time he was completing his doctoral thesis in the Americas, funded by the University of Wisconsin, his interest in night terrors began to interfere with his concentration on tried and tested ethnographic studies. The patterns in the data, similar to what he found in Newfoundland, and gathered from tribesmen's tales of night-time phantoms during his peripheral fieldwork in northern and southern Guatemala, unleashed ambition in his system like molten lava. His original doctoral study of folklore and occult systems soon developed into a specialisation in what seemed to be a universal malady of sleep disturbances, directly related to some form of witchcraft. Hart had found religion.

This was his chance to make an original contribution, attain his own niche in the sprawling and encyclopaedic reaches of anthropology. That in itself was hard. What had not already been written? As an undergraduate at the University of Wisconsin, he remembered gazing at the library's Anthropology section and being swamped with a sense of futility. What could he possibly add to it?

Opportunity, clean and pure, presented itself, and his doctoral study blossomed into a book-length project. The choice of title – *Transcendental Magic* – and original synopsis were cautious, but flavoured with something fresh, only raising the eyebrows of those scholars he'd expected to be averse to new ideas. The conclusions he'd drawn, connecting many states of mind previously disregarded as mental illnesses or drug-induced hallucinations to rare but actively effective occult systems, he'd saved from his tutors and banked for the book.

His angle was radical, avant-garde, and would encourage a serious expedition into neglected regions of society and mind, extinguishing the New Age flimflam and spiritual hocus-pocus that tainted his subject like indelible ink.

And now the evidence is within his grasp. In St Andrews he's stumbled, from a whim, into the first signs of an epidemic of fear and confusion. His own winning lottery ticket to original thought. It is actually happening around him. No one will expect part of the sophisticated Western world to be disturbed by something as inexplicable as the night terrors. That is the milieu of naked savages in hidden tropical depths, not the domain of modern Great Britain.

Before Scotland, the closest he'd actually ever been to a night terror was in steamy Santiago al Palma, a village in south-western Guatemala. Hart arrived six months after the execution of the local shaman, the nagual, and his entire family. Amongst a Mayan tribe, Hart saw the devastation allegedly caused by the shaman. In the second month of his fieldwork, a guide took him to a deserted village in a valley. At the nearest missionary station he was told the natives of the blighted settlement had willed death upon themselves, believing they had been cursed. An official in a government land-reclamation office confused this with an outbreak of yellow fever to explain the reported hallucinations and near disappearance of the entire population of the village.

But officialdom failed to warn Hart off, and he proceeded into the jungle with the guide, catching amoebic dysentery from bad water before eventually making contact with the survivors. Two gnarled elders, hiding in a neighbouring settlement, who smoked a foul tobacco to keep the insects off their leathery skin, explained to Hart that six months after the initial wave of night terror, described as a plague of bad dreams, that swept through their village, neighbouring tribesmen resorted to extreme tactics. By this time half of the village felt *its* embrace in sleep, others had fled, and the neighbouring hunters, afraid of the contamination spreading, slaughtered the local shaman. As a result of his death, the epidemic of night visitations ceased overnight. Allegedly, the original shaman had invited something into himself, described by the villagers as a 'Win', an evil-doer. But Hart had only seen the bones – the scorched bones of the shaman's clan, and the remains of the victims – all that remained of the Win's feasts. One of the elderly tribesmen saw the barely disguised horror on Hart's face after describing the plague of nightmares they'd suffered. Infants and youths were stolen from their beds and found half eaten miles from home.

He then explained to Hart how the shaman had been caught transforming, and quickly despatched. It had been necessary to dismember the shaman and his infected family before torching their remains. 'If you commune with the dead and feast on the living,' he instructed, 'you give up your right to live.'

They had ways of dealing with unwelcome hosts, Hart learned, and knowledge as old as the steaming depths of the forest about them. And the words of their own patron saints to expel unwanted companions, that whispered and waited, full of hate, only rising to the surface when the time was right to breathe the air of man. The community had exercised their own brand of social control over a deviant in Santiago al Palma, but now those technical terms that served an anthropologist – 'social control' and 'deviant' – seemed to lose their weight. This phenomenon defied scholarly language. It was a realm of nightmare.

From Guatemala, Hart travelled to the Amazon Basin, excited by a journal article reporting an outbreak of demonic possession amongst the Mundurucu Indians. Once more, he arrived months after a violent backlash from terrified locals, but a line of thin poles, set back from a waterfall and shadowed by dark-green foliage, brought him to his knees in shock. On top of each pole a brown head had been placed, mounted above grisly remains in wooden bowls that still buzzed with crowns of flies.

A possessed sorcerer and his disciples had been exorcised by the most bloody means a head-hunter legacy could devise. Hart lost his appetite not solely as a result of dysentery.

Word of mouth outlasted any missionary's bible in that lost region of the Americas. And again, in the Amazon villages, he glimpsed more of the insanity surrounding the night-terror legacy. According to witnesses, a dozen teenagers had disappeared within the course of a few months, each of them having complained of a sleeping illness. The Mundurucu Indians blamed an errant sorcerer – one of a caste of holy man feared for centuries, predating the Spanish conquest. The ritual execution of the sorcerer followed. It was merely a way, his academic discipline would instruct, for a culture to deal with a scapegoat. But Hart began to think otherwise. He had seen the ravaged remains of the children's bones in the undergrowth – the victims of the sorcerer and his night terrors.

Once again, when the sorcerer was executed, the epidemic stopped.

Old footsteps left heavy prints. The further Hart looked the more evidence he uncovered. In the thirties a French trader called La Faye had written a short book about nocturnal manifestations of spirits throughout Asia. A man had to get down on all fours and understand the world in different tongues, and that is what La Faye had done with the Kachin tribe in Burma, detailing how, in 1934, a contagion of the night terror, or the Hpyi, had been ruthlessly suppressed, resulting in the executions of some ten tribesmen believed to have been possessed by the Hpyi spirits.

Different names, different places: from the highlands of New Guinea to the frozen ground in Newfoundland, Hart chased night terrors and the people who dealt with them. Old tongues and strange magic protected the tribes. Bloody executions and ritualistic magic were accepted without doubt as cures. But what do they have in St Andrews?

Having reviewed European occultism as an undergraduate, he knows something of witchcraft, and the 'evil eye' myths of Greece and Ireland, but night terrors? There is little written from an anthropologist's perspective on the occult in Europe, so his knowledge suffers limitations. It is more the role of an historian to delve into the sinister offshoots of European culture, while the anthropologists concert their efforts in Asia, Africa and the Americas. As far as he knows it takes belief, real belief, hallucinogens, self-discipline, and an entire hierarchy of traditional practice and lore to even get close to an aberrant spirit. In Europe, Christian belief has taken man out of nature. Mystics and visionaries have gone. Science and economics are the new faiths. So how has something broken back through? It cannot just occur: where is the ritual, the knowledge, the decade of mage-like study, the creation of the right environment for contact, and the final leap of faith in St Andrews? Where is the source?

EIGHT

Illumined by something more than the first stars and the moon, the sky remains bright. It's as if the night is unwilling to release the sun completely after it has baked the ground hard and warmed the stones of St Andrews throughout the long day. From the air, the orderly skeleton of streets in neat rows of interlocking white and grey, lead to the fallen cathedral and the Eastern harbour beyond.

Amongst the cathedral's tombs and graves, still protected by walls beaten by coastal weather for centuries, the lonely sentinel of St Rule's Tower stands, solid and rectangular between sands East and West, the sea to its front and the town in line behind. Like a stage, the cemetery is lit by the electric lights on the perimeter walls and only awaits its players.

Elsewhere, the slow airs of late summer have drowned the town in deep slumber. Within firm walls and behind curtains that sway and then brush together it is time to sleep. Sacred sleep. Sleep from the heat; sleep after a day in the hot office and shop; sleep from the drowsy meander the day makes toward nightfall; solace in sleep after evening hours endured before flickering television screens. Some of the town lights, however, have refused to wink out; some people read by lamplight or laugh in early-hour gatherings where glass after glass of wine puts back the time for bed; others are unable to settle, and a few will not allow themselves rest.

Maria checks her bedroom door-lock for the third time in an hour before returning to her black tea: no sugar. Cupping the steaming mug, she watches the slice of lemon float in the dark liquid: no calories in citrus fruit. Strained eyes in her thin but pretty face flick across to a brass alarm clock: two minutes to midnight. Would Chris forgive her? His perfect face smiles back from the photograph beside her clock, framed in pewter.

'What's wrong with you?' he'd shouted that morning in a voice she often heard bellowing from the rugby pitch – a voice he uses when he demands the ball from a team-mate, when he believes he can reach the touchline and control the game. A voice she hears when he's drunk and angry and someone has dared disagree in the pub. 'I can't touch you anymore. You keep pulling away from me. What's the matter with you?'

But how could Chris even begin to understand? Those big brown eyes, with a solid and ever-confident stare, beneath a floppy fringe, would mist at the very first sign of an expressed emotion, or doubt, or inner query, or at anything not as material as a computer or car. Maria envies him: able to charge through life in a blazer and silk tie, his thoughts ordered meticulously like his possessions and neatly pressed clothes; able to do things that are instantly justifiable to himself, or not do things because they aren't right, because he says so. There are no abstractions or subtleties in Chris's life – he can hold the world in his hands as something measurable and tangible, like concrete.

'You scare me. Did you throw up again this morning?

Christ, girl, I don't understand you. No one can stay awake for that long. It's not right. It's not normal. Listen to me, don't roll your eyes or shrug your shoulders. Get something from that doctor.'

'But I have had some sleep. And I missed my appointment.'

'Yeah, for two hours this afternoon while I watched you. I can't do this every day. Eat a proper meal and get some rest for God's sake. I have training and work to do.'

Maria hates him. Maria loves him. And at least her anger and hunger may keep her awake for the third night running.

The little brass hammer on her clock smashes between the bells announcing midnight with a tinny racket. Maria flinches and spills her tea. She rushes across her room, her small and wire-thin body casting strange shadows in a chamber illuminated by three strong lights: one in the ceiling, plus two desk lamps. She pushes the clock's hour hand forward until 1 a.m. and stops its clamouring. Then she returns to her chair. The clock's bell is a lookout and the changing of its noisy guard has become a familiar routine, a successful ritual to stave off sleep – because sleep wants to drift before her eyes, deep languid sleep beneath a thick duvet, so she's wrapped up and healed in a warm cocoon . . .

Maria's head drops across her chest and jars her neck. Snapping herself awake, she stands up, furious. Stay angry, that is the answer. Stay brittle and annoyed at the slightest thing: at every inanimate object, at food, at Chris, at anything. But don't fall asleep. Just two more days of this, the thesis will be complete, and then she can go home and sleep for a week.

It is somehow all connected to this room in New Hall and

the university. Maria refuses to believe she's mad, or frigid as Chris says when baffled and hurt that she will not open her bedclothes to him, as she has done every other night since the first year: back in those halcyon days when their sweat would dampen the clean white sheets, and her hot face would nestle across the broad chest of the man two blonde girls had fought over at the KK ball. They made love every-where: in the afternoon, late at night when tipsy and ad-venturous, and first thing in the morning, all sticky and basic. He had selected her; she had said no. He had pursued her indefinable airs and quick tongue, sensing something unknowable but within the classification of a suitable girl. And eventually she had succumbed to his hesitating attempts at romance, until the tall figure was her own: handsome in the classic sense and always in control. And so they had loved and then slept. Slept through heady summer after-noons, as she lay on his hard and flat stomach, when her whole body became heavy with a pleasing, satisfied fatigue.

Maria jolts awake. Leaden eyelids spring apart. A noise startles her and now it's too late. Something scrabbles on the wall outside, beneath her third-floor window. A whimper detaches from the back of her throat.

Desperately, she wants to run to the door and escape the prison cell, tinted a pastel shade, that once was her little home and now only seems to trap her in a stink of new carpet. But her skin is alive with a familiar attack of cold pinpricks: not quite pain, but a spread of numb bloodless lethargy.

After moving as far as the bed, she collapses upon it, her brain starved of oxygen and blood. Phosphorescent lights explode in her sight. Maria hauls air into her lungs and claws her fingers on the thick red duvet, before each digit switches off, one by one, until she is still, deathly still, except for the heart-beats and startled breaths inside.

The curtains are closed but she senses it out there, grinning as it hangs from the ledge like some giant bat. And the sounds of something dragging itself up a wall find their way into her room. Then she hears the voice: a low babble and incoherent mumbling of old words and . . . her name, 'Maria.' Just to hear it makes her want to change her name. She'll remember the rasp of its tone if anybody calls her Maria again.

If? Again?

The lights go out. There is just one click and they are all doused together. Enveloped with panic, she feels the voice again creep through her pores like winter cold, to freeze her bright spirit until it shatters, until she does not know herself amongst the vile things that chase other vile things through her imagination. Maria closes her eyes. She cannot abide it; the thought of seeing it will snap her mind like a dry twig.

Out there, in the dark room, the curtains now swish over a window she remembers locking. Who opened the window? Did it make her? And there is the thumping sound of its weight dropping to the floor after it has spilled over the sill, followed by the rustle of something moving across the floor to her bed.

She hears a hiss of excitement from somewhere near her feet. A sniff too and then the fumble of thin anxious limbs as they begin the search. Maria tries to scream, and pushes her heavy muscles to move her arms and legs, but they will not obey. She can stand no more. Her eyelids unroll. Her lips part and she sucks at the air, to suddenly pull the stench of a slit whale belly into her mouth.

Something dark smothers even the faint light that seeps beneath her door. The smell is unbearable and her stomach convulses, sending an involuntary seizure up to her mouth.

It prods the bedclothes. Then its movements quicken the moment it finds the shape of her legs beneath the duvet. Now it's pulling itself up the bed. Onto the bed. She can't bear to look and shuts her eyes. But the dark creates an anticipation the safe cannot imagine. And as she senses it rising above her, the exhalations that come are tainted with eagerness.

'This stuff is good, but not that good,' Tom says, one eye squinting through the smoke, the other closed. He has draped his slender body, stripped to a pair of cobalt-blue jeans, across the couch in their new living room. 'You used to be such good company after a smoke,' he continues, attempting to provoke Dante into becoming the early-hour companion he is accustomed to. 'A couple of toots and you would be off, man. Your mouth running like a Porsche trying to keep up with your mind. What's up?'

It is an effort to speak after the three joints they have smoked this evening, following an excellent pasta dish and fresh fruit salad with yoghurt that Tom effortlessly rustled up with a fag drooping from the corner of his mouth as he sang, his tight musculature revealed in a white vest as his arms flipped, sprinkled and stirred.

No wonder every woman fancies him, Dante muses; he can cook, as well as sing, play a guitar, light up a party. Tom never stops. Not for a second. Always talking, always making a noise. Is he the real talent? Dante thinks of his books and ideas. Are they worth a damn? He estimates he will have to live for three centuries just to get the gist of what Eliot knows. It all seems hopeless.

A small orange lands on Dante's lap and gives him a start. Anger coils in his belly, fires through an arm, and feeds the hand that returns the projectile at more than double its previous speed. Leisurely, Tom raises a hand and catches the orange. 'Feisty,' he says, and then winks at Dante. After casting a black look at Tom, Dante returns his gaze to the blank wall above the fireplace.

'You should be on top of the world. Today, you met your idol. But you have just sulked.'

Dante sighs. 'I'm not sulking. Jesus.'

Tom starts to smile. 'Sorry, man, but I don't see a problem. You said he was brilliant and charming. OK, a little intimidating too, but you still met him. Eliot Coldwell. Chewing the fat about books and shit. How many people get to do that?'

Still annoyed that he's not been entirely honest with Tom, Dante's feelings are further exasperated by the profound sense of stupidity the meeting with Eliot stirs up in him. It should have been a fairy story meeting of kindred spirits, the mentor and his disciple, but instead, if he is really honest, he returned home ridden with a sense of ignorance and a growing suggestion of unease. A pile of dusty encyclopaedic books on the floor before his chair serves as a reminder.

'I didn't tell you everything, Tom.'

Angling his head, Tom studies Dante.

'It wasn't all books and compliments.'

'I know,' Tom says. 'There was that beautiful freaky Anne Bancroft secretary.'

'It wasn't her, man. Today made me realise that it's too late. That I have missed the ferry. Spent too long in rock clubs wearing fuckin' cowboy boots. I'm just too far behind, it's like I can't catch up. In fact when the boat left the dock, I wasn't running down any pier, mate, to arrive just too late. I was still in bed, on the other side of town, fast asleep.'

Tom chuckles. 'I've told you before, don't smoke this stuff if you're down or in a crowd. It'll make you paranoid.'

'It's not the dope, Tom. Eliot is really cool, but . . .'

'What?'

'I don't know. He mentioned something about him changing. You know, his personality, and there was just this, this air about everything he said. Kind of negative. Not like *Banquet* at all, and he even slated that.'

'I'll tell you what it is, it's a classic case of first-day nerves. You meet a guy, who's like the biggest influence on your life, in a university, surrounded by all this Greek salad. Man, it's bound to rattle you. But it's the first day. As soon as you learn to play the game, it'll be plain sailing. You're a clever guy, a stone's throw away from a boring intellectual. You'll be a nerd by Christmas.'

Dante cannot prevent a smile from creeping across his face. Suddenly, he feels foolish and guilty for persecuting Tom in his thoughts.

'You just have to learn to count your blessings,' his friend continues. 'Look at this flat. People would pay eight hundred a month for this in Brum. We get it for two, right by the sea and the castle.'

'Bishop's Palace,' Dante corrects him, feeling warmer inside.

'Excuse me, Mr fuckin' professor. It could be a bishop's outhouse for all I care.'

'Sorry, man,' Dante says, his voice breaking with laughter.

'I'm going to come over there and kick your arse in a minute. I'm trying to help and you're taking the piss.'

Unable to stop laughing, Dante's eyes water. He can't remember being so pleased to have his friend by his side. Giggling too now, Tom stares at the side of Dante's head, his own shoulders moving up and down. 'Man, you have really lost it. You'll never make a rock star. You have no stomach for drugs. Look at you man, after a couple of toots on this cheroot.'

With a gasp, Dante wipes the tears from his eyes. 'Buddy, sometimes I wish you had breasts. I'd get down on one knee. You do me the world of good.'

'Which reminds me,' Tom says. 'Did I tell you I nearly scored today, with a chick that sells cigarettes and lottery tickets in the supermarket? Legs like a gazelle and a voice like honey.'

'No you didn't, but this is my surprised face. Be careful with the locals. This is unknown territory. I don't want some tattooed Scot kicking the door down in the middle of the night, shouting "Morag! Morag! I love ya. I'll foockin' kill him."'

'Man, what am I, an amateur?' Tom says, smiling.

Dante sinks deeper into his chair. 'God, I feel better now. And you're right about this place, mate. Cracking flat.'

'Yeah. Eliot wouldn't do this for anyone. Remember that. The force is strong in you, mate. He knows it.'

When they first arrived, the day before, the modern interior of the flat amazed them. The sight from the street of the cramped stone front of the building furnished each of their imaginations with an impression of a twee decor. But there was nothing floral or busy about the interior when they let themselves in. No porcelain bric-a-brac or hideous scented dolls propped up on pillows. Instead, the old structure had been gutted and modernised in clean and plain terms.

Tonight, their candles are alight at strategic points around the living room, and while Dante was with Eliot, Tom has shopped, unpacked, and arranged their acoustic guitars on stands by the patio doors, which open out to a large garden they share with the flat above them. 'Have you met the neighbours yet?' Dante asks.

'No, but I saw an old woman peeping at me from the window. I'm amazed she didn't call Johnny Law. Imagine seeing a couple of long-haired gypos carrying a Marshall amp into the flat downstairs?'

'There goes the neighbourhood,' Dante adds, and they both laugh – the breach closed and the protective circle drawn for the night.

The hard cold thing between Maria's hands is a gravestone.

She wakes, bent over. She struggles to breathe and flashes her startled eyes about – a pretty deer stunned by the high beams of a sleepwalk. A forest of tilting headstones stretches off in every direction, only rearing up in their shadowy processions to mill about the thick perimeter walls, or to part by the eroded cathedral remains and lonely St Rule's Tower in the centre of the churchyard.

The stars and streetlights struggle to penetrate the ground where Maria stands, all thick with black grasses and mildewed stone figurines. She's barely able to see her own legs or to distinguish the hard shapes that corral her inside this thick copse of worn tombstones. Every object seems indistinct but almost alive – as if vibrating from the hidden energies of night. To her right, a thick wall, encrusted with upright tombs, dulls the sound of the sea. To her left, forlorn St Rule's Tower stands beside the chipped and spectral silhouette of the Priory's east gable, which joins the dark archway straight ahead of her.

Dank smells fill her nose and mouth: a thick and cloying reek of decay, wet leaf and dripping urn. A place summer has forgotten. Here and there, dotted like false hopes in the black, drowning sea of forgotten names and worn markers, a luminescent halo rises off new marble, a final sign from the newly dead, the last brightness from lives gone and never destined to return.

Standing straight, Maria's entire body shakes from nerves and the breaths she takes quickly. She moves a leg and bangs a naked shin on stone, solid and impatient with living flesh. Pain revives her enough to still her confusion and, immediately, her instincts advise flight. She should not be down here, miles from New Hall, with no recollection of having arrived. It is too dark, too quiet, and too still – a place of finality and reluctant rest, not for the living and never at night.

Moving clumsily, she crosses wilted flowers and avoids sloping gravestones, to reach the path running under the arch. It cuts between the cathedral and the western cemetery, and leads to the main gate. One of her fingernails catches on a leaning headstone, then her knees scratch against an edge of another stone that has crumbled, and finally she stubs the toes of her left foot against a square marker hidden inside the cold grass. Never has her body felt as weak and vulnerable as it does amongst these hard rocks that long to shipwreck a body fleeing for the locked gate.

Memories come back to her when she least wants them to, making her recall the whispers in her room, and the dark presence that issued them. She will definitely see the American doctor tomorrow. Why did she have to fall asleep and miss her appointment this afternoon? If she'd gone she might not be here. But right now, she has to get out. There is a police station on North Street, by the cinema where she fell in love with Ethan Hawke, and there are taxis down there too. Just get out, and get out fast.

But Maria only makes it to the path, near the ruined cloister, and not much further. Because something is moving in the ruins, amongst the flat tombs, near the old and vanquished altar. She sees a shape. It is hunched over, and lopes across the flattened grass and the paving stones where the building once broadened out in the shape of a crucifix. It moves quickly, craning a head back to test the air with a face that is mercifully indistinct. There is no strength in her legs.

Desperate, she wants to bolt toward the gate and Dean's Court beyond, where South Street and North Street meet. She should shout for help too, and wave her arms in the air. There is a car outside Dean's Court – a black car, an Audi with tinted windows, and its tiny red brake lights are on so someone must be inside it. But she stops herself. For a moment, nothing in the world will allow her to remove her eyes from the exposed cathedral innards. This is how people must feel, she thinks, when they come face to face with a bear in a forest, or a leopard in a jungle. They freeze.

There is more movement in the remnants of the hallowed walls – a flit from shadow to shadow. Something is leap-frogging over the smooth stones and then darting left and right as it draws closer. Once more her instincts beg her to flee, but she realises she'll have to cover the thin gravel path, one hundred feet long, to reach the gate and the safety it promises. And it's so far away and she's never been good at running. Sobs rear up inside her and tears smudge her vision.

Don't panic. Don't panic. Don't panic. Run!

Pointed stones stab into the soft palms of her feet, so she screws her toes up and runs awkwardly on the balls of her heels, moving her arms in flutters to sustain a balance. She tries to keep her vision steady and focused on the gate, on sanctuary, but something pulls her eyes to the side – the left side, where the remains of the cathedral glower and seem to raise their last standing stones like arms above wailing faces. Something is keeping pace with her, crouched over but moving as if it glides. Every step she takes brings it closer in an effortless streak to the apex of an invisible triangle where their paths will meet. But she tries, she really tries to reach the gate despite the cuts on her feet. An attempt at escape is better than facing it back amongst the stones and shadows.

Screaming, Maria flings an arm out when it comes for her. It sweeps forward like a black sheet blown by the wind, across the jumble of stone and the milky patches of grass. And it comes so fast. She tries to pull her body into a tight defensive ball, and she wants her eyes to remain shut, but, at the last moment, as it moves into its embrace, she can't help looking and she finally sees the hungry thing's face.

*

'Shit!'

'Jesus, did you hear that?' Dante shouts, sitting bolt upright in the chair that has cuddled him into a stupor.

Tom is already on his feet, eyes wide. 'That was a scream. God, that freaked me.'

'Was it real or someone mucking about?'

At the banality of his friend's question, Tom raises both eyebrows. The awful wail, resounding with distress and terror, could not have been the result of play-acting.

'We should go and look outside.'

'Yeah, right,' Tom answers.

'Where did it come from?'

'Over there,' he says, pointing over Dante's shoulder toward the wall separating them from the neighbour's house.

'What's over there?'

'The coastal path, that runs between the cliffs and the cathedral.'

They look at each other for a long time, both minds locked in persuasive theories concerning foxes, rare Scottish nocturnal birds, and the habits of drunken students. An image of a severed arm drifts into both minds. No one would want to go toward the cathedral or pier after hearing that noise, not on their second day in town, and not after such a trying one.

Slowly, Dante and Tom reclaim their seats.

NINE

The golf ball lands on the road between the Links and the West Sands, bounces twice, and then disappears without a sound into the dunes. Colin McAllister raises his face to the early-morning sky and shouts, 'Jesus wept!'

Walking slowly in the direction of the vanished ball, he bites down on the rage threatening to break from him, a rage capable of destroying his expensive equipment. At first light, he ventured onto the Old Course alone to practise through nine holes: nine holes he should have mastered long ago. But today, like too many others lately, just as he is about to swing, a single thought will jostle into his mind and distract him. The feeling and not thinking technique collapses and the resulting strokes send ball after ball shooting off at infuriating curves to fall at random destinations. A miserable chain of inept shots has already ruined the morning.

And it started as such a fine day too: the sky already blue, winter kept waiting, the neatly shorn grass with its sweet smell, thick and bouncy beneath his shoes, and bird song. A quick round of golf, a good breakfast at the club, and then a morning paper: that was the plan.

With his shoulders hunched and his stare locked on the dunes bordering the beach, Colin makes his way across the narrow strip of tarmac dividing the Old Course from the sea. Between his gloved fingers, a golf club hangs limp and trails behind his body like an unwanted toy. As he crosses the road, the spikes of his shoes grate on the stones, and when he climbs over a wooden stile to gain access to the beach, not only do his checked trousers flap irritatingly around his thin ankles, but he becomes conscious of the label in his red pullover scratching at his neck. It will be one of those special days reserved for the retired – a conspiracy of petty trifles and constant pains in the joints, reducing optimism to ashes. There are too many days like this.

'Relax,' the doctor said during his last blood-pressure check-up at the Memorial Hospital. 'Get some exercise and fresh air. Take up a sport, but nothing too strenuous'. He remembers looking forward to his retirement for over twenty years. But taking up golf is emotionally and financially the single biggest mistake he has made since leaving the company.

Hacking at the long grass in the dunes with his custom-made iron, he begins the search for the ball. The club should have been covered and put back with the others – its material value exceeds even that of his new 'wood' – but it has let him down, failing to live up to its graphite-and-alloy promise. Churlishly, he believes this alternative use of the club as a strimmer will register as punishment inside its gleaming but treacherous shaft.

When his arm begins to twinge, he stops the flailing and lowers his head. When he opens his eyes, the uneven and spiky grasses swim beneath his feet. Pain runs from his left shoulder to his elbow and something tightens inside his chest – something he cannot rub better. Prickles spread across his scalp, killing the warmth beneath his hat. Brief recollections of his first heart attack dry his mouth and his thoughts slide toward panic. He doesn't want to be suffocated by agony and fear again, to lose his dignity by groping around on all fours trying to find the breath for a scream, when his mouth becomes nothing more than a silent, sucking hole.

Concentrating on the white toes of his new golf shoes, he tries to calm down, and pats his trouser pocket for the reassuring rattle of the bottle of angina pills. Slowly, the pain dims from his arms and the steel band relaxes its tourniquet from around the hard pipes of his heart. In silence, he makes a solemn oath to see the doctor in the afternoon.

He feels the sweat dry between his shoulders and under his hat. Cold now, he begins to wander around in hesitant circles, breathing through his nose. The movement helps and warmth returns to his skin as his heart kick-starts his circulation back into motion. In his mind, he sees his heart as a small lump of gristle, its stiff valves barely able to open so the thin blood can pass through and sustain the rest of his meagre frame. 'Damn you', he says to the failing organ, allowing a spurt of relief to reactivate his determination to find the ball. No, a golf ball won't kill him. The brief spasm has passed. Just got too excited, that was all – something to be avoided at all costs, the doctor said. But the golf ball will be found. It means nothing as a physical entity, but he will seek it on the principle that trifles cannot be allowed to undermine a man. Some sense of order has to be maintained or you may as well be dead. The ball is there to entertain and relax him, not to defy him. It must know its place. Even if it takes all day, he will find the ball. Maybe when it is back in his hand he'll spit on it for nearly killing him before throwing it away, to show the bloody thing he's beaten it but cared not a jot for it. Madness, his wife would think, but she doesn't understand.

The ball could be anywhere, though. Has the momentum of his slice sent it through the grass to find a dark and secret place in the scrub or in a sandy hollow? Maybe it is peering out right now from one of the squat clumps of weed that grow like cacti from the sand dunes – peering out and laughing at him. 'I'll have you,' he swears. 'Cut you in half with a hacksaw and bury you in a dustbin. You shan't take me down.'

To summon the concentration required to conduct a thorough search, Colin shuffles forward through the first set of dunes and glances at the sea. The tide is out and the surface of the distant water is flat. That is how calm he wants to feel. But with the ball at large it will be impossible.

As he turns to inspect a hillock his foot slips a few inches forward. Regaining his balance, Colin peers down at his feet. Anger smoulders again. Dog shit – all he needs on a pair of new calfskin shoes. Reluctantly, as if scared of what he might find hanging from his sole, he turns his foot sideways to inspect the mess. Something glistens. A dark brown smear between his cleats and in the grass where he stands. After taking a step back, he bends further over to glare at the stain. Whatever it is sticking the grass together, it doesn't look like excrement. It looks like oil. Heavy sump oil, only it is reddish and brown in turn at the edges – the colour of hard fried bacon. Colin steps away, one hand windmilling for balance, not liking the texture or shine to the stuff he realises is blood.

He stamps his foot on the ground and then scrapes it backward to remove the blood and whatever it is that has collected to thicken the spill. After rechecking his sole to satisfy himself that the sticky fluid has been wiped free from his shoe, Colin ventures forward to inspect the wet and matted area of sand and verdure.

Immediately, he notices something odd about the grass: it has been flattened down around the dark smears to form a trail, the width of a man's shoulders, that leads over a small ridge and down into a crevice between two sandy hillocks. He's developed an aversion to blood after the last war, and any visit to a hospital still tightens him up inside: too many mates gone in and not come out. Perhaps a dog has caught a rabbit here. He hopes it won't be too messy.

Carefully, he moves up the side of the trail where the grass is long, and then peers down into the little sandy valley that slopes away to join the beach. But it is not the sight of a dead rabbit that greets his eyes.

After the initial double take, he twists away and falls onto all fours. Clarity of thought and vision disperse as he scrabbles back across the dune. Murmurs in his heart turn to rapid palpitations and then to quakes of crippling pain. Urgent breaths die in his parchment mouth. He crawls back through the trail of blood, soiling his trousers with bright streaks. It is blood from that wretched thing on the beach, propped up beside his golf ball.

Forced to stop crawling by the lightning in his ribcage, he rolls onto his back and releases his grip on the golf club. Staring at the sky, with his useless legs splayed in the mire of clotted sand, he moves his head from side to side and mouths the word 'No'.

There are no flies: it is a fresh kill.

Is he in danger? Is the killer still nearby? He must get up

and find a phone box. Stay calm, he tells himself, don't push your ticker, let it settle down and then find someone.

But his attempts to remain calm fail. Back into his mind bursts the horror of what he tried to crawl away from. He's never seen such a tortured statement of a human body, not even on a beach in Normandy. The thing in the sand was once a woman, of that he is sure. Scattered items of clothing didn't give the gender away, but what was left of the breasts did.

There was no sign of hair on her head, or even skin on the silhouette of her thin body. Peeled wet, she looked like a sculpture made from red clay, still moist from the touch of an artist's watery hands. And perhaps it was the curious animation about the thing down there in the sand that brought the fresh attack of searing cramps to Colin's heart – the manner in which it was sitting bolt upright on the beach with crossed legs. Or maybe it was the grin on the taut face staring back at him, beneath eyes that would never blink again.

Little pinpricks of light cluster before Colin's eyes, and he turns his head to retch on the ground. So as not to choke, he raises his head and spits a long tendril of mucus off his bottom lip, but he lacks the strength to spit properly and the bile clings to the front of his Pringle sweater. With only the grinning thing for company, chest pains make sure he is unable to move from where he lies in the dunes. And only when he hears the sound of something lifeless being dragged through the long grass does his heart stop in its struggle to beat.

TEN

Dante sits cross-legged on the floor of the lounge with a collection of books laid before him: books, cumbersome in size and hardbound, that Eliot gave him in an old leather satchel following their walk on the pier. There are so many, and each looks as indigestible as tough meat.

A second cup of tea fails to revive him after sleeping so late. His nerves are still jangling after so many joints the night before. And after that awful scream, they stayed awake until five, speculating, until the night gave way to a dawn the colour of orange-peel marmalade. Oddly, not since childhood can he remember feeling so grateful for the birth of a new day.

Sunlight gives the flat a nourishing yellow warmth, and the distant sound of the sea makes him eager for the outside world. Towers, ruins, mysterious alleys made out of stone and cooled by the shade, wait beyond their front door. He hopes to explore the town for at least a few days before going to Edinburgh – a place neither of them has ever seen – and the thought of a jam with Tom also appeals. The sentinel of Eliot's old books, however, anchors him to the spot. He will have to make a start amidst the enticing smell of the salty bacon Tom cooks. There was an impatience in Eliot the previous day as he hastily selected the books from around his desk. Saying little, besides murmured assurances of their importance to his studies, Eliot insisted he read them all thoroughly. And, as he is due to meet Eliot at the Orientation on Friday, where he'll be accompanied by Beth, it will be smart to create a better impression than the one he made at their introduction. He needs to gain a feel for Eliot's references, a broader grasp of Eliot's academic field, to inspire confidence in the man he's been asked to assist. Power reading, accelerated learning, discipline, a new sense of order – maybe these things will undermine his drinking, smoking, late sleeping, and notion of damning personal ignorance. He'll learn about history, religion and philosophy. The perpetual cycle of aimless guitar practice, drug taking and unhealthy introspection will be broken. He'll be saved by knowledge. He should be grateful. Can't he see that? After making the effort, the first aperture of enlightenment concerning the mystery of Eliot Coldwell will open. Lyrics, concepts for songs and melodies will then flow, before he sweats for perfection on the acoustic project, like he did with the first album. He just has to make a start: the rest will follow.

'Breaky's done. Self-service you lazy arse,' Tom calls from the kitchen.

After shaking his unruly hair off his face he raises the first volume from the stack. It is heavy, bound in worn leather, and frayed around the front cover. Gold lettering on the spine has faded and the spine crunches when he opens it to the title page. He sees the title: *Bendanti*, and the author's name, Carlo Ginzburg. The print is small and the pages thin. It smells of his grandmother's bible, with the red dust mites that spin around the pages whenever it is opened. The thought of reading this one suggests migraines and a bleeding nose.

Tittering to himself, he places it on the unreadable pile and picks up a slimmer volume, written by Sir Richard Francis Burton. Isn't he an actor? Dante puts it beside his left knee to start a pile for more accessible volumes.

The next one is titled *Historia Naturalis Curiosa Regni Poloniae*, authored by a P Gabriel Rzacynski. Without delay, he shuffles it behind him. His swiftly rummaging hands uncover something by Voltaire, titled *Questions sur l'Encyclopédie*, but on opening the volume he finds it to have been printed in French, so it also finds a home on the unreadable pile. Does Eliot think he understands French?

And the next one follows suit – incredibly old and held together by thick rubber bands: *Lettres juives*, by the Marquis Boyer d'Argens and printed in 1737. Dante carefully places this one on the coffee table, frightened to even have such a delicate thing in his hands. After glancing across the other spines, the dull knot of futility expands behind his eyes. There is Leventhal, Gallini, Goulemot, and something called the *Gnoptik Fragment* with no author cited. Eliot called this 'the first batch', but even the ones he can read will consume at least a month of concentrated effort.

He can see the reason: Eliot wants him to read the influential works of other scholars, dilettantes and explorers of the unknown – men who inspired his longing for change and adventure. But these titles seem especially archaic and obscure. None of them is even cited in *Banquet*. Perhaps it is a test, or an academic exercise to induce the right state of mind in the man selected to assist Eliot's biographical second book. Nonetheless, he expected handwritten journals, old photographs, press cuttings and stories told around open fires – things more vivid and immediate. Eliot only ever published *Banquet for the Damned*, creating an overnight sensation in 1956 before a scathing critical backlash saw it out of mainstream print. And no one is more familiar with the book than he, but Eliot dismissed it and made him feel stupid, maybe even a little resentful. And why was Eliot so vague about the new project? Does he not trust him? They'll never get started if this reading list is merely the beginning of what he has to pore over. If only there were a faster way to catch up. But who is he to argue with Eliot Coldwell? Every book will have to be read, carefully. If he hadn't been invited to Scotland and provided with the flat, he'd be tempted to suspect delaying tactics on Eliot's part.

Dante shakes the notion from his head, wondering if his ingratitude can be measured.

Gentle strokes of a plectrum against the strings of an acoustic guitar slip beneath the door of Tom's room, and become a distraction before he's finished a cursory flick through the Richard Burton tome. As his eyes stare down at a yellowing page of cramped text, he imagines the onyx neck of Tom's guitar cradled between his friend's supple brown fingers. Instinctively, he wants to rush through and play the rhythm to the seductive lead. It is the arpeggio for *Black Wine* he can hear. A bluesy ballad from Sister Morphine's first album, with a dreamy country quality throughout the chorus, evoked by Tom's winsome harmonising and slide guitar. Tom is singing now, in a hushed tone, and the song sounds especially sad as it drifts through the flat.

They wrote that song together, huddled around the electric fire in Dante's room in their house in Northfield: he,

Tom, Punky the drummer, and Anneka, the last bass player. Sprawled between overflowing ashtrays, and huddled around an empty Jack Daniel's bottle, the song came to them like a gift. Dante remembers how they looked in the flickering light from the four black candles that some Goth girl had given Tom after a fling: lank hair and gaunt faces; silk shirts hanging over ribs with too much definition; a blue-grey pallor to their skin in the dim light; flesh unused to sunlight. Rock' n'roll orphans lost to melody, legs clad tight in leather, drunk and stoned, but absorbed in the song someone began in D. Content together.

A bit of speed, coke if it floated for free, and plenty of skunk to help them along in those days. Time never mattered and neither did poverty, an empty fridge or signing on in Selly Oak. Everything seemed easier back then, with something special pulsing between them, whispering that it could go on forever.

Dante sighs and decides he will read the books, as much as he is able. After all he loves to read novels. But not today, with the sun out and the town to explore on a late summer's day. Eliot will understand; he and Tom need to settle in. The dusty minutiae of occult histories can wait.

ELEVEN

'Leather jeans. What were we thinking?' Dante says. 'What kind of impression are we going to make?'

'The right one,' Tom replies, casually. With his fingertips he pinches the black silk shirt off his collar bones and stares down his body, his face lit with pride. The untucked shirt sways over the belt buckle that supports his skin-tight leather jeans. Tossing the unruly mane of hair from off his face, he says, 'What is this, a fuckin' costume?'

Dante shakes his head and sucks on a cigarette. There is no point in arguing – Tom went to his own mother's funeral in jeans and then dressed in brown leather trousers to watch Beechey, a friend of theirs who leaped to his death from a block of council flats, laid to rest. He would not change for anyone and people were never offended by Tom's clothes; he added a chic touch to anything frayed, faded, or torn. With his easy gait, his height, and the chiselled face enhanced by his raven hair, he should have been a model when the agencies were recruiting long-haired men, but it was too much of an effort for Tom, and the thought of going to a gym had appalled.

It is nine o'clock and still light. Dusk washes above the town in a dark-blue skyscape, mingling its lofty depths with purple and black streaks of cloud – a science fiction sky,

Dante muses, with the stars almost airbrushed between the drifting vapours. The kind of sky you see on the covers of Prog Rock albums. He likes that about Scotland. You get those skies up here.

Turning from the silent Scores, they enter the rear lawn of the Quad through a garden gate, and emerge behind the immensity of St Salvator's College. As they marvel at the multitude of broad windows, the path leads them between large glass globes of white light, mounted upon black iron posts. The lawn they circle has been mown as flat and perfect as an English bowling green and is bordered by high walls thick with ivy. It separates the Quad from the Scores, and only the higher gables and turrets of the other colleges are visible over the wall. Following the path, they walk beneath a small arch into the Quad proper. St Salvator's tall square tower, with its red clock face, stands opposite them with an arch at either end. Parallel fifteenth-century halls run down from the chapel, all lit from within to cast an amber glow over the paths and darkened central lawn of the court, of which Lower College Hall provides the base, completing the square.

'This is it,' Dante says, turning to survey the front of the palatial building. They walk toward the stone staircase, which narrows as it rises to the large wooden doors – now open to welcome the cool night air and guests. Dante and Tom drop their cigarettes, grind them out beneath the soles of their polished biker boots, and then kick the little flat butts under a holly bush.

'You know,' Tom says, his grinning mouth signalling the approach of raucous laughter, 'it's gonna go like really quiet when we walk in. Everybody is going to stop talking and then turn around to look at us. All of these professors and their uppity wives.'

'Stop it. I'm bricking myself as it is,' Dante says, but he too feels the first tremor of hysterics.

'Man, I'm going to lose it in there, I swear,' Tom says, his shoulders already twitching.

'No you're not,' Dante warns, his whole body stricken with fear, and his mind now conjuring a picture of them both racing back out of the Orientation, laughing, with tears on their cheeks. When one of them becomes possessed with hysterics, the other inevitably joins in; it has been the same since school. He hesitates at the foot of the staircase, not daring to catch Tom's eye. The caution is unnecessary; Tom skips up the stairs and disappears through the doors. Dante is compelled to follow.

Resplendent with a high ceiling, the long walls of the hall are covered in vast oil paintings housed in ornate rectangular frames, featuring dignitaries from the university's long past, all assuming gigantic poses. They glare from under powdered wigs or push their chests out, invariably clad in black, with massive pink faces and white eyebrows beneath imperious foreheads. A long table, covered in a white cloth, has been erected on the left side of the hall and twinkles with a hundred glasses. Between the glasses, a host of platters is filled with food.

Several of the guests, dressed in formal attire, but not black tie, turn and look at Tom and Dante. Their eyes do not linger for long. Dante feels his chest tighten and his leather trousers set like concrete around his legs. 'Come on, let's find Eliot,' he says to Tom, who is making eyes at the food and drink.

Dante steers himself through the centre of the crowd, which is predominately male and middle-aged. He looks around for Eliot, ever anxious to avoid the occasional pair of curious eyes that turns toward him. After he passes through the main body of the gathering, he checks the seats lined against the walls by the small round tables at the head of the room, where people sit and eat. Tom is no longer behind him, lured away, no doubt, by the promise of food. Then he sees Janice, from the School of Divinity, on his left, and he smiles at her. The smile is not returned. She twists her pale neck and whispers into the ear of the man on her right, his face distinguished by a long jaw. He immediately looks up at Dante, and stares right at him, his face unmoving, the intensity of his look only broken when he turns to mutter into Janice's ear.

She keeps her haughty face turned to Dante and continues to watch him as he back-pedals through the crowd. He knocks against a man clad in tweed, wearing a bow tie. He apologises, then flees to find Tom.

And as far as he can see, Eliot is not here. Maybe he is late, he hopes, holding back any paranoid musings about being stood up. The only eyes upon him are those of Janice and the tall, long-jawed man, now joined by a squat bald man in a three-piece suit. They have followed him through the crowd and seem content to hang back and stare.

Dante turns his back on them; there is no law against assisting Eliot and he's been invited to the party by a member of staff. He can think of nothing, besides his inappropriate clothes, capable of provoking such a reaction from three strangers. What is it in their eyes: disapproval or apprehension?

Before he can take another step toward the distant shape

of Tom's sleek head, a hand falls on his shoulder from behind. Dante swivels about to find himself staring into the face of the fat man who previously stood with Janice and long-jaw. 'Hello there, I'm Arthur Spencer. Hebdomidar of the university. I hear you've been asked to attend to some important work. With Eliot. Eliot Coldwell.' The voice is pleasant and the large bald head gleams like an opaque marble. Confused, Dante accepts the hand, which is pudgy, pink and hairless. He shakes it gently, as if a firm handshake will bruise the man's scrubbed paw. But at least the eyes are friendly: small, blue, and enclosed by pink-rimmed eyelids and gingery lashes, the skin resembling uncooked pastry as they close and then tremble after a blink.

'Not exactly,' he replies, but likes the sound of what the man has suggested. 'I don't really know what my role will be. To help with research and things, I guess. While I put some of his ideas to my own music. Oh, sorry. I'm Dante. Up from the Midlands.'

'Well, I am afraid you will get little from him tonight, Dante. Eliot has failed to appear. It's a dreadful shame, you know,' he adds, with a gentle shake of his head, expressing pity as if Eliot were ill. 'But wait here and I shall get you a drink.' Arthur Spencer bustles to the refreshment table, pausing once to greet another member of the faculty congregation.

There is no way around it: Eliot has failed to show. It is a 'dreadful shame', the man said. What is he to make of this? What does he actually know about Eliot, beside the stories in *Banquet* and a handful of letters reiterating the individual's need for a purposeful vocation? Eliot loaded him down with books after a strained and sometimes spiky first meeting, and now he's been tailed since arriving at the party.

131

Arthur Spencer returns, holding two glasses of white wine, mincing his way on small nimble feet between elbows and heads thrown back to laugh at punchlines Dante has not heard and does not expect to understand even if he did. Arthur offers the glass. 'There you are, sir.'

'Cheers.' Despite his dismay, there is something he wants to like about the Hebdomidar. Besides a couple of shopkeepers who sold them cigarettes, this is the first friendly face he's encountered in St Andrews. He forces himself to remember the man's surname. 'Mr Spencer?'

'Arthur, please,' the Hebdomidar says.

He gulps the Chardonnay down and relaxes. 'You said it was a dreadful shame?'

Arthur takes a breath, cocks his head to one side, makes an attempt to speak and then stops.

'What?'

'Well, how well do you know Eliot?'

He welcomes the inquiry; it gives him the opportunity to seek reassurance. 'I met him a couple of days ago, for the first time, and he was all right then.'

Arthur smiles, and nods at what sounds like a familiar story. 'So the research, and this talk of his book. How did this come about?'

'*Banquet for the Damned* is my favourite book. Our next album will be a conceptual record about it. And I've been writing to Eliot, on and off, for a year. A few weeks ago, he suggested I become his research assistant. To help with his second book, so I jumped at the chance. To meet him more than anything. And it'll help our music. You know, being close. It's an acoustic project.'

'Really,' Arthur says, frowning. 'You mean to say you never met the man before? Extraordinary.'

'Yeah, never even spoke to him on the phone. Maybe I should have done, before he went and arranged our accommodation and everything.'

There is a perceptible hardening of the man's features after his mention of accommodation. 'We?' he asks.

'My friend, Tom, came too. He's the guitarist in the band.'

'I see. And you had no, how shall I put it, no prior knowledge of Eliot other than his book and the letters?'

'That's right. But don't look so surprised, we were desperate to get out of Birmingham. It turned into quite an adventure, with that arm on the beach and everything.' Dante wants to continue and tell Arthur about the scream, but the man becomes immediately uncomfortable at his mention of the arm. There is an awkward silence, until Arthur ends it. 'You are a writer?'

'No. Besides lyrics for songs, if that counts.'

'But Eliot has a publisher for the second book?'

'I don't know. Maybe he'll write it first and then, you know, look around.'

'Look around, of course.' Arthur seems to deflate with relief. Then his face adopts a quizzical expression. 'Do you think a publisher will be receptive to a book by Eliot?'

Dante nods. 'Of course. *Banquet* is a classic. It's a crime it's still out of print. But things do come back and what Eliot said is important. Although,' Dante adds sheepishly, 'you might not think so.'

'On the contrary. It's a fine read. Although I haven't perused it for years. A little unsavoury in parts I fear, and there are far healthier ways to achieve enlightenment than experimenting with the black arts.'

'I see that as just a metaphor, for raising your consciousness. You know, like with poetry or meditation.'

The man nods, studying him for a time before speaking in the tone of a confidant. 'Well Dante, it may surprise you, but I have known Eliot for practically all of my adult life. We were at Oxford together.'

'I envy you that,' Dante says, out of his depth again.

'He has always been a good friend. But . . . and this might be hard for you to digest, particularly after coming so far, Eliot is not the man he was.'

Dante holds his breath.

'I can see confusion in you already, Dante, despite your admiration for him. But there have been hard times in his life and it is best that you are made aware of certain facts. It's only fair that I put you in the picture. He has problems. Serious problems. He is subject to embarrassing digressions and, well, some quite abnormal behaviour. You see, I doubt whether he's capable of writing the book.'

Arthur sighs. 'This is so hard. I find it so touching that his book has been such a positive influence on a young man, and on a musician too. But Eliot has been unwell recently. You could say he never really recovered from an unconventional youth. And to be absolutely honest, and you deserve nothing less, it was his travelling and certain episodes that *Banquet* was based upon that began his illness.' He emphasises the word 'illness', and raises his eyebrows as if to impart a further cryptic embellishment.

'But don't take this the wrong way, Dante. He was once a force to be reckoned with, and made an excellent contribution to his faculty. But that was some time ago.' The man's voice softens. 'I tell you this in confidence. There are alcohol problems. And I'd hazard a guess that Eliot needs to attend to his personal problems now. Rather than launching into a new project. It's all quite serious, I'm afraid to say.'

'I don't believe this,' Dante mutters. 'It can't be right.'

'I know it must be difficult for you.'

'But the other day he was fine. I mean he was lucid and clever and –'

'There are rare moments of clarity, but on the whole, I am afraid . . .'

'What about his partner, Beth. Can't she help?'

Arthur closes his eyes for a second. 'Dante, perhaps we had better sit down.'

They sit on the other side of the hall, beside the refreshment tables. A short distance away from where they sit, Dante notices Tom. He holds a plate loaded with food and he speaks to a young blonde woman in a black dress. She stands close to him, smiling.

'Dante,' Arthur says, as soon as they are settled, 'Beth and Eliot have an unconventional arrangement. I am really not sure it is my place to divulge so much, but I think their days are numbered in this town. St Andrews is a quiet place. Young people come here to receive an excellent education, and there really is no room for the more unconventional aspects of academia. If you follow? A great risk was taken in inviting Eliot to lecture here. It was only his considerable knowledge of religion that encouraged the university to go out on a limb and invite a somewhat controversial figure here in the first place. Beth was a student of Eliot's, and their relationship did not befit his position. I am afraid he has let a great many people down. His students, his friends, and ultimately himself. I suppose I am trying to tell you that Eliot has been unethical. He lost his effectiveness a long time ago. Perhaps even in the fifties. Prison must have been hard for him.'

The words fall like axes. 'Prison?'

Arthur nods. 'Turkey. And Haiti.'

By looking at the floor, Dante attempts to conceal his shock.

'Over the last few years,' Arthur continues, 'Eliot began to drink again and suffer from certain lapses of memory. And, well, the rest has been a rather unfortunate mess. I am afraid he is incapable of taking lectures, and hasn't produced a credible paper in years. It is only through the generosity of another of our circle from Oxford, the Proctor, that he is still with us in a consultancy role.'

Dante sinks into his chair; the sounds of clinking glass and scraping cutlery amplify to a swirling clutter of noise in his ears, and his head feels unnaturally heavy. The voices in the hall are louder now, mocking, laughing at his impetuous journey and pitiful hopes of escape. If what this man says is true, he has driven four hundred miles to assist a man ridden with dementia. But what this Spencer says makes sense. It explains Janice's reaction when he first went to the school, as well as Eliot's cryptic dialogue, and the eyes of the staff tonight.

Arthur's voice seems to drift across to him from another dimension. 'So sorry, Dante. If there is anything we can do to help . . . Perhaps we can assist your interest in Eliot with our recollections. After all, we knew him in his prime. And what a prime. Captained his county, you know. One of the first to climb . . .' Arthur's voice trails off. His jowly face suddenly reddens.

'I believe I may command the best position to impart my résumé, Arthur.'

Dante sits stunned, bewildered by both Arthur's reaction and the unexpected sound of Eliot's voice. Arthur rises from out of his seat, wearing embarrassment on his face like clown paint. There is something else too, setting that grin fast and making his small eyes flick about. It appears as if he is frightened. Arthur Spencer looks down at Dante and mumbles something about a visit to his office on North Street.

'Sure,' Dante says.

'Bloody fool,' Eliot says, watching the Hebdomidar move away through the crowd on his journey back to Janice and the long-jawed man, who still watch with a keen interest. 'Over there, Dante, are three clever debunkers. You know what a debunker is? A person who lacks imagination, Dante. Who can only thrive in the material world. Their dull creed replaced spirituality with a new god of economics. But what has that achieved? People are dissatisfied, bored, unfulfilled. Those three can do nothing but mock the intuitive and the creative. Like us, Dante, who flee the everyday world and seek a meaning through our endeavours. We are the fortunate ones.' The words are bitter and come fast, Eliot's breath polluted by whisky, his eyes struggling to focus. But Dante finds the words exhilarating and far closer to what he loves about *Banquet*.

Eliot then slumps into the chair Arthur Spencer vacated. The speech appears to have exhausted him and, as he leans forward in his chair, he winces as if suffering from back pain. For a while he looks past Dante and glares at the trio across the hall, who finally turn their faces away. 'Forgive me, Dante.' His words are softer now. 'We were friends once. Good friends.'

Dante nods, inspired by Eliot's words and angry at himself for even daring to doubt the man. People like the Hebdomidar are clever orators, capable of playing with your emotions by feeding you lines. Every genius is despised in his own time, and he knows a thing or two about envy: the band scene at home is brutal. And, after all, what is a Hebdomidar? He has no idea, but the name conjures an association with administration. Maybe this Spencer is a money man. And Janice runs an office. How could they understand Eliot? 'I hear you,' Dante says.

'I know you would never doubt me, Dante. It is important that we trust each other. Am I right?'

'Absolutely.'

'Good. You would do well to steer clear of them. There is unfinished business and I do not want it interfering with our collaboration.'

'No. Not at all. I'm all yours, Eliot. You can trust me.'

'I know,' he replies, but looks away from Dante.

From where he is sitting, Dante can see that Eliot has closed his eyes. 'Are you all right?'

Eliot nods, but keeps his head bowed until the moment of pain has passed. 'Beth is here,' he says. 'She has plans this evening with –' he pauses, a struggle to remember the end of the sentence he's begun '– with friends, but would like to meet you before. You should meet her. She looks marvellous tonight.'

'Sure.'

'But there is a slight problem, Dante. You see, she refuses

to come inside. There is bad blood here, between Beth and certain members of staff. I can only apologise, but you must become accustomed to our habits. I suppose I have always been on the run from something. An outcast if you like. And Beth, somehow, became tangled in a little unpleasantness too. But don't worry, I have faced far greater perils than a trio of bureaucrats.' He pats Dante on the shoulder in a fatherly manner. 'Can I ask a favour, Dante?'

'Yeah. Of course.'

'Spend some time with Beth. You'll like her. Get to know each other. I suspect you may become close. I think it is important if so much is to be shared.'

He feels uneasy again. Surely Eliot's not suggesting anything amorous? He has to calm himself and stop being so malleable. 'You won't be there?' he asks, a touch of nerves registering in his voice. But Eliot is distracted again; his eyes wander about the hall. Dante is about to repeat the question when Eliot turns to face him. 'She won't bite you, Dante. Not unless you want her to.' The malicious grin is back.

In addition to feeling foolish, confused and now awkward, he struggles to dampen his suspicion. 'I'd love to meet her. We can get talking about the work.'

'Yes,' Eliot interrupts, his grin turning into a fragile smile, as if he were disappointed that Dante has failed to accept some voluptuous and tempting bait. 'I have something to take care of, but you should go to her. She's outside. Waiting for you.'

Rising to his feet, Eliot suddenly gasps. One tremulous hand reaches to his back. Dante scrabbles to assist him, but Eliot bids him sit with a waft of the hand. 'Wait until I'm gone,' he adds in a whisper, and then staggers from the hall, leaving Dante alone. Not being asked about his progress reading Eliot's books is fast becoming the evening's only salvation. He considers finding Tom, to discuss the alarming exchange, but notices his friend is still closing the gap with the blonde by the refreshment table.

Becoming almost psychotic for a nicotine fix, he leaves the hall after Eliot has gone. And the benefits of the night air, outside in the deserted quadrangle, are immediate. He sits upon the stone wall by the holly bushes and front steps, and finds his cigarettes in his denim jacket. It is darker now, the last vestige of twilight having deserted the sky to summon a greater silence and a legion of new shadows into the court. Leaning back, he takes several long draughts of cigarette smoke into his lungs and tries to get his thoughts straight. Nerves prevented him eating much of the salad Tom prepared for dinner, and the one glass of wine he's guzzled makes his head spin. A sudden influx of nicotine into his system turns his brain-judder into a dizzy spell. He looks around for Beth.

No sign of her, and where has Eliot gone? They've said virtually nothing to each other since his arrival, and now he won't even stay around to introduce him to Beth. Instead, he has to go outside and find her for himself. What is it all about? Can the man only tolerate his company for brief periods of time? And this Beth: what is Eliot trying to suggest about their working relationship? Looking at the sky, Dante dares to whisper, 'Don't let my hero be a fucked-up, alcoholic pervert.' Then he sniggers, looking forward to unloading it all on Tom. And thank God he has Tom with him. Here he is, sitting outside after being warned off by the university authorities and deserted by his host, while Tom closes in for the kill on a babe in a designer dress. There is little he can do but shake his head at another preposterous situation in his recent life.

And where is this Beth? Eliot said she was waiting outside, but there is no one in the Quad, just him with his visions of an early return to the Midlands. If things continue to get much worse, what other choice will he have? Trying to explain the whole improbable mess to Tom will be awful, before the packing of their bags and the journey back down the M6 to a greater uncertainty. And, if he is honest with himself, Birmingham is out of the question. They now have nowhere to stay, no parental support left to drain, and not even a friend they can bunk with. Everyone in their crowd is already living four to a damp house, on housing benefit and only crawling out of bed to sign on or to rehearse in a studio. Ill, drunk, crazy, unpopular: Dante has no choice other than to give Eliot the benefit of the doubt. He looks at his cigarette, to acknowledge an old friend, and reminds himself of his own creed: to distrust anyone like the Hebdomidar who wears a suit.

'Dante,' a far-off voice calls.

He starts at the distant sound of his name and looks up. Across the dark grass of the central court he sees a young woman. She stands between the wide arches of the chapel's cloisters. She is tall and dressed in black. Her hands are concealed in the deep pockets of a long winter coat that sweeps around her ankles. Her hair is dark and pulled back from her narrow features. The face, although indistinct, suggests refinement to him: pale, the eyes large, and the nose thin.

Peeling himself from off the stairs, he begins a slow walk across the lawn, puffing on his cigarette as if it were his last. As he approaches, she raises a hand, gloved in leather, and waves to him. On her distant face he senses a smile and he returns the wave, hesitantly.

From about fifteen feet away he is able to see her more clearly: her skin white and smooth across her high cheekbones, her mouth wide and lips generous. In her early twenties, he guesses, and at least six foot tall in her heels.

Smiling, he sidles toward her. Huddled within the confines of the coat, she seems reluctant to emerge any further into the Quad. Her lips are painted a bright red and return his smile. Her teeth are perfect but dark, or so it seems. Must be the shadow. When he stands before her, she lowers her astonishing eyes, as if glancing down with embarrassment at the realisation that a blush has stained her cheeks.

'Hi, Beth,' he says.

Something pulls taut inside of Dante when she laughs. The sound hums from the top of her long nose, which wrinkles in a way he thinks delightful. She offers a gloved hand. 'Hello, Dante.' The sound of her soft Highland accent makes him go warm inside, and he remembers Tom mentioning the voice of the checkout girl. It was like honey, Tom said, and he understands the comparison: smooth, sweet.

He stops smoking and as he accepts her hand, he cradles her thin fingers, and only through a conscious act of resistance does he quell the urge to stroke the soft leather of her gloves. She smiles again and lowers her eyes to the ground, where the tips of her patent boots peek out from beneath the hem of the woollen coat. Dante struggles to find words, any words, and finds himself unable to do anything but stare at her with a mute wonder, while still holding onto her hand. Is she Eliot's lover? What did the Hebdomidar suggest about their relationship? And how can Eliot trust any man around her, let alone encourage them to meet her? Is it all a game?

He thinks back to *Banquet* and the descriptions of Eliot's free-loving exploits in his exploration of Tantric rituals. Surely Eliot was not suggesting that anything intimate should pass between them?

Squeezing his fingers into his palms, he tries to defend himself against the unreal night, with its arboreal smells, old shadowy stones, and big fairy-tale globes on giant candlesticks.

Like someone who has watched him for years and never had the courage to speak, Beth continues to smile at him. She seems bashful, but eager for something too. A notion of love at first sight comes to him. Is this what it feels like when you see a stranger and know something significant and unspoken has happened that will never vanish? 'You must be cold out here,' he says, imagining words are unnecessary, as if communication could be telepathic between them.

'Just a little,' she replies, and he marvels some more at the melody in her voice.

A silence falls between them. Dante raises his eyebrows; he is nervous, and considers another cigarette to hide behind.

'I am sorry that we had to meet like this,' Beth says. There is something in her manner that makes him presume she is relieved to see him. 'But you came, Dante. I am so happy. Your letters were lovely.'

His voice seems to originate from outside his body. 'You read them?'

'All of them. And I want to make it up to you. For all of this. You have every right to be angry.'

'Angry?' Dante says, transfixed by her. 'I'm not angry, Beth. I'm grateful. It's a dream come true. It's an honour to meet Eliot. And you . . . You took me by surprise. I'm sorry for staring like this.'

'Thank you,' she says, and as her stare pierces him, the hairs rise along his spine, from the nape of his neck to his tailbone. She moves forward, her coat covering a hush of static as her long legs descend a stair between the chapel arches. Leaning forward, her smooth face moves closer until it nestles against his cheek, where she leaves a cold kiss. A press of lips that pass tiny arctic prickles across his skin and encourages him to close his eyes. 'Eliot wants us to become friends,' she whispers, bathing his face with her sweet breath. 'We have so much to share, Dante. We both have a bond with Eliot. A bond existing before we even met him.'

'You liked *Banquet* too?' he asks, unable and unwilling to open his eyes in case she vanishes.

'It was the reason I went to him.' Her voice is strong in his ear, and her slender body sends out little charges of electricity across the narrow divide between them, stinging him in a way that feels good.

'You were a student here?' Dante asks. He opens his eyes, but it is hard to focus. Her blurred face is at an angle, and occupied with a study of his mouth.

'Yes,' she says.

'And Eliot, he is all right, isn't he? The Hebdomidar said he had an illness.'

Beth steps back, away from Dante, the look on her face mischievous. 'He is well enough for me.'

'I wasn't suggesting anything,' he stammers.

Beth smiles. 'I'm teasing you already. Sorry.'

'No worries,' he says, instantly relieved that she is not really displeased.

She stares past him and into the distance. 'It may surprise you, but you were my idea. I saw your pretty photo that came with the music. And I knew you would be right for him. Your arrival is important to us. We are so close now.'

'Why do you have enemies?' he says, astounded that anyone could hold anything against so fair a girl.

'They?' she says. 'They are nothing. Even though they want to remove us, Dante, they are nothing. They can't even imagine what we have seen. What you will see.' Beth looks up at the sky and a tear moistens the corner of her eye. Her bottom lip trembles. Dante feels a surge of emotion inside, a need to comfort her, to do anything to soothe her. His hands make an ineffectual movement forward and then fall back to his sides. He wants to say something meaningful, but he is still full of the beautiful young face, as if this sudden longing has become a seizure. 'I'll help,' he whispers, a lump in his throat.

'So much has happened. And we need you now.'

'For what?' he hears himself ask.

'There isn't time for me to say. We must meet again.'

'Anytime. We could . . . You could . . . There's coffee back at mine. It's still early. I could take you home later.'

Beth shakes her head and dabs her eye. 'Meet me in St Mary's Court the night after tomorrow. Come at eleven. There will be time for us then. Tonight, I just wanted to see you. For his sake.' Her eyes widen just enough to suggest the unthinkable, and Dante feels his stomach turn over. His vision dances, drunkenly, and he blinks hard, as if trying to stay awake in a warm car on a long drive. She turns to go.

He feels a sudden pain in his gut. 'Wait. At least let me walk with you.'

'No,' she says, with her back to him. Then she issues a gentle little laugh, as if to mock but also cherish his ardour. His face reddens, and he feels dizzy again. His head fills with a swarm of recriminations, doubts and ecstasies as she walks away. He loses his balance and takes a step back. What is he thinking? She could be involved with Eliot. Didn't Eliot refer to her as his partner? But what does that mean? It seems like such a tame expression, lacking in commitment: an association without an emotional tie.

Her soft voice floats through his confusion. 'You'll know soon.'

He nods and struggles to understand her strange signals, but she has already folded away, through the dusk of the cloisters. And as she goes, he sees her face in profile, looking out toward the Quad's perimeter walls, black with ivy and rustling with draughts. In the dark, her eyes appear to have closed, and her lips part to suggest the anticipation of a passion about to be requited. And then she is gone from sight and all he can hear is her heels tapping as she runs away from him, across the cobbles and through the arch to North Street.

He wavers on the path, stunned. He feels sleepy, as if she has physically fatigued him, but he is ecstatic too: a schoolyard princess has smiled, a crowd has roared, his voice has reached an operatic peak. Anything seems possible. And she kissed him; he can still feel the alien frost of her lips freezing through him.

Unconsciously, he finds himself walking through the arch after her, testing the air for her perfume with his nose and tongue. He looks along the wide tarmac river of North Street, hoping to see her with some equally delightful friend. But Beth is gone. All that remains of her is an imprint of her face in his memory, set alight by eyes so green and clear they astonish him. Eyes that read his letters and understood him.

Dante pulls his cheeks down with his fingers, the way he does when trying to wake up and shrug off a doze. The wine must have been strong, he guesses. Maybe the sea air and the shock of Beth's beauty have added to the effects of the drink and have deepened this muddle in his head. He is reminded of being drunk in a rock club, where sensual opportunities lurk around the flashing dancefloor, and new faces look across to lure him over to fresh mouths: the high Tom could never resist. Something has come to life in him.

He turns back into the Quad and combs his fingers through his hair. How long has he spent scratching around in Birmingham, when all this was waiting a mere road trip away, like some beautiful dream you try to return to every night? Dante crosses the lawn and, as he walks back to the hall, he thinks of Tom inside with the blonde girl. Tom's contact with her reassures him. Competition between them for Beth could prove fatal. And all he wants now is another opportunity to be with Beth, alone. It will be for the best.

Something runs down the Wynd at speed, on the other side of the Quad's western wall. Dante pauses to listen to the skittering sounds. A new breeze stirs through the rose bushes and the ivy. He shivers. A dog? He feels relief when the sound fades . . .

Whistling, he tries to shake the remnants of the dizzy spell from his head; he still feels odd. With a yawn, he fishes inside his pocket for a cigarette and decides to head for home. Eliot and the Hebdomidar have worn him out. He just wants to roll a fat one, open a cold beer, and allow nothing else to interrupt his thoughts of Beth.

TWELVE

He knows the story well: why the tunnel is there, who built it beneath the castle, and how it once worked, for a short time, to belay the Catholic French as they besieged the Bishop's Palace. The invaders threw cannon shot from the town centre to break the walls, and the ardour of the defence of John Knox and his Protestant supporters. But why he should be standing in the tunnel, shivering, with no watch on his wrist, and only dressed in the underwear he climbed into bed wearing, is a mystery to Mike Bowen.

He's been here before, in the castle grounds, against his will, and well after the sun has set. But never has he been this far within it, deep inside the bowels of the crumbling fortifications that overlook St Andrews Bay. Before, he awoke near a parapet, or found himself sitting on one of the lawn-courts inside the decrepit walls, having crossed the drawbridge, or climbed a fence bordering the moat without any recollection of having done so. But to actually have made his way through several Wynds from Dean's Court to the cliff edge, and to then descend the mineshaft, built nearly four hundred years before: this is a new development in his case of what the American doctor called night terrors.

He is at the bottom of the tunnel, at the east end of the defences, having crawled down the smooth brown stones, damp with seepage, to where the mineshaft begins, before it crosses beneath the Scores to the place it originally met with the burrowing French; in the middle of the road, where a subterranean skirmish took place to push the Holy Roman warriors back, for a time at least.

Extraordinary; no other word for it. His presence here is beyond his orderly and above-average faculty for reason. How did he not wake on this nocturnal journey to the mineshaft? In the amber glow of a security light, situated at the summit of the tunnel, he looks at his hands and the soles of his feet. They are black with grime from where he's walked, unshod, and then scrabbled down as if to find something after midnight in the mineshaft. Or rather, he now feels, it is as if he's been summoned to this place by something in his sleep. The presence, the hallucination, or whatever it is that visits him in his mediaeval chambers at Dean's Court, or appears beside him in the university library, is responsible.

Mike rises to a crouch and dismisses the idea as suddenly as it strikes him: it is ludicrous. Despite the dark and the silence underground, profound save for the far-off murmur of the tide against the black rocks, his reason fights back and answers the instinctive and primal cry of terror inside him. 'A sleepwalk,' he says aloud, to comfort himself with the sound of his own baritone. 'Nothing more,' he adds, his voice quieter. But is this not the conclusion of something that first began that afternoon? On the top floor of the library, in a study cubicle facing the sea, where he has been disturbed before?

Earlier that day – less than an hour before the library closed at ten in the evening – he swore he was not alone while he worked between the Theology and Ancient History sections. As far as he determined, in the still and silent top floor, where only the odd flicker of a strip light or gurgle from a radiator could be discerned, no other student was working. There was no sound of the fire doors by the stairwell opening or closing, or any noises of heels scraping along the linoleum of the aisles. No one else was there with him, not even the two librarians on duty, as he made the final amendments to the bibliography of his thesis. And yet, when he left his seat to seek out a volume in which to double-check a page reference, or be certain a publication date was this and not that, and that it was published at the University of Massachusetts and not by the Cambridge University Press, he became aware of a presence. Nearby, in the next aisle, or at the end of the column of books he searched through, just beyond sight, he was sure he saw a shadow. Or heard a whisper. Or maybe, out of the corner of his eye, saw someone move quickly. Twice he called out, embarrassed at having to do so, and inquired if anyone was there. Twice he went unanswered.

Never prone to flights of fancy, and absolutely certain, as certain as any intelligent man could be, that there is no such thing as the supernatural (as fascinating as it was, in the interests of folklore and mythology), he still felt distinctly uncomfortable. It was a little colder in the library than usual too. Perhaps the lowered temperature set his nerves on edge, because he became prone to occasional glances over his shoulder, and began a frequent peeking into an aisle before entering it, as if to avoid the shock of coming across another scholar he'd mistaken for something else. Even a man with little imagination would not have felt at ease in the library that evening.

His ears were the first things to play tricks on him. While at his desk near the window, he heard a quiet voice repeat a word – more a hiss than a whisper – as if the speaker were learning to pronounce the word. It had sounded like 'You'. Like someone was trying to get his attention, quickly, and knew of no other name to call him by. 'You,' 'You,' twice more, as he tried to concentrate on the bibliography and its minefield of cross-references.

He stood up and said, 'Look here. It's not funny. Who is it?' And he left his snug cubicle with its view of the white breakers and grey troughs, out there in the unusually excited sea, and peered down every aisle, half a dozen near him, where the mutterings must have arisen, if they had sounded at all. And seen no one. Nothing besides a flutter of something at the base of the last aisle, although it could have just been his eyes, or his mind telling him he should see something because someone had spoken nearby. But he thought he caught sight of someone, or the end of their garment at least, or the last of their shadow, as it flitted from view the moment he poked his head out.

He turned sharply at the sound of something falling to the floor with a rustle, back where he'd been sitting. That was the last straw, to turn around and see your own overcoat upon the table, where it had been upset from the window-sill, lying as if face down with the shape of a body still inside it, on the desk where his books and folders were open.

Then he fled, angry at the prankster, angry at the draughts in the building (to have shaped his jacket so), and angry at himself for running to the fire doors, taking little backward looks at the corridors of books, disused terminals and empty desks, all left in his wake. But still he made his way to the ground floor, with some haste, and reported the disturbance to the first librarian he came across. And before he'd properly gathered himself too, which made his cheeks redden when he thought back on the affair over dinner. 'Someone is messing about upstairs,' he said to the man on the front desk, with whom he was on nodding terms after his three years of study in the library. The man gave him a quizzical look, and seemed ready to offer the wry, patient, though condescending smile of a librarian disturbed by a fool, but corrected himself at the last moment, convinced perhaps by the sincerity behind the complaint.

They climbed the stairs together, saying little to each other, and entered the second floor. All was how he had left it. Near the desk where he'd been working, Mike spoke. 'Right here. Every time I get into my work, some idiot whispers something, and then runs down the central aisle when I investigate. And it's not the first time it's happened.'

The librarian smiled and turned his back on Mike. Saying nothing, and only announcing himself by the squeak of his rubber-soled shoes, the librarian walked into the midst of the Classics section and peered about, probably bemused by the fact that Mike was working late in the library rather than drinking over at the West Port with the rest of the postgrads. When he stopped, at the end of a bay that ran thirty feet long before it joined the main concourse of the library, the librarian did something that Mike thought unusual. He rubbed the outside of his arms and moved his shoulders in the slight but perceptible way that shoulders move when bodies are cold.

With Mike in tow, the librarian then walked down the central concourse, looking left and then right into every aisle until he reached the far westerly wall, before turning and walking all the way back. 'No one up here besides you, I'm afraid. And a particularly strong draught. There must be a window open somewhere. I'll check them when we close. In about twenty minutes,' he said, as if to prompt Mike to leave and allow the staff to go home.

Immediately, he read Mike's dissatisfaction. 'I've been on the front desk for the last two hours, and you're the only person to have gone upstairs. Sorry,' he added, accompanied by the smile Mike had begun to find detestable, as if he were being pitied for getting spooked on his own, in a well-lit library, as the midnight hour drew close.

So what is wrong with him? Disturbed in the library, and now to be crouching in an underground passage beneath the castle, shivering, in just his smalls. And how the temperature drops, he thinks, the closer you get to the sea. With that thought, he turns and begins to clamber back up the tunnel, moving on the balls of his feet and the palms of his hands. It is a difficult space to move through, and impossible to make quick progress with gravity against you and the inhibitions of space preventing a man from walking upright.

But he gets no further than six or seven feet upward when something moves behind him, with a heavy sound. If he's not mistaken, something has just been dragged across the stone floor, like a thick covering, reminding him of the sound of the gym mats at boarding school, pulled by obedient boys into place behind the vaulting horse.

Turning his head, he stares back into the throat of the tunnel, toward the pit, where it opens out in a rough cavern, hewn from the sandy rock. In the base of this cavern, he knows, from his many visits to the fortifications, there is a manhole and an iron ladder descending ten feet down into another, deeper chamber: the only visible part of the mine-shaft proper still open to the public. There is a cave down there, no bigger than the living room of a town house, with a low ceiling, uneven walls, and a metal grate to stop the curious and the foolhardy from walking any deeper under the town. Down there – the sound has come from down there. And whoever, or whatever, is making the sound is at it again: dragging something across the floor to the ladder that connects the mine to the tunnel he is currently cramped up inside.

A dog perhaps? Lost, seeking shelter and unable to resist the powerful scents of a dark cave, it may have fallen down the ladder to the lower annexe and hurt its legs. 'Who's there?' Mike calls out, after clearing his throat, his body frozen into the undignified crab-crawl he is making back up the tunnel.

No answer.

'Are you all right?' he asks, after suddenly thinking of the possibility of a person having fallen down there: a drunk, or student on a dare. He's heard reports that such things have happened in the past. 'Can you hear me?' he asks, his voice insistent.

The dragging noise ceases, but is immediately followed by the clink of something hard against the metal of the ladder.

One of his legs starts to shake – from the cold, from this sudden plummet in temperature, he tells himself. The shakes seize hold of his jaw next and he has to swallow hard to regain the power of speech. Not moving, but taking a quick glance up the tunnel, in order to estimate how soon he can cover the ground on limbs curiously strengthless, Mike calls out again. 'Will you answer me?'

There is a momentary pause in the clinking sound – a noise that follows the pattern of hands mounting the rungs of a ladder – and a sigh is announced. A sound of air passing from a mouth, but not from exertion, from excitement. And then a rustle and the clinking of fingers on the rusty rungs recommences.

Something moves in the shadows around the manhole. 'You,' it says. And other things are muttered – too low for him to hear, and too quickly for the patterns of ordinary speech – before Mike begins his ascent in greater haste than before.

One foot slips backward as his toes fail to find purchase. His knees graze against the floor of the stone chute. His breath grows loud in his ears, and his mouth opens, ready to cry out.

He makes it no further than the neck of the tunnel, and knows with all the power of his logic that the moment he heard the scrape of bone and the flap of rags against the walls of the well, he would get no further.

But how could he have guessed his body would descend the tunnel at so great a speed? Or that whatever seized him by the ankle would be so insensitive to the cries he makes as his naked torso, with T-shirt now ruffled around his throat, is dragged across the rock floor to the pit? And then down the manhole he goes, and into the grave beneath it.

THIRTEEN

Running as fast as he is able, his bare feet skim across the surface of an empty field. Blades of long grass catch between his toes and then snap away. Stalks of the thicker weeds whip against his shins and around his calf muscles to leave a sting. Under a clear blue sky, he flees across this seemingly endless grass, bordered by tall trees of a dense summer green; a place he's not seen in years, but one that is instantly familiar to the vague sense of consciousness he possesses in the most harrowing of dreams. This is a place he's not run through since a child, and only then as he slept while the twitches of his eyelashes kept time with his pounding feet.

But tonight, things are as vivid as they have ever been. It is as if he can smell the pollen of midsummer, and feel the warmth of the sun on his skin, and see the whites and yellows of the butterfly wings he has startled into life and then quickly passed. And he knows where this race will lead and how it will end.

Aware it is a dream, but unable to wake himself, Dante finds himself in the grip of a terror so strong he even tries to call out to himself, to stop himself from running any further through this grass toward the centre of the pasture. He wants to shout out and warn himself that he is alone, that no one for miles can hear him, that the field is disused. But still he runs, and so fast now he begins to lose his balance, right in the middle of the field. And as his head lurches forward, his legs buckle, his knees clash together like dull cymbals, and his hands start crazy windmills in the air, he prepares for the anticipated fall.

One of his feet lands in a hollow on a patch of uneven ground beneath the sea of unmown grass. The leg straightens and jars his body from ankle to neck. But the momentum of his charge carries the rest of his body over, jack-knifed in the middle, so the top of his head faces the earth and his arms fly backward and his fingers point at the sky. Braced for the snapping of his delicate neck, he closes his eyes and puts himself in the dark. But the top of his head never strikes the earth, his neck never twists, and his body never flops over in an ungainly gambol. Instead, he carries on falling, straight as a stone dropped into a well, without his shoulders or ribs or legs touching the sides of that which he plummets down at such speed.

There is the sudden sound of a wind blowing up through the hole, which instantly replaces the sounds of the birds and insects, back up there, above ground level. Now everything is dulled, shut out, and finally silenced. Even the lights go out when the sides of his shoulders hit the walls of the giant soil pipe which runs in a vertical line from its opening, in the middle of the disused field, to the centre of the earth. Down it travels, through miles of damp clay, reddy brown and tiered with strata of worm and root and thick, endless, soundproofed earth.

His fall slides to a stop. His shoulders are jammed against the sides of the red pipe; the soles of his bare feet face the coin-sized portion of sky, at the mouth of the hole. The pipe has narrowed as it descends, hundreds of feet down, until something man-sized has eventually become lodged, head-first, below ground.

In a split second, he tries to do several things, fails, and the full realisation of his predicament hits him. First, he tries to move his arms, but they are stuck fast; the force of the fall has lodged him in the tunnel, air-tight and upside down. Then he instinctively attempts to bend his knees. No use; he can only widen his ankles a fraction, and his kneecaps strike the smooth side of the pipe the moment he attempts to bend his legs. He tilts his head back an inch but the crown of his skull also hits the solid wall of the pipe.

When he screams for his mother and his father, as he did so many years ago, his voice is high-pitched, but smothered by the infinite darkness he stares down and into. Unable to wriggle back up, with gravity against him and his shoulders squeezed tight and stuck fast, he realises in a fraction of a second that no matter how much he wants to see his family and friends again, to enjoy Christmas and walk on the sun-baked sands of family holidays, and to exult in every joy of childhood, he is trapped. Stuck forever; confined in the earth like a dead man in a coffin. His voice fails; hysteria follows. From the back of his brain and down into every muscle, bone, tendon, fibre and molecule of his body, the coldest panic fills him up.

Dante wakes. He sits bolt upright in bed. His heart whacks the sides of his ribcage. Staring about himself, in a mess of wet sheets and duvet, he sees that he is no longer trapped underground. It was a dream. He is at home, in the flat, in his bed, facing the window that overlooks the East Scores.

Dante gives immediate thanks to God that it is nothing more than a nightmare, and that he is awake and not buried alive with the blood rushing to his head. If there is a hell, that would be it for him: the soil pipe in the middle of a deserted field. He hopes to God there is no such thing as hell.

Rubbing his hands over his face, he knows he cannot risk going back to sleep in case he finds himself running again, at speed, toward the pipe. It is the same realisation he grasped as a child, when he waited for the morning light to drift through the curtains of his room, and only then would he doze until his mother woke him with a call for school.

But why has the dream returned? No sooner does he begin this train of thought than he stops thinking. Something has just moved, at the end of his bed.

Dante feels his body go cold; he swallows but is unable to move. He squints into the dark. He can see the shape of the wardrobe, the edges indistinct and almost vibrating in what little light the moon emits through chinks in the curtains. Beside the wardrobe is the windowsill and the shape of something before it, interfering with the thin lines of seeping light.

Hunched over, with something about the head, like a hood, or some manner of swathing, the figure sits and, he is certain, watches him. Dante closes his eyes and then opens them, trying to banish the vision – the residue from the awful dream. But as his eyes refocus, he sees that it is still there. Waiting.

'Shit,' he says. But he only has enough air to say that, and nothing more. As if stirred into life by the sound, the intruder stands up, quickly, and rises to an unnatural height, so the top of its head is lost against the murk of the ceiling. It moves past the bed in a quick upright glide, no more than a foot away from the base of the bed-frame. Dante feels every hair stand upright on his body. A cry is stifled in his throat. His eyes water. He prays for his heart to stop before it comes for him.

But when it turns, with a swish of air, it moves toward the closed door of his room and away from his bed. Its outline disappears against the dark wood of the door that the moonlight fails to illumine, even in part. And through that black rectangle of door, it carries on moving, right through and into the hallway, without a sound.

Wrapped in his duvet, Dante leaps from his bed. He scrambles across the room, the carpet rough against the soles of his bare feet. Stretching one hand from the folds of duvet, he slaps his palm against the wall, fumbling for where he remembers the light switch to be. His fingers brush across it, return, and then click the light on.

For a moment, as the light bursts from the bulb, he winces and flinches back, expecting to see the intruder reaching for him.

There is nothing there. No one in his room and the door is closed. Everything is as it was before he climbed into bed; still orderly, beside the clothes he wore that day, now strewn about the floor where he left them. Pulling the duvet up around his shoulders, Dante sits on the corner of his bed, still in shock, with his instincts telling him it is all an omen, that it has a meaning, that he is in danger and must leave. Never has he felt this so strongly about anywhere he's slept.

He struggles to think of sufficient cause for the return of his childhood haunting, and then for this imagined intruder. The move from Birmingham and all that has befallen him since has been something of a roller coaster, with his spirits rising and falling and finding no middle ground. But has he been unsettled enough to dream of the pipe, and then to see something at the foot of his bed, waiting for him to wake?

There is something especially vivid about each experience, as if they were stronger and clearer than it is natural for nightmares and waking visions to be. And it is the worst place he can think of to have such thoughts, being so close to the rotten cathedral, with generations of old bones hidden under its cracked slabs, and across the road from the castle, with the memorials on its pavements to those burned to death, or hung from windows – a hundred yards from his bed.

With heavy eyelids, he went to bed on a high after meeting Beth, having returned home to smoke a quick joint. He should have passed out and not woken until at least eleven the following morning. There is no call for such a disturbance.

Lighting a cigarette to keep his hands busy and his mind occupied, Dante wanders through to the kitchen, hastily turning on every light he passes. After switching the kettle on, he finds the novel he was reading before they left for Scotland. He'll sit this one out, like he did as a child, until dawn breaks. And then, and only then, will he allow himself to close his eyes again.

FOURTEEN

Was her mouth stuck in an enticing pout? Was there a becoming cluster of freckles on the bridge of her nose, and a subtle hint of rouge on high cheekbones? He can't be sure, cannot remember, but he does know every part of her face seemed to draw him toward the green of her eyes. Precious eyes, revealing little of the thoughts flitting through the mystery and dark of her pretty head.

In the light of midday, after the worst of his shock at the night's disturbances has passed, Dante lies on the couch and tries to recall Beth's face from the night before. But the more he tries to visualise her features the more indistinct they become. It is as if she has mostly escaped from his memory, to leave only an impression – an enchantment for him to obsess over. Eventually, his desperate efforts to remember her begin to spoil the magic, so he settles on the prevailing sense that she is exquisite to look at, and that he'll meet her again, soon.

But who is she? A student embroiled in an affair with an old wanderer and academic, attracted by a fierce intellect and its unconventional tastes? He can hardly see her dancing in nightclubs or enjoying the company of a regular circle of girlfriends. Beth is no ordinary girl. There is a wisdom in her. Something older than her years wrapped up in something childlike, like tenderness. A combination of maturity and vulnerability. And wasn't that what he saw and craved in Imogen too? But Beth goes beyond his fixation with Imogen. And Beth sweeps aside the tired attitude he's adopted toward girls since that disappointment. He feels as if, after only a brief introduction, she's reinvigorated something meaningful inside him, made him rediscover an intensity of feeling he's either forgotten or given up on.

But is there not the danger of disappointment also? She'll demand the finest clothes and eat special foods; she'll rocket across the sky in first class, and wear sunglasses by rippling turquoise waters, while palm leaves shudder above her. She's the kind of girl he's seen in London, with that cold, focused beauty, who strides across airport marble, indifferent to admirers, or sits alone at a cafe table, listening to some exclusive whisper from a chic mobile phone. Beth will want an extraordinary man; age will be of no consequence. How can he compete? Maybe she'll experiment with a musician for as long as he proves interesting and his scene stays valid, and then she'll be gone to a painter in Milan, or a terrorist in Paris. She has choices and lovers, her leather cases are full of expensive clutter, her windows are watched by drawn faces, sapped of blood by the rents in once confident hearts. The very thought of her past, her expectations and moods, makes him feel acutely fragile; he can almost taste the beginnings of his own despair.

Toward the end of their brief contact, in the shadow of an old church, she seemed distracted too. He remembers the flutter of ecstasy on the child-queen's face the moment she left him. Something he's occasionally seen captured on a model's face in a fashion shoot, featured in a copy of *Tatler* or *Vogue*, when he's leafed through pages reeking of opened perfume samples in a doctor's surgery. What was she looking for in the Quad? What did she sense with her divine face? Was it a friend she planned to meet? Eliot said something to that effect. But who can say how these strange circles of Sloanes operate? They live in a different world. He guesses he would only come into contact with them in places like St Andrews, the Oxford of Scotland, where the students have money and boarding-school peers with unbelievable names. This is an alien place, with its cool air, hidden interiors and stone crevasses. He is still so far from learning its language.

Warm and relaxed, he lies in the crater his body has moulded around itself on the sofa cushions. While his mind brims with doubts and promises of something extraordinary that Beth might provide, he uses these impressions of her to obscure the fright he's received but still fails to explain to himself. Drawn from the first cigarette of the day, smoke curls about his flat belly and hangs over the green glass of the ashtray, placed between the golden belly ring and his tattoo of the Def American record label, inscribed around his navel. Cold glass feels good in the centre of so much warmth. Smiling, he wonders if Beth will ever trace a long fingernail around the fine lines of the tattoo. Most of his girlfriends have been fascinated with it.

But caution is everything. He is a hard-luck champion who eats chips with a tarnished fork; he belongs in bedsit land and on night-service buses. A man who has made his choices and now lies in a different bed. So what does Eliot want with him anyway and why should Beth care? Some high-brow undergraduate would have been more suited to assisting Eliot with his work – not a man who lives in biker bars and plays Faster Pussycat covers for drinks.

And as he idles in the strong sunlight that falls across him from the garden windows, Dante wonders if they are toying with him. Is he a new curiosity to be tossed between sharp claws? Is he crazy for travelling so far, hastily setting sail in a rusty boat with the closest approximation to a male prostitute for a companion – his best friend, to the end?

Beyond the windows, the new world continues to glow, trapped in its infinite summer. The sky is blue again, and the country a lush green around the clump of majestic architecture perched on this jagged harbour. Amongst the rush of emotion and thought that fires through him, and then suddenly changes course and alters into fresh feelings and contradictory notions, Dante can identify excitement. This is an adventure he's fallen into, and the thrill-seeking part of him relishes it all. St Andrews, with its bickering academics and bloody history, is waiting to be discovered. He feels like a warrior from a Robert E Howard novel, wading ashore on some forgotten isle to tremble before the sight of distant black spires.

But despite his ecstatic first impressions of the town, when he was overwhelmed by the sea and the sunlight, he's become aware of something else. Although the place radiates the elegance and romance of any well-preserved site of antiquity, there's another feature so well hidden he only catches flashes of it, when particularly alert. A quality not entirely pleasant, if he is honest. Perhaps that taints his impression of the town, affects his feelings for Beth, heightens his suspicion, and gives him nightmares. It is possible. Because St Andrews possesses its own peculiar brand of darkness. It is hard to define while he gorges his senses on the freshness of a new and spectacular environment. But, all the same, it is there. Every monument to a martyr burned slowly for heresy speaks of injustice, and every skeletal ruin of church and tower hints at death. Nights have shadows deeper than any city and the impenetrable, almost oppressive, grey stone reminds him of a great and ornate mausoleum slab, dropped into place to cover forgotten plagues and unrecorded tortures. Here exists another threat, an old and clever one, like organised religion, he thinks, remembering the teachings of *Banquet*.

Whistling drifts into the lounge from the bathroom and breaks his train of thought. Dante sits up in bed, alert to the sound. Impatience in the performer spoils the melody he can hear Tom whistling. It's the tune for *Sweet Child of Mine*, which Tom always recites when trifled. When Tom joins him in the lounge, he stands in the middle of the room and lashes the lid off his Zippo against the seam of his jeans, before striking the flint down his thigh to create fire. 'Where did you piss off to last night?'

Dante stretches his legs out and mumbles through a fake yawn. 'Oh, I got tired. I was just like a fish out of water. How about you?' he adds, to change the subject.

'Don't change the subject. You never even said goodbye. I saw you with this fat guy and then you were gone. Was that Eliot?'

'No, it was the Hebdomidar, and you were busy with that blonde. I only saw Eliot for a minute.'

'I wanted to meet him.'

'Busy man, Tom. Not a scratcher like you.'

Tom raises two fingers at Dante before disappearing back into the kitchen to rummage for milk.

'You dehydrated?' Dante asks.

Tom nods on his way back to the lounge. His eyes go wide over the rim of a plastic one-litre bottle of semi-skimmed milk.

'Did you cop off with that lass?'

Tom sneers, then burps.

'Well?'

'Been here three days, and already I'm the strike-out king of Scotland.'

Dante starts to titter. He knows what's coming. 'Tom, you cannot expect every girl to shag you on the first night.'

'Why not?'

'Cus this ain't a rock club in Birmingham five years ago. These girls are different.'

'You're telling me. We drank a bottle, she was eating out of my hand and all I said was "fancy a walk?". She was just like stunned and made some pathetic excuse.'

'Tom!' Dante cries out, trying to conceal his mirth. 'Where were you last night? It wasn't Eddie's, man. It was an academic soirée. That girl wasn't going to throw her reputation away on some long-haired tramp she just met.'

'Fuck you. I had my best shirt on.'

'You've got to move slow, man.'

'The day I take advice off you about chicks is the day I shoot myself.'

They glare at each other for a moment; both faces are tense.

'Sorry,' Tom says after a pause. 'That was low.'

'Damn right it was low.'

'Come on, cut me some slack. I've got a hangover.'

Dante turns away and stays quiet.

'Don't mess around, Dante. I said I'm sorry.'

'Drop it.'

'No I won't. I'm a prick. I don't deserve a girl.'

'That's right, you don't. Think before you open your mouth.'

Tom sighs and drifts over to the chair. 'You know what I'm like. Man, I have to get laid. Maybe it'll be better when the students come back.'

Dante shakes his head in exasperation.

'What?' Tom asks.

'Nothing.'

'Come on, Dante. We're on holiday, man. Why are we arguing? All that is in the past, and this place is the shit. I just need to find my feet.'

Dante sighs. 'Don't break anything in the meantime.'

'I promise. You won't know I'm here.'

'Time for work,' he says, and returns his attention to the pile of Eliot's books, gathering dust in the corner of the room.

'Fuck that,' Tom says. 'Let's go for a walk, check out the beach –' he sniggers '– Who knows what we'll find? Then we can go out and eat tonight. Hit a few bars.'

'Nah, I have to read Eliot's books. I'm seeing him tomorrow night.'

'Why at night?'

'Dunno. And Tom, we have to save money. I'm not blowing the stash in some pub. I have to make a start.'

'We've been here three days and we've seen nothing.'

'And the cash won't last forever.'

'Don't worry, man.'

'Tom, are you deaf? I am going to read today.'

'Touchy. What's up with you?'

Dante shakes his head. 'I had no sleep last night.'

'You kipped in here. What's that all about?'

Feeling uncomfortable, Dante adjusts his slouch on the sofa and lights a second cigarette. 'Bad dreams.'

Tom laughs. 'So you were a fraidy cat and couldn't sleep in your own bed.'

'I kid you not, it was awful. A dream I used to have all the time as a kid. And after I woke up . . .'

'What?'

'You'll piss yourself, so I'm not telling you.'

'Sod that. Tell me.'

'I saw a ghost or something.'

Tom raises his eyebrows, but he doesn't laugh. 'No shit.'

'At the end of my bed. There was like this figure sitting on the floor. Then it stood up and walked straight past my bed, and went through the door. I freaked and came in here.'

'So that's why all the lights were on this morning. You must have been spooked.'

'I haven't shat myself like that since I was about ten. It's weird.'

Tom looks into the garden. 'Funny, that.'

Cocking his head at Tom, who now looks pensive, he asks, 'Why do you say that?'

'That scream. Remember that scream the other night?'

Dante nods.

'Well, I heard it again last night. Not the same voice, mind, but a different one. Right across the road from my room. Came from the cliffs or the castle. It was really faint, like it was far off or down by the sea. But it was awful. At first I thought it was the wind or something, then I swore I heard someone yell, "help me". They said "God help me" or something like that. Funny we should both get freaked.'

'I didn't hear anything in here, but I believe you. Something's up with this place. Last night when I was walking home, I heard this kind of dog or something, running on the other side of the wall by the Quad. And then I get the nightmare, and see that ghost thing.'

They look at each other, both faces serious for a moment, before each mouth breaks into a broad smile – a smile so broad Dante can see Tom's one gold tooth at the back of his mouth. Then they are laughing until tears fill their eyes. 'Edinburgh,' Dante says. 'We need to get out of town for a day. Let's take the Wagon up to Edinburgh.'

'Fuckin' A,' Tom cries. They punch each other's fists and Dante makes his way to the shower.

FIFTEEN

Hart sits on the couch and bites into an apple. Deep in thought, he gazes across the room at the orderly lines of buildings printed on his town plan. On the far wall of the lounge, between a mirror and lamp, he's tacked the large map of St Andrews and the surrounding country. Three red pins on the map represent night-terror activity. Having the map gives him what feels like a greater sense of control over the investigation, and it supplies him with something to focus on when idle.

And there have been a lot of idle moments since his first two interviews. Besides two inquisitive phone calls from students not suffering from night terrors, a spokesperson from a local Bible group, and someone who phoned three times and hung up without a word, the early momentum of his research has lapsed over the last two days. But he dares not venture too far from the flat in case he misses another call. Maria, the girl with a nervous voice, never showed for her interview, and neither Kerry Sewell nor Mike Bowen has been in touch since the first interviews.

Kerry lives in Salvator's on the Scores and woke on the pier in the Eastern Harbour. Mike Bowen lives a quarter of a mile away in Dean's Court, across the road from the castle grounds, where the scholar of Classics repeatedly found himself walking after midnight. Maria, he knows, lives in New Hall, on the western side of town above the Golf Links. No more than a mile away from West Sands, where an arm was found a week earlier – something he gleaned from a local paper – and where Ben Carter incinerated himself.

From what he's gathered in other fieldwork, and through his macroscopic reading, the intensification of night-terror incidents never spreads beyond the confines of a small area like a single village, one side of a street, or sometimes a solitary room. But the St Andrews phenomenon stretches across a square mile. Maybe it's increasing or spreading further afield, beyond his knowledge, but he has nothing to rely upon for information beyond the response to the flyers he's posted – many of which have already been covered over by university clubs and societies advertising for the new intake of students. Will any more red pins pierce the map in the coming weeks? Or will it suddenly stop? Is there an innocent explanation? Something escaping from local industry into the air or water, perhaps? Or could it be auto-suggestion from the lecturer who ran the paranormal meetings? Which poses the question: how many students attended and are now suffering from sleep disorders? Maybe some declined to come forward or have already fled the town limits.

From what he understands, until the main wave of students returns from summer vacation, only fourth years and postgrads have stayed on in the town between June and September, to finish their dissertations. At least the present student population is small, but soon it won't be. And the one link, uniting his three victims, is a past involvement with Eliot Coldwell and his paranormal society, during the previous academic year. The link is still tenuous – no form of ritual magic was performed at the gatherings, and each student claimed the meetings consisted of nothing more than discussions or exercises in meditation – but it is all he has to go on. Though Coldwell has become the biggest frustration of all. Every time he's phoned the School of Divinity, the administrator has abruptly told him Eliot is not in residence. A request for the lecturer's home number was also denied. Finally, his three trips to the school on the Scores, the day before, all ended in disappointment; the administrative staff exchanged knowing glances with each other before claiming, and sincerely too he intuited, that Eliot makes only the rarest of appearances at the school. So where is Coldwell, and how long can he afford to wait for the man to reappear?

Sitting around drinking Scotch through the afternoons and evenings of his first week has also begun to create a series of grisly reactions in his stomach. After Nigeria, his sleeping and eating patterns are still off-kilter, and the whisky only serves to make his insides feel hot and loose. It is still unwise for him to venture too far from the bathroom. Landing amongst the early tremors of what he instinctively feels is an impending quake of night-terror activity aggravates his stomach further. Thwarted, he's waited out two days, drinking, while his mind winds itself through stages of anxiety, excitement and disappointment on an hourly basis.

Licking his lips and smoothing his beard away from his mouth, Hart rises from the couch and hovers by the hospitality cabinet. He steps forward, slides the glass door open and places his hand on the neck of a new bottle of Scotch. Releasing it, he stands back. Then repeats the motion. The third attempt at resisting the whisky fails, and Hart's hand returns from the cabinet clutching the neck of the fresh bottle. 'What the hell,' he says, and breaks the seal. He takes three long gulping slugs, gasps through the afterburn and then reclines on the sofa, feeling dizzy. He places a fresh tape in the Dictaphone and begins recording:

'Occult history of the Northern Hemisphere must be looked into. Conduct research in the university library on the possibility of relevant occurrences in this locale. No epicentre appears to have formed for the recent activity. Early indications suggest the attacks to be random and occurring across a wide area. Check on Mike Bowen from Dean's Court –'

The phone rings. He drops the Dictaphone and speeds across the lounge to the phone, mounted on the wall in the reception. 'Hey now, Hart Miller.'

'Have you seen Maria?' The voice is surly.

'Maria?'

'You know who.'

'Who's this?'

'Her boyfriend, and I want some answers.'

'We got something in common.'

The man goes silent. Hart prompts him: 'I'm not prepared to discuss my investigation with anyone not directly –'

'Oh, come on. You're not even a proper doctor. No wonder my girlfriend lost it. She's stressed out and you should have known better, instead of filling –'

'Hey listen up, buddy,' Hart barks, feeling whisky-brave, his pride stung by the kid's attitude. 'I haven't even seen Maria. She blew off her interview. So chill.'

For a few seconds, there is just the sound of two men breathing across the static distance.

'I can't find her.' The young man's voice is about to break around the edges. Hart hears him clear his throat.

He softens his tone. 'When did you see her last?'

'It's been two days now.'

'Maybe she's with a friend or something.'

'I've seen her every day for three years. She never goes anywhere without telling me first.' The man has become impatient again; the volume of his voice rises and his tone becomes shrill.

'OK. Right. Cool it. You keep shouting and my phone goes down. You hear me, buddy?'

Silence.

'Can't hear you,' Hart says.

'Yeah,' the voice replies, still petulant in tone.

'Now who are you?'

There is a pause. 'Chris.'

'So, Chris. You're looking for someone to blame. But I'm not responsible here. I've been in town like five minutes. But there's one thing I do know: people like your girlfriend have suddenly begun to experience nightmares. A special kind too. Like nothing they've known before. They get frightened, they behave strangely. Maybe you even stop recognising them. That can happen. A few individuals have been to see me. But your girlfriend was not one of them. She called for an appointment, sure, but she never showed up. And hasn't answered my calls either. I'm concerned too. Got me?'

Silence.

'I take that as a yes. So allow me to get things straight. Maria takes off a few days back and there's no word since. Am I right?'

'Yeah.'

'Would she go home?'

'No. She left her door open and all her things are still in

her room. Her neighbour heard her leave after midnight, on Monday night.'

'Go on.'

'With someone.'

Hart presses his forehead to the wall. 'Any ideas who?'

'Maria would never fuck around. And I'd kill whoever took advantage of a sick girl.' Chris's voice is rising again, to something mean.

'Dude, I never said she would. This is something totally beyond anything that Maria would ever do. You two are close and she tells you everything.'

'Right,' Chris says, putting his voice back together with an effort.

'And you have no idea where she could go.'

'No.'

'She been sleepwalking?'

'She said so. She asked me to watch her, but I couldn't. She doesn't understand. I have things to do.'

'Sure. This is not your fault. She was frightened and unless you have suffered this first-hand, you cannot understand what these dreams are like.'

'Come on, mate. We're talking about dreams here. They're not the cause. She's bulimic. That's how this started. You can't help.'

'Don't hang up,' Hart says. 'Tell me where you've looked.'

Chris sighs, exasperated. 'I've checked out her friends. Then I phoned her home and frightened her mom. The police said she doesn't even qualify as a missing person yet.'

Hart speaks quietly but firmly. 'Chris. Listen to what I have to say. Don't freak out. Just listen up.'

'What?'

'Have you had a nightmare recently?'

'No,' he says, irritated by the question.

'Good.'

'Why is it? I told you, this dream thing is ridiculous.'

Hart interrupts. 'Did you attend any of Eliot Coldwell's group meetings?'

'What's that got to do with anything? My girlfriend's gone missing and —'

'Just answer me. Did you go?'

'To that load of bollocks? You got to be joking.'

Hart takes a deep breath. 'Might still be a good idea for you to leave town, Chris. Just for a while.'

'What?' the man bellows.

'Leave town, yes. There is evidence to suggest . . .' Then Hart gives up and moves the receiver away from his ear.

The verbal barrage continues from a distance. 'My girlfriend goes missing and you say I should leave! Why would I leave? What exactly would that achieve? Who'd find Maria then? Waste of time! All you Yanks are the same! You're all full of shit! And if I find out that Maria's been there, you're dead.' The phone clicks down at the other end.

Hart exhales. He is unable to be angry. He drinks another four fingers of Scotch and settles back on the couch, feeling more impotent than ever. But as he ponders Maria's disappearance and tries to decide whether he should speak with the university authorities, the phone rings again. Standing up too quickly, he staggers across the sheepskin rug in the lounge. Tiny red flashes fall through his swooping vision. He snatches the phone from the cradle and prepares for more abuse. 'Hey now.' His voice is thick. His mind inflexible.

'You the nightmare guy?'

Hart breathes a sigh of relief; it isn't Maria's boyfriend. 'Yessum.'

'I need to see you.'

'Sure. What's your name?' he asks, excited now, feeling the spirit of the investigation suddenly reanimate in the flat.

'Oh yeah. Rick.'

His words slur. 'When's good for you, Rick? How about now?'

'I can't. Not today. I got something on.'

'Tomorrow?'

'Yeah. That's cool. What time?'

'Will you be up at ten?'

'I'll be up at nine. I live with a prick who wakes me every morning.'

'Ten's fine then.' Hart gives Rick the address of his flat and takes Rick's phone number. 'Before you go,' he adds. 'Did you go to any of Eliot Coldwell's meetings?'

'Waste of time that was. I was told we'd get paid. I wasted three Friday nights.'

Hart raises the phone in triumph after he says goodbye to Rick. Another one; that makes four. Maria has disappeared and there has been no word from Kerry or Mike, although Kerry admitted she intended to leave town. But Mike? He would hang on to the end because of his thesis. Hart makes a decision on the spot: to satisfy his curiosity, and to placate the bad feeling Chris's phone call has instilled in him, he'll go and check on the scholar from Dean's Court.

Pale-faced, a little unsteady on his feet, and feeling as if his stomach has been replaced with a torn paper bag, Hart walks to Dean's Court from Market Street. In the bright sunlight, his head hurts too and he hates himself for thinking about the next drink. It is an effort to restrain himself from entering the dozen pubs he passes since leaving the flat. Getting liquored is all he feels up to after being yelled at by Chris. Conflict is not something he expected, not from the students. Is he losing his touch? And what the kid said about him not being a proper doctor cut deep. As an undergraduate in Chicago, he always drank heavily for confidence. At five-four, with legendary acne, he grew a Robert E Lee beard to cover it. Two proofreaders adjusted his Master's thesis because he was skunk-drunk when he wrote the final draft. What he then saw in Guatemala gave him a rock star's liver and, he guesses, another ten years to live unless he climbs on the wagon.

People need him in St Andrews. He has to lay off the booze. But the situation is impossible; if he starts spouting the truth about night terrors they'll say he's a crank with the looks to match.

Cursing himself for a moment of self-pity, Hart reminds himself that Mike Bowen's safety is first on the agenda. He hopes to God Mike Bowen's failure to answer his phone is nothing more than a case of the guy cracking Latin rocks in the library. But if he's gone missing too, Hart knows he has to go somewhere important, and soon, with his information. It's still too early to start making a noise, and he needs to speak to this Coldwell character before he goes to the authorities – even if it means forcing a confrontation with the lecturer, or doorstepping him at home.

Passing under an arch set in a high stone wall above a cobbled terrace, Hart enters the gardens of Dean's Court. Poplars, oaks and chestnut trees cast shadows across the ancient well, and lush grasses surround the fourteenth-century hall. It's made from grey stone and has an arbour dividing it from a modern annexe overlooking South Street. The steps leading up to the large wooden front doors are smooth and slippery with the wear of centuries, and the expansive reception smells of polished oak, old books, floor wax and dust: just like every university library he's ever worked and slept in since his teens. The air is cool inside, the hall quiet, there is no glare from sunlight, the rug feels soft beneath his feet. He is feeling better already.

Against one wall, festooned with black and white photographs, a coat of arms, and an engraved honour roll of past Deans, Hart sees a wooden roster, divided up into little slots containing the names and room numbers of every resident. A tiny wooden slide is pulled across the slot to indicate whether the tenant is in or out. Under Mike Bowen, room fifteen, the slide has been pushed to the right, revealing the word IN on the white card beneath. A good start.

'Can I help you?'

Hart turns to his left, quickly, and then groans. He clasps a hand to his clammy forehead.

'I'm no that ugly,' the woman says, her accent broad.

'Rough night,' Hart says. When he opens his eyes, he sees a handsome long-haired brunette, in her mid-thirties he guesses, descending the staircase to the reception.

'Hey now,' Hart says, but his voice lacks its usual music.

'I'm the sub-warden,' she says, and smiles, pleasantly, but confidently enough to make Hart aware who the boss is at Dean's Court.

He offers a hand which she takes quickly and drops just as soon. 'Hart Miller. I'm looking for Mike Bowen.'

The sub-warden stops smiling, either because she's smelled the dead rat in his mouth, or his mention of Mike is cause for concern. 'Aren't we all,' she says.

'He was helping me out with some research. And I can't get hold of the guy.'

The woman seems concerned. 'Well, he's no been in his room since yesterday evening, and he's missed two meals since. Students are supposed to tell us if they're to miss meals. And as for leaving his door open again. Well, it's no safe.'

'Safe?' Hart asks. His stomach goes all tight.

'Things have gone missing before. He's been told. A room is only secure if it's locked.'

'Oh right. The security risk. Any idea where he's gone?'

'No.' It is not what Hart wants to hear but he likes the way she says 'No', as if the word is passing through a tunnel like a breath of wind. 'You and Mike friends?' she adds.

'Hardly. Met him just the once, but we have something to finish up. I'm not a student here. Just visiting is all.'

She cocks an eyebrow, as if longing to indulge in gossip, even with a bearded stranger. 'Mike's a strange one. Students! The top five per cent they say, and he canne even shut his door after him. The cleaners found it wide open this morning, and he's no been back since last night.'

Hart feels a chill pass through him. He swallows. 'He left last night and hasn't showed since? But he usually shows up, right? After leaving the door wide open? Did he leave any messages? Did he have any plans for today?'

'Is there anything you might tell me?' she asks, her face grave.

'I'm studying sleep disturbances. A rare form of them, and Mike was helping me out.'

She frowns with concern. 'Is he all right?'

What could he say? He looks at the floor, and thinks of his promise of confidentiality. 'Sure. I reckon so. Bad sleeper is all.'

'Really,' she says, distracted, trying to equate Mike Bowen with a bad night's sleep. 'I'm sure he'll turn up,' she adds, her tone upbeat again.

Hart smiles. 'The moment he shows, get him to phone me. Or even better, get him to swing by my place. It's Hart Miller. Tell him I called, would you? He's got my number.' He turns to leave the hall, feeling a little sick. A cool breeze waits for him by the front door. He pauses on the reception mat. As he turns around, it crunches and spikes against the soles of his boots. 'Mike's a smart kid, but I'm worried about him. There's something going round, like a flu, or so I've been told, and it makes people a little loco. Has anybody else had it, or been taking off in the middle of the night and leaving their doors open?'

The sub-warden places both hands on her hips. 'Really. I've no heard of that, except for a rumour about the Hong Kong thing.'

'Must be that,' Hart says, nodding, but it's an effort to give the woman a smile of reassurance.

'Mike is a one-off,' she mutters, and shakes her head. 'I've never met one quite like him before and I don't expect to again.'

'Me neither,' Hart hears himself say, automatically. His fragile smile has begun to ache under his beard.

The sub-warden's eyebrows rise in surprise. 'As for the

others going off walking in the middle o' the night, I can't help you there. I've no heard it was catching. Are there many at it?'

Hart leaves the hall without another word.

SIXTEEN

'He's a bastard! A selfish, egocentric bastard, and I'm going to tell him tonight. Even if it comes to blows.' Jason speaks before a captivated audience of three. His friends lean across the table in the pub, their mouths open in amazement at the long list of grievances that Jason airs. They begin by laughing; every student has horror stories about shared housing, but Jason's have become legend. By the time he finishes the lengthy account of his roommate's crimes, his three friends stop laughing and shake their heads, incredulous, but thankful they have not spent a year with Rick.

'Fife Park,' one of them says. 'It just attracts those types. They always go for the cheapest accommodation.'

'Yeah,' another chips in. 'Same in Albany last year. We had one just like him.'

'But his parents are loaded, aren't they?' the third questions.

'Damn right!' Jason shouts, his blood up after a fifth pint of Caluden Ale. 'He's a typical spoiled Southern ponce. Never had to work a day in his life, never washed a fuckin' dish, and his mummy and daddy bail him out after every failed course. He's a piece of shit.'

Laughter roars around the table.

'What are you going to do?' one of the delighted specta-
tors asks.

Jason takes a deep breath. 'Well, he's soiled every dish, cup
and spoon since the other lads left in May. There is nothing
left to use. It's all in the sink, or strewn across the table. You
know, some of the scraps on his plates are actually rotting.
So I am going to put all of it in his room. On his bed. No,
under his disgusting bedclothes that have never been washed.'

'Fantastic,' one of his mates says.

'Then,' Jason continues, only pausing until his friends fall
silent again, 'when he comes back from the pub, pissed up no
doubt, and finds it, I shall demand a sum of money for all
the bread, milk, tuna, bog roll, cereal, olive oil and God
knows what else of mine he's been using all year.'

'He'll never pay. He'll just lamp you.'

'Good! I want him to take a swing, because it's all been
building up inside me for a whole year. It's been eating me,
so I can't sleep, or think, or work. Single-handedly, he's
ruined my fourth year. He's changed me. My personality.
And it will all come out. It'll just explode . . .'

His friends start to snigger now, uncomfortable and a little
nervous. Jason's eyes have developed a far-away gaze, and
his bottom lip trembles. His hands clench until his knuckles
crack and look like they are ready to pop through the skin.
Two of his friends pass cigarettes around the table while the
third considers patting Jason on the shoulder, but soon
thinks better of it.

'I'm going home now,' Jason says quietly in the uneasy
silence, and leaves the table.

'Jesus. He's going to murder Rick,' someone says, once
Jason has left the pub.

'He deserves it. You heard what Rick called Jason's girl-friend.'

'Yeah, but what if it goes too far? Jason could get into some serious shit.'

'Serves Rick right. Anyone that turns a good-natured lad like Jase into a psycho has got it coming.'

Rick launches a crumpled beer can down the bank toward David Melville Hall. The empty missile drops short of the ground-floor windows. In retaliation for the beer can's failings, Rick stamps on the first bicycle he passes. The mountain bike has been left chained to a lamppost, and rattles against the concrete pole after his foot makes contact. Nothing falls off the bike or snaps, so he swears and carries on down the gravel path that passes the Sports Centre. He staggers here and there, corrects himself and then continues to walk in a straighter line. Then he considers going back and pulling the saddle off the bike frame, but it seems like too great an effort.

Can't be arsed.

He's never liked Jason, not since the first day of term when he asked him if he minded not smoking while others ate. But it is not just the eye-rolling or the petty hen-pecking comments about the dishes; there are other things he dislikes about the man, and he will tell Jason about them all, tonight.

Rick has failed the year, and has not been sleeping well. Jason knows this but continues to nag him about the kitchen. Nightmares have left Rick reluctant to pursue the usual sixteen hours of sleep he has become accustomed to after a drink. The dodgy gear he scored in an Edinburgh club must be the cause of the dreadful imaginings that now seem to pounce every time he closes his eyes. There is plenty of bad acid around, but the shit he took in July was rancid. He's been off drugs since the nightmares began and, as an alternative, chooses to drink more heavily. Maybe he should try to get sleeping pills from the Yank sleep doctor, the quack who he's supposed to see tomorrow morning.

Rick left the pub at nine-thirty, having expended the last of his parental contribution. He will have to borrow some money to phone home and ask his dad for more cash. But right now, all Rick can think about is a cigarette. He's desperate. Maybe he can ask Jason for a couple of fags – those cheap roll-ups he smokes. And then ask him for change to make the call home. But he must make sure to do it before they have the row. That will be more diplomatic. Rick grins. Turning a familiar corner on the path, he breathes a sigh of relief; this is the last leg of the tiresome walk from town to Fife Park.

Something scuttles under the hedgerow next to his left foot. Rick flinches and then bends over to peer through dark leaves and bracken. A bright-red pheasant darts away through the undergrowth, its tiny head bobbing up and down above a bulbous body. 'Fuck,' he says, before feeling the sudden rush of adrenaline dissolve in his muscles. He exhales noisily. It is vital he fights off the fatigue that immediately tries to establish itself, created by a lack of sleep and worsened by the effects of too much beer. He will have to be alert for Jason. He can take him though; the guy is soft.

High above, the sound of a jet from the Leuchers airbase ripples across the horizon. As it is still light enough to catch a glimpse of the distant golf course and sea from the path he walks, he might be able to watch it fly over. Could be something more interesting than a Tornado. Usually, the planes come in pretty low from out at sea, practising bombing runs on Iraqi targets, and the noise is deafening. He turns and looks to the horizon, visible between and over the top of the dreary concrete of the North Haugh building and Andrew Melville Hall, arranged below the hill he crosses, on the summit of which the budget halls of residence, David Russell Hall and Fife Park, have been built.

As he scans the purple expanse of darkening sky, something in the distance catches his eye. Rick stops, and looks across the dark-green leaves stretching across the furrowed acres of root crop to the distant wood. Is someone standing in the field? He screws up his eyes. In the dark, from this angle, it almost looks like a man standing up with his head bowed. But it would have to be a man on stilts because no one is that tall.

Rick moves closer to the fence and places his hands on the top strand of wire. He's never seen anyone in the field before, not even a farmer. No, it can't possibly be a man. It is a tree, surely. The thin trunk only resembles a torso in poor light from a distance, and those other things that hang down like long arms must be the branches. It is just the black silhouette of a dying tree that he's never noticed before. But despite the cushion from fear that a belly full of alcohol provides, something about the distant shape makes him feel uneasy. It's not the kind of thing you would want to look at sober.

The jet is coming closer now and, for a moment, Rick wishes he were in it. He carries on walking, and averts his eyes from the ugly thing perched in the field. But his senses stay alert. He has an acute notion of being watched. Impulsively, he looks back to the field. The tree has vanished. The field now resumes its natural appearance, empty except for a forest of root-crop and an occasional hovering seagull. Rick stops walking again and goes back to the fence to take a keener look. His eyes sweep across the field from left to right. Although his vision judders a little from the drink, he becomes absolutely certain that the figure has disappeared. It can't have been a tree in that case. It must have been a man. But no one can move that quickly. They were standing near the centre of the field and could not possibly have made it back to the trees in only a few seconds, or hidden in the crop, because it grows no higher than a man's ankle. The air seems colder now. But then he's stopped moving, and that would explain why he now shivers. Time to move on, because staring across the field, in the descending dark, hurts his eyes. He shakes his head and carries on.

Got to be the acid.

Has a residue of LSD stayed behind in his synaptic fluids? He has a hazy recollection of many horror stories about bad trips. People hallucinate for sure, but recently, he's only been freaked while he's asleep, or just after he's woken up. The beer must have jogged the chemicals loose and made him think he's seen a man standing in the field.

Walking quickly now, Rick heads toward the first outcrop of sloping grey roofs that forms the periphery of David Russell Hall. Above him, the jet passes. Its rush and roar crack the sky, but he chooses not to lift his eyes off the dusty gravel before him. Not until a sudden flutter of movement beside him brings him to a standstill. In the field something has flitted across the green stalks of the crop. He sees it from the corner of his eye. Something dark moves, flares up like a bear on its hind legs, and then quickly sinks to the ground.

Wheeling around as fast as he can, Rick loses his balance

and places his weight on his back foot to stay upright. Some-one is there, crouching behind the thin fence, pressed against the wire. In the split second of shock he endures before it moves, he thinks it looks like a heap of sacking, thrown over something long, and all covered in shadow. He feels that where there should be a face, it is bowed. The shape appears to be kneeling. It trembles. Or is it readying itself to leap?

'Who . . . ?' he says, but his voice is lost as the jet flings its screaming power above the field and path. And when the thing stretches out arms, the shriek leaving Rick's mouth is gone too, as if the plane has sucked every competing sound into a vast and rapacious vacuum.

'To leave your dirty dishes for someone else to clean is . . . is . . . It's immoral. It suggests a sense of superiority. You are deliberately coercing someone else to clean up your mess. Someone you consider inferior,' Jason mutters to himself as he walks. His head is down between his shoulders, and his eyes look no further than the pieces of smeared, broken and unwashed evidence revolving through his mind. It's an obses-sion; a neurosis. It has taken over his life. How many hours have been wasted in one year with these constant specula-tions about Rick and the true extent of his inconsideration? It eats into everything: his relationship with Julie, his thesis, his sleep. Everything has suffered. He hates going home.

Jason turns into the Strathkinness High Road and swal-lows. The countdown to confrontation has begun. Between the small trees and occasional car, the wide sprawl of grey barrack-like flats becomes visible: Fife Park.

Jason jumps over the tiny perimeter wall and then takes a shortcut across the grass to the flats. The entire settlement looks deserted. Besides himself, Rick, and half a dozen post-grads locked in over the summer, Fife Park emptied back in May. Even the warden has gone on holiday – which is particularly trying because Rick has yanked the door off the oven and broken the seal on the fridge. Life in the flat resembles camping; he's been eating off camping equipment, and his diet has been restricted to freeze-dried foodstuffs and food in tins – all stashed away in his room so Rick cannot pillage the stocks.

He has to confront him tonight. The walk has sobered him slightly, but if he does not pursue the issue now then the prevailing sense of injustice, and the sheer loathing he has developed for this individual, will haunt him for the rest of his life. This demon must be exorcised.

Jason stops walking when he hears a scream. It seems to shoot like a bullet from a building near the carpark, and then ricochets off every window and grey wall in the little lanes that run between the flats. The scream starts off somewhere near a second soprano and rises higher, as if the vocal cords responsible are being stretched taut. Taking his hands out of his pockets, he tries to determine from where the sound has originated. It's hard to tell; the echo obscures it.

Hesitantly, he walks down a path between two aisles of the small triangular-roofed buildings to where his flat is perched, on the end of a row, before the carpark and rubbish skips.

Did anybody else hear the scream? Is anybody else in Fife Park tonight? He is apprehensive and a little annoyed; the scream has interfered with the concentration of his thoughts and anger – it has taken a lot of beer to prepare for this final showdown.

Jason crosses the square front lawn before his front door, and peers through the grimy kitchen windows next to it. Television is switched off. No one in. He steps over the rusty bicycle, left chained to a bush by a previous tenant, and hops over three stuffed bin bags outside the front door. He tries the door handle. It's unlocked, so Rick may have come home – although he does have a habit of going out and leaving the front door unlocked.

Jason walks into the reception. The lights are out in the hall and on the staircase. The familiar smells of damp old newspaper, and the blocked sink in the kitchen, engulf him. He flicks the light on and notices that the coat pegs, just inside the door, are empty. A scruffy denim jacket with a wool lining is usually a sure sign that the wastrel is in. Rick must still be out then, and he has left the door unlocked.

'Bastard,' Jason says, and wonders whether he should go back outside, while it's still light, and investigate the scream. He supposes he should; it might be a girl in trouble. If it proves to be a false alarm, he can then return to the kitchen and start loading up a bag with dirty dishes, destined for Rick's bed.

But just as he's about to leave the flat, Jason hears something else, a dull thumping sound. He hears it coming through the ceiling. He strains his ears and looks up in the hall. The ceiling is stained with brown rings. But there is no sound now. He purses his lips. The walls are thin; sometimes you can hear the neighbours' every footfall. But the flat next door is vacant; the tenants left months ago, and the sound definitely originated from upstairs in his flat. He remembers locking his bedroom door earlier, and the other two rooms on his floor are empty. Rick's room is downstairs; if Rick is home then he has no right being up on the first floor. Maybe it's an intruder. Standing absolutely still, he waits downstairs, and listens to the ticking sound that comes out of the hall light.

There it is again: a muffled suggestion of something being moved across the floor upstairs. It could be a bed or something. But who would want to steal Fife Park furniture? Jason tries to quell his anxiety. He takes a deep breath and ascends the stairs. Has that bastard Rick broken into his room looking for food or tobacco?

The sounds continue sporadically, issuing through the wall opposite the tiled staircase he climbs. Jason reaches the first-floor landing, stands outside the stinking toilet, and looks across to the heavy wooden fire door. He visualises the plain walls of the corridor and the three bedrooms beyond the door – two empty, the third his own. The muted sounds seem to be emanating from the end room, where Ivan used to live, beside the attic space. Dare he go through the fire door?

Suddenly Jason has a new theory, and he exhales with relief; it must be Rick in the loft, amongst all of those boxes. Maybe he's packing, planning to go home. Feeling calmer, he's suddenly annoyed with himself for being so jumpy. He opens the fire door and enters the upstairs hallway, which is dark.

Jason feels his body stiffen again. Surely Rick would have turned the hall light on in order to pack and then carry out the boxes from the loft? He flicks the light on and waits for it to sputter into life. 'Rick!' he shouts at the attic door.

The thumping sounds stop.

'Rick! What the fuck are you doing in there?' he shouts, trying to incite confidence by raising his voice.

No answer. Just a faint shuffling sound.

'Shit,' Jason mutters, and looks behind him at the fire door. Deciding against flight, he then rushes along the hall and fumbles with his keys, before he finds the right one and unlocks his own door. He sneaks into his room and looks about for the cricket bat. He'll need a weapon.

Jason returns to the hall with his Duncan Fearnley, size six, clutched between rigid fingers. He remembers the light switch in the attic is just inside the door. He'll fling the door open, knock the light on, and confront the thief. He holds the door handle. He pauses for a moment. He yanks it open.

Pitch black in there: just a hint of sloping roof timber and a new smell, mingling with the dust and woody-loft tang. Something smells raw, and above it, hanging in the warm roofy air, Jason can smell something rotten. He slaps a hand around for the light switch, and picks up splinters in his palm from a wooden beam. His fingers scrape against brick-work and then find the small plastic square of the light fitting. He flicks the light switch down.

Among the breeze blocks and insulating foam and before the padded water tank, Jason sees his roommate. Or, at least, the remains of him. The hand closest to Jason's foot is waxy and pale. The fingers are bent in toward the palm. There is a foot too, still inside a wet boot, and the dark bulk of a torso near it, stripped of shirt and wiped red.

The room seems to spin. Then his vision telescopes. The ceiling rushes at him and then falls away; the walls lift upward and then judder back down. In the half-focus of his shock, he sees the head: eyelids closed, mouth shut, the back of the skull moist.

Empty cardboard boxes, stacked neatly in the far corner

of the attic, suddenly tumble forward and bounce over wretched Rick, making some of the separated bits twitch. The beating of Jason's heart pauses. And what comes through the scattered boxes and over his streaky flatmate threatens to shut his mind down, forever.

Instinct only allows him to pause in the attic for a second, but that is long enough for Jason to see something feeding. Its teeth are obscured by what looks like a pale fragment of cloth, flapping like a rag in a dog's mouth, but the eyes, yellow above wet bone, brand themselves into his soul. He falls backward through the attic doorway.

How he makes it down the hall to his room will remain a blur in his memory, but somehow he manages to turn from the makeshift abattoir and crawl back to his haven. He vomits beer and chips through his nose and mouth, and it splashes across his legs. Once inside his room, he collapses against the door and locks it from the inside.

Then the shaking begins – in his legs, under his ribs, and along his jaw. Unable to feel his feet, he stumbles across his room and prepares to drop from the window. It is a miracle he screams but once, and only when something begins to paw at the outside of his bedroom door.

SEVENTEEN

Hart arrives at Fife Park on foot – puffing and sweating after the walk from town. A solitary police car passes him as it leaves the main drive to join the Strathkinness High Road. Through the windscreen he notices the two young officers staring at him. 'Who is that crazy guy with the beard?' Hart whispers, and indulges himself with a chuckle.

He enters the shabby residential development and wanders through the cluster of buildings, looking for numbers on the peeling doors of the flats. He presumes they are arranged sequentially, and looks for 37, where Rick lives. The student did not show for his ten o'clock interview, but had seemed pretty keen to meet with Hart when he phoned the day before. Unwilling to delay any longer in contacting the young man, Hart set out for Fife Park just after ten, a little angry with himself for not insisting on seeing Rick right away. Not only should he have a third interview recorded – more ammunition for his case – but after the vanishing of Mike Bowen and Maria, nothing can now be left to chance. If something has happened to the kid he'll never forgive himself. He makes another quick resolution to lay off the booze and chides himself further, when he remembers the two glasses of whisky he needed to just get started that morning. 'Who am I, Aerosmith?' he says to himself with a scowl.

If he cannot persuade the students who called him to leave St Andrews, the least he can do is keep an eye on them. It is too early to go to the college authorities. He needs more proof on tape: frightened voices, unusual narratives of disordered sleep, similar dream experiences, a connection, a case.

Despite the blue of the late-summer sky, Fife Park has a grim feel to it. Neatly cut grass on every lawn, and the swept concrete slabs of the paths, only serve to make it look like an institution. A boot camp or low-security prison. The linked flats could be empty birdhouses with their pointed roofs and drab grey sidings, or a temporary mock-up of a town designed for nuclear testing. He's seen similar in Nevada.

Spotting the warden's hut, he ambles up a path to the front door. A CLOSED sign has been hung behind the wire-strengthened glass, but he knocks anyway. There is no answer, but he hears the sound of a car door slam on the other side of the warden's hut. He makes his way toward the noise. In the carpark that opens out before him, he sees a young blond man hastily packing an ageing Volkswagen Golf. 'Hey now,' Hart says, smiling.

The man pauses – the muscles in his arms strain around a television set. He stares at Hart for a moment and then looks away, continuing in his attempts to squash the TV set down and amongst the softer bags he has crammed into the boot of the car. *If they ain't laughing at my beard, they're ignoring me.* 'Forget to pay the rent?' Hart says.

'What?' the student asks. His face is red from the battle with the television set; a rivulet of sweat trickles from his temple and through his sideburns, making them dark and shiny wet.

'Nothing. It's just you being in a real hurry an' all.' The young man carries on with his packing. 'I'm looking for number 37.'

Immediately, the young man stops forcing the television into the car, which has begun to rock from side to side from his efforts. He turns to face Hart. 'Do I know you?'

'No. But I need to find number 37, because one of the guys who lives there didn't show up for an interview this morning. That's all. Don't fret. I'm no cop. With hair like this I wouldn't even make undercover.' The man's young face never moves. 'Can you tell me where number 37 is?' Hart insists, speaking slowly.

The student appears to be in a daze. Hart walks away, shaking his head, when the young man finally speaks. 'I live in 37.'

Turning around, Hart's brows rise above his glasses. 'You do? That's great. Don't look so worried. I ain't no bailiff, brother. Your TV set is safe.'

'Who do you want?' the student asks, ignoring another attempt at humour.

'Rick . . .' Hart flicks open the top pocket of his denim jacket to find the surname on his notepad, but the man's reaction to the mention of Rick stops his fumbling. He slams the hatchback door shut and then slumps against his car, with both of his feet stuck out as if to prevent himself from sliding down to the tarmac. He covers his face with his hands and rubs his eyes. 'You all right?' Hart asks.

Nodding, the student pulls his dirty fingers down his face, slowly.

'You Rick?' Hart presses.

'No.'

'Do you know where I can find him?'

'You don't. Nobody does.'

'Mind telling me why?'

'Are you a tutor?' the student asks, now staring at Hart with an intensity that makes him feel uncomfortable.

'No. I'm an anthropologist. Just visiting. And Rick was going to help me with my book.'

Shaking his head, the young man begins to grin, and then laugh as if he has nothing to laugh at but the hopelessness of everything. 'Rick was an anthropological curiosity all right. What's the book about: socially dysfunctional rich kids?'

'Things that go bump in the night, actually,' Hart replies with a smile, trying to relax the kid. But the smile shrinks from his hairy cheeks when the student's face blanches. 'I think you better tell me what's going down at 37,' Hart says.

The man nods a reluctant assent. He motions for Hart to follow him.

'Rick's dead,' the student, who nervously introduced himself as Jason, tells Hart once they are seated in the scrubbed and meticulously clean kitchen.

Hart puts his cup of coffee back on the table. 'Dead?'

Jason nods. 'I saw him last night. What was left of him in the loft space. I called the police early this morning.'

'Why not last night?'

Jason raises his frightened eyes. 'After what I saw upstairs, there was no way on this earth that I was leaving my room until daylight. And I had to be sure it had gone. It was outside my room. After it killed Rick. So then I was going to jump from the window, but I heard it go down the stairs.

Then it would have been outside the flat, so I stayed put, in my room until first light.' The way Jason, in all sincerity, is referring to this other party, shrivels Hart's balls. 'I called the police this morning from the phone by the common room, and they came right away. But it was all gone from the attic where I saw him. There was nothing there. I don't know how. There must have been stains.' Jason swallows. He seems to be on the verge of tears. 'Then they opened Rick's room and found some acid in one of his drawers and accused me of wasting their time. They were really on edge. Nearly bloody arrested me. They asked me loads of questions. I think they put me down as some kind of idiot suffering from hallucinations. Then they just sat in their car, for ages, and watched me pack. They said it was the second prank call they had received in a week.'

Hart leans forward. 'The second?'

'Yeah. Some golfer was found in shock on the beach and claimed to have seen something down there. He'd had a heart attack and a stroke, but the fuzz didn't find a thing. They reckon people are freaking out because of that body part they found washed ashore.'

'Jesus,' Hart whispers. He slumps into his plastic chair.

'And now they reckon that everybody is claiming to have seen a body. But I did. I know I did. I don't take drugs. I know what I saw and it made me puke.'

'You saw Rick?'

Jason nods.

'This was last night?'

Jason nods again. 'I thought they would blame me. We didn't get on. He was a messy bastard. Awful to live with, but I wouldn't have wished that on my worst enemy.'

'What exactly?'

'There was someone in the loft with him.' Jason's voice dies. He covers his eyes with his hands.

'You saw it?'

'Sort of. It was . . . It was . . .'

'Go on.'

'It was eating him.'

Hart stares at Jason's face for a long time before he pushes his stubby fingers behind the lenses of his glasses, to rub his own tired and red eyes. Jason stares at Hart, whose turn it is to be distracted and pale in the face. 'You seem to know a lot about this?'

'That's why I'm here. It's something I've been researching for a long time.'

'You believe me then?'

'Wish I didn't.'

'Who is it?'

'I don't have a clue. Not as to specifics. But I think something has returned to this town. Something old that most people would never believe in.'

'You mean like the devil or something? I mean hang on, that must have been a man I saw up there.'

Hart sighs. 'Did it look like a man?'

'No.'

Hart raises an eyebrow. 'Well then. It's all too much for people to believe in, Jason. They need colour footage these days. I don't even bother explaining anymore. Just keep things to myself, mostly.'

'Amen to that,' Jason replies. 'It's so crazy, though. I thought I was going to be arrested for murder. Especially after what I said last night in the pub about Rick. I didn't have an alibi, I had a motive, I was drunk. But the police only slapped my wrists about making prank calls.' Jason starts to laugh with disbelief.

'Jason,' Hart says, his voice low, his stare fixed on the young man. 'Did you see anything before last night?'

'Like what?'

'A shadow. Near Rick's room.'

'No. Nothing. I spend most nights at my girlfriend's place. I couldn't stand being around Rick. I was ready to . . . Well, you know.'

'He got under your skin.'

Jason nods. 'Messy bastard. Poor sod.'

'Place looks fine to me.'

Jason smiles, sadly. 'I cleaned it this morning for the last time. We all lost our deposits because of Rick. But the least I could do was wash his dishes one last time. A kind of good-bye.'

Hart turns his tired face to look up at the ceiling.

'You want to go up there?' Jason asks.

'I better.'

'You're on your own.'

'That's fine.'

'I'll give you five minutes and then I'm out of here. I've got to lock up and post my keys through the warden's door. And anyway, you won't see anything. I went in with the police. There's nothing there. Not a drop of blood that I could see, and the police didn't look too hard once they'd found the acid. I've begun to wonder myself, now, whether I actually saw anything. Maybe it was like my subconscious or something.'

'Do I need a ladder?'

'No. Just go up the stairs. Then go through the fire door and turn right. It's at the end of the hall.'

Hart leaves Jason to his packing and makes his way up to the attic. After he has opened the loft door, he has to fumble for the light switch. With the light on, he moves into the narrow storage space and crouches down on the dusty floorboards. Peering under the boxes scattered about, he notices several dark patches on the wooden boards and fragments of carpet. Could be oil, and the stains look old. Maybe there is something for forensics, but Hart is relieved the police have not taken samples. They would immediately start looking for a serial killer or something – wasting their time and getting in his way. When the time comes to act, the police will be useless. Hart shudders. Then it will be time to forget a rational approach. If he's learned anything from South America, it will be a time to act quickly and to go somewhere insane. Can he?

Hart lifts his face and squints at the low ceiling. 'Who are you?' he whispers. 'Why are you here?'

EIGHTEEN

South Street is deserted. The disintegrating cathedral at the top of the street surveys all of which it once was master. And at such a quiet hour, the sight of so many blackened chimneystacks above the houses, shops and college halls, with their attic gables ominous atop worn stone fronts, makes Dante's neck tingle with excitement. He checks his watch under a streetlight and realises he is five minutes early.

From a tourist-office map he located St Mary's College, and walked from the flat on the Scores to find it tucked behind the walls of upper South Street. An arch leads to the college buildings and the court they surround. It has been burrowed into a plain stretch of stone wall, obscuring the actual court from the street outside. One of the iron gates in the arch is unlocked. Dante steps into a narrow brick annexe and the courtyard opens out before him. Dim globes light the paths, and subdued nightlights glow within the ancient buildings to create an enticing gloom in the court.

Hesitantly, he makes his way forward, until he stands before the oak tree at the head of the main lawn. Around the wings of the court, like a smaller version of the Quad, a ring of academic halls creates shade and protects the hush of the garden. There are cupolas and decorative turrets, worn plaques and coats of arms above the archways and broad windows, whose panes of glass are divided into little squares. Dante thinks of his guitar. He would like to sit down on a bench in the stillness and dark, to allow the impressions and contours of history to press in on him. He wonders what he could find on a fretboard to capture the atmosphere of the court. Blues scales were not cold enough. He'd have to brush up on classical arrangements.

'Dante.' Beth's voice startles him. It drifts from out of the shadows in a corner untouched by the orange lights that create a tarnished sheen on the black grass. Dante walks toward the belltower, its walls blanketed with ivy, from where the voice has risen. He peers into the murk around the tower but can't see Beth. 'Beth, where are you?'

He hears a giggle and stops walking. Squinting, he peers through the fountain of spiky tree branches that falls away from a skeletal thorn tree, next to the belltower. From behind the blackened tree trunk, Beth unwraps herself, smiling. Swathed in her dark coat, she approaches him, slowly, and seems to glide and pour through the gnarled branches and twigs until she reaches the edge of the lawn. Her feet never make a sound. She laughs again and wrinkles her nose with delight. 'This is my favourite tree. Mary Queen of Scots planted the little shoot in the soil.'

'It's kind of an ugly tree, though.'

'Ugly, Dante? Isn't there beauty in age?'

'I guess, but it's tilting to one side and has that calliper thing at the bottom, to hold it up.' Dante pauses when he sees Beth's expression change to disappointment. 'Sorry, Beth. I shouldn't knock your favourite tree.'

She smiles and lowers her eyes. 'It's one of my only friends here, and you should be nice to her.'

'I promise. And this place is, like, beautiful.'

'Isn't it. So little has changed. Walk with me and I will show you things.'

For balance, she removes her hands, gloved in leather, from the deep pockets of her coat and steps over the guard-rail that protects the tree. Dante holds out an arm and she takes his fingers to steady herself. For a moment, as she raises a leg, her coat parts and reveals a long limb encased in patent leather to the knee. Immediately, Dante's eyes are drawn to a glimpse of slender thigh, shimmering beneath a thin gauze of nylon, before the heavy drapes of her coat sway shut to conceal it from his eyes. Beneath her coat, the rest of her body is clothed in black too: a leather skirt on her slender hips and a black woollen rollneck sweater to hide the pale skin of her throat.

'Thank you,' she says, and stands close to him on the gravel path. Dante's chest tightens when he looks into her eyes, wide and laughing beneath heavy lashes. His face reddens and he becomes glad of the dark. 'I'm so pleased you came,' she says, and slips an arm around his elbow. 'Shall we walk?'

Dante fumbles for his cigarettes with his free hand. 'Love to.'

Gently, Beth tugs him down the gravel path where the loose pebbles crunch and slide beneath their feet. But when he ignites his Zippo she pulls away. He glances at her and watches her face and how it has become wary of the flame. Disapproves of smoking, he guesses. Or maybe he is spoiling the effect of the dark. In any case, he lights his cigarette and quickly douses the Zippo's blue-yellow fire.

'See the little sundial, Dante?'

'Oh yeah.'

'And this is St John's Arch.'

'What's left of it.'

'A ruin has its own magic. Old, forgotten things do.'

'They do. I'd like to try and catch this on my guitar. We usually play blues and Tom's the wizard, but I think we could get something from this.'

'Are girls impressed by musicians?'

Dante's jaw hangs slack. Beth throws her head back and laughs. Then she squeezes his arm and Dante is hit by a cloud of perfume as the scent disperses from the fur collar of her coat. 'We were thinking of a gig somewhere. Is there like an alternative pub in St Andrews?' he asks, trying to recover lost ground. Beth stays silent. As if his babble is of no consequence, she just smiles up at the looming heights of wall and mildewed roof-tile above them.

'Does Eliot know you're here?' Dante asks, hesitantly.

'Down here, Dante.' They leave the courtyard and walk into a narrow wynd where the dark air feels heavy. Chestnut trees form an arch overhead to blot out star and moonlight, while the hedge shields the gully from the court lights. On their right, the wall is smothered with ivy and occasionally indented with an indistinct doorway. It prevents the distant town lights from intruding upon the court.

'Can't see where I'm walking,' he says.

'Let me be your eyes, Dante. I know this well.'

'You spend a lot of time here?'

'When I can. This is my favourite place. One of my family died here.'

'You're joking.'

'No. They took her from Parliament Hall and stoned her in the street.'

'When?'

Beth laughs and cuddles into Dante's shoulder. 'Long time ago. Look here, we go past the fir tree and the path takes us back to the courtyard.'

Despite the delight of having Beth's lean body pressed into his own, he misses the light, so he can look at her again.

'The night frightens you,' she whispers.

'No, I love the night. Spent most of my life in clubs. But all this would be clearer during the day. Why couldn't we have seen this earlier and then had a drink? Made a night of it.'

'Too many people. What about the solitude you can find at night? That's the best. It excites me.' Dante feels his groin immediately stiffen. In the company of this beautiful girl, he feels curiously powerless. Could he refuse her anything?

On their way back to the courtyard, they pass a mediaeval building with a little brass plaque on its door: BIOLOGICAL AND MEDICAL SCIENCES. 'This is the old library,' Beth says, and she pauses by the wooden door, which is studded with iron bolts. 'And next to it is the Lower Hall. It was once the Parliament Hall where the estates met. It's changed since,' she adds in a sad refrain.

'It's all great, Beth. I'm used to wet concrete and council estates. You know, I was amazed that there is no litter or graffiti in St Andrews. But the age of this place, it's kind of eerie. Don't you miss nightlife and stuff?'

Beth never answers. She releases Dante's arm and walks across the central lawn. She sits on the wooden bench before the monument. Sheltered beneath overhanging oak branches and huddled on the bench, her shape becomes undefined but thin, and blends into the black-green ivy that covers the stone and brass behind her.

After sparking up another cigarette for the fragile comfort its glow offers, Dante follows her to the bench.

'Tell me about your friend?' she asks, as he sits down, near but not against her.

'Who, Tom?' he replies, and fights to conceal his disappointment at her inquiry.

'Umm, Tom,' she murmurs, releasing the sound of his name from her lips with a little pout.

'Well, he's my best friend. More of a brother really. We go way back.'

'Does he have pretty hair like you?'

Dante chuckles. 'Yeah, right down to his bum. Hides behind it.'

'You must have so many girlfriends.'

'Hardly. The band was popular once. We were big fish in a small pond. Although, at the time it felt like we were at the centre of the universe. But things change. It was time for a new start,' he adds, sadly.

Beth crosses her legs and her coat slides off her knees. The hem of her leather skirt slips back and Dante's eyes catch the glimmer of something pale. 'I like –' the words stick until he's cleared his throat. 'I really like your style, Beth.'

'My style?'

'The way you dress. It's very chic.'

She smiles and looks down her body, distractedly. 'I wanted you to like me. I was so keen to meet you and very nervous the first time. I get so used to my own company.'

'Do you have any friends here?'

'Some.'

'Do you go out much? I mean, shopping and things in the day?'

'Not really.'

'Why?'

'I'm needed.'

'By Eliot?'

She moves against him. 'Sometimes.'

'Like as a nurse.'

'No.'

'Evasive creature, aren't you?'

'Maybe you would run away if I told you everything.'

'Try me.'

But Beth laughs: at him, he thinks. He removes his eyes from the girl it hurts to look at. It's the only way to keep his head straight. 'So where do you and Eliot live? I only had the address of the school.'

Her face turns toward him. 'Out on the west side.'

'Nice out there?' Dante asks, feeling as if he is fighting with a blindfold, desperate to peek over the top and see her again, to enjoy even a moment when her eyes are upon him. But Beth stays quiet. 'Did Eliot say when he wanted to see me next?' he asks, looking down at his boots.

'No.' The sound of her voice is closer now.

'How shall I approach things with him?'

Her breath cools on the side of his face. 'Have patience, Dante.'

'I'm not knocking your boyfriend, Beth. I just want to know what's going on.'

'Don't call him that.'

'What?'

'My boyfriend,' she replies, and it seems to have been an effort just to say the word in relation to Eliot.

'Isn't he?'

'You've been listening to gossip. Idle tongues should be cut out.'

Elation at her not being romantically connected to Eliot should be rising and warming through Dante, but that comment about cutting tongues out makes him uncomfortable. Her voice went deeper too when she said it, at odds with her beauty. 'Look Beth, I don't want to pry into your private life, but –'

She cuts him off. 'Dante, will you promise me something?'

'Sure.'

'Don't pry. I don't like questions. Once, a long time ago, I was asked painful questions. Too many questions by terrible people.'

Breaking his resolve, Dante finally looks at her face and watches a change spread like a thin and soundless ice beneath her alabaster skin, now appearing dead beneath the false colours of toner. Her gloved hands grip the bench and he hears a knuckle crack. The hard seat becomes harder beneath his buttocks. Police, he thinks. Maybe she's talking about Johnny Law. She's had a crazy youth and was busted for something. That's why she turned to Eliot's book. Wasn't he roughly the same? But the emotion suddenly drains from her, rage vanishing in the time it takes to beat one lash across a panther's eye.

'You are a loner, Dante. Like me,' she says, and her face attains a strange vacancy.

'Is that why Eliot wants me? Wants us to be close?'

'We want you to be with us. You wrote to us and we

understood. The unseen world in *Banquet* touched you. But a book is only words, a shadow. Why not give yourself to something that is real?'

'What? I mean, like a cult?' he answers, feeling uneasy, and silently praying she will laugh at his suggestion and then vigorously deny it.

'To be more than you will ever be alone. To be with someone powerful.' Her voice sounds older now; the bashful girl has gone again, with her prickly kisses and gentle hands. Her thoughts have wandered, unhooked themselves from the present and blown away to a place he doesn't understand. 'This is why you came to him,' she says. Her eyes widen with excitement. 'This is why I gave myself to him. I don't remember much about the time before him, and I don't want to. Everything is different now, Dante. I see and hear things I never did before.'

Dante stares at her, dazed. What has Eliot done to her, with his scarred hands and talk of sacrifice? Drugs maybe. Has the mescaline-eater found an apprentice? 'I will help him, I want to,' he says, cautiously. 'I think I owe him. But how can I help? I'm a musician. You and Eliot keep dropping hints about this great adventure. But what is it? Where do I stand in all this? I mean, are you talking about drugs? I smoke dope, Beth, but the rest is shit. Did you try things with Eliot?'

Tilting her head on one side, she looks at the floor, and although her lips move he can hear no sound. It is as if she is hearing something whispered to her from an earpiece. Her face becomes dreamy, the green eyes distant, the body lifeless under the long coat, like a beautiful marionette left in a corner.

'Beth,' Dante asks. 'What's wrong?'

She turns to face him so quickly he flinches.

He swallows. 'Sorry, too many questions. But I need to know what it is you want from me.'

She moves her face closer, with her chin raised. And before he can ask another question, she closes the gap between their lips. Against his mouth her lips part. He can see the whites around her irises and smell her strange breath cooling on his face. He thinks of wet stones, dying summers and deserted beaches. 'You are special,' she whispers, stretching her arms out to hold his hands. One of her thighs presses against his own. 'I knew you would be special.'

Dante feels like he is floating before her face. Before anything real starts between them, it's like she is already hurting him, and it feels good. 'He will take you, and your friend,' she whispers. Are they about to kiss? Blood rushes in his ears and he fails to suppress a noisy gulp in his throat. 'You are right for him,' she murmurs.

Not thinking, he reaches an arm around her shoulders. Beneath the coat, where he expected softness to be, she feels brittle. Still, he draws her body closer until her perfume drowns him: a drowsy pine forest in her hair, a heavy draught of juniper berries on her throat. She angles her face against his cheek. Her lips brush against his skin until her mouth returns to his and smothers his breath. Cold kisses sprinkle ice particles down his back. Dante surrenders to her mouth.

Suddenly, she clutches his cheeks with her leather fingers and bites his lips. Streak lightning crackles through his head and blinds him. Sharp aftershocks of agony bring tears to his eyes, and there is a muted sound of something ripping inside his mouth as her teeth go to work.

But the pain is good. Good enough to overcome his instinct to pull away. Blood me, he wants to whisper. No longer does he think of her confounding wiles or her ability to leave every question unanswered. She's promising something decadent and painful that he suddenly craves, to take him somewhere where he can make pacts with writhing, binding things that will leave him paralysed and powerless. And yet still he will yearn for them. Toward her pallid, beautiful face he falls again, asking for the shock of her betrayals, shared with moments of her attention that will exhilarate and inspire. Laying his throat and heart open to the sweetest pain, he bites back at her mouth, knowing his desire for her is a trapdoor he wants to drop through – to feel his entire weight jolt at the end of her rope where it will dangle and wait for more.

But just as suddenly as it began, the kiss ends. Beth releases Dante's face and sits back to pant in the dark beside him, her lips smeared with blood or lipstick. He does not care. The smudged image of her face watches him, eagerly. It is as if she is now using extraordinary powers of will to restrain herself. A little whimper for more mewls from his throat and dies on his tongue. She looks insane, slovenly, a hysteric; the mouth gaping, the stare crude, the body slumped, thighs open. Torture pornography against a black surround.

Coppery blood mingles with the taste of the silvery lipstick she's smeared across his teeth. His limbs are heavy, his body drugged. Shaking his head, he fights the faint, only aware of his need for more of her. Slowly, he moves forward to engage the delicious, biting mouth again. Gentle hands spread wide across his chest and stop him. Baffled but pushing against her hands, Dante implores her for more with his eyes. But his head is like lead and lolls to the side, while one of his feet skitters uselessly through the grass as an unnatural warmth relaxes his body. Thoughts become vague until everything around him seems insubstantial, and even her face blurs in the soft focus of his dimming sight. Forcing one eyelid open, he can barely see her thick lips, crimsoned and spread wide across the dark teeth. There is only a suggestion of her face before him now and it peers into the gloom behind the bench. The private ecstasy on her face is no longer directed at him, but at something he cannot see that makes her lips move but produce no words.

'Be still,' she whispers, as both of his eyes close. She moves away from him.

'No,' he mumbles.

'Be patient.'

She leaves the bench, but Dante keeps his fingers entwined with hers. 'Wait,' he mumbles, just managing to squeeze and hold on to her hand, until her movements to free herself pull him groggily to his feet. She wraps her arms about his waist and whispers, 'Keep your eyes closed for him –' her stomach presses into his erection '– promise me. It's for the best.'

'Promise,' he says, and Beth kisses him, once on his broken lips and then once on his forehead.

When his eyes open, he finds himself slumped on the bench, alone. Peering between eyelids sticky with sleep, he cannot see Beth. The court is silent, save for the distant sound of a car engine, idling somewhere beyond the walls. He tries to move, but his limbs have become numb, as if anaesthetised, and his neck is stiff with cramp and cold. All he wants to do is fall back into sleep. He is reminded of the occasions when he hears his alarm clock ring early in the morning and he can only find the energy to turn over in bed and shut it off. It is as if Beth's wonderful poison is warming through his blood. She has filled him with her delinquency and beauty until he is drunk with her. Beth is strong wine, sweetened in obsidian cellars. She is rich brown heroin shot through the groin. An acid moment before stainless steel where the angles of the world are tilted.

Falling in and out of sleep, he then experiences a curious inner vision, in black and white, as if it has been left behind by her presence. From above, he sees himself, pale and naked, curled up on the night sand, amongst dunes spiked with coarse grass, beneath an unnaturally bright moon. On this desolate strip of beach, a figure appears in the distance. At first its shape is indistinct, but it gains ground rapidly. Long thin arms become visible, and they are thrown into the air as it rushes forward. Flapping like a tattered flag around a crooked ivory pole, some kind of winding or swaddling linen hangs from the spindly figure. Like thin notes from a bone flute, Beth's whispers swirl about him and move the black sand on which he lies. As if on her command, he arches his back and exposes his throat to the hungry thing in rags.

Through the delirium he suffers on the wooden bench, the last part of his consciousness warns that he is not alone in the court. All around him a breeze rustles through the trees to become a murmur of voices, as if suddenly the place has filled with nervous courtiers who sense the approach of a ruthless king. The old halls seem to inhale and hold their breath inside bleached stone lungs, as if they too have been warned of the approach of an unwanted guest. A guest the halls and lawns want to be quiet and still for, hoping he will pass by. Something creeps through the shadows and along the stone walls. He can feel it coming.

A part of Dante wants to surrender, to relent and expire, convinced that a full comprehension of the stranger will equal a terror and panic no man would willingly face. To lie still and listen to the melody of the whispers and the rhythm of a slowly approaching tread on the brittle grass, heralded by the bony crackles of parting oak twigs, is easier and his end will be without pain.

And then the court seems to breathe out, trying to expel the foul air that has seeped in. Suddenly, there is laughter in the distance, in the street, the highway of the living. Someone calls for a taxi. Dante is distracted. He suddenly struggles against the desire to drift away and give up. A rush of impressions enters his dimming, dreamy thoughts. Brightening images of familiar faces shine like white lights through fog. He sees Tom's laughing face, which makes the silver earrings shake in his ears. He remembers the warmth of sunlight on his blinking face and how tea tastes with two sugars, and how beer smells after the little gassy pop beneath a levered bottle top. His fingers twitch for Ernie Ball strings on nickel frets. A distorted D-minor chord roars somewhere at the back of his brain, and he hears the crackle of old vinyl under a diamond stylus. Dante snaps from the trance and opens his eyes.

For a brief and fleeting moment, as if he has emerged into a new dream, the world has changed. The buildings around the court have slumped against each other and the roses have withered against the walls. Trees are petrified. Woody smells and earthy scents have been replaced with the malodour of age. A phosphorescent light contaminates the air. Somewhere in the distance, he thinks he hears a bell peal with forlorn clangs. Blinking, he moves stiff arms, so his cold fingers can rub the sickly nightmare from his eyes. He is aware of how heavy and empty his head feels, like an old iron pot swinging on the thin handle of his delicate neck. And as he tries to gather his senses, he becomes aware of a presence behind him.

This impression of company soon manifests into a rustling sound behind the bench. Despite the dark of the court, he also detects the suggestion of a great shadow, rising from leaf mould to stand amongst the tree branches. Without looking, he knows someone now stands upright and close to his back. When he hears the sigh, he runs.

And falls.

A stiffness in his limbs and muscles brings him down against the gravel path, which spits under his weight and cuts his palms. Panic and pain drain his mind of the dirty water of the vision. Sensing the presence of something old, but more than a man, waiting to satisfy a profound appetite and now so close to doing so, he is compelled to grope and clutch his way back to the distant street. This is survival. He wants to live and knows truly, for the first time, his life is under threat.

As he crawls on his belly, his shirt twists against his chest and stones crunch against his face. Sharp pieces of grit spike against his skin and force him to try and find his feet. Rising from the ground to all fours, he glances back at the copse of trees that circles the bench. A peek motivated by terror and made quick by reluctance verifies that something is moving.

It looks like a shadow, swaying like a giant black kite caught in a tree. Swaying when there is no wind. Stay, it seems to plead, when it reaches for him.

Another burst of laughter explodes from outside the gate, followed by the gritty sound of feet scuffling along paving stones. Someone yells 'Taxi' again, and the voice is loud and warm and living. Dante looks toward the entrance. The narrow brick arch and the iron gates are only a few feet away. Headlights swirl across the curved brickwork ahead of him and flash through the iron poles of the gate, lighting a path toward salvation. There is a squeak of brakes and a hydraulic wheeze as a car sinks down on its tyres. He does not want to die in here.

He runs. His boots slap off the paving stones. The urgent beats of a heart speeding up tell him he is running at full throttle. He is nearly free when something drops to the ground behind him, back by the bench. It makes the sound of loose bones shaken in a gourd.

Unable to look behind, he flees, off-balance as his right boot skids and then slips on a cascade of polished stones littered before the tunnel. Stumbling, he slaps a hand against the cold brick of the arch to keep himself upright, knowing that if he goes down he is finished.

Through the gate, he can now see the wide boulevard of South Street. There is an idling saloon car at the kerb, resplendent with glossy white paint, and an orange light on the roof, painted with black letters that read TAXI.

Dipping his head, he leaps through the tunnel, firing himself off his front foot, like he is taking a long jump back at school, unconcerned where he will land. But something, with a long and determined reach, swipes at the back of his head.

219

It catches a tendril of his hair and tugs, bringing tears to his eyes, making his head jerk back. His eyes are suddenly confronted with the smooth curving bricks in the ceiling of the arch. Dante grunts and twists his head. He falls sideways and then rights himself. The lock of hair snaps from his scalp, and his head shoots forward, plunging through the open half of the main gates. He emerges into an explosion of yellow street light; his lungs wheeze, his body moves too fast to control.

Behind him, a force rears up and then smashes against the closed half of the gate. A miasma, spiced with rot, belches from the stone arch of St Mary's Court and hangs like a cloud on the street. Dante slams against the taxi and plants his hands on the car bonnet with a bang. He glances up at the two tipsy pedestrians who stand by the open rear door of the car. They see something in Dante's face that kills their bleary-eyed camaraderie. 'I have to get away,' he says in the strange, matter-of-fact voice of the truly shocked.

They nod and then look at the trembling iron gate of St Mary's Court. Dante moves around the car, steering himself with his hands, tasting tar and blood in his mouth, until he finds the open door. Slumping his body across the rear seat, he whispers, 'Drive.' Uneasy, but unwilling to argue, the driver turns to stare at the long-haired youth with the ashen face who sprawls on the back seat of his car. The driver releases the handbrake.

NINETEEN

And even in sleep, Dante can smell the damp concrete. Sleep has transported him back to the cellar and rehearsal space of the band's house in Birmingham. Silhouettes of the drum kit and Marshall amplifiers, covered with rustling polythene sheets, rise up from the depths of the vision. A single light-bulb illumines the four walls. White paint gone yellow with age peels off the powdery bricks. Water pools on the floor where he lies. The ceiling is lost in darkness.

A gust of wind blows the wooden coal hatch down, built into the wall at the bottom of the brick staircase that runs into the cellar from the ground floor. And with its clatter two figures become distinct. 'He's here for you, Dante,' Beth says in the dream.

'No,' he tries to say, but his voice dies. It is hard to breathe, let alone speak. When he tries to move, there is no strength in his arms and legs, just an infuriating numbness, like an attack of pins and needles spreading over his whole body. All he can sense is the dead weight of his own shape. It is useless and cold.

Eliot stands beside Beth, smiling. 'I needed someone stupid,' he says, and then laughs in his wheezy way. 'An idiot was required.' Beth laughs too. It feels like his heart will break. His face screws up but no tears will flow; even that part of him has stopped working. He just grunts.

'They used to put people in the ground for him,' Beth says.

Dante's voice returns. He whispers, 'Not in the ground. Please God. Not in the ground.'

'Yes, darling,' she says. 'Underneath everything.'

'It's required,' Eliot adds. He nods his head too, looking grave now, the smirk gone.

Beth and Eliot look behind them at the coal hatch. Something comes to life, in the hollow at the bottom of the coal chute, where it is clogged with wet leaves. A small shape flops down from the drain cover above. Inside the chute, the shape stirs and then moves. Catching skeins of greyish light in the place where its face should be, the thing's head is no bigger than that of an infant. Wet where the winter light touches it, the creature mewls like a lamb. Then it drops to the floor of the cellar with a plop, as if it has slipped into a pail of oily water. Unable to see, Dante can hear it, travelling across the uneven concrete floor toward where he lies. Now it is harder to breathe than before, and he is unable to turn his head.

'See,' Beth says. She seizes his jaw and turns his open mouth towards the sound of its coming.

'Put him in with it,' Eliot says. With one foot, he then presses the sole of his shoe against the side of Dante's face. It is gritty where it touches his cheek. 'Put the stupid bastard in.' Useless, his numb body is rolled into a hole that has appeared in the cellar floor. Curled up in the foetal position, he drops several feet down and into the ground, below the surface of the floor and into a concrete basin, which seems to have been moulded for the shape of his body. It holds him fast. Against the sides of his head and along his spine, the hard stone hugs him into a ball. Eliot removes his foot and moves from sight, only to reappear with Beth, both of them struggling under the weight of a thick concrete slab. 'Once you're in, you just get forgotten about. *Oubliette*, you imbecile. It means to forget.'

Hysteria boils inside Dante. A loud rushing sound like seawater, frothing through a tunnel, fills his ears. The air is thin and although he gapes like a fish, he is unable to breathe. Slowly, the slab is lowered and the light dims. Just before everything goes to black, something slips from the cement floor of the cellar, and drops into the tomb with him.

Sitting up violently, Dante wakes and spits the chewed corner of his duvet from his mouth. The cellar has vanished, and his room reassembles around the bed. Mackerel light shines through the wispy curtains, and the outside world is silent except for the far-off whisper of the tide below the cliffs. Pulling his knees up to his chest, he backs into a corner and struggles to suppress a sob. He holds his face, and tells himself it was nothing more than a nightmare. Then he peers into every corner of his room, and searches for any sign of a visitor.

The vapours of sleep clear from his mind and are replaced with shock. Desperate for an answer, he tries again to remember what preceded the nightmare – what exactly occurred in St Mary's Court to induce the terrible dream. It is as if Beth left him suspended in the tendrils of some sudden sleeping sickness, vulnerable as a sacrifice. It is like nothing in his experience, to have been so aroused and then so frightened. And were they alone? When Beth left him on the cold bench, he remembers a sense of a presence behind his back. Something yearning for him, excited. Something he never quite saw, but something he heard as it rose up behind him. And he ran desperately, as if his life depended on escape. But ran from what? He's known danger before: the expectation of a biker's fist that would turn his nose to squelching gristle; the foolhardy step before a hurtling bus; a sliding foot on the edge of a cliff in Cornwall, on holiday as a child. He remembers the dryness of real fear and the way words evaporate before they become sound. And the kind of ether it leaves at the top of the nose, hormoney and rich. But never has his own fear been so ever-present and yet diffuse, and not able to fix on any one individual or place. It just hovers inside him, waiting for something he cannot understand to reappear.

Here he is again, scrunched up on a corner of his bed, afraid for his life without understanding the threat, and all within a week of arriving in Scotland. What was on Beth's lips? Were they coated with some plasma that sedated him and then fooled his eyes with living shadows? Vague and evasive Beth. Beautiful, cold and estranged Beth. She emerges from the same intoxicating breed of woman that disturbs sleep, kills appetite, and clouds every thought. She is everything a muse could be. It is like the first time he saw Imogen in a rock club. Then, there was a flash of eyes, a pale shoulder turning through a cascade of hair, her perfume on a draught of air, a smile triggering a dizziness inside him until his stomach seemed to drop away. Same thing with Beth, only it goes deeper. With Beth there is terror. It is as if Beth walks him between this world and the next.

You are right for us, she said. But what did that mean?

What has she planted in his head? Maybe the whole seduction routine is trickery, a plan to stir him up with her beauty and indifference until he believes anything she and Eliot say. Eliot has changed her; she said as much. *He wants you to be with us.*

He is losing control. With one philandering episode after another, he expected Tom to drain him in St Andrews, but now he's on the slippery slope, threatening their new start and putting the second Sister Morphine album in jeopardy. And all because of a girl.

Too afraid to sleep, he makes himself comfortable by sitting up in bed with the duvet wrapped around his chest and the bedside light switched on. Nothing will make him sleep again. Something is wrong with the town; he can feel it and has felt it since they first blundered across a severed arm on the West Sands. Tonight, he was in real danger. And the dream. It was too real. He was suffocating. He actually felt it. Just like before when the night took him back to the soil pipe.

But who can he confide in? And how can this anxiety be articulated without him appearing mad? He has to see Eliot. Even if he has to go as far as forcing a meeting by barging into his study or home, wherever the hell that is. There is no other way to get an answer. Maybe Eliot is doing something up here he shouldn't be doing, and something has gone wrong and now he is involved.

Dante lights a cigarette and places it between his swollen lips. He winces when the filter touches the flesh Beth's teeth have opened. He pulls his toes under the covers and keeps lookout for the people who buried him alive. And it is then, listening to the gentle sounds of early morning, with the initial shock of the nightmare subsiding, that he becomes aware of something in his body. Tickling the back of his throat with a threat to rub it raw in the coming hours, combined with a dull ache hovering in the wings of his brain, something unclean has begun to flourish in his blood.

TWENTY

'Wake up, shit-heel.' Dante walks into Tom's room at nine, unable to sit alone any longer with either his thoughts or the worsening effects of the virus. Tom rolls over in bed and squints at Dante before looking at his watch on the side cabinet. Yawning, he collapses back into the crumpled pillows. 'What's the deal, getting me out of the sack before twelve?'

'I need to talk to you, and seeing the morning for the first time in ten years won't do you any harm.'

'Fuck the morning.' Tom sinks his tanned shoulders back beneath the duvet.

Watched by Tom's one open eye, Dante places a cup of tea on the bedside cabinet and then sits on the bottom of the bed with his damaged face turned away.

'Something is definitely up,' Tom says. 'A cup of tea and a wakeup call. What's going on? You couldn't wait to see the back of me last night, and you ditched me at that party.'

Dante smiles. 'Did you sleep all right last night?'

'Why?'

'Just answer the question, butt-munch.'

'Yeah, I did. But it's a wonder I managed to sleep at all.'

Dante turns more of his face toward the top of the bed. 'Why do you say that?'

227

Tom sits up in bed and reaches for the nearby packet of smokes. 'Last night, when you were with Eliot, I did a little reading. Skimmed through some of those books he gave you. Most of it was boring. You know me and books, I can't concentrate for long. But a couple of them freaked me out.'

'But no nightmare?'

'Nah, but I should have been up all night. There was this thing in one of the books about a German witch cult, who ate kids and stuff. Horrible. Why do you ask?'

'I couldn't sleep. Bad dreams.'

'What like?'

'You know, old stuff. Claustrophobia stuff I had as a kid.'

Remaining quiet, Tom lights a cigarette. He then asks Dante how the rendezvous with Eliot went. With a stomach immediately swimming at the thought of his planned visit to the School of Divinity, Dante stands up. 'Hard work. Can't get to grips with the guy at all. He might have some problems. So I'm off to see him in a bit, to try and get my head around it all.'

'Hang on,' Tom says, squinting in the dim light. 'What's wrong with your mouth?'

Dante freezes and raises a hand to his scabbed lips. 'I drank too much last night and gobbed it.' Moving to the door quickly, he adds, 'I won't be long. I'll see you in a bit.' As he leaves the room he can feel Tom's eyes studying his back.

Breakfast is skipped too: the virus seems to be growing with the heightening of his temperature, and the anticipation of barging in on Eliot is enough to kill even his mightiest appetite. From the flat, he walks to the cliffs beside the castle.

Gazing across the sea, he fills his lungs with salty air and then lights another cigarette. The events of the previous night have dimmed with the bad dream. Was he just spooked, cast in a panic, imagining someone was behind him? And his recollection of the trip to St Mary's now seems to be nothing but a collection of half-formed images his mind struggles to erase or fully recall. The beginning of the night, when he met Beth, and then the ride home in the taxi, are clearer than anything that transpired in between. He remembers the driver glancing back at him via the rear-view mirror, saying things like, 'If you needed a taxi that badly, why didn't you go down to the rank? You only live around the corner. What good's it doing me?' But he ignored the driver and was just relieved to be moving away from the court. He even astounded the man by leaving the change from a tenner for a tip.

What is happening to his head? Is he seeing things because he's ill?

But the sense that someone chased him through the court prevails, no matter the effects of daylight and reason, and he remains convinced that Beth manipulated the whole scene. An impression of her stretching her beautiful face toward a third party, after kissing him like a savage, remains clear in his recall. He remembers her becoming distracted in a similar way in the Quad, on the night of the Orientation, when she heard running feet on the other side of the west wall. Was someone with her then too?

Banquet for the Damned is full of Eliot's carefully recorded visions and bodily sensations induced by hallucinogens. There are transcripts of his dialogues with spirits in Egypt, Tunisia and Libya. Could Beth have slipped something

229

into his mouth when she kissed him? Did he hallucinate? She could have laced her cold lips with one of Eliot's exotic cocktails. People did it in the sixties.

He'll have to be quick this morning with Eliot and then get back to bed. He is dizzy now and wants to puke. His head swims and the back of his skull aches. Dante drops the cigarette and smashes it under his boot. Nicotine is making him feel worse.

He walks across the gravel drive and up to the School of Divinity. Once inside, with the door closed behind him, Dante hurries past the pigeonholes and secretary's office on his way to the stairwell. Mercifully, the school appears deserted. Janice's keyboard is silent and save his own careful footsteps on the stairs that wind down to the basement, he can hear nothing on all three floors.

Feeling increasingly hot beneath his clothes, he enters the basement corridor. By the time he reaches the door of Eliot's study, a sweat has broken across his forehead and his armpits are clammy. Although he felt rough back in Tom's room, at least he was lucid. But whatever is burning his skin now, and lighting flares inside his skull, seems to have accelerated its effect the minute he entered the School of Divinity. Not nerves this time, but a fever. Something is rim-shotting a snare drum inside his skull with a crowbar too, which breaks into a painful swelling, capable of popping his eyes out. His breathing is ragged and he can feel a slop in his lungs, summoning the rust of blood to his mouth. He thinks of news reports about meningitis in universities. But then maybe it is just flu. It's always the same when he kisses a new girl. It's possible he's caught something contagious and fast-acting off Beth. It will just take his body time to acclimatise to her bacteria. The thought turns his stomach. He knocks on Eliot's door.

There is no reply so he tries again, knocking even harder. He waits. Hammers the wood again. On the other side of the door, he then hears a voice, or at least a groan. After knocking again and listening hard for a response, he tries the door handle. It creaks around one full turn and the door opens. Wiping his brow, Dante walks into the dark humid office.

Something stinks in here. In Eliot's undersea world, the fumes of stale booze and unwashed skin fill the air. Dante nearly gags, coughing instead to clear his throat. In response, there is a slow movement over by the desk. Someone moans and shifts their weight in a chair. Squinting through the gloom, he tries to identify the fuzzy shape in the dark corner. 'Eliot?' he whispers.

Only a little sunlight struggles through the curtains behind the desk, but in it he can see the shape of a man, slumped across books and papers, with one arm stretched out beside the silhouette of a whisky bottle. 'Eliot?' Dante asks again, tottering further into the dank study. He bangs his leg against something before the desk and staggers sideward. Thinking better of swearing, he moves around the chair he's stumbled over, and makes his way to where Eliot sleeps. 'Eliot. It's Dante. We need to talk.'

A messy grey head rises off the desk into a band of sunlight made grubby by the unwashed drapes. Coughing, the figure shifts about on the chair before pushing its legs out. This is not the confident figure that strolled the length of a pier or sent his debunkers running for cover, but a sunken, waxy-faced drunk. After belching, Eliot chews something that has gathered in his mouth. Dante winces at the smell emanating from his dishevelled clothes – the same linen suit he wore to the Orientation. One lapel is now streaked with a stain. 'You all right?' Dante asks.

'Water,' the deep voice gasps, before losing itself in a second ragged fit of coughs. Preferring the stale basement air to the stench in Eliot's room, Dante wanders back down the corridor and finds a bathroom on the left side. From the waste-paper bin, he grasps a plastic cup and fills it with water. Stumbling back to the study, he spills half over his hand. Upon re-entering the room, he watches Eliot attempt to stand. When he succeeds in getting his back straight, Eliot then clutches his forehead and slumps back into his chair. With reluctant fingers he proceeds to pull something from his mouth that looks like a tendril of wet hair.

Wiping his nose, which drips with a milky sweat, Dante places the plastic cup before Eliot. With a shaky hand, Eliot cradles the cup from the desk to his mouth and gulps at the water. When it is gone, he drops the cup on the floor. Turning in his chair, Eliot fights with the curtains and unlatches a window. The curtains sway and Dante is instantly glad of the cool breeze that slips through. Muttering, Eliot pulls the curtain aside to illumine the stranger in his study. With Dante suddenly swathed in white sunlight, Eliot makes no effort to speak or move. Breathing heavily, he just stares at Dante, his weathered face etched with surprise, or is it disappointment?

Swaying from side to side, with the fever now coating his entire upper body with sweat, Dante leans against the desk. 'We need to talk. About Beth.'

'Not now.'

'Yes,' he says. 'I'm worried.'

Eliot stares at him. Yes: it is dismay he can read in Eliot's expression. 'Is there a problem?' he asks, looking nervous, or agitated.

'Maybe.'

'I only asked you to spend time with a beautiful woman. Do you like girls, Dante?' The voice is stronger now, bassy and verging on impatience, as his worn face begins to clear of its initial bewilderment.

'That's not the point. Is she all right? I mean, does she need help?'

Eliot slouches in his chair. After a moment of silence he begins to laugh derisively, and his pointy body shakes beneath the greasy shirt and loose tie. Tottering on the spot and wiping the sweat off his top lip, Dante flushes hot, but not from the fever. 'Sit down and have a drink,' Eliot says, with what appears to be amused despair, which makes Dante feel ridiculous. But of more concern than the impression he is making with Eliot is the illness, and he begins to wonder if he'll even make it back to the flat without fainting in the street. Nausea forms a slick in his belly.

'Sit down before you fall down,' Eliot says, in a voice that seems to be travelling to him from a great distance. Briefly, Dante's vision breaks up into white pinheads of light. A fresh convulsion lurches in his stomach. He claps a hand over his mouth and runs to the bathroom.

Gripping the cold porcelain of the toilet bowl, he vomits. Gasping for air, fearing suffocation, and aware of his disgrace, Dante presses his forehead against the rim of the bowl and spits a bitter residue off his bottom lip. His stomach, now empty, still insists on contracting to release a series of dry belches up through his body.

Moving across to the sink, he dunks his head under a stream of cold water and splashes it down the back of his neck. It runs under his shirt and freezes against his spine. Feeling a little better, but astonished at the sudden attack of nausea, he drinks from the cold tap and yanks a dozen paper towels from the dispenser to mop his face.

When Dante re-enters the study, too delicate to feel shame, the window is wide open and the curtains are drawn, half-way across the rail. The whisky bottle is uncapped on the littered desk and he can smell fresh alcohol fumes. There is another spasm in Dante's stomach but nothing follows through. 'Came down with something last night. And these dreams I get . . . I need to go home.'

Eliot just stares at him, but if Dante isn't mistaken, the man now looks alarmed. Pushing himself away from the chair that he holds to support his weight, Dante turns back toward the door. Every careful step sends a shudder of agony through his head.

'Beth is a strange one,' Eliot says, his voice uncertain. 'Maybe she's hasty. It'll be good . . . for all of us, if you accept her.'

'She was not alone last night,' Dante mumbles over his shoulder, wanting nothing more than to reach the door. 'I could swear she brought something . . . someone with her. She made me feel strange. She made me sick.' When he turns in the doorway, he doubts whether he is making any sense, but some part of him still hopes for a response.

Eliot's face is ashen. With his eyes downcast, the man reaches for a glass of whisky, his scarred hand unsteady.

Another ripple of nausea passes through Dante. His skin goes cold all over. As he crosses the threshold of Eliot's study, he thinks of hospital. The room now seems to darken again as if something has moved in front of the sun. He cannot remember ever feeling so weak and now the desk seems so far away too. As he tries to focus on the distant figure of Eliot behind the desk, the light snaps out in his mind.

How he has come to be slumped against the secretary's door is a mystery, but now someone is speaking into his ear. They are shaking one of his shoulders too and holding the rim of a mug to his lips. He guzzles the water, having lost so much fluid with the sweats, and thinks he'll die without the mugful of liquid in his stomach. Gradually, his vision clears and he stares up at Janice Summers. She is crouched over him, her handsome face stricken with worry, and she holds a hand against his forehead. The palm feels cool. He reaches for the hand. In his delirium, it flatters him and pleases him that she would care. An enemy.

'You're not well. You should go home. You are not to come here. Do you hear me?' She speaks quickly, her lipstick-tinged breath especially sharp in his nose. When he tries to move, every joint screams along his back.

'Can I get you a cab?' she asks.

Dante shakes his head and forces himself to his feet. His head weighs nothing and a river of perspiration turns cold between his shoulder blades. 'I'm going home,' he says, and moves away from Janice.

By the time he reaches the flat, the worst of the nausea has mercifully passed. Fresh air and sunlight revive him enough to get through the front door. Stripping his leather jacket and damp shirt off, he stumbles to his room. 'Tom!' he shouts, and then flops onto his bed. He pulls the duvet around his shivering skin. Tom appears in the doorway, as Dante kicks his boots off beneath the sheets. 'I'm sick.'

'No shit,' Tom says. 'You looked pasty this morning. What is it?' he asks, unwilling to come into the room.

'Virus. I felt bad last night and again this morning. But over there, at the school, it was crazy. I puked. I'm getting these attacks.'

'Settle in,' Tom says, and inches away from the door. 'I'll get you some juice.'

Dante buries himself beneath the coverings. And when Tom returns with a glass of orange juice, Dante is asleep.

TWENTY-ONE

It is like spending your last ten-spot on lottery tickets and hoping for the billion-to-one odds of winning the jackpot. Within minutes of cracking open the first book at the university library, Hart is overwhelmed by the sheer magnitude of occult history before him. The futility of the venture strikes him immediately.

In the deserted divinity and theology section a surprising number of tiered columns, each packed with hardcover tomes, are concerned with the question of witchcraft in the British Isles. Seated near to this ocean of information, he is walled inside a cubicle with his first, cursory selection of books. He sits near a window on the second floor, overlooking the gardens below and the West Sands in the distance. But the view does nothing to ease his mind. He is living amongst the shadows of centuries of occult lore: book after book filled with stories and records and allegations of witchcraft, possession, diabolism, and the inevitable persecution in Scotland.

As he reads, he slurps Scotch from a ceramic hip flask, which he bought from the Rainbow Tribe on the final Grateful Dead tour, and begins to wonder which seat Mike Bowen was frozen into. Looking around every few minutes, Hart makes sure the two students in nearby study booths are still there. It is only mid-morning, and Mike may have been paralysed at night, but an instinct for self-preservation will not allow him to relax.

Students are vanishing, limbs are being washed ashore from the German Sea, and after Jason's story about the visitation in Fife Park Hart has stopped sleeping. Something has been seen in St Andrews; it is corporeal, its manifestation tangible, whole in its horror, complete in its intent. He shifts in his seat; it is like some huge and rising indigestion is making his skin too tight for his body. It passes, and leaves him dizzy and cold and unable to form a thought or do anything but stare at a thin blue pen mark on the laminated surface of the cubicle desk. For a while he holds his head in his hands and it all seems unbelievable, utterly preposterous. He then makes another attempt to read the book open before him. But on the page the words swim, and he is more conscious of the smell emitted from the old bindings than he is of the meaning of the sentences.

Concentration is too difficult to summon. Thoughts of the people he has met, like Mike Bowen, or the youngsters he has talked with recently, like Rick and Maria, pop into his head. They are not dead. How can they be? To be taken by something not of the same world that he is now sitting, breathing, and thinking in? It is absurd. 'No, no, no,' he says to himself, to cut through the pandemonium of impressions, emotions, and confusion that swirls inside of him.

In the next cubicle, a man with a podgy face and a goatee beard hears his muttering. He looks across and smiles at Hart, as if to acknowledge a kinship with another struggling student, who has waited for too long to begin his thesis and now sits, stunned, before the heavy thought of where to begin. Hart smiles back, knowing his face is white with anxiety, and then turns back to the book he no longer even sees. Droplets of sweat fall from the hair in his armpits. He takes his jacket off and wants to hang from the window until he is dry.

No, no, no; the idea of an aberrant spirit operating in this town is preposterous. There has to be another explanation. As he sits on an ordinary chair in a library where computer screen savers click on, and where pages are turned and chairs are occasionally and discordantly scraped about him, he tries to convince himself of it. But a contradictory idea soon strikes him: the ordinariness of life about him, with its distractions and monotony and routine, has allowed others to overlook the first suggestion of the shadow that now creeps through their town.

He closes his eyes and tries to empty his head of the clamour in there. He manages to steer his thoughts off and into the emptiness of inner places where thoughts haven't even begun to form yet. He stays like this until his body relaxes and the sweat dries on his back. Hart opens his eyes. He begins reading again.

But after three hours, the utter randomness of his reading pays dividends in an even greater frustration. His concentration is barely active and he takes in little of what he reads. He knows it's unlikely he'll even secure a gist of what is happening in the town by sitting in the library stabbing at certain chapters of randomly selected books. It takes an hour to read a chapter of one of the larger books, and will involve a day's labour to finish a book in its entirety. Will he happen across something significant by quickly turning half-read pages? Skim reading is rarely of any use and, for some, it has taken a lifetime of study to chronicle the occult, before any synthesis of its occurrences in these haunted isles was achieved. But what else can he do? He is only here because of his desperate desire to improve his understanding of the problem. The trip to the library is an attempt to stay active. And if he is honest, he has nothing else to do. After Rick, no other student has made contact for an interview, and with the first wave of students he interviewed now missing, there is little for him to do with his time other than sit around the flat drinking. And still, he has no idea how many people have come into contact with Eliot in the first place, and whether they have been affected, and if not, why certain members are selected by the night terrors while others have walked free. There is at least one active apparition, but he knows little else. If the Frenchman Laforgue is right, an infestation of one malign influence can spread its influence like a plague, until the aperture from which it has entered is slammed shut. Are people suffering right now who have not seen his flyers? Kerry said Eliot's group was popular with lots of people, but if they fail to call him how will he know of them? It seems unlikely that records were ever kept of a membership, and if such deeds exist, who owns them? It would take official pressure to uncover information like that.

Returning his attention to another of the twelve books on Scottish witchcraft, Hart glances at the docket detailing its loan history inside the front cover. It has not been withdrawn from the library in ten years. He sighs.

After another two hours, he ascertains that many people have been tried as witches in the northeast of Scotland, tortured, and then horribly disposed of, but little else. He suspects their deaths were the result of accusations made through fear or envy, sanctioned by religious intolerance, and that the hapless individuals were all innocent of the charges brought against them. That is the tone of every book; the authors disbelieve in the existence of any supernatural basis to the stories. The last story he reads is concerned with an old and solitary woman accused of witchery, who is stuffed into a barrel by an enraged mob, which is then covered in tar, ignited, and finally rolled into a river so she will both suffocate and burn. Her imagined helplessness, confusion and terror in the moments leading to such an inhuman punishment depress him. He wants to flee this, and all of the books, and all of his questions, with another drink.

Restless, he scrapes his nails on the underside of his chair until his cuticles hurt. What he needs is a definitive guide. And as every clue in the town leads to one man, he has to be found. Even if it carries the risk of arrest, Eliot Coldwell must be hunted down and forced into confessing what he knows. Hart closes the book. All he can do here, he has done.

He stands up. 'Stake-out,' he says to his neighbour with the goatee beard.

TWENTY-TWO

At five in the afternoon, Hart is still watching the School of Divinity from inside the castle grounds. It has begun to rain – the first sign of winter since he arrived in town – so everything is now wet. What little sunlight penetrates the faded grey of sky turns the concrete and stone to the colour of his own despair.

For a two-pound admission, he's been able to stay inside the castle for hours. With his arms folded on a wall, he stares across the moat and the Scores beyond it, and into the first-floor window of the School of Divinity. He can see the top half of a blonde woman's head, bent over a keyboard. It is Janice Summers, who turned him away on his first two visits to the Divinity faculty. And if she catches him in the building again, knowing full well he is not a student and is probably harassing Coldwell, she has every right to phone campus security or the police.

The same feeling of futility that overwhelmed him in the library returns. 'This is twentieth-century Scotland, for Christ's sake,' Hart mutters. Despite his academic background, when it comes to confronting a figure of authority, or a representative of reason, he suffers diffidence. Anything he says to them about his studies into night terrors, by way of explanation, always sounds preposterous. It's why he prefers to work in the developing world, where there isn't an innate inability to fully comprehend a connection between chants, trances and sacrifices and the notion of night terrors. He'd be wasting his time here, telling them his suspicions.

Right before him, from the coastal path to the Russell Hotel, are lines of gleaming cars parked beside the pavement. A Galaxy transporter plane shakes the town as it comes in to land at the Leuchars airbase, and there are television aerials on every roof. Technology has replaced mysticism. And everyone who lives in this town is so tangled in the mesh and mess of their lives, what time or energy do they have to hear him out? He'll be seen as nothing but an entertainer, or a laughable asshole at worst. It makes him feel adolescent. Will he not be just inventing another anxiety to add to their pile? This is the modern world; people don't just sleepwalk and disappear. Things cannot materialise in rooms and make off with the occupants. And if he, in this time of night terrors and missing youths, becomes discouraged and cannot believe in his own work, then no one else will.

He forces himself to remember the distress on Kerry's face and the thin pitch of her voice: a young mind made witless by terror. Jason in Fife Park was the same. Something has happened here that is defying logic and traditional wisdom. And it must have started somewhere, with someone.

Hart sighs, restless. Above all, he is tired of being silent. He is worn out by the thoughts that come with being alone.

He moves to the drawbridge, wondering when the administrator will leave for home, and when she does if she will lock the front door to the building. It is still the summer vacation, but that afternoon he's seen dozens of students enter and then leave the building by the front staircase, which connects the first floor to a gravel carpark out front. The town is slowly filling up. And it isn't just the greater presence of feet on the pavement that warns him of this; the very air seems to zing with the presence of new visitors.

But after another hour, as the light fades and the evening chill deepens, the only person he can see in, or near, the school is Janice Summers: the guardian, deep in concentration, with the characteristic frown marking her distant profile. Time to move. 'Don't be a pussy, man,' Hart whispers to himself, determined to do something before the cycle of solitude and too much thought beats him up again.

Hart leaves the castle. Stiff in every joint and now numb from the cold wind that blasts over the stone ramparts and hits his back, he pauses near the gutter of the Scores opposite the school, and rehearses a plan. He'll sneak past the secretary and find Coldwell's study first. Then, at the very least, he can slip a written demand for an audience under the door. In the unlikely event that Eliot is in residence, he'll push his way in and demand answers. Contrary to his nature, he'll have to be assertive.

But what is making it hard for him to place one foot in front of the other in order to cross the road? Why has something like indigestion suddenly lodged behind his sternum at the thought of confronting Coldwell? Is it fear of the police? For when they eventually tie all the threads and reports of missing persons together, they will look for a suspect, and the more he probes and connects himself to the vanished, and the more people see of his hardly inconspicuous beard around town, it won't be long before an angry Scottish cop rubber-hoses him in a cell downtown. But police questioning, if he's honest with himself, is nothing but a secondary concern. Something else keeps him dithering behind the walls of the castle: fear of the unknown.

If night terrors spread in a contagion, and if the sleep-walkers and the vanished all knew Coldwell – the source, like the Nagual in Guatemala – it is possible he is putting himself at risk by making contact with the lecturer. Unwittingly or otherwise, Eliot might be responsible for the spread of terror. Hart has little idea how the occult practices in the West work – whether a hex, a rune, a spell, a rite, or a drug makes a victim susceptible to possession or a haunting: it varies from culture to culture. The Nagual allegedly cast spells, but not every anthropologist agrees. Some speculate it is an animal or dead spirit infesting a witch's body and generating a transformation into the night terror. Others speculate it is connected to the animism he studied in Africa, where the witch doctor's transformation into an evil spirit, or Win, occurs after a long period of preparation – sleeping in cemeteries, worshipping a devil, and making calculations with the zodiac. Laforgue thought it was a form of vodun, or voodoo: an ancient and closely guarded ritualism passed from holy man to holy man until one turns rogue and goes for the virtuous like a tiger in a herd of baby goats.

Newfoundland has a closer connection to the Old World's necromantic past; where forsaken rites and blasphemy are performed in order for an individual to be endowed with powers to leave their body at night to prey upon neighbours or rivals. But a college lecturer and a black mass? He finds it hard to accept. And to whom can he turn if he is able to discover such a thing: the Vatican? The Jesuits blame demonic possession on anything from Ouija boards and tarot cards to rock'n'roll music, which he also feels is hardly

Coldwell's style, as none of his interviews reveal anything untoward about Eliot's paranormal group. There are thousands of similar paranormal meetings, held all over the world, run by the curious, or mystics, or cranks, or just plain housewives, and he's never read an account of night terrors occurring as a result. But isn't it also a total ignorance of what exactly the town is facing that leads to the swift ends of its victims?

'Let it go, buddy,' he whispers, and crosses the road to the School of Divinity.

Sticking close to the school wall, he realises that if he keeps his head down, it might just be possible to walk up the front staircase without being seen by Janice Summers from the office window.

Hart creeps up the stairs, his body bent over. He holds his breath until he reaches the top step, and then peers through the windows set high on the front door. The main reception is empty.

Entering quietly, and leaving the front door ajar, Hart shuffles over the welcome mat and then looks about for clues. Straight ahead, beside the stairs, he sees a wooden board mounted on the wall, similar to the one in Dean's Court, announcing the residential status of staff. There are more than twenty studies spread over three floors in the school, but Hart's flitting eyes quickly lock onto the name 'E Coldwell'. Beside it, stencilled in neat black lettering, is the word BASEMENT. The wooden slide is slipped into the OUT position. He'll leave a note then, with his phone number, just to let Coldwell know he is being watched, and then he'll take off the way he's come in.

Beside the secretary's door, he spots the BASEMENT STAIR-

CASE sign on another plain white door. Crossing the reception with his teeth gritted, Hart tucks his long hair behind both ears and listens for any sign of the administrator. Slowly, he turns the handle of the door to the basement. It makes a dry metallic squeak before rotating one complete turn. He eases it open and slips through. Walking at the side of the stairs to avoid the creaking middle, he makes his descent around two bends to the basement. The scent of radiators reheating dust fills the corridor.

Walking down the passageway, Hart checks all the doors on either side of him. They are all unlabelled. At the very end, the last study by the fire escape, he finds a door marked 'E Coldwell'. He knocks to make sure the lecturer is out. But, to his surprise, from the other side of the door, a man clears his throat. A muffled but elderly voice then says, 'Who is it?' The tone is expectant.

Hart stands back at the sound of someone approaching the door from the other side. 'Mr Coldwell,' Hart says, fighting to keep his voice straight. 'My name's Miller, Hart Miller. I was wondering if –' He stops talking at the sound of the door being unlocked from the inside. The smell emitting through the narrow gap, which reveals one glinting eye set against the gloom, is one Hart is long accustomed to: the odour of stale booze greets him every time he opens his own front door or climbs into a tent on a field study.

'I no longer see people,' the voice says. It is slow and tired, as if the mind behind it is preoccupied with physical pain. But there is relief in the voice too, as if Eliot is glad the intrusion is not the one he's been expecting.

'It won't take a minute,' Hart says to the darkened crack in the door.

'I no longer teach here.'

'I'm not a student,' Hart replies. 'I only want a few minutes of your time. It's very important I see you now.'

'Sorry.' Eliot begins closing the door.

Hart panics. 'I'm here about the missing students.' His voice sounds thin and absurd in his own ears. There is a pause in the closing of the door. It opens a fraction wider. Half of a worn face, with an eye as wet and red as that of a beagle hound, peers out. 'Who are you?'

'Not a cop. But it won't be long before one is standing right here.'

'Who are you?' Eliot repeats, agitation entering his tone.

'Let's just say I'm a visitor from overseas who heard a few things. Things that tie in with my chosen niche of study. I've been rooting around this town and I don't like what I found. And your name's all over it.'

Eliot regards him for a moment and then says, 'It no longer matters.'

'What?'

The scarred face weaves about, and the rheumy blue eyes blink slowly as if even that is an effort that requires concentration. Eliot then begins to look to either side of where Hart is standing, as if he is looking for collaborators, an ambush. 'Goodbye,' Eliot says, after ascertaining that Hart is alone.

'Wait. Is it a coincidence that students who signed up for your paranormal society have vanished?'

The half-seen presence of the man beyond the door suddenly takes a firmer shape. Eliot straightens up, holds the door tighter. The voice is faint. 'Let me have the last of it in peace.'

'Last of what? Or are you gonna make me take a little

sleepwalk down to the surf? Turn my legs into driftwood.' Hart frightens himself at the thought of what he's just said. But it affects Eliot too. The expression on the shadowy face confronting him could wither a cornfield. The drunkenness vanishes from Eliot's voice: 'If you're as clever as you think you are, then stay away from me and keep your inquiries to yourself.'

'Because it's not safe,' Hart says, his voice softer. 'But what is it? Did you bring it here? You gotta tell me, sir. I know my field. Been to Guatemala, the Amazon Basin and Nigeria. And I'm finding the same fingerprints in St Andrews. You started something and I wanna know what. Maybe I can help.'

A long, wheezy, and cynical laugh is hardly the reaction Hart expects to spill through the door following his offer of help. It has taken both balls and no brain to even offer assistance, and now the guy is laughing at him. Anger replaces fear: 'Jesus, buddy. Don't you care about the people who have just disappeared? I ought to slap that grin off your face.'

Eliot counters his outburst with a whisper that makes Hart wish he'd never ventured into the basement. 'If you are touched, you'll wish you'd listened.' But in saying this Eliot has been forced to remember something dreadful – Hart can see that. His head drops and he shuffles his feet just to stay upright.

'You giving me a chance? Did the others get one?'

But the door closes and Hart is alone in the corridor again. He takes a step forward and hammers a fist against the door. 'I'll follow you until I know,' he shouts at the wood. There is no answer, but he hears the weight of a man slump against the other side of the door. 'I won't go. Some of your students are still in danger, if it's not too late. I won't go. Do you hear me?' There is no response. Suddenly conscious that others, upstairs in the building, may have heard the exchange, he sits on a chair near the study to calm down and to begin his third vigil of the day.

Forty minutes later, still sitting in the basement, he hears a phone ring inside Eliot's study. It rings for a long time before Eliot takes the call. Hart presses himself against the study door, his ears keen. But Eliot says nothing and Hart hears the receiver replaced. He keeps his ear to the door. There may be a footfall, but nothing more, until he hears the sound of someone sniffing. It is followed by one or two muffled words that Eliot repeats to himself, that he cannot make out, and then he hears the sound of someone – Eliot – crying. In the emptiness beyond the door, in the silence and darkness, Eliot Coldwell is weeping. But he doesn't sound like a man. He sounds like a child.

Hart steps back from the door. While he wonders whether he should knock, the door handle turns. He takes another step back. The door of the study opens and Eliot comes through backward and then starts when he sees Hart still standing in the poorly lit corridor. Gathering himself Eliot then walks past as if they have never met.

'Sir, we have to speak. Please. Do you know what's happening here? Do you intend for it to continue?' Hart follows in the slipstream of stale sweat that trails behind Eliot.

The lecturer stops and turns around, his movements slow. He looks lost and confused, his body especially thin, as if malnourished. The palms of his hands are bright red and his fingers have the appearance of being useless, and permanently cupped into his palms. 'Who are you?' he says.

'Hart Miller. An anthropologist. I study sleep disorders. If you can't speak now, come and see me, please. I'll beg if it makes a difference. On Market Street, opposite Grey Friars. Please. I'm going out of my mind with this.'

Eliot regards him for a moment, and his lips move as if repeating what Hart has just said. 'You can't know,' he then says, softly, his punished face pale in the shadows of the basement, the lines by his mouth creasing the flesh deep. 'It's not safe to know. And if you believe what you claim to, you are in danger.' Eliot turns and continues to walk to the basement staircase. Hart follows. When he places a firm hand on Eliot's shoulder, the old man flinches. Below the sound of their scraping feet and the swish of Eliot's overcoat, Hart thinks he hears the old man whimper.

'Sorry,' he says, automatically.

Eliot leans against the wall, hunched over, his eyes screwed up. When they open they are full of fear. His face twitches and he shivers, or does it just seem so in the failing light? His mind wanders, and he says something Hart does not hear. This is no great necromancer; the man is finished. He is drunk and unwashed and his memory is shot full of holes. 'Sir, you need help.'

Eliot looks at him, his eyes wide like an innocent afraid of the dark. 'They're here. After a while you can feel them.'

Hart feels his body go cold; a cloud passes over the sun in the world outside the School of Divinity. At the end of the corridor, the light that penetrates the dusty glass of the fire escape dims, snuffs out.

'Listen to me,' Eliot says, sounding as if he is trying to

catch his breath, his body no more than a thin silhouette in the new darkness. 'If you follow me outside, you're finished.'

Hart swallows and takes a step back. 'How?'

'Because it's too late to undo what has started. Get out while you can.'

'I can't.'

Eliot pushes himself away from the wall. 'Then be damned,' he says, and begins to mount the stairs, every step taken in reluctance. Hart can see that. He gives it one more try. 'OK. I'll leave. You'll never see me again, I promise. I don't want to be hunted down like they were.' Eliot reacts when he says 'hunted'; one of his liver-spotted hands nudges at the wall for support. 'But,' Hart continues, 'I have to know what it is. What came through.'

Eliot breathes out, exasperated. 'Rhodes Hodgson,' he says, unable to even meet Hart's eye. 'See Rhodes Hodgson in the archive. Ask him about the work. If you believe what he tells you, you have a name for it. Nothing else can be done.' And then Eliot is gone, around the last bend in the staircase and into the reception.

TWENTY-THREE

Back inside his flat, Hart closes the front door, and then leans against it to make sure the lock has clicked shut. Quickly, he walks into the kitchen and scribbles the name, Rhodes Hodgson, onto a piece of notepaper. He sticks the note on the tack to which the wall calendar is suspended. He sits down, to take in what Eliot just suggested, confirmed even, to put it together. But before he knows it has happened, he is back on his feet, pacing. He pours a drink and looks at his street map without properly seeing it.

After the confrontation, he's never felt so isolated in St Andrews. He has no companion with whom to share his suspicion and fear. To do something, anything, to hear another person speak, he turns the portable kitchen radio on and then walks to the window in the lounge. Before the glass, he rubs the palms of his cold hands against his temples, trying to slow things down inside his mind.

Outside the sky has darkened. More rain soon. A sheet of cloud tints from grey above the town to black on the horizon, promising a storm. People below in Market Street are looking at the sky, their faces full of blame. A car horn sounds but he cannot hear a single bird. Soon it will be night.

On the radio, tuned to a local station, two journalists talk with a government minister and a local councillor. A member of the Wicca religion joins the discussion. Hart is too distracted to listen. He continues to pace the living room while they argue.

Has he just met a man at the end of his reason? Eliot was drunk; that was certain. But what did he mean when he said he no longer saw students? Has he been fired? He jumped at the touch of a hand and then talked in riddles about 'they'. That you could feel *them* coming. That *they* were near. Are he and Eliot now alone with this knowledge? Or has the man merely lost his mind, while he's been strung along by the suggestion that something truly extraordinary has occurred in St Andrews?

On the radio, the journalists harangue the minister about support for local agriculture; it has been the worst harvest in Fife and Perthshire since records began. The beef industry is on its last legs. What can be done? the councillor asks. Rural community is at risk. In response, the minister recites the amount of money already spent in assistance. Then the Wicca priest talks about an imbalance in the cycles of seasons. No one seems to take much notice of him. The debate is interrupted by the local news. A freight ship founders off the coast. Two crew members are lost, swept away; the coastguard rescued the survivors. No one expected the storm. The news and the weather add a synthesis to his day, to these times: everything is bleak and he wants to escape it. Is it all becoming too much for one man alone?

Hart tries to make a sandwich with a few odds and ends he bought from the Metro supermarket the day before. The sight of the hardening slices of bread and the slabs of cheese on the breadboard make him pine for a hot meal. Besides soup, he's lived off cold cuts and whisky since his first day in town. Gouges of hard butter refuse to be spread across the bread, which rips in his hands. Holding it together with his fingers, he bites into the messy sandwich and then puts the bread back down. He chews at the mouthful, but the thought of swallowing makes him feel sick. He empties the chewed bolus of bread from his open mouth into the kitchen bin.

An increasing discomfort in his stomach, flashing hot throughout the day, is now compounded by a noisy churning. His stomach must be empty, but he is too nervous to fill it. He pours himself a glass of milk, in case these discomforts are the start of an ulcer. Drinking the milk, Hart kneels down to check the answering machine. The digital screen signifies that two messages have been recorded in his absence. Snatching a pad and pen off the coffee table, Hart feels his stomach tighten with anticipation.

The first message clicks on but the tape remains silent. Someone phoned, waited for the end of his pre-recorded message, and then hung up after a pause. The second message follows the same pattern. Hart rewinds the tape, annoyed, and listens again. It may only be interference, but it sounds as if there might have been a suggestion of someone breathing among the crackles on the phone line. Both messages were left in the last hour. He presumes it is the same person, reluctant to leave their name and number. A scared student? Maybe he'll never know.

After turning the kitchen lights off, he douses the lounge lights too, save for his little desk lamp, and moves across to the window, facing the street, to draw the curtains. Dusk casts a spell of gloom across the steeples and towers. Out at sea, the oncoming night sweeps the darker clouds to shore. Heavy drops of rain begin to hit the windowpane. He wants to shut it all out.

Just as he draws the curtains to the centre of the rail, something catches his eye. Standing still, amongst the last few pedestrians who scurry to car doors or the awnings of stores for shelter, is the figure of a young woman. Oblivious to the scurrying human traffic, or the now lashing rain, she stands against a wall on the other side of the road, with her face turned upward. She is looking right at him.

The face is pale where it can be seen through the folds of a dark scarf and straight black hair, and her slender silhouette seems to stretch, with the early-evening shadows, away from the dull amber glow of a street lamp and into the shadows of a nearby wynd. Screwing up his eyes, he tries to see more of her face. It is alabaster, bleached into the grey, unlit stones behind her. There seems to be a strong definition to the face and a hint of eyes impossibly large. But beside these vague suggestions of beauty, discernible from thirty feet, the solitary girl makes Hart uneasy. Her stare is unbroken; it seems to face him like a threat. Moving back from the thin slit in the curtains, he swallows, and wonders what he should do. He considers waving to her, but the thought of attracting her attention unnerves him further.

Hart pulls the curtains further across the small brass rails and retreats fully into the lounge. He begins an immediate rubbing of his mouth and then wonders, despite his reticence for contact, whether the girl is a student looking for a nightmare interview. He thinks of the phone messages. She is certainly young enough to be a student, but then he never printed his address on the flyers. Unless one of the other interviewees passed on the information, there would be no way of her knowing where he lived.

He douses the desk lamp, so she won't see him peeking out. Licking at his beard, he moves back to the window. Opening the drapes a fraction, he peers down into the street. The girl has gone. He leans further against the window and looks up Market Street to the monument and cobbled market square, and then down to the Student Union building. There is no sign of her.

Hart closes the curtains. There is no telling who she is or why she was eyeing the flat. Maybe she was waiting for a return call from the phone box nearby. And just as he is considering the possibilities, the trill of the phone gives him a start. Hart puts a hand against his chest.

Picking up the phone, he clears his throat. 'Hey now.' There is no response. Standing still, taking shallow breaths through his nose, he listens, then says, 'Who is this? I know you called earlier. Don't be afraid.'

They hang up. He listens to the tone, transfixed, until a recorded message tells him to replace his receiver. He obeys the electronic voice and moves about the flat, turning every light back on. On the radio, the announcer begins an emergency shipping forecast.

TWENTY-FOUR

'I thought you were going to snuff it,' Tom says, standing over the bed while Dante sucks at a carton of orange juice. He pauses only to breathe the cool and salty air blowing through the open window in his room, before returning to his desperate thirst.

'Look at the state of you,' Tom says. 'You should see your hair. Man, it's like plastered to your head and so knotted.' He lets Tom carry on, sensing the relief in his friend's voice. When he sits up in bed, the slight movement tires him instantly. Beneath his body, the crumpled sheets twist beneath his body, and the creases dig into his skin like twigs beneath the groundsheet of a tent. 'Do you want to know the worst thing? You pissed yourself,' Tom adds.

Dante feels well enough to blush.

Tom winks. 'I won't tell anyone.'

Through the open window, a weak grey light and the noise of hungry gulls flood into the room. Welcome sensations. They revive him sufficiently to make him aware of the chasm in his stomach. 'I didn't have any breakfast, I'm fucking starving.'

Tom laughs, and shakes his head with disbelief. 'Which breakfast was that? You've been out of it for ages. All yesterday, and last night too. I had to call a doctor. You've been delirious for twenty-four hours, mate. And you're lucky it's a small town. He was here in half an hour and gave you an injection. In the arse. I had to hold you down. He took a blood sample too, and I told him to send it to the tropical medicine lab. I thought you had malaria. Never seen anyone sweat so much.'

'What did the doctor say?' Dante asks, stunned by the news of how long he has been incapacitated.

'Pretty clueless. Your temperature was way up, but there's some kind of Hong Kong chicken flu going around. Could be that, he reckoned.'

'Jesus,' Dante mutters, feeling more vulnerable than ever before. With no family to run to, he feels helpless. Being ill makes you feel it more than anything. And what if Tom hadn't been there? Dante shrugs the thought away.

His memories of the virus are hazy. There are dreams he can't recall, and then periods of wakefulness in which he remembers being terrified of something, but the more he thinks about it, he's not sure he was even awake. But the sense of not being alone, while he suffered in his room, has survived. 'It was awful.'

'You're telling me.'

'It wasn't like a virus. Only at the start. Were you in here the whole time?'

'No way. I got better things to do than watch you sweating cobs and crying like a baby.'

Dante rubs his face. The skin is covered in a gritty layer of salt. 'Run me a bath, buddy.' Tom leaves and begins knocking things over in the bathroom. 'Tom! There was someone in here with me, I swear. Was the window open?' he shouts above the sound of the taps.

'What you bitching at now?' Tom asks, as he wanders back through to Dante's room. He stands in the doorway and shakes drops of water from his fingers.

'I said, was the window open when I was sleeping?'

Tom looks at the window. 'Yeah. I opened it last night. It stank in here. But it was only open a touch, and I put the latch on too.'

'Did you hear anything strange while I was under? Maybe the sound of someone else in here with me?'

Tom laughs.

'No, I'm serious.'

'Man, this is St Andrews. What are you trying to say, that someone broke in?'

Dante exhales; trying to explain is ludicrous. 'No. Not exactly. It's just that I was certain that someone was in here, standing by the bed.'

'Man, you couldn't testify to anything. You were hallucinating. You kept sitting up in bed and swiping at things and pointing. That's why I called the quack.'

Whatever raged through his body was powerful, capable of making him see things. Something he's started to do recently. One of his uncles had schizophrenia. He swallows. His suspicion, however, at the idea that it was something else, with no medical explanation, refuses to subside.

After a hot bath Dante wraps himself in towels and moves back to a clean bed, changed by Tom while he soaked. Propping himself up with pillows, he sits, trying to dissect his impressions of the viral attack, when Tom comes into the room, holding a letter between two fingertips, his eyes narrow with suspicion. 'I almost forgot to tell you. This arrived last night. Hand delivered. Someone just dropped it on the mat. Nice linen envelope and it reeks of perfume. Are you holding out on me, mate?'

As he snatches for the letter, Tom pulls it out of reach. 'I nearly opened it when you were under. It's a miracle I didn't. Any ideas who it's from?'

Dante loses his temper. 'Just hand it over!'

Tom's face stiffens. He drops the letter on Dante's lap and stalks from the room in silence. Closing his eyes, Dante whispers a prayer: 'God, let me be well again.' He sighs and stares at the envelope before him. His stomach flops over when he smells the perfume. Beth's scent for sure. How could he mistake that? Suggesting a mystery that is addictive, seductive, physically manifesting by way of a slight intestinal tug and a pang in the chest. It is a smell that haunts him, though he still rejoices that she has made contact. But as he holds the unopened envelope he also feels the same unease he experiences around certain rock-scene acquaintances: the unpredictable ones who turn psycho after a few drinks, with anyone fair game for their compulsive violence. Beth is like that. She twists things; she is unpredictable. Another reason he doesn't want Tom near her.

To assuage his guilt at having snapped at his friend, Dante thinks of Imogen. And then Sophie – Punky's girlfriend and heartbreak-onhold – whom Tom slept with, breaking the band apart as a result. On the issue of women, above all others, he has to be firm with his friend. Especially here. He begins to feel sick as he wonders if Tom would ever cross him over a woman.

Raising the envelope to his nose, he inhales more of Beth's essence. He shudders involuntarily, and remembers flashes of things, confused and dismembered fragments of the last time they met; he sees her beautiful deep-water eyes and how they developed a hungry, detached gaze. He sees her full and bloodied lips, her hands in tight leather, her long thighs, and recalls her rambling, infuriating talk. Tearing the gummed flap open, he withdraws the letter.

> *Dante*
>
> *You are wrong to distrust me. Perhaps we should start again. Come to the West Sands tomorrow night, with your friend if you like. I like to walk there at night, at the far end by the river estuary. There is something Eliot and I need to show you. Everything will make sense if you come. Please do not let us down.*
>
> *Beth*

Exasperated, Dante slumps back into the pillows, the paper loose in one hand. The note was delivered the day before, so she wants to see him tonight. And Beth must be angry on account of his visit to Eliot, who was drunk again, from what he can recall as the fever struck. What do they want from him? Feeling drained and too weak to play this game of theirs any longer, which has done nothing but make him jump at shadows, have bad dreams and fall ill, he decides that if anyone has a right to be angry, it is him. Maybe he should go and confess his fear and his failure to understand what it is they are doing to him. Although he loathes himself for considering it, there is always a chance Beth is nothing more than a girl wrapped up in Eliot's games.

Someone he can save. He closes his eyes and thinks of her lethal mouth. It gives him pleasure.

What is he thinking? Dante clasps his face with both hands and does his best not to cry out with frustration. She is poison. How can he still kid himself? She bewitched him with her beauty and her seductive mouth and with all of her hints about great secrets about to be shared, as if he'd been selected for some astounding revelation, and is now annoyed because he won't play the role of her doting, trusting mallard. She and Eliot are conducting an experiment. He has to give himself some credit; suffering from low self-esteem doesn't make him stupid.

It is over. He admits it to himself, hopelessly smitten as he is. Everything is over: the trip, the research, the acoustic album. He and Tom are leaving the moment he feels up to it. 'Fuck it,' he says. 'Fuck them.' He'll tell them tonight, even though it will be tantamount to madness to venture from his sickbed. What if he has another attack? No, he'll take the risk, get it out the way tonight, before he gives himself too much time to talk himself out of it. The worst of the fever is over. And the bowing and scraping before Eliot and Beth is over too. This will be an opportunity to tell them exactly what he thinks of their bullshit. They will be together and he won't even need to get out of the War Wagon. He can keep the engine running. He smiles at the irony: here he is, twenty-six years old and frightened of a girl.

'Tom,' he cries out. 'Get in here, buddy.'

TWENTY-FIVE

Turning at the top of Market Street and cutting through to North Street, Hart catches glimpses of the sea in the distance, with its grey pallor and choppy surface. A wind from the southeast, thick with rain, plasters his hair and beard to his face. He thinks of ships sinking out there in the cold and indifferent waters. Winter has set in, quickly and unpredictably. Things are going to be harsh up here. He can sense the energy and violence in the sky, making him think of snow and gales. The ruins and the old buildings around him take on a haggard, desolate character he never noticed when the sky was blue.

After every few steps, he stops and glances over his shoulder, not sure whether it is his imagination or his sixth sense that assures him he is being watched. After the strange phone calls, he only slept a couple of hours before morning, and only then because the sky had lightened outside his curtains and made him feel safe.

Instead of entering the library from the North Street access, at the front of the building, Hart ducks into the mediaeval alley – Butts Wynd – to enter from the side. By the English Language Learning Centre he finds a connecting arch leading to the library. In the poor murky light, the glass of the building matches the colour of its aluminium struts. Parts of it gleam in the wet: a fragile modern experiment amongst ancient foundations.

Someone turns the corner and comes quickly into the arch. Hart's vision jumps as he flinches. They pass him with rain trailing off the hem of a black raincoat. It is a young man, a student carrying books from the library. He gives Hart a confused look as he passes. Breathing out, Hart tries to offer a conciliatory smile to the stranger. But, by the time he's gathered his wits, the young man is gone. He hears himself say, 'You jumped me,' but there is no one to hear him.

Pulling the note from his pocket, he glances at his own crabbed handwriting to remind himself of the librarian's name: Rhodes Hodgson. Curiosity overcoming fear, he runs across the courtyard to the library. Pushing through two sets of doors, he then sweeps the security bar to one side and approaches the long counter on the ground floor, empty except for the two librarians who stand behind their angled computer terminals. The smell of laminated covers and polished linoleum makes him feel instantly safer. 'Hey now. Can you tell me if Mr Hodgson is around?'

The woman says, 'Rare Books, just down the stairs,' without looking up from her work.

In the basement, he opens a security door and enters a tiny office, with windows that look over the vault and main reading room. As Hart gazes at the ceiling-high shelves of bound books in the reading room, another female librarian, this one smaller but just as distracted as her colleague upstairs, approaches him from the vault area. She smiles and asks if she can help.

'Sure, I'd like to see Mr Rhodes Hodgson.'

'Oh. I am afraid he is very busy, preparing for the new semester. Are you sure I can't help?'

'I need to see him in person. Can you tell him Eliot sent me. It's very important.'

'And your name?' she asks.

Hart surrenders his name and she walks away. Through the glass window, Hart then watches a tall, neatly dressed and elderly man shuffle into view, emerging from behind a tier of overloaded racking as soon as the message is delivered. He peers at Hart through the thick lenses of his glasses. The grey eyes behind the magnifying lenses are full of surprise.

But Hart immediately intuits something amiable and well-meaning about this figure, despite his connection to Eliot. Softened by age and civilised by knowledge, he offers the impression of being immensely comfortable in his own skin. There is something relaxed about the way he walks too, mis-construable as weariness, as he enters the office. Standing still, with his mouth slightly open, the man continues to stare at Hart. His breathing rasps across his dentures and thin lips. 'Eliot sent you?' he queries, the voice English, cultured, and surprisingly deep.

Hart smiles. 'Yes. He recommended you.'

'Are you sure?' the man asks, frowning in disbelief.

'Oh yeah. I saw him yesterday. He gave me some refer-ences to help my research.'

'Yesterday,' the man says, baffled.

In the presence of the elegant archivist, Hart suddenly wishes he had worn clean clothes, becoming conscious of his grubby trousers and creased combat jacket, the shoulders now dark with rain.

Hodgson's thick eyebrows rise. 'Well, well,' he says.

'Forgive my surprise, only Eliot has been rather scarce for some time. Is he all right, or should I say better? I've heard all sorts of things.'

'You know Eliot,' he says, unsure of himself, laughing nervously, and raising his hands in the air with mock exasperation.

Rhodes Hodgson nods and gazes at the wall behind Hart. Confounded, he then shakes his head. Hart is reminded of his dad, whenever he reads something in a newspaper that confirms his deeply held suspicion that the world is a circus. Rhodes snaps out of his daze and stretches his hand forward. 'If you see Eliot again, please, please, tell him to come and see me. Tell him I absolutely insist upon it. Always fascinating working with him. Regardless of his troubles. No longer on the staff, I hear?' Rhodes says, peering down at Hart over his glasses. Hart stays silent and just grins foolishly, trying to think of something to say. 'Anyway,' Rhodes adds, looking disappointed that no information is forthcoming. 'How may I assist you?'

Hart takes a breath. 'Well, I'm looking into witchcraft in the area. This town. A history and so forth, and Eliot recommended I check out his most recent studies. He said that everything he knew, you knew, if that makes sense.'

Rhodes seems flattered; he smiles. 'Well, he's probably referring you to his last project. I assisted Eliot's research for some time. For his second book, you know. Five years in the making, although I doubt whether it will ever be finished. But it was a fascinating theory.'

'Really?'

'Yes. I acquired several resources for him, from all over the place. Particularly from the continent, if my memory

267

serves.' Rhodes wanders across the office and holds the second door open for Hart. It leads to the reading room. 'What is it you are studying? Something in conjunction with Eliot?'

'Er . . . There seem to be overlaps. I take the anthropological angle on folklore. Nightmares particularly.' Hart pauses and watches the man's face for a reaction. Rhodes waits for more. 'Umm, what I call night terrors connected to witchcraft.' Hart watches his face keenly again, eager to spot give-away signs.

'Witchcraft?' Rhodes says, smiling enthusiastically but innocently. 'Then Eliot's your man.'

'Were you two friends?'

'In a professional capacity we were close. Though I wouldn't count myself fortunate enough to be called a *friend*. Eliot has always been a very private man. He has his interests and they are sufficient, I imagine. One of the last true scholars.'

I bet, Hart stops himself from saying. He follows the librarian into the reading room and stands beside a large rectangular table. 'Please take a seat, and I will be with you shortly,' Rhodes says.

Hart removes his jacket and settles into a chair. Rhodes pulls a small grey footstool across to a row of shelves and pulls two bulky volumes down. Pieces of torn paper are visible along the top of the books to indicate pages marked for later reference. 'What was Eliot's angle, for the new book?' Hart asks.

'A history, I suppose,' Rhodes says, over his shoulder. 'Of the witch's familiar. There was more material than I imagined once we got started. So much of it held in private collections, though. Little still in print. But we tracked down some valuable resources. We began tracing the origins of a certain fourteenth-century Hungarian cult, although they may have been around since the earliest Manichees. Eliot seemed to think so. He actually traced, if not their influence, a similar pattern of events, all over central Europe. Eventually, his reading led him to Scotland. Very academically rigorous, Eliot, despite what you may hear from other quarters. That is, as long as the subject interested him. Eliot has the strangest tastes, as I'm sure you know.'

'Uh-huh,' Hart says.

Rhodes places the two massive leather-bound volumes on the table before Hart, the smell of old books puffing around his face like dead pollen. 'Bit of light reading. Those winter nights must have flown by,' he mutters to himself. It will take days to read them both. He doesn't have the time. 'Was there a certain part in these that Eliot focused on? I appreciate you sorting them out, but I'm on a really tight schedule.'

Rhodes strolls around the room, unhurried, his hands clasped behind his back, while his face becomes a parody of an intellectual's delight in an opportunity to express his expertise. Hart smiles. 'Well, I suppose I can offer a brief outline of his initial study. Although it will be brief,' Rhodes says. His eyes are shining and seem bigger and not so sleepy anymore behind the lenses of his glasses. 'As I mentioned, I only assisted Eliot's secondary reading.' He wafts a hand about, distractedly. 'Assembled his bibliography and assisted with the footnotes. And those two volumes, both written in the late twenties, provide a fair summary of Eliot's original speculations. And yes, they'll take some reading. Rather heavy going from a historical perspective, like the Reverend

Summers. But I liked working with Eliot, because his own travels gave him more precise insights than the authors of these two books, who I assume wrote in a cloistered environment without the benefits of fieldwork.'

'Amen to that. You don't have to convince an anthropologist. But why did Eliot come here, to St Andrews?'

'I can only suppose it was in the interest of continuing his work. I never thought he was a man interested in a conventional career. The lecturing, it's fair to speculate, would have been secondary to the further cultivation of his interests as an explorer. We have amassed one of the best occult collections in Britain here at the library. Most of it bequeathed, but all of immeasurable benefit to him. I believe he had friends here too, who secured a lecturing position for him. I think the scandal over *Banquet for the Damned* had subsided sufficiently to make him a safe bet, if you follow.'

Hart nods. 'Can you tell me anything about these books? You know, why he'd be so interested in them specifically?'

'I can certainly help with the Blackwood, who by the way wrote in a slightly antiquated style and it's heavy going. That of the gentleman dilettante, not unlike C W Ceram, but without the wit. Blackwood had time at his disposal to amass an extraordinary compendium of occult occurrences. He rants a little, we felt too, from a very orthodox Catholic standpoint. You know, convinced that Satan or some such nonsense was behind every evil in the world, but his historical material is really very, very good. Indispensable. The particular section that interested Eliot concerned the Hungarian society, or witch cult. Made particularly poignant by its dependence on the familiar.'

Hart frowns in concentration while Rhodes paces about

the reading room, occasionally glancing across at him, as he continues with his recollections, flushing at times with a topic that obviously enthralled him in the past. 'It was the summary of the Kresnik inquisitors' findings, at a celebrated trial held in the northeastern region of Hungary in the late 1400s, that really excited Eliot. You'll find it in chapter five. I remember copying it for Eliot. Fascinating piece. You see, as the trial progressed, the witnesses began giving statements about the witches' exceptional powers for divining and summoning, following the use of strong hallucinogens prior to ritual. Ecstatic ritual. I daresay, you are aware of Eliot's own digressions with these substances, a long time before it became fashionable?'

Hart nods.

'Well, it was claimed that the nine accused had spread an epidemic of animal disease, tempests to ruin the crops, human illnesses and so forth. We can assume someone had to be blamed for natural consequences, as was the way of things at the time. But what enthralled Eliot was the evidence stating that the coven was served by, and indeed served, an emissary. An ancient spirit with something of an appetite for sacrifice. From that, allegedly, their power came.

'There is a passage in the Blackwood describing how the coven delighted in a rather gruesome practice of –' Rhodes pauses, his eyebrows rising over his glasses '– of dismembering their victims, and removing the skin or bones prior to a cannibalistic orgy. All rather distasteful. And their Sabbaths involved dreadful inversions of Christian services. You can feel the author holding back on specific details, and he loses his impartiality by vehemently condemning the accused and, would you believe, taking sides with the inquisitors.'

Hart moves around on his seat, uncomfortable and unable to feel the benefits of the radiator's warmth.

'But what is also extraordinary about this case is the leader. These weren't the usual unfortunate crones on trial here. No, the leader of the cult was a woman of noble birth. It was her influence that must have prolonged the coven's activities. Her name was Kazparek, I think. You see, it was some time before the church put an end to the activities of her coven. She'd had something of a field day until the ecclesiastical authorities were compelled to intercede. Forced to, because of the monstrous nature of her crimes.

'The head inquisitor, a fiend called Kolosvar, called Kazparek a "devil" and a "whore", amongst other things, at her trial. In fact, he didn't consider her to be human. Nor did he ever cease to be amazed at her resistance to torture. It was only when the astonishing beauty of her face was threatened with a hot poker that she cracked.

'And it was from her confession that so wide a range of diabolical crimes has been recorded. It's why I can remember the case so well. Her testimony, and it's all in the Blackwood, detailed the seizure and consumption of, I recall, some fifty infants and youths over a period of six years. Including her own son, would you believe.

'The other eight in the coven were burned alive in a mass pyre, but Anna Kazparek survived the flames. On account of her title. But she was banished from Hungary. I think her lands and wealth was confiscated too, but one can't help but think she got off lightly.'

Rhodes takes a breath and rocks back on his heels. Hart sits still, increasingly distressed at the thought of what Eliot has been meddling with. He wants a drink, and feels utterly humbled by Rhodes Hodgson's encyclopaedic knowledge.

'Blackwood, however, pursued her to Germany, where a similar group surfaced. This would have been fifty years later.' Rhodes begins to smile. 'Impossible, I know. But she allegedly recruited a new coven made up of rebellious nobles. And again they acted according to the will of their familiar. Their emissary.

'The coven was known as a Wahrwolf society. Something Blackwood attributes, like other scholars, to the Werewolf legend. This time their notoriety arose from their wearing of human skins, usually those of abducted youths, in the form of raiment. There was the same pattern of forbidden rite and unholy mass as in Hungary, preceding all manner of social ills again. Though this time they seem to have added to their dark talents. The Wahrwolfs had mastered the ability, while in a trance, to provide a new mobility for their deity. It allowed the spirit to move at night and wreak a rather grisly fate upon a chosen victim.

'A bishop, I seem to recall, became their nemesis in Germany, and once more the coven was ruthlessly exterminated. The leaders too this time.

'Blackwood's story then leads to the 1500s, in Poland, and yet another emergence of a similar cult. In Poland they called them the *Upyr*, which Blackwood believes to have evolved into the vampire myths. The *Upyr*'s blasphemous and murderous activities were so widespread and of such a magnitude they were described as a plague.'

Hart runs his fingers across the smooth surface of the table; a coincidence?

'Anyone visited by the *Upyr* at night would succumb to

fevers and what have you, sometimes with terminal results. Once again, there was a plague of blood-letting, the disappearance of infants, and cannibalism. Their goal: the absorption of their victims' souls into their god's corporeal body. A blasphemous inversion of taking Christ's body and blood into the body, by devouring parts of the victim. In order, you see, for their deity to exist and for their powers to continue. The church believed the *Upyr* to be a direct inversion of Christian sainthood.

'And this was the crux of Eliot's argument. He believed the witch, werewolf, and vampire traditions were one and the same thing. Different places and times afforded them different names, but the familiars became crucial. A hangover from pre-Christian times. There seemed to be some pretty compelling evidence too, that these things actually existed.'

Rhodes pauses to look at Hart. 'Oh, I am sorry. I must be detaining you.'

Hart clears his throat. 'No. It's very good of you. Please go on – really.'

Rhodes refolds his hands and resumes his pacing, unaware of how painful some of the material is to Hart. 'The *Upyr*, it was discovered, entered their trances after taking opium or datura. The drug enhanced their professed abilities to direct the familiar and allow it to attain corporeality elsewhere, so it could perform its foul business. Either at the home of the bewitched or at a more convenient location, where the victim would be transported and devoured. Once an opening had been attained in one household, it was said the relatives of the initial victim also became susceptible to attack.'

Hart's eyes feel like they are burning in their sockets from

the strain of watching the steadily pacing and relaxed bib-
liophile, while he struggles simultaneously to maintain his
composure. Rhodes moves behind Hart, leans across him
and begins leafing through the Blackwood tome. His eyes
light up, brighter than ever. 'Ah, right here, chapter seven. It
gives details of how Cardinal Kossa rescued the large Polish
town of Lublo with his pitiless persecution of the *Upyr*. The
plague ended with large-scale burning, beheading, and skew-
ering, I believe you'll find, over a two-year period. Nearly
three hundred people died. Mercenary soldiers were even
employed to execute the church's decree. In each case, the
heart of a *Upyr* was removed and burned, after the removal
of the limbs from the torso.'

Hart rubs at his face – these are echoes from Guatemala
and the Amazon Basin.

Rhodes pauses to glance at his watch. 'Oh, I say, I really
must be getting back to my work, but I still have the copy of
the Wilkins. Must think about sending it back to its home in
Massachusetts. Been waiting for Eliot's say-so. I'll mark the
relevant section. You really must read it. The story emerges
right here, on our doorstep in St Andrews.'

'Thanks,' Hart says. 'Thanks for the information, Mr
Hodgson. It clears up some of the more difficult things that
Eliot has been telling me.'

'Quite all right. I really miss working on the project. You
can see why it stuck in my mind. And do please tell Eliot to
get in touch. I have given up calling his office. He never
seems to be there. And then I heard he was ill for some time.
One doesn't really know what to do in these situations.'

'No,' Hart agrees. 'But . . . Did Eliot actually believe these
things – the familiars – existed?'

Rhodes laughs, cheerfully, before answering, 'I shouldn't think so.'

'But why did he research them particularly?'

The librarian raises an eyebrow. 'You have me there. Mythical figures perhaps? And he was an expert on Agrippa of course, and something of an authority on Crowley. Both men allegedly summoned a familiar that never left them.'

Hart swallows. 'Did he ever mention his paranormal group?'

Rhodes appears pensive for the first time. 'He referred to it once or twice, and I know there was a bit of a stink over it. Never went myself, but his assistants did. They came here with him sometimes.'

Hart leans forward. 'You remember them?'

'Oh yes. There was a very pretty girl, who came at the end of last year, I believe. Or was it earlier this year? I can't remember when, but I believe she was helping on the project, with his regular research assistant, Ben.' Rhodes pauses, looking almost guilty. 'That poor lad, Ben Carter.'

'I heard about that,' Hart says. 'He died on the beach.'

'On the sands, the West Sands,' Rhodes answers, obviously reluctant to continue with the story, but Hart presses on. 'But the girl. She all right?'

'I presume so. Never really knew her. Beth was her name. Eliot was very fond of her.'

'Was she really tall? With bones like a supermodel? Dresses all in black?'

'That's a fair description. You don't know her?'

'No. But I've seen her around.'

*

After Rhodes Hodgson leaves the reading room to potter in a distant confine of the vaults, Hart remains in the basement, with a copy of the Wilkins volume, *A Geography of the Black Arts*, open on the table before him. And, as Rhodes warned, Wilkins's passion was for Scotland.

The first marked chapter begins with comments about the Scots' ability for second sight. Even as late as the eighteenth century, Boswell and Johnson were documenting the phenomenon amongst ordinary people. Not to mention the reverence attributed to those in possession of an extra sense. And psychic abilities, thought to belong to the region between death and resurrection, had been highly prized and cultivated by the witch covens of Scotland since the dark ages. Hart begins to enter familiar ground.

Oblivious to the passage of time, Hart settles into the warmth in the basement, his eyes soothed by the clear yellow light. Stretching out his legs, he resumes reading about the proliferation of the Brown Man myths. Legends that draw him further into Eliot Coldwell's world and to a remarkable set of coincidences. Parallels to what he has so far uncovered in the town.

When Wilkins writes of St Andrews's birth in 870 as an ecclesiastical centre, he mentions the uneasy alliance of the barbaric Pictish religion and Christianity. Wilkins guesses that the strange fusion of Christian belief and Pictish myth, occurring at this time, created a subversive undercurrent of pagan belief. But one fused with Christian superstition that fostered witchcraft. More importantly, it led to the continuation of a profane worship of the 'Brown Man'.

Historians placed the figure as a strange amalgam of the Greek god Dionysus, the deity of Athens called Melanaigis, or the 'Black One', and Pan, the leader of satyrs. Elsewhere in Europe, the Gallic stag-god Cernunnous was cited as an influence for the 'Brown Man', while the Romans, busily building Hadrian's Wall to keep 'it' and the Picts out of England, wrote of it as Dispaster, god of the underworld. And by the time the Papal Bulls were brought to the town, the Roman Catholic belief in good and evil associated the deity and the worship of it with the devil.

Wilkins detailed the survival of the 'Brown Man' cult with a plethora of quotes from bishops and officials, defaming its dreadful rites. In the seventh and eighth centuries attempts to suppress the 'mumming' dances only succeeded in forcing the cult underground. The 'mumming' ceremonies involved the ancient ritual of dressing like the figure in order to rejoice and exult in its honour. The witches, as Wilkins referred to them, would drape themselves in the skins of cattle or the cerements of the dead and literally become wild animals. Others would dance naked, but daub themselves in darkly coloured clay. The feverish dances and ecstatic worship would become orgiastic, in the hope that a union with the god could be achieved. At the Sabbaths, it was believed every conceivable perversion was performed, including cannibalism. Sacrifice of the young was particularly popular and was always preceded by a strange backward dance. Back to back, hand in hand, the witches would skip backward and shake their heads in a frenzy until an animal madness was induced to prepare the coven for the arrival of the Brown Man.

Wilkins's next chapter takes Hart to the Reformation and the height of the Scottish witch persecutions. In 1643, both John Kincaid of Tranent and John Balfour of Corhouse, master prickers and witch finders, were summoned to St Andrews. Their business: the celebrated interrogation and trial of one Lady Anne Muir for her 'wickedness, impietie and hyneous abominations'. In Anstruther, Dysart, Culros, St Andrews, and other regions on the Fife Coast, her name was associated with chaos, fear, and every expression of black magic. Barley and oats had rotted for successive harvests; cattle were said to have been cursed and calves were still-born; ships were wrecked and their crews perished; people in the towns became inexplicably ill with fevers. Anne Muir and her malignant carline, or dark familiar, were believed to be responsible. In due course she was, therefore, cleansed of impurity by pain and fire.

It seems that Anne Muir, in Wilkins's version, was a gentlewoman of great beauty, and had masqueraded as an epitome of nobility and grace. And only when her titled rivals at court began to protest against the nocturnal visitations of 'a misshapen thing in rags', was she charged with witchcraft. The investigation soon discovered a coven of 'persounes, aucht wemene and three men', all in her service and allegedly responsible for the devilry in St Andrews. Hart knows ordinarily he would find the reported hysteria and language in the text vaguely amusing, but he finds it difficult to even read parts of the story. Those passages detailing her suffering at the hands of her inquisitors are particularly distasteful.

After an immersion with her followers in the Witch's Pool, Muir suffered an inexorable agony under the implements called the *Turkas* and the *Bootes*. Her fingernails were removed with pliers, and pins were inserted to their heads in her fingers. Soon after the *Bootes* were put in place on her legs, crushing and bruising them until they were deemed 'unserviceable'.

In Wilkins's summary, it was claimed that the devil had entered her heart so deeply that even her blood was unclean and black. And yet, no confession was forthcoming, even after the *Pilliwinkes* were attached to her already tortured fingers. It was, however, the binding and wrenching of her head that destroyed 'her excellent beauty' and broke the resolve of Muir.

Apparently dead from her injuries, she was partially torched and then buried in consecrated ground. Her coven were 'burnt at a steake till they be dead' and their ashes were scattered to the winds. After their demise, the Brown Man, who had been known to drag the sleeping town youths from bed by their hair, was not seen again.

It sounds like a typical reaction from zealots, ridding themselves of guilt, confusion and fear at the expense of an innocent woman. An example of the town's puritanical malice. But the information is frighteningly coincidental and matches his night-terror research at a fundamental level. What's more, Eliot wanted him to see the material. And Ben Carter killed himself as a result of studying it.

And would it sound so implausible to him, Hart muses, if he heard about it in Africa or the Amazon? Perhaps enlightenment, technology and secularisation haven't cleared Europe of the oldest science of all – the occult.

The appalling fate of so many witches gives him a new perspective on the town too. He finds it hard to comprehend the sheer scope of brutality and injustice occurring within a stone's throw of where he currently sits. Despite the veneer of tranquillity in present-day St Andrews, he begins to imagine a power of unrest beneath the solid rock of the town's magnificent structures and ruins. Could such stains ever be removed?

When he nears the end of the long and detailed accounts of merciless torturers and seemingly ridiculous accusations, Hart finds a specific commentary on the Brown Man of St Andrews:

It seems almost certain that the witch, Anne Muir, was in possession of a familiar. From a covenant with the devil, she owned or was owned by a spectre. The worryings, molestations and nocturnal hauntings were thus made by her Brown Man in the town of S Andrews. Cloaked in invisibility and projected through sleep, it inflicted severe and sometimes mortal wounds upon its victims. There are suggestions that the spectre grew in corporeality, clothed in the fear and blood of the poor wretches visited. Similarities can be drawn with the terrible black dwarf, called Filius Artus, the familiar of Lady Alice Kyteler of Kilkenny, and the black thing called Grimoald, that accompanied Cromwell after his initiation with the rabbi, Menasses Ben Israel, in Amsterdam.

Anne Muir's Brown Man allegedly resembled the satyr: terribly emaciated and thin-legged with a coif or cowl for its scant raiment. It was said to have accompanied Muir to every social function. At the Bishop's Palace after the estates had met in Parliament Hall, certain guests (among them Mary Campbell – who we can only assume was gifted with the second sight) were filled with a suffocating anxiety and unease upon Anne Muir's entrance. Mary Campbell's faint, and the unnatural epilepsies of two serving girls, were believed to have resulted from a sighting of the Brown Man in all his glory, at Muir's side. It was said to have assisted in the churchyard-Sabbaths and was even noted to sit behind her in church service, its smile matching hers, as they mocked Christ the Saviour and the sanctity of the church by their very presence. In the street at night, it was seen behind her, and there were several sightings of its abominable face at the windows of Muir's residence. Even King James VI of Scotland, in his famous Daemonologie *has written: 'To some of the baser sort of them he obliges himself to appear at their calling upon him . . . which he shows unto them either in likeness of . . . an ape, or such-like other beast.'*

It is quite possible that the Brown Man is also connected to King Arcan, as described in the anonymously authored, and frightfully illustrated, An Elizabethan Devil-Worshipper's Prayer Book. *Arcan, drawn from life, was pitch-black and long-toothed.*

But even that is not as upsetting to Hart as the final passage detailing Anna's Muir's trial. It seemed that *Muir was defiant to the point of death.* When he reads of her final cries, in the cathedral where she was tried, he goes dizzy. *She cursed the town as she was led to torture. Her work had been postponed, but her last words promised that the Dies Irae – The Day of Wrath – would still destroy S Andrews.*

After Hart closes Wilkins's *Geography of the Black Arts*, he sits for a long while, unable to move. The profoundest fear he can remember seems to pull his shrivelled balls up inside his body. It is difficult to even see straight. Hazy but irrepressible images of something thin and brown prance through his imagination.

'Still here?' Rhodes says, breaking Hart's trance. 'Nearly two. We close the archive soon, you know. We'll be open later this evening, and again tomorrow. But I'm afraid I'll have to turf you out now.'

Hart turns his ashen face to the old librarian.

'Was it of any interest?' Rhodes asks, looking concerned.

'A real page-turner,' Hart rasps.

Rhodes sniffs and nods toward the book. 'Grisly stuff, aye?'

'Yeah. I can't thank you enough, Mr Hodgson.'

'Quite all right,' he says, distractedly, and begins rummaging along the top shelves of the reading room. Hart says goodbye to the elderly librarian and then makes his way back up the stairs to the ground floor. If Eliot sent Hart to the library to find the truth, then the town faces the biggest threat yet in its long existence.

Unable to face the door to his indefensible flat right away, Hart goes looking for a drink. After a morning of revelation in the library, he needs to be among the ordinary people who walk the streets. He needs to breathe the cool air of the everyday world and buy whisky.

Choosing a pub at the end of Market Street, he orders a beer and a double Scotch chaser and disappears into a quiet corner.

What is he to make of the information? Perhaps Eliot's obsession provides the only answer. The man may have eaten too many rotten mushrooms and sunk his mind into too many occult histories to be sane. Did he sway the students' minds into believing they experienced visitations from the Brown Man? Maybe he used hallucinogens on his paranormal group, and everybody was suffering from psychotic delusions. But what about Beth? Can there be a coven? Something Eliot started and maybe lost control of? Through hypnotism, maybe Beth believes she is Anne Muir.

But Hart has a hard time trying to convince himself and ultimately fails. Eliot's passing beyond sanity, and his move outside the boundaries of taste and common sense, as with so many shamans Hart has studied, may have led to a connection with something even older than the town. He just doesn't know enough about Eliot. His *Banquet for the Damned* was a defiant cry against too great a dependence on empirical thought, and Christianity's increasing departure from practical spirituality. It was dismissed as some half-assed Hindu phenomenology about seeing a meaning in everything, about raising your consciousness to a level where a man could see new truths. A novel, but quickly repudiated attack on the passivity that eroded the true scope of a person's inner life. And Eliot belongs to a school of thought that believes a certain proportion of the population, when properly trained, can harness what amount to psychic abilities. That must have been the purpose of his group. If Wilkins is to be believed, Scotland would have been perfect for a scholar of second sight. But to practise black magic? Mike mentioned something about Eliot communing with the dead, and Kerry said his group went underground. Isn't that how it always starts? When the world loses faith, because you can't produce results, crude and often disastrous short cuts are pursued. So many shamans basically do the same thing in a misguided attempt to regain favour with their tribes. Eventually, they unwittingly give life to something unholy.

Hart begins to wonder if he can risk digging any deeper.

He buys another Scotch. He thinks back to the phone messages and the girl across the street with the white face. Whoever has taken a sudden interest in him, if indeed it is Beth, knows where he lives.

For the rest of the afternoon, he only feels comfortable in the society of others. The rain continues to fall on the town, and only the excitability amongst the students, who arrive by the hour in a steady trickle, alleviates his gloom. He feels peculiarly sensitive to the cold, and finds it hard to keep his concentration on anything. Lack of sleep is catching up on him, but he still wants to delay going home.

After eating his first hot meal in St Andrews at a Chinese restaurant, he finally walks back to his flat at nine in the evening. One or two cars move up and down Market Street, but the weather keeps most people inside.

Outside his street-level door, he pauses. Could someone be in there, right now, waiting for him in the dark? Hart unbags the whisky bottle he bought from the supermarket before it shut, and creeps up the stairs. If anyone moves inside, he'll use the heavy bottom end of the bottle to bust their head.

But nothing comes at him when he climbs the stairs, nor when he opens the door and quickly slaps the lights on. He creeps from the lounge to the bedroom to the bathroom, trying to swallow his heart that beats against his Adam's apple. Cupboards and drawers are opened; the bed and couch are looked under. Nothing has been touched since he left that morning.

Hart stows the groceries away and then slides the heavy wooden couch against the door to barricade himself in for the night. If they try to burn him out, he'll leap from the window like Arthur Brown with a singed beard. Chuckling to himself, Hart secures the flat and congratulates himself for not running out on the most daring and insane experience of his life.

But the moment he's finished, the phone rings.

TWENTY-SIX

Silence on the line. Every molecule in Hart's body stops moving. 'Who is it?'

No answer. He strains his ears. In the distance, from the other end of the connection, he hears a car pass and what sounds like a door slamming shut. The call is coming from a public phone box. 'Come on, speak to me,' he says, hoping to sound friendly, but the strength is gone from his voice. The phone clicks down at the other end.

Pawing his beard, Hart lets the phone receiver go loose in his other hand. He becomes conscious of the silence in the flat. No cars pass in the street below. He wants to hear at least one. There are no gurgles from pipes or drip drop, drip drops from taps in the bathroom. Checking his watch, he sees it is ten after nine. He thinks back to the pale-faced creature he saw outside yesterday. He rushes to the lounge window. Through the curtains he sees the street is empty. But as he looks out at the town, he starts to feel strange. A curious discomfort. One that grows until it overwhelms him, taking control of his movements, emotions and thoughts.

Dizzy, he feels as if his body weighs nothing. He sits down, like he's just stood up too fast with no blood in his brain. Then his temperature plummets, all over and down and into his boots. His scalp prickles. A feeling of acute nausea rises up the back of his neck and makes the top of his skull icy. You can feel them, he thinks.

It is a struggle to get his breath. He stands up and tries to move about, half-blind, through the lounge. The only thing he concentrates on is breathing fast enough to keep up with his heartbeat. Maybe closing his eyes will relieve the attack, or the spasm, or whatever it is. But the moment his eyelids shut, concealing the room from his eyes, he is afflicted with an unexpected vision.

Like an unwanted slide, slotted into a projector in error, he sees a woman in a dark room, its heavy wooden door shut behind her. She is bent over a deep crib fringed with lace. Dark drapes are pulled over the greater part of the cradle. She wears a bodice and long skirts, but he cannot see her face. Laces criss-cross up the front of her chest to her slender neck, where a spray of fine red dots speckle the marble of her throat. 'No,' Hart says aloud, and opens his eyes. Did he hear the sounds of breaking gristle and the slide and crunch of teeth on the thin bones of a child?

'Jesus,' Hart says, and leaps away from where he's been standing as if that part of the floor is responsible for the imagining. But on they come, the quick flashes of things he has never seen before and would never have imagined independently. Shaking his head, he tries in vain to remove the canopy of dark sky, heavy with rain, that now stretches through his mind. Beneath it stands a triangular pyre of kindling, some of it green and fresh and wet, through which thick plumes of black smoke try to grow from red innards of fire. Tied to a roughly hewn post of wood is what resembles a doll in white rags, dirty with smoke. Then he sees its face, wet with tears, blackened and crimson like bacon. And he sees its head, hairless and partially bound in strips of linen.

Hart falls down.

Across a white beach, where the sand looks like salt and the sea like oil, comes a figure fast. Low to the ground, moving at such a rate that speed and distance are impossible to judge. Agile as a monkey, it kicks up puffs of sand and comes at him, driven by a motive he takes for hunger. The vision passes.

Hart scrambles to his knees and then his feet. He whimpers and uses his hands to snatch at things for support, a sofa leg, the top of the coffee table. A glass hits the rug and bounces onto the wooden floorboards. Something smashes but it isn't the glass. Turning toward the sound, he sees the lens on the wall clock is broken. A long crack runs through the glass and then divides at the top of the case. Hart seizes his jacket and runs to the door of the flat. He heaves the couch away and descends the stairs three at a time.

Down on the desolate street, he shivers. A cold breeze sweeps up from the west and blows a piece of litter across his unlaced boots. His head is suddenly, mercifully clear; the nausea and dizziness pass, but his every nerve hums like a live wire. Tucking his head down, Hart runs across the road, away from the flat, at a slanting angle toward Grey Friar's Street – the nearest exit from Market Street. He drops to a crouch at the corner of Grey Friar's, inside the canopy of a building society.

He zips his jacket up to his throat and looks for somewhere else he can hide. But there isn't time. A car approaches from the top of Market Street by the monument. There are no headlights warning of its approach. It becomes a long black saloon that crawls to the kerb outside his flat. The door to the flat is still open and he has left all the lights on upstairs. He can see the orangey glow they make from the top of the staircase. He pushes himself as far inside the entrance to the building society as he can. The tiles on the floor freeze his hands; the glass feels cold enough to stick his face to the windows.

He can hear the engine of the car idling. There is the sound of two doors opening and being slammed shut, followed by a scuffle of heels on the pavement.

An age seems to drag by and Hart remains still and silent, shivering with cold and the fear he can taste like a mineral in his mouth. Whoever is now inside his flat is taking their time. He begins to wonder if it is the police. Maybe he's been turned over to the law and plainclothes detectives are tossing the place right now. He tries to force the theory to make sense. He's been spouting off about missing students and it is only a matter of time before the disappearances of Rick, Mike and Maria are investigated. He's met Mike, interrogated Rick's roommate, and spoken to Maria and her boyfriend on the phone. Every path leads to him. But why didn't the police come straight away? And are the local constabulary capable of psychic attack? Because that's what it was, up there in the flat, where he thought himself safe with a couch against the door. He tries to banish the residue of the visions that assaulted him inside the place he knew as home. Thank sweet Jesus he left when he did.

Hart takes one tentative peek out of the doorway, but draws back quickly at the sound of hurried footsteps descending the stairs of the flat. They scuff off the tarmac and scurry around the car. He hears a door open and then slam again. The car's suspension springs creak down from the added weight of a passenger. But the car continues to idle at the kerbside. Wondering why it doesn't drive off, he peeks back at his flat.

His breath catches in his throat and his body tightens to a cramp. The tall woman he saw earlier watching him from the street has paused before she climbs into the front passenger seat. If Hart isn't mistaken, the bleached face with the closed eyes is sniffing at the night air. No longer able to feel his legs, or hear anything save the thunder of his heart, Hart eases his head back inside the doorway and closes his eyes. He remains in the same position for another ten minutes after the car has driven away.

Two taxis pass by and the cold begins to ache in his ankles. He can't stay outside all night. He has to go home. Unsteady on his feet, he stands upright and then drifts across the road, longing to cradle an assault rifle over one arm. Carefully, he enters the unlit staircase. The lights are off upstairs but the door that opens into the lounge is still open.

Creeping up the stairs with his teeth set in a mad grin, he nods his head up and down, and blows short breaths out of his mouth in an attempt to calm down. Another shock and he is sure his heart will go bang.

Peeking around the doorframe into the dark lounge, Hart stretches out a hand, flicks the light switch on and shouts 'Police!' He ducks back from the door and prepares to flee down the stairs in expectation of something in pursuit. With all of his remaining courage he waits for a few seconds to pass. There is no sound of movement from within. The flat remains quiet and nothing comes loping from the door he hovers outside.

He enters the lounge. 'Bastards.'

Whoever forced entry and then searched the flat has been thorough. The cushion covers have been turned inside out and the couch is on its side. The Ecuadorian rug has been thrown into a corner. Drawers have been yanked from the desk and turned upside down. The computer is smashed, the tape recorder spews coloured wires, and his Dictaphone machine has been stomped underfoot. Even more alarming, his books, papers, and cassette recordings are gone. Hart staggers across the room. Bits of black plastic from the obliterated answering machine crunch beneath the soles of his hiking boots.

Things are just as grim in the bedroom: mattress against the wall, split pillows, tossed clothes. Stooping down, he pulls his rucksack out from beneath the iron bedframe. 'Motherfuckers.' His passport and travellers cheques are gone. The bathroom follows suit. The pink candlewick mat is in the tub and the medicine cabinet doors are wide open.

He walks back through to the lounge and slumps on the floor. Holding his head in his hands, he looks up to see if the phone is still intact. But his eyes never move any further than the large map between the mirror and floor lamp. Every red pin, from the little plastic pot he keeps them inside, has been stuck haphazardly across the map. Hundreds of tiny red balls cover St Andrews from the Western Sands to the Eastern Harbour. At the top of the map, on the blue strip representing the bay, someone has scrawled the words *Dies Irae* in what he hopes is red lipstick.

TWENTY-SEVEN

Although the most active part of the illness is gone, Dante still moans every time the Land Rover bounces over a pothole or bumps across a ripple of tarmac while he drives, alone, through the town toward the sea. Despite the cold of night, a light rash of sweat creates a sheen on his forehead, and there is something tattered about his breathing in between the occasional coughing fit that leaves a taste of cigarette tar and blood in his mouth. He makes the usual vow to give up smoking and to appreciate his health once he's made a complete recovery. And that will be at a time, if he can remain resolute through the impending confrontation with Beth, when the debacle of his journey to Scotland will be a few hundred miles behind him.

Once he passes the Old Course and clubhouse, now darkened and deserted, the silhouette of St Andrews town, spiky against the sodden blues and blacks of night, glowers down at him from up on its perch, as if it too despairs at the scruffy sick man in the beaten-up truck. Which is precisely what he thinks of himself as he glances at the distant spires and towers through the driver's-side window, watching them grow smaller between the far-off trees, where they rise behind the walls on the cliff tops. Tonight, the town seems especially unforgiving, as if it relinquishes responsibility for those not shielded within its stone and beneath its timbers now the sun has waned. Its rocks and foundations have survived revolutions and atrocities and weathered countless storms, and he doubts if he has ever felt so vulnerable as he does now, away from sanctuary and alone.

Once his business with Beth and Eliot is finished, there is no option left for him but to flounder away, back into a pitiful, transient life, in England. Despite the initial hiatus of his arrival, his awareness of yet another defeat has been ever-present, and grown stronger since the first meeting with Eliot. It is just the way things seem to happen in the life he's made difficult for himself by choosing to be a musician. What has the trip north achieved? He's doubted his mentor, deceived his friend, and run from shadows.

Nearing the place selected by Beth, he suffers a fresh pang in his stomach. 'What a mess. What a fuckin' mess,' he says, in a quiet, flat voice to himself.

He passes the sea wall, and slows the Land Rover down to listen to the ocean waves pause and sigh before the roar when the waters are suddenly confronted with stone and sand again. He always wanted to live by the sea. Maybe he can go and sell pasties on a beach in Cornwall, or work in a bar in Spain, now that Scotland is finished. On the journey back, he'll make sure to drive right past Birmingham, and not even stop for cigarettes, in case he becomes caught in the city's magnetic field and sucked back to the very place he started from.

Definition in the landscape ebbs away from around the Land Rover as Dante passes the last outcrop of buildings connected to the clubhouse and putting green of the Old Course. With both hands on the wheel, he swerves the War

Wagon around snaking bends, and makes it hiccup over the speed bumps near the last carpark at the start of the West Sands. The narrow road then straightens, with the golf links on one side and the dunes on the other, and carries him away from town and closer to the oblivious sea.

A final glance in the rear-view mirror reveals the town lights as mere dots about the now indistinct sentinels of St Salvator's and the castle. One quarter of a silver moon adds a bright light far up in the sky that fails to illumine much on the ground. Ahead of him, the coastline slips into a depth of night that throws the weak beam of his headlamps back at his eyes, and the dunes huddle together in the cold, like the bowed heads of giants with tufts of grass for hair. And over their hunched shoulders, the sea at high tide is as black as pitch.

Dante wonders how he will find them. The beach road stretches for at least another mile toward the Eden Estuary. Beth instructed him to meet them where the dunes flatten, near the river mouth. On the map there is an observation point there, before the road ends, but no streetlights. He thought the beach was lit at night. Anxious about passing it in the dark, as his headlights only light up the tarmac in front and not the sides of the road, Dante slows the clattering and wheezing Land Rover down to a crawl and pulls his window all the way back in the frame.

'Shit!' Something runs across the road. He stamps on the brake. The Land Rover fish-tails on the sandy tarmac before coming to a stop. Breathing hard, he peers out of the cabin. Whatever the hell it was has vanished. The headlights cast only a brief smear of light on to something running across the front of the vehicle, low to the ground, with its head turned away from the light. A black dog or a dark, freckled deer, perhaps, disturbed from the undergrowth by his lights and the sound of the engine. Fleeing animals always add a sense of urgency and immediacy to the dark when they run through high-beams. That's all it was, he tells himself. He drives on, shaken.

Now, all he can concentrate on is his recollection of the scream, heard on his second night in town. And then he thinks of his last visit to the sands, and how the discovery of an arm prevented a return to the shore. The thing that ran across the road makes him regret leaving the flat. What was he thinking? He trusts neither Eliot nor Beth, and they want him and Tom out here in the middle of the night? What can they say, or show him, only at night and not during the day? He thinks of turning around and driving back. Anger forced him into this reckless journey; his impetuous need to end the Scottish adventure brought him out here, alone. And if he is honest with himself, was it not also a desire to see Beth that brought him to the sands? And does she not know that he will come? He swears at himself.

Moving forward, slowly, he looks left and right, backward and forward, until his neck begins to ache. After another hundred metres, the left side of the road opens out to a wide grass verge, which in turn is gravelled to serve as a carpark. This has to be the place. Turning off the tarmac, he rumbles over the loose stone chips scattered over the hard mud that has been grooved by tyres when wet. His visibility is limited to twenty feet on all sides, so he keeps the engine running and the headlights on. It has gone twelve and if they are here, they can't fail to see his lights – the only lights this far out. With the engine idling, he fumbles with a cigarette. His nerves hum. His voice is ready to break into soprano, and his foot twitches to plant the accelerator pedal against the metal floor.

'What the . . .' There is a boom and a crash close to his ear. Something slams against the side of the Land Rover's fibreglass hardtop and nearly shuts his heart down. Dropping the lit cigarette, Dante twists in his seat to gape at the passenger side of the vehicle that has been struck. Echoes from the crash still resound in his ears. For a moment, he is too shocked to focus, but when his vision clears there is nothing to see but the silent darkness beyond the grimy glass of the windows. Depressing the clutch, he pushes the gearstick into reverse. Just as he is about to rocket backward, a figure appears between the headlamp beams. Someone stands upright, swathed in black, with their head bowed.

Dante jumps. His foot leaves the clutch and the Land Rover kangaroo-hops to a spluttering stall. He peers at the dashboard. His fingers scrabble for the keys and the ignition button. When he dares to look up again, he stares into Beth's smiling face.

Dante swears aloud. She is playing a game. His heart thunders like a drum kit inside his chest. Sweat dries to shivers. Beth turns her hand, palm upward, and beckons to him with her index finger. In the distance, the grin on her white face strikes him as both sly and superior. Something inside of Dante reacts against it. He feels foolish and angry. It wasn't funny, her startling him like that. And the noise of her hitting the Land Rover was horrible; it sounded like an animal. The whole vehicle rocked from side to side and the noise was deafening.

And where is Eliot? Is she alone? He thinks of his fright in

St Mary's Court and his anger turns to caution. He restarts the Land Rover. Beth's smile vanishes and a pleading enters her expression. She tilts her head to one side and then mouths the word 'please' at him. Her black overcoat falls open. A satin slip shines against her breasts and hip-bones. Against the dark material, the beam of his lamps reflects off the white of her throat and the pale cleavage below. Never has she looked so beautiful, so dead, so eager.

Dante opens his door and steps out. When his boots touch the gravel, he struggles to remember how he came to be standing there. He just obeyed her; there was no choice.

The silence on the beach is deeper, the air heavier, and only the cold against his cheeks helps to earth him. 'Beth,' he says.

Raising her chin, she arches one brow above a mad eye, and pouts her dark lips. And then for a moment her face trembles with rage, before she throws her head back and laughs like a hysteric. She must be drunk. He stays by the open door of the Land Rover with his hand tight on the handle. But Beth's laughter ceases as quickly as it began. She dips her head to smile at him, sweetly. Then she walks toward him. Slender legs, booted to the knee, but left pale to the hem of her slip, steal his gaze from her eager face. His feeble resistance dissolves into the dark.

When she is no more than a single step away, her expression turns fierce. He flinches, but she is too quick. Clutching his cheeks with her hard fingers, she kisses his mouth, tearing at his lips with her teeth. He cries out, tries to pull away, but she pinches the skin of his face hard, immobilising him with pain. The scabbed wounds on his lips break open with a ripping sound he feels more than hears. It makes him feel sick.

He tries to breathe through his nose as he chokes on the perfume clouding his face, before it slips up his sinuses and dulls his mind like morphine. When his body goes limp against her, she withdraws her face to laugh.

Unwinding her arms from his back, Beth steps away from Dante, leaving him tottering on the spot and wiping at his lips. 'Oh precious,' she whispers, her expression now that of the little-lost-girl the first time they met. But her eyes remain wide, disabling his ability to look away. He tries to speak but can't remember how. His face is numb, his mouth traumatised. 'I told you to wait,' she says. 'Why couldn't you wait? You didn't trust me. We were wrong about you.'

He feels a sharp pain in his stomach, which becomes a desperate need to placate her, to make her want him still, but she turns on her Cuban heels and marches away across the gravel, out of the headlight beams and through the grass to disappear amongst the dunes. 'Beth. Wait. Beth! Wait! It's not like that!' he shouts. But she is gone. Dante leans against the Land Rover. 'Beth,' he calls, weakly, 'I'm not well. Don't make me chase you.' Sulphur smoulders in his lungs.

His desire to stray no more than a few feet from the Land Rover grinds with his need to see her again. Her quick and savage introduction arouses a lunatic desire in him. It blinds him, douses his fear. He feels reckless, and trembles on legs that feel especially thin and useless as he calls her name. She never answers, so he crosses the gravel part-way, slowing down when the sensation of loose stones beneath his boots gives way to the cushion of dune grass.

And soon he is shouting with annoyance. His resolution to stay near the War Wagon is broken, forgotten. He stumbles over pieces of driftwood, and twists an ankle on the uneven ground where the dunes begin to rise. Ascending the first hump of sand, he falls into the harsh grasses growing through the damp sand. They stab at his face and poke an eye. And he is reduced to sitting with a hand pressed against a wet and stinging eyelid, shut tight. But at least the pain revives him, helping him to think straight for the first time since she kissed him.

Back on his feet, he climbs to the top of the nearest dune. Bending over, he swats the sand from his knees. When he straightens, Beth is standing in front of him. 'Jesus!' he cries out, and staggers back. And he is about to shout at her, when she removes her long coat. She looks down her body, her face concealed by her hair. 'When you left the court, we were punished.'

'What?' Dante asks.

'You were told to be patient and not to ask questions.'

'Can you blame me?' he asks, baffled.

Beth makes a little muffled sobbing sound in her hair.

'What's going on, Beth? Tell me.'

'There is another, Dante. He wants to meet you.'

'Who?'

Beth raises her chin and shakes the hair from her face. A creek of tears shines on her cheekbones. She sniffs and then turns around to show him her slender back. She slips a tiny strap of her slip off one shoulder. The silky garment slides down her pale back. There is a shadow under her scapula. Dante moves closer and the shadow becomes a large bruise. He winces. 'Shit.' As his eyes accustom themselves to what thin light the moon transmits, he catches a glimpse of something that resembles a giant black orchid, with a smattering of red petals around it. The evil flower covers half of her back. 'Who did this?' he says, his voice tight. From his bad eye, tears stream hot and sting his face.

'One whom I love,' she replies, a tremble in her voice.

'Eliot?'

When she answers, her tone changes again. It is soft and hushed, as if she is speaking of someone of great importance. 'Pain can be a reward.'

Dante swallows but stays quiet. He has no idea how to react; what she says seems to diminish him. There is nothing in his experience to compare with the seductive horror of her suggestion.

'Are you afraid, Dante? Of offering yourself to something greater than you could ever be alone?'

He wants to say 'you need help', but is afraid of setting her off and making her violent again. She is ill; this is clear to him now. Schizophrenic even. These mood swings explain it all. There are at least two distinct personalities active in her: she switches from this young and vulnerable girl to something sadistic and out of control. And Eliot is responsible. He keeps her and controls her and beats her. He lures impressionable students into his twisted games, and then uses them as playthings. It is all starting to make sense. Maybe he uses narcotics and some kind of suggestion to beguile and then control his victims. It explains the illness. He must have been drugged. No wonder the Hebdomidar tried to warn him, and it is no surprise that Janice reacted so strongly to his association with Eliot. The Hebdomidar mentioned all of this at the Orientation, and he failed to connect the clues because he was so smitten with Beth and in awe of Eliot. But now, the penny has finally dropped and he'll go straight to the police, and he'll take Beth along as proof.

'We thought you were the one for him. But you couldn't understand,' she says, adrift in her own world.

'Shut up, Beth. Cut the crap,' Dante answers, his voice quick. 'I know more than you think. I know what's been going on, and I want you to come somewhere with me. Tonight. I want you to trust me on this.'

Beth glares at him. Her teeth are revealed in another mad grin. 'Do you think Eliot is my master?' She laughs, crazily, at the sky. Dante looks over his shoulder at the silhouette of his Land Rover. 'Beth, you're coming with me. I've had enough of this.'

'Fool,' she mutters behind him, in a deeper tone of voice. He is shocked to hear her speak like this; it contradicts her youth, spoils her beauty, is incongruous, as if her face and body are a façade to conceal something far uglier. 'There are greater ones to serve than broken men, who only now begin to realise what has begun. And you are privileged. Our lord is hungry. He will take you in his arms tonight, and you will truly know him.' She comes for him without a sound, closing the distance between them with one step. Her arms are colder and thinner than ever as she embraces him. Her hands disappear beneath his shirt. Fingernails tear into his back. Dante cries out in pain. He tries to pull himself free, but she smashes her face against his neck. Immediately, her teeth become busy on the soft flesh. With her fingers locked behind his back, close to his spine, she prevents him from pulling his arms free, and when she begins to squeeze him with her bony arms, the breath is forced from him, and then his ribs began to shift and groan. Overwhelmed by her unnatural strength, and a fear of suffocation, he stamps about in the sand, trying to shake her loose. But his desperate staggers only succeed in toppling them to the ground.

As they roll in the sand and wet verdure, he kicks his legs about, and tries to call out, but his squashed and winded torso can produce no sound beside a rasping noise that vibrates in his throat. Blind with panic, he is sure he will pass out.

When her grip suddenly loosens around his chest and he is able to draw some air into his lungs, she begins to lap at the deep abrasions on the skin of his neck. Her tongue is dry as a cat's and she makes a snuffling sound as she suckles his throat. The sound is worse than the pain that preceded it.

And then she breaks away from his throat, moves off his body, and sits crouched down beside him. She stares into the dark nearby.

Unable to move from shock, Dante looks in horror at the lipstick and blood smeared about her mouth and chin, making her look slovenly, like the insane hybrid of a harlot and a clown. 'He comes,' she mutters. Then tilts her head back, with her eyes closed and her dark mouth open. A desperate scream issues from her mouth. It pierces his inner ear and he rolls his head from side to side to ease the pain.

Beth falls silent, and she looks like a young and pretty girl with chocolate around her mouth. 'He's here for you,' she whispers, and then lowers her lips to his forehead. He flinches. She kisses him, tenderly.

Dante peers up at her, still too shocked to speak or react. And too stunned to avoid the hard punches that soon rain against his face from left and right, Beth making soft grunting sounds as she strikes him. And through the blood and confusion that whirl about his head, he hears her knuckles crack.

When the storm of violence concludes, Beth is gone from him, leaving him numb and half-conscious in the sand. Through his concussed haze, he hears the noise of her feet as she runs away, into the night-blackened dunes.

And in the distance, he hears another sound. Faint, but growing. A sound that makes him feel an instant and profound chill. It is like a sail billowing and snapping against the rigging of a ship when struck by a sudden gust of wind far out at sea. But it grows louder as the sound travels through the night at speed, toward where he lies in the dirt. His mind wants to collapse – to flicker out like a candle's flame before a draught. Only some basic instinct for survival motivates him to move his arms and legs. He rises to his hands and knees as his senses collect to deliver a terrible conclusion: she's blooded me, she's prepared me.

The sound is close now. It is all around him, circling just beyond his vision, carried by a frozen wind that skims off the sand. Remembering the sound of old bones flung through St Mary's Court, he clambers to his feet and staggers about on the spot, fighting for balance. The blood deserts his brain and he nearly falls as he stumbles toward the Land Rover.

Beth screams from behind. A scream of anticipation and wild animal excitement.

Dante runs with tears in his eyes. The pain in his chest, from where she squeezed him, makes him move slowly, barely able to stay upright. When he reaches the gravel of the car-park, he notices a movement on his right side. The motion is joined by a faint sound: not footsteps, but a suggestion of something being dragged or dragging itself across the ground.

It stays level with him, keeping pace, content to stalk him from a close distance.

Screwing up his eyes, he sees a shape, or a long shadow, crouching near the turf, before the grass drops away to the beach. He thinks of breaking into a sprint, but knows the idea of the shadow moving more quickly in pursuit will stop his legs with fear and possibly his heart too. Hysteria gains momentum inside him. A sound squeezes out of his throat – a thin note of anguish that trembles and threatens to grow into a scream. Should he shout? Who would hear him? 'Beth,' he says, in a weak voice. 'Beth, call it off. For Christ's sake, stop this,' he cries, as if he is being menaced by a dog while the owner looks on.

She laughs again, like a lunatic pleased after performing some awful deed with a child and a sharp implement. 'Our lord is here. He's here for you, Dante. Just for you.'

In the distance, just audible above Beth's voice, Dante hears a car engine. He looks over his left shoulder and sees headlights approaching, down the beach road. It is the only sign he needs. Forsaking the Land Rover, knowing he will never reach it, Dante suddenly breaks into a sprint toward the road, adrenaline neutralising pain. As he runs, he shouts and waves both arms in the air. But no sooner has he begun to run as fast as he is able, than a wind of pursuit flares up behind him. 'No!' he cries out, and stumbles. He looks back, only once and quickly too. It is sufficient. He sees the silhouette of something long and thin, close to the ground, coming after him.

Ahead, the car turns from the beach road to the open area he runs across. Hope surges. They've seen him. Hope peaks. He wants to cry out. Hope dies.

As if he is whacked by the boom of a boat, something hard thumps his back and knocks him down so quickly his hands never have a chance to break his fall. Before his face hits the earth, his ankles are clutched and slapped together. In the next instant he is being dragged backward toward the sea at an incredible speed. Whatever holds his ankles runs twice as fast as a man. His arms flail and his body skims over the stones and litter and bits of broken turf, as if he is being dragged behind a horse. If he is taken to the sand, he knows he is finished. Using all the might of his lungs, Dante screams.

For a moment his body is airborne. He seems to be flying, feetfirst, backward and through the air. In both hands, he clutches handfuls of grass from the turf he's just departed. When he lands, facefirst in the sand, the air is forced from his body, and consciousness is slammed from his head.

TWENTY-EIGHT

The voice is coming from a distance. For a while, it is as if someone is talking to Dante in a dream he is just about to leave. But when he wakes and opens his eyes, he realises the voice is no dream fragment; it is being spoken in the real world by a woman with a quiet but firm voice, who is pointing a torch at his face.

'He's awake,' she says to someone standing nearby. The light hurts his eyes. Pain erupts all over his body. He stays still, terrified to move in case the pain gets worse. He clenches one hand. Damp sand crushes in his palm and slides between his fingers. With the other hand he shields his eyes from the torchlight. 'Dante,' the woman says. 'It's all right. You've had a fall. Can you tell me if you're hurt?'

He groans.

'Tell me where it hurts,' she says, her voice soft.

'Sure he's no pissed?' a man's voice says from behind her.

'Canne smell anything on his breath,' she answers the man.

It is now that the full impact of the night's events crash into his mind. He suddenly remembers Beth's attack, the thing that prowled around him, the chase, being dragged to the sea, and then . . . nothing. But he is alive.

Dante sits up quickly, but immediately grips the sides of

his head; the pain is so great his eyes water. 'I'm not dead . . . drunk. Not drunk.' It sounds like he's sleeptalking. The initial wave of agony subsides inside his skull. He keeps his head still. 'Who are you?' he asks, speaking slowly, feeling the shape of the words on his tongue.

Anxious, the man and woman move away from him. 'We're police officers,' the woman says. The torch beam shines in his eyes again. It blinds him. 'We saw your vehicle from the beach road with the lights on.'

Dante puts a hand to the patch of stinging skin on his throat and winces when his fingertips touch something wet. He looks up and squints until the male officer lowers the torch beam from his face. Now he can see their silhouettes. She is a head shorter than the man and neither of them wear hats. 'What happened?' the man says, his tone brusque.

Dante closes his eyes. His ribs hurt and there is something else bleeding on his back. He can feel his T-shirt sticking to the skin where it stings: a cut from when he was dragged across the ground. But what can he say to the police? His first feeling is an overwhelming gratitude. Inadvertently, they've saved him from the sea. From death out there in the dark and cold water. He shivers. His arm would have been found in the surf, eventually identified from the tattoos on the upper part. Tom would have identified it.

'What were you doing out here?' The woman's voice hardens with suspicion.

'I came out here to meet someone.' He pauses; they wait. 'It turned nasty.'

'You saying you were assaulted?' the man asks, his accent strong.

Dante nods.

'By who?' the male officer asks, losing his patience. The two officers exchange glances. 'Up on your feet,' the man orders. 'Come on.' He stretches an arm down. Dante fingers the sleeve of the man's jumper. His arm is limp and it feels as if there is no strength left in the muscles. Impatiently, the policeman seizes his elbow with a tight, practised grip and pulls him, sharply, to his feet. 'You been drinking, pal? Aye? Drugs maybe?'

The woman stands to one side. She is leafing through his wallet, which is how she must have learned his name. 'Says here your address is in Birmingham. Long way from home, son.'

'Yeah,' he says, and smiles with relief at her reminder of a place that is familiar to him: another world, away from this madness. The smile is not returned. Their expressions remain severe. She is pretty, but her face has gone tight and her eyes are hard.

'What are you doing here, pal? And who assaulted you?' the male officer asks.

Dante panics. What can he say without sounding like he's been taking drugs? What if they make him take a blood test? He and Tom have been smoking weed since they arrived. 'It's difficult,' he mumbles.

'What's difficult?' the man says, his torch in Dante's face again. 'You tellin' me you don't know who assaulted you? I'm not inclined to believe you, pal. We find you lying on the beach in the middle o' the night. What were you doing, staking out your plot before the tourists come down tomorrow?' Many take a similar line with him on account of his long hair and appearance. People's first reaction is distrust, their second ridicule. Not caring for the man's tone, which has become not only sarcastic but condescending, Dante says, 'No, pal. Nothing like that.'

The officer stiffens at the tone of Dante's voice and the mimicry implicit in his answer. 'You're well enough to back-chat me, son, you're well enough to come in and do some talking.' Dante's right arm is seized behind the elbow.

'OK. OK,' he says, and struggles to untangle his arm. The iron fingers clench tighter. 'I'm sorry. I don't want to argue. It's just that I've had a shock. I've been unconscious –' his arm is released '– just let me get my bearings. My head is killing me. Please.' The woman moves closer to calm things down. She looks at her partner, who takes a reluctant step away from Dante. 'I'm not a troublemaker,' Dante says, and his voice trembles. He looks at the sea and then down the wide expanse of sand, still dark, and indifferent to what has befallen him. A place to die, where the wind and water and sky will carry on in their circle of tide and rain and day and night forever, unconcerned. He is frightened again and can't think straight. 'You came just in time. I want to thank you . . .' His weak voice fails him.

'That's all right,' the woman says, and touches his shoulder. Dante wipes his eyes.

She smiles. 'Let's go up to the car and have a wee chat. How's that sound?' Dante nods. All three of them climb away from the sea toward the patrol car parked beside his Land Rover.

Dante stands in the bathroom. He grips the washbasin to stop the shakes. Rinsing his face under the cold tap revives him, but does little to calm the storm inside his skull. It's all an illusion. It must be. This can't be real. It was just a big guy. Someone strong that finished Beth's dirty work. Unconvinced, he then slumps down to his knees and closes his eyes. 'I'm losing it,' he whispers.

Something raggedy and long flings itself through his mind. Immediately, he opens his eyes. He is back in shock. He takes deep breaths. He tries to kill the image. An illusion? Something was expecting him on the dark beach. Whatever it was, it came with Beth at the end of a night they intended to be his last. A final rendezvous at the climax of Eliot's plot where, all along, from their first exchange of letters, something in St Andrews has been waiting for him, or has been promised him.

But murder? No way. That happens to other people. 'No,' he says. Gripping the lime-green bathroom mat with both fists, he flicks his wet hair out of his eyes and says, 'No,' again and again, until his voice rises in a feeble attempt to erase the image of the thing that stalked him by the sea. Through the wall he hears Tom stir – a muffled and far-off rustle of a sleeping body turning in bed. Dante winces and kills the flow of water still streaming from the tap. Tom will have to be told, even if he ends up thinking his best friend is mad.

Looking at his watch, he sees it is four in the morning. There was an hour at the police station on North Street as he tried to talk himself out of a night in the cells. And then the next two hours in the emergency ward, having his cuts and bruises attended to, finished off the most harrowing night of his life. Three stitches on his neck from her bite, and a weight of salve-soaked dressings on his back and stomach courtesy of her companion. 'Superficial wounds,' the doctor with the slender face had said, with the cheeks scrubbed and pink under the hospital striplights. 'Just cuts and grazes.'

Because of the injuries the police officers had been forced to take his story seriously. He was Eliot Coldwell's research assistant, or so he told them, and had begun to see one of the lecturer's students out of hours. A girl called Beth who seemed to be having problems. When he met her late that night, she and a third party – an unknown assailant – attacked him for no reason he could gather. There had been no provocation, although she claimed he had disappointed her terribly by expressing concerns about her mental health to Eliot. Not a convincing story, he thought, looking at the unconvinced faces of the police officers, but it was all he had. Although he was desperate to inform them that the unknown assailant wasn't even human, he held his tongue, fearing a drug test. They took it all down in a notebook, but the male officer was clearly unimpressed from start to finish.

But what mystifies him most is the time immediately after Johnny Law rolled up. Where did Beth and her companion flee to? There was no one around when the police found him. The male officer went off and searched about, flashing his torch here and there amongst the dunes. There were no other cars out there, no buildings to hide inside, and not a single soul had been sighted. They had vanished.

'They,' the male officer said, sarcastically, 'must have been long gone by the time we found you.'

'No,' Dante insisted. 'It was your interruption that saved me.' *From death*, he wanted to add.

But it was just him they found, alone on the sand, and they were sick to death of students wasting their time with their drunken foolery, and noise, and rucks in the streets with locals. They only enjoyed a brief respite over the summer months when most of the students left the town, but recently things had been as busy as they were in Raisin week. 'What was that?' he asked.

'What was Raisin week? A festival,' the policewoman said, and she rolled her eyes at the very mention of it. Then they took Eliot's address at the School of Divinity. Questions would be asked. But Dante was unsure about pressing charges, and was still foolishly wary of implicating Eliot, out of an unshakeable, stubborn, and infuriating sense of his greatness.

All he wanted, he said to the officers in conclusion, was to grab his mate, get out of town and drive home. This seemed to please the male officer, but they would still need his town address should further inquiries be made. When he provided the flat's address on the East Scores, the officers exchanged glances. 'What?' he asked.

'Do you know the man who used to live there?' the woman cop asked him.

'No,' he replied, and gave them the date of his arrival in town. The male officer looked at him with suspicion. 'So you have no connection with a man called Ben Carter?' he asked. Dante shook his head and wanted to know why this caused concern. They believed he was telling the truth – he could see it in their faces – but neither gave him an answer to his question.

The male officer said it was probably best that he was going back to England after all. 'Some strange things have been happening,' he added, more to himself and for his partner's benefit than for Dante's.

'You're telling me,' Dante said to prompt them. 'I turned up the day they found that arm.' At both officers looked uncomfortable. 'Know whose it is yet?' he asked.

'No,' they said in unison, and the interview was over. Then the grumpy male cop took him to the hospital for repairs, staying silent all the way and not even looking him in the eye when Dante said goodbye outside the entrance to the Emergency Room.

Casualty wards in Birmingham were dreadful places in the early hours. On three occasions, he either took Punky to casualty for a stomach pump, or collected the drummer from casualty after a stomach pump. He saw fist fights, nurses assaulted by drunks, hysterical women, kids wheeled to and fro with blue faces. But in St Andrews, at the Memorial Hospital, it was a different world. He was the only patient, so the staff – a young doctor and a sweet nurse – saw him immediately, and were careful not to question him too closely about his wounds. It was obvious they assumed he'd been in a fight. With his tattoos and messy hair, they thought he was a brawler, the type that attracted and caused street violence. It would have been no good trying to explain otherwise. A dog and angry girlfriend story was too lame for a repeat telling. From casualty, he then took a cab to North Street and drove the War Wagon home from where it was parked outside the police station.

Regaining his feet in the bathroom of the flat, the stinging pains on his back cry out again, tender body parts harassed by the simple touch of his shirt. The bite on his neck is not as deep as he expected and doesn't trouble him greatly, even though the teeth marks immediately went septic. 'Dirtiest mouth on the planet,' the young doctor said, swabbing his throat. 'Did you know that even the dog bite is cleaner than the human?' One of his cheeks is bruised and he has a fat bottom lip from Beth's punches, but his face has slipped into a welcome numbness since he swallowed the painkillers he was given at the hospital. Even his ribs that Beth crushed offer nothing more than a tender sensation when he inhales, but his back continues to give him hell.

The doctor spent some time inspecting his back. 'You were bitten? What did the other fellow do, pick you up in his mouth and run with you? Nasty,' he added.

Curious and anxious about what he might see, Dante slowly removes his shirt. A trickle of sand falls to the tiled floor of the bathroom. He turns around and peers over his shoulder at the reflection of his back in the bathroom mirror. Then he peels the corner of dressing off the part of his skin that hurts the most, stretching from his waist to the small of his back.

'Jesus,' he says. Standing under the electric light, he moves from side to side to fully reveal the extent of the flesh wound. He keeps his eyes in a squint because he can't bear to see it clearly. His sallow torso now resembles something on a mortician's slab. It is as if he was thrown amongst a legion of small beasts during a feeding frenzy. Small incisions, encrusted with coagulating blood, are surrounded by others that are still raw and fresh. It covers his entire lower back. Spattered between the cuts and evil bruises is a series of painful blue indentations pressed into his flesh by fingertips. Bony fingertips. But it is the marks over his kidneys that make him dizzy with shock. He grips the sink, steadies himself and then looks back at his reflection. Teeth marks. It looks as if a large mouth has dislocated its lower jaw to clamp his skin between sharp incisors – wanting to break through and kill. Around the entries the teeth have made into his skin are what resemble long and inflamed bruises from where his skin has been stretched. It is like the doctor suggested: that he's been picked up in a mouth and carried.

Down on the sands, the last of his fever, his anxiety at meeting Beth, and her manic behaviour may have transformed the evening into something surreal and dreamy. But here are the physical scars, again, resulting from a few minutes in her company. The attack was savage, the assailant determined and merciless. There have been no illusions in St Andrews after all. It is for real.

Beth is insane. Not weird, kinky, beautiful, a mystery in furs and leather boots, like he wanted to believe, but insane. She hypnotised him or drugged him back at St Mary's. Same again on the West Sands where body parts wash ashore. Only down by the sea, where it is more remote and easier for her, for them, to work, she tortured his helpless body in some kind of blood sport – a perverse sadistic rite – a prelude to a snuff movie, where the tide and wind swallowed his cries.

Awe-stricken by the weight of his thoughts, he stands mute, displaying his broken skin to the mirror until his legs weaken and he can look no more. But even when his cuts are covered again, the bandages only conceal his battered nudity; the flesh itself still harbours the sensations of thin fingers and dirty teeth.

Dropping his head, Dante fights to hold the tears back. When was the last time his mind was clear, when he was able to think and act rationally? He needs Tom, who will shake his perfect head and smile, before suggesting a fresh escape and a new plan. An involuntary shiver wracks his body, and Dante thinks of his bed. Will sleep remove her terrible scream from his mind? It still seems to echo around his skull, tainting his thoughts with its awful sense of excitement. And beneath the painful abrasions on his skin, the virus might still be groping about, looking for a chink through which to rise.

'Eliot,' Dante whispers, as he creeps across the quiet hallway to his room. The man he wants to immortalise with music has deceived him. How many years has he spent quoting from the book, feebly transferring its message to half-drunk musicians? How many times has he rescued it from second-hand bookshops and offered it as a gift to someone he thought would benefit from Eliot's wisdom? Eliot wants him dead, mauled by Beth and then offered to the thing in rags.

The first glimmer of anger begins to smoke and then flare through him. When the bedroom window is closed and latched, the front door and patio door locks secured, Dante slips into bed. He winces as he lowers his punished body to the cool sheets. He'll pack up first thing and hit the road before ten. It is the only thought that offers any comfort. But sleep brings no relief; there are other things that demand his attention under the cover of slumber.

TWENTY-NINE

When Dante's eyes open, something lies beside him in bed. His desperate need to flinch and turn away is denied. A numbing paralysis weighs him to the mattress, damp beneath his skin. It is the extreme attack of pins and needles again, shutting everything down except for his shallow breaths and faltering heartbeat.

His eyes flick left, right, up, down. He can see the pale ceiling of his room and the simple lightshade corralling a bulb he wishes were on. The bare walls appear distant and barely reflect the faint traces of yellow streetlight creeping through a tiny parting in his curtains. An attempt to clench a fist fails; it is no longer there. The hand seems to have vanished from his tingling wrist, like a blind man who has groped off the end of a pier.

Beside him in bed, a head turns on the pillow. Droplets of sweat freeze against his scalp. The pillow dips beside his right ear. There is a faint exhalation and then silence. Something rests against his cheek. A head. He can feel the outline of a large face, a flat forehead, with eye sockets and no nose beneath – just the edges of something dry and sharp.

A petrified cry escapes from his throat. Panic slaps around his skull, like a dizzy child crazed with terror in a burning house. The bedfellow stirs and the movement of its limbs creates a rustle beneath the sheets – black snakes in long grass. Suddenly, it sits up. Dante's eyes flick to the right – a frightened rabbit, trapped in a tunnel beneath a large shadow, expecting the end.

Upon narrow shoulders, an indistinct face opens its mouth and utters a rasp of delight. Something long and thin reaches across his body. Hard fingers grasp his arms and hold them tight against his body. Then the shadow rises and moves across his vision before it settles down, spider-like, covering the bed. Dante closes his eyes and stops breathing. Like a sack of sticks, he hears its creaks and rustles. Outside his clamped eyelids, a face lowers itself. The embrace becomes a crush.

Dante's naked body hits the rough texture of the carpet beside his bed and he wakes with a scream. Moments later, the door blows in and the overhead light is swatted on. Tom stands by the bed, panting, dressed in just his shorts, his hair tousled and his eyes wide with shock. 'Jesus Christ! I thought you were being murdered!' Tom slumps against the wall and tries to catch his breath.

They stare at each other – Dante pallid, his face stricken, Tom about to speak, but in shock. They stay silent. Gradually, the horror of Dante's bruised and lacerated body is comprehended by Tom. He raises his eyes and pleads with Dante for an explanation. Dante begins to sob and covers his face. 'Tried to kill me,' he gasps. 'The window. Must have come in through the window.' He stares at the locked window. The curtains are still.

'Dante, look at you.' Tom's voice is unsteady with emotion. 'You're all cut.'

Rising to his feet, Dante looks about the pastel-shaded walls of his room. He touches the furniture. Everything is solid, real, in its place, and he is alive. He wipes tears from his eyes. Twisting around, he checks the bed. Slapping his hands down on the crumpled bed linen and mattress confirms the departure of the uninvited companion. Dropping to his knees, he peers beneath the bed, half expecting something to reach out and grasp his head with long fingers.

Nothing there.

A hundred-watt bulb and the yellow of sunrise bring reason back to his mind. But his recall of whatever made him scream in sleep dims, infuriatingly. Something was beside him. But what?

Tom's hands shake; he is angry now. His tanned face whitens, his head cocks at an accusatory angle. 'Where the fuck did you go last night? I heard the War Wagon's engine. I checked your room. You went out.'

Dante sits back on the mattress, catching his breath in the early-morning charm of sunlight and cool air. He glances across the broken skin on his torso. 'Jesus, look at me.'

'I want fuckin' answers, mate!' Tom shouts. 'I know what makes those marks.'

Dante closes his eyes and sighs, so thankful to be awake, so grateful to be alive, to see Tom again and hear a milk bottle swept off a neighbour's doorstep, to hear birds and the distant shutting of a car door.

'Say something,' Tom says, exasperated.

Dante reaches for his jeans. He has to get up, smoke a fag, drink some tea, shower in hot water, force the small routines of living into the sick and drunken haze he's been wading through for days. Tom moves into the room, watching his friend's poorly balanced struggles to get dressed. He stands close to Dante, his eyes warning him of a serious fracture in their relations. 'Just a smoke and a cuppa, Tom. And then I'll give you the lot. The mess that I've got us both into.' Speech is such an effort for him. His entire coating of skin now stings or aches after every movement. When he tries to walk around Tom to get to the bathroom his friend places a firm hand on Dante's shoulder and shakes his head. 'No more bullshit, Dante. I want to know what's going on with you. You're covered in fuckin' bite marks, for Christ's sake.'

Dante nods. 'Just let me wash.'

When he finishes washing and sobbing he finds Tom waiting for him in the living room. Tom smokes a cigarette and watches Dante take the easy chair opposite the sofa. Nervous, Dante begins the confession.

Ten years of living in each other's back pockets produces frequent conflict, usually only resulting in slight confrontations. But at times something else will take over, something blood-hot, and they stop just in time, and bite back on the words at the last moment to save their bond. On this morning, however, it seems as if the very foundations of their friendship, supporting them for over a decade, are under threat. For once, Dante muses, it is because he is in the wrong.

'You kept that from me?' Tom says, incredulous, after Dante nervously recounts the fuller version of his liaisons with Beth. 'I can't believe you never told me. I've been kicking around this flat day after day, jerking off, looking after you, going insane with boredom. You know, I started to think that this whole deal in Scotland was a mistake. We don't belong here. I only kept going because of you, keeping all of my doubts to myself, because this was Dante's trip of a lifetime. He was going to meet Eliot Coldwell.'

'Tom, I know it sounds bad –'

'Damn straight it does. For Christ's sake, Dante! All this time you've been fucking about with Eliot's wife. If anyone was going to commit adultery up here I thought it would've been me, but it was you and some tart into bondage. Look at the state of yourself. You don't have a fuckin' clue! How could you do it to the guy that wrote *Banquet*? You've read it a hundred times and turned it into lyrics. He's an old man with a young girl, and you fuck her.'

Something hot flinches inside Dante. 'Tom, forget sex. It's not like that.'

Tom refuses to look at Dante. 'Sure.'

'Tom, I'd never met anyone like her before. Beth was like that muse I was always telling you about. I thought she was the one. Instantly. She seemed so beautiful and so weird. And it was Beth who asked us up here. The letters, the research job, the flat – she claims that everything was her idea. She read *Banquet* for all the same reasons I did. We seemed so alike. How could I have resisted her? I didn't know what I was getting into. Eliot manipulated the whole thing. He wanted us to get together for a reason. You have to understand how I was pulled in.'

Tom looks at the ceiling. Shakes his head in disbelief.

'Try and understand, Tom. I couldn't tell you. I had to know where we were standing. If we could pull this thing off. I didn't want to worry you with all this in the first week. I mean we're here five minutes and I get fuckin' typhoid or something and . . .' Dante pauses, swallows. 'There's more, Tom. It gets worse.'

'How could it get any worse?'

'Hear me out . . . I don't trust Eliot, let alone Beth. I don't know how to say this, but I doubt if Eliot asked me up here to assist his research.'

'What?'

'It's crazy, I know. But being his assistant was just a ruse. Something is going down that Eliot started. I don't know what. Maybe some kind of cult. And I'm their fuckin' sacrifice. It's all starting to make sense to me and I'm frightened, Tom. I'm not kidding. I want to leave St Andrews. Today.'

'You're out of your mind. She's made you paranoid. You never could handle your emotions with a girl.'

'Please, please, just listen. What about these nightmares I've been having? I thought it was because of the virus, but it's not. They're connected to Beth. The dreams are like a prelude, an introduction to something. Same with the time I met her in the court. They're offering a glimpse of someone I'm supposed to meet.'

'You're the only fuckin' nightmare,' Tom cuts in.

'Tom! You're not hearing me. Beth told me something about a third party and she acts all weird whenever she speaks about him. And I don't think this other party is a person. I mean, it's not a man.'

'What the fuck are you on?'

'It sounds crazy, I know. But I saw it last night. Or a part of it. The thing from my dreams that I can never remember properly when I wake up. Don't you see? It's all connected. At first I thought I was seeing things, being ill and susceptible and somehow dreaming the whole thing. But now I know it wasn't. It's real. That's why she asked me out to the sands last night. And in the court. They have something, Tom.

Something up here with them. They were going to give me to it.'

Tom closes his eyes and dips his sleek head between his legs. 'I've heard some bullshit in my time, Dante, but I never thought it would come out of your mouth.' He looks up. 'We came up here to get away from the crazies, remember? I don't know what the fuck that woman has done to you, but she's made an arse of you. A real arse. Do you think you can sneak off behind my back and shag some crazy bitch and then fob me off with this shit?'

Knots of frustration tighten inside Dante until they produce a burning sensation in his chest. 'Is that all you care about, Tom? All you ever care about, the allocation of female affection? That's why you're pissed off, isn't it? Because for once I got the girl, without you getting in first. Without taking over and rewarding me with your cast-offs, like I should be grateful. You don't care about everything falling through. Or the fact that we've been deceived, and that I'm ill, and in trouble. You just can't stand the thought of me meeting someone first. It offends your vanity. I've never been more serious in my life and you call me crazy. I nearly died, for fuck's sake.'

Tom's face colours. 'You selfish bastard. Why did you bring me here? Because without me you'd be isolated. You might think you're some kind of radical outsider, but you're not. You're a misfit and a fuckin' dreamer. You meet some arty bitch, some brainy beauty, who gets off on being the centre of attention, who craves it, with some weird-ass psycho sex shit going on, and you think, you convince yourself, she's the one. You betray Eliot and you ditch me. You've been single for so long, your desperation is calling the shots.'

Dante knocks his mug of tea over. 'Fuck you! How can you talk of betrayal? You knew how I felt about Imogen and you just had to have her. You took her when you could have had any girl in or out of the rock scene. And then she became everything that was good for you and you still chucked her. And now you try and judge my problem by the yardstick of your fuckin' bitterness. By your inability to ever accept even a smidgen of imperfection. Your own friends, best friends, can't trust you. You fucked Punky's girl and it killed the band.'

'She was no good, and you know it,' Tom blurts out. 'I did him a favour. If it wasn't me, it would have been the next guy that made a pass. She was going to dump him anyway because of his drinking.'

'Bullshit! You know how he felt about her. That's why he was drinking. The kid always had problems, but he loved that girl and he worshipped the fuckin' ground you walked on. You just couldn't resist flexing your power. Proving that you could have any girl going. Even a mate's. Everyone knows you're beautiful. Every girl wants you, but you always have to prove it. You're poison. That's why the band has two musicians left. You fucked it up. The straw that broke the camel's back. You're fond of gazing into mirrors, mate, but the one I'm holding up reveals a little more than your fuckin' bone structure.'

'Enough,' Tom says, clenching his fists. 'Say another word and I'll break your jaw.'

Dante turns his face away. A thick clot of something cold closes his throat down.

*

They do not speak or even see each other for the remainder of the day. Both guitars remain silent, as if neither man can bear to touch any symbol of their companionship. The melody and rhythms are gone.

Tom stays out of the flat all day, and only returns for a brief spell in the early indigo-tinted evening, before Dante hears him leave the flat a second time, taking the Land Rover with him. He will go on a bender, that is for sure. After wandering around the town all day in a sulk, he will drink himself stupid and end up breaking a window or blarting in the street.

After laughing, humourlessly, Dante speaks aloud in the empty flat, 'We are truly pathetic. A pair of teenage girls. We ought to be ashamed,' only stopping himself when he longs for an opportunity to share the notion with Tom.

Unable to concentrate on anything in his room, Dante shuffles about the flat. Whether messing with a snack or slouching on the couch, the cuts and bruises on his body refuse to let him concentrate on anything, or relax or forget. Every time he sees Eliot's collection of books, stacked into the small wooden bookcase in the lounge, he wants to boot them all over the floor. They seem to mock him: a symbol of adolescent delusion. All he wants is to leave. There is no way he can spend another night in the flat.

THIRTY

'Where are you, buddy?' Dante calls out, but the wind snatches his words from the air and throws them away like a handful of sand.

He wanders around the East Sands and harbour. There has been no sign of Tom for twenty-four hours. The beach here is not as spectacular as the West Sands, but the thought of going back there fills him with dread. He just needs to be outdoors, to clear his thoughts of conspiracy, and the fretting and paranoia. But even nature seems to have turned against him. Screwing up his eyes against the salt spray, he spits a tendril of hair from his mouth and replaces it with a cigarette. Out at sea, the water is a dull grey. It stretches between the rusty shallows to the thin dark line of the horizon. The clouds look like dirty snow and move sluggishly to erase any peek of brightness above them.

The late summer has given way to skies that remain dark after sunrise, and brood throughout the day as if impatient for the return of night. The change in the weather occurred suddenly. It is as if he was deceived on his arrival by the bright sun and blue skies and their false promises of eternal spring in this coastal suntrap. Now the weather shades the morning brightness and swallows the afternoon light, threatening a long and terrible winter.

And somewhere under these unfriendly skies, Tom also walks alone with his thoughts. But where? He took the Land Rover and only returned yesterday evening to take his share of the money. Something Dante only discovered before he left for the harbour this morning. To his lasting shame, and Tom's equally enduring indifference, neither of them possesses a bank account. Following the non-payment of his student debts, and Tom's irregular employment history, at the age of twenty-six it has been deemed by banks and building societies that neither of them can be trusted with a cash card. Hidden inside a guitar case, their stash of paper notes was to have been carefully meted out in Scotland until the second album was finished. An early division of their means was never envisaged when they left Birmingham.

He's paid no attention to their troubled friendship since they arrived. But after everything that has happened so quickly and unexpectedly, how can he blame himself for the confrontation? In truth, it has been brewing and threatening to spill over for years. Tom's relationship with Imogen loosened the pin from the grenade destined to go off since they began living exclusively in each other's pockets, for the five years following Dante's graduation. Perhaps it isn't natural for two grown men to have grown inseparable. Has the band been an excuse to spurn an ordinary life? he wonders. Was it a sophisticated refuge for two misfits? Does it represent their failure at life? And even if they have talent, what does it mean if they are now destined to lose their friendship and song-writing partnership? If only Tom understood what he's seen in St Andrews, what he alone has experienced, then it would be different. They could escape together.

Three Tornado jets crack the sky and break his trance.

They shriek beneath the clouds like black, spiky dragons and then drop down, beyond the town, into the narrow crevice of the Eden Estuary. Dante turns his collar up and walks back along the beach toward the pier. The wind pushes at his back, like the hand of an annoyed guardian, determined to hurry him along. Resisting it, and increasingly angered at something else he is at the whim of, he deliberately makes a slow drift toward the town until the weather responds by launching a new offensive against his bowed shoulders. Rain adds a serrated bite to every gust of the punishing wind. By the time he reaches the fishing vessels bobbing inside the oxbow harbour, he has little idea whether it is the sea spray or the rain that proves most effective at slapping his numb head and stinging his exposed earlobes.

Following his first and reluctant night alone in the flat, he packed their bags and then cleaned the flat of their nervous occupancy, a means of keeping himself busy and a reinforcement of his decision that he and Tom quit St Andrews without delay. But he waited alone in the flat, staying awake all night and dozing through the morning that followed, occasionally disturbed by the sound of an engine more powerful than a car rumbling down the East Scores, at which he had rushed, in vain, to the front door hoping to see his Land Rover idling at the kerb. At times he would stop his agitated pacing about the lounge and his room, overcome by an urge to laugh madly at what has befallen him in Scotland. But he never dwelt on his stay for long before the unpleasant images blew into his mind, ragged and animate fragments from dreams and darkened beaches, flung forward from where they had been banished, before he stopped the train of thought, clutched his face, and, by an act of will, forced them back whence they had come.

In the past, when times were hard, playing the guitar was good therapy, and he was always able to withdraw for days and reach inside himself for a song. Or reading a book could be useful in counteracting his tendency to wallow in doubt or fear. But not now. Those distractions seem trivial. A struggle between life and death, between friendship and abandonment, occupies him completely. This is the biggest challenge of his life, and he can focus on nothing but the imagined return of his friend.

Buffeted and whipped by the wind, and slipping over twice to muddy his knees, he climbs around the bottom of the pier and makes slow progress up the grassy hill to the cathedral and the Scores. Never has he felt so insignificant – a plaything at the mercy of an old place that shuns the outsider. The sea spits at him, the wind shoves him, and the town now refuses to please his eye since it has swallowed Tom. Its graceful lines become the edges of cruel defences, the crumbling walls of the castle and cathedral a promise of ruin; windows are empty black sockets, the wide streets an arena for him to stumble and trip through as he is persecuted from the pavement. All the doors are shut to him.

Back in the town, scant drifts of people look past him as they hurry by. No one will meet his eye. Shop assistants look askance at his drawn and bruised face. They serve him quickly to encourage him off the premises and on his way.

His only consolation, and a blessing he counts hourly, is that there has been no further sign of Eliot or Beth. If he had seen either face again, now having grown in his mind to detestable proportions, he is sure he would have fled to the nearest railway station, guitar in hand, and leaped upon the first train bound for England.

And what more can he do but wait for Tom to return to the flat? The thought of going to the police and filling out a Missing Persons report makes him feel both afraid and foolish. And there is always a chance Tom has driven back to Birmingham. For years, Tom's impulsive behaviour has driven Dante to either quick-fire rage or silent exasperation. But his annoyance has always been a transitory thing, and their reconciliation was always inevitable on account of their fears of losing each other. They have no one else. There is no safety net in his estranged and disappointed parents, their collective of resentful lovers, or the casual rock-scene acquaintances picked up over the years. But who can Tom go to? He must have fled to someone. Of that Dante is certain; Tom can never exist on his own for long. And that only leaves Imogen.

In a phone box, on the westerly end of North Street, he finds himself overcome by a sudden anxiety. He raises the receiver and replaces it three times. If he is honest with himself, separating himself from Imogen was a major motivation in his desire to leave Birmingham. Just hearing her voice on the phone still causes him pain, and watching Tom and Imogen together was, at times, unbearable. He still blames Tom for conveniently shelving his guilt over breaking up the band by launching himself straight into a new distraction with Imogen. But if that was Tom's motivation, then it was his own too. Tom seduced her before he had a chance to assert his own designs. They both saw Imogen as an escape from the mess Sister Morphine had become. And Tom's effortless triumph fuelled most of his animosity. He hates himself for it – it makes him sick with guilt and a sense of chronic immaturity.

Mistakenly and sullenly, he'd presumed Tom was set for life with Imogen, which bore the consequence of them parting anyway – at least from the suffocating and increasingly quarrelsome bond that had developed between them. Ironically, he even began to fantasise about a new start in life without Tom or the dregs of the band, in the form of a new and solitary vocation somewhere near the sea – a new musical trajectory under Eliot's direction. And when Eliot's unexpected invitation arrived, it had to be an act of fate, creating a chance for him to escape his muddled and resentful life.

But everything is clearer now. His departure from Birmingham was partly founded on his desire to hurt Tom for securing Imogen as his own. Back home, as the War Wagon was serviced, his bags packed, and his goodbyes passed around the rock scene, his friend could only watch – unsmiling, never participating, saddened. And just as they were about to shake hands, it was then Tom changed his mind about *their* girl and decided to tag along. 'Things aren't working out with Imogen,' he said. And it was all he said. Suddenly, as Dante also secretly hoped, the relocation to Scotland did not have to be faced alone, and Tom no longer had Imogen. No matter how hard he chided himself, he was unable to prevent himself secretly rejoicing over Tom's decision. Revenge was his, but now it seems manipulation and self-pity ask a heavy price.

Rubbing his stubble, Dante stands in the phone box and listens to the rain rattle against the tinted glass. His double standards aside, can he phone her after she denied him the chance to say goodbye? Blaming him for dragging Tom away from her, Imogen hung up the moment she heard his voice the day before they left for Scotland. 'Fuck it,' he whispers. Less than two weeks later, with his life in tatters, Dante punches out a familiar number on the telephone's metallic keypad. He swallows when he hears the distant sound of Imogen's phone ringing.

What can he say? Imogen, it's been a nightmare. Tom's binned me after a fight and I can't find him. Eliot is a dangerous necromancer. I contemplated an affair with his young girlfriend, thinking she could provide a replacement for you, and she tried to feed me to the Grim Reaper on our first date. He begins to grin, humourlessly. The truth is ludicrous.

'Hello,' Imogen says, her voice distant, and made more so by the noise of passing traffic outside the phone box.

Dante closes his eyes. 'Hey, Kitten.'

There follows a silence, permeated by a clicking on the line, somewhere out there in the distance of wires and poles standing in the rain. He expects her to hang up. Then decides to end the silence and his discomfort made unbearable by it. 'Imogen, I'm sorry. I know you're still pissed with me, but it's an emergency.'

'Really,' she says, instantly dismissive.

'Tom's the reason I'm calling. I need to know if he's come home.'

Silence.

'Is he there?' he prompts.

'Why would he come here?' she answers, an inflection of hope in her voice.

'Has he been in touch, then?'

'No, and I doubt whether I'll ever see that bastard again. My choice now, not his.'

'I know you're still sore, but –'

'Don't patronise me with sympathy.' Her voice trembles. 'You're as much to blame as him for what's happened.'

Dante swallows. 'Imogen, I never wanted to stir things up again. But I had to phone. I had no choice. About Tom –'

'Why should I care? I wouldn't give a damn if he dropped dead.'

'Funny you should say that.'

Imogen speaks in a thinner, breathless voice. 'Oh God, Dante. Something's happened to him.'

'I don't know. He's disappeared. Yesterday morning, we had the biggest fight of our illustrious friendship so far, and he took off in the Wagon. He still hasn't come back. I just wanted to make sure he hadn't turned up in Brum, before I sue him for stealing my granddad's motor.'

'Don't scare me like that. I've been having some dreadful dreams since you left. And I started to feel that something had gone wrong.' Dante stiffens. 'Dante. Are you still there?' Imogen asks, concern in her voice.

'Yeah. Still here. Something you said threw me a bit.'

'What did you say to make him take off?'

Dante sighs. 'A few home truths.'

'Time someone did.'

'Yeah, but now I wish I could take it back. I'm such a hypocrite with him. Always have been. It was the last thing I should have done. Everything just got on top of me. Things haven't worked out in St Andrews. In fact it's been a nightmare from day one. Let's say this place has opened my eyes to a whole new world.'

'What do you mean? I don't understand.'

'Long story.'

'You're not making sense, Dante. Where's Tom gone?'

'I have no idea. He just took off.'

Disappointment enters her voice because Tom hasn't run to her. 'Well, as you're the only person he ever listened to, it's your problem. I've washed my hands of him. Your friendship was always unhealthy. It's no surprise he's left you. It was bound to happen. All that coercion has finally backfired, Dante. But don't worry. He won't have gone far. He'll be shacked up with some bimbo who doesn't answer back, and when she's up the stick, he'll come flouncing back to you with some idea about a tour of Australia. Then you can have him all to yourself again.' Imogen's voice falters. She stops talking and starts crying. Earlier that day, he doubted his spirits could fall any further. He was wrong. 'You OK?' is all he manages to say.

'No, I'm not bloody OK. How would you feel? I have one year left at university, my whole life ahead of me and he just deserts me. It was all a mistake. I wasn't trying to entrap him. He knew my feelings about abortion.'

Dante can no longer feel his legs. 'What?'

'How can I bring a child up on my own? I live off an overdraft. I still haven't told my mum and dad.'

It is as if the blood has stilled in his veins. Dante clasps a hand to his forehead. 'Shit. Imogen, I didn't know.' He can hear her sniffing over the static on the line. He swallows the lump in his throat. 'Tom never said anything. I just can't believe it.' You poor, sweet girl, he wants to say. We deserve everything we get, he wants to shout. Guilt chokes him. And beneath that, and not for the first time since he's befriended

Tom, he feels like a rueful parent, summoned to a head-master's office after school hours because his child has been disruptive again. 'I don't know what to say,' he offers. 'I really don't. This is so fucked up. Why didn't he . . .' But everything makes sense now. Their argument must have upset some brimming vat of remorse inside of Tom. 'What are you going to do?' he quick-fires without thinking.

'How do I know?' she sobs back.

'Oh Jesus, this is just too much,' he says to himself.

'Don't bother yourself with it. It's not your problem.'

Dante clenches his jaw. 'Don't say that. When I find that fuck, I'll really kick his arse. Do you think I'd have let him come up here if I knew you were pregnant? Jesus, Imogen, you know me better than that.'

'I didn't know what to think.'

'I promise you,' he says. 'I'll sort this out. I'm going to find him and slap him awake.'

'I don't want him back, Dante. I mean it. I couldn't stand him dragging his heels. He'd never be faithful. I'm through with him. I told him before he left.'

It's going to be a beautiful baby with you two as parents, he thinks, stupidly. 'Look Imogen, my money's running out. I don't have any more change. I'll get in touch again, soon. I'll send – Shit! I'm down to ten pee – I'll send a card with the address on if you need to write in an emergency. OK?'

Imogen sniffs.

'I'll sort this out, I promise. Just hang in there –' After a series of infuriating beeps, the call is terminated.

By the time Dante has called in at a dozen guesthouses on Murray Park, his clothes are sodden. The rain hits his head from all sides as he darts between the tall and sombre Victorian buildings. Carried by whining gusts of wind, it whips through the hard valleys of the streets, as if seeking him out to slap his face whenever he turns to stare its fury down.

Ringing the doorbells of every guesthouse, he watches the owners shuffle through their warm receptions, warily, to peer at him through the glass or crack in the front door. Trying to smile with water dripping off the end of his nose, he asks, over and over again, if anyone called Tom has made a booking within the last two days. Each time the answer is 'No'. He struggles from one house to another until his jeans are plastered to his legs and his waterlogged leather jacket has doubled in weight.

Anger at Tom pushes him up the left side of the road; desperation pulls him down the right. The futility of the venture grows after every disappointment, but he has to stay busy, to provide a focus for the maelstrom of thoughts dizzying him. He begins to suspect Tom may have travelled to one of the outlying fishing villages or even vanished into Dundee or Edinburgh; it's a gut feeling that tells him Tom is no longer in town.

In the very last guesthouse on the street, an old woman, holding a large dog by its collar behind the glass of her porch, shouts 'No vacancies' three times before Dante forces his aching jaw to move so he can ask the familiar question. She then wanders back to her guest book and leafs through the rigid pages, while the dog watches Dante as he stands swaying and dripping on the front steps. When she finally turns and says 'No,' Dante experiences a weary glow of relief; at least he can go home.

He runs up North Street, past the cinema and Arts Centre,

to take a short cut through the Quad and rejoin the Scores. Tight jeans rub the tops of his thighs and his underwear clings inside the crack of his buttocks. With an aching back and wet socks wearing blisters on the rear of both heels, he cries out with relief at the sight of the craggy castle and entrance to the East Scores: nearly home. Through a murk of rain and fine sea spray thrown up from the cliff-base, he passes the School of Divinity and turns the gentle bend before the winding coastal path begins. When he next sees Tom, he wonders if it will come to blows.

'Bastard!' he shrieks, the moment he sees the War Wagon, parked outside the flat. He breaks from a jog into a breathless sprint. He flings himself against the front door. His numb hands fumble with the keys and he drops them twice before the door is unlocked. 'Tom!' he yells as he staggers through the warm hallway.

Silence.

He rips the clinging leather jacket from his back. It has become like a diver's wetsuit, and one arm, turned inside out, catches on his watchstrap. Swearing, he stamps on the other empty sleeve to remove the jacket completely. A spasm of pain erupts from the cuts on his back. He grits his teeth against the discomfort. Banging down the corridor, he throws the two bedroom doors open. On each mattress the bags he packed that morning are still huddled together awaiting the evacuation. There is no sign of Tom.

Clawing wet tendrils of hair from his face, Dante runs into the lounge and then the adjoining kitchen. Neither offers any evidence of Tom having returned. Confused, he races back to the bathroom, yelling 'Tom' at the top of his voice. But in there too, everything remains as he left it –

clean, empty spaces around the toilet and bath with its misty shower curtain.

He plods back to the lounge and slumps on the floor, panting with emotion. He clenches his teeth to suppress the imminent and explosive rage he is sure will wreck the flat if it breaks loose.

The Land Rover! It strikes him then. Maybe Tom left a note in the War Wagon. Through the fog of anger and frustration, he leaps to his feet, and then winces as his sand-papered thighs scream at the contact of wet denim on raw skin. Wasting no time, he pulls his sopping jacket back on, squelches down the hallway, and throws himself back into the storm.

It is perfume: faint, but still present. Among the smells of petrol, oily metal and damp seat leather, Dante can smell perfume in the War Wagon's cabin. It lingers on the driver's seat. Tom has not driven the vehicle home to the flat, a woman has. He immediately thinks of Beth and sinks back into the seat in despair, his head empty, his ears only hearing the patter of rain against the cabin roof. But no, this is not Beth's scent; he would know that anywhere. Dante sits forward and sniffs. This fragrance is different; it's not something he would associate with a young girl.

There is no reply. He bangs the door again with the side of his fist until the wood rattles in the doorframe. 'Eliot, I'm not going until you open this door!'

Yanking at the handle again, a strange sound erupts from his throat – something sharp-pitched and animal. His black hair hangs in spiky streaks across his wet and pallid face.

'He's not in there.'

Spinning around, Dante sees Janice. She stands at the other end of the basement corridor, by the stairwell door. Despite her elegant presentation in black, the senior administrator is nervous. The make-up and hair are immaculate, but there is something especially pinched about her already thin features, and something frantic about her usually cool, dismissive stare. Dante walks toward her. 'Where's Eliot? I want to see him now!'

'He won't be coming back. His contract has been cancelled,' she answers, her chin raised.

'What the fuck does that mean?'

'He's been fired.'

Dante rests a hand against a wall and stares down at his boots. 'This is too much,' he whispers.

'I doubt if you'll see him again.'

Dante looks up, sharply. 'Who, Eliot or Tom?'

Janice's expression signs a confession. She swallows.

'He's with Eliot, Beth and God knows what else. Isn't he?'

'I don't know what you mean.'

'Bullshit!'

Janice flinches, and takes a step backward to the foot of the stairs. Her body shrinks into the dark. Dante follows her, trembling with frustration and rage. 'My mate Tom has vanished, just like I was supposed to. You know what I'm saying, don't you?'

Janice turns to run up the stairs, but Dante catches her by the arm on the first bend. 'Let go!' she shrieks. But he grabs her other thin arm and presses her body into the wall. She tries to raise her knee and stab it at his groin. But her tight skirt restricts the movement, providing Dante with the opportunity to push her flat against the white plaster of the wall. The weight and force of his tensed body trap her fast. Their noses almost touch. Her eyes are wide with fear. 'I'm not as dumb as you think, lady. Eliot and his screwed-up girlfriend tried to give me to something. Did you know that?'

She turns her head away, her features crumpling.

'I didn't work out,' he says. 'And so they've turned their attention to Tom. Gullible, impetuous Tom who can't keep his dick to himself. Beth will take advantage of that, won't she? He's been gone since yesterday, Janice. You can understand why he needs my help, or are you a part of Eliot's little coven too?'

'Stop it!'

'No! I saw the way you looked at Eliot way back on that glorious day when the great man shook my hand. You and Eliot have history. I don't care what kind of crazy shit has been going down in this quaint little town, but my patience has run dry. I want answers now.'

'I warned you. I told you not to come back.'

'But not loud enough. Eliot's out of control and I found out the hard way. What's he done, Janice?'

'I don't know.'

'Liar!'

Janice begins to sob. The strength drains from her arms. She collapses against him, her thin wrists going limp in the tight fetters of his hands. 'I saw Eliot with your friend . . . Yesterday.'

'Where?'

'In Eliot's study. Your friend went down there.'

'Two guilty boys. A sheep and a wolf!' Dante pauses to breathe deep. 'And?'

341

'Don't know. They were still here when I went home. I haven't seen either of them since.'

He watches her eyes keenly for the slightest flicker of deceit. 'You're lying.'

Janice stops crying. Her glossy lips part, and she bares her bright teeth in a snarl she speaks through. 'I don't know anything else, you little shit. And there are at least five members of staff in the building, so if you don't let go of me I'll make sure they hear me scream.'

'Yeah! And we can both go down to see Johnny Law and explain the mysterious disappearance of my friend. Now, where does Eliot live?'

Janice swallows. 'Strathkinness. The faculty cottage. But he loses the residence with the job.'

'But he'll get some time before the eviction. Eliot works fast. Two dates with Beth and Tom will be dead.'

She shakes her head. 'I've said enough. And I've heard enough. I won't have anything more to do with this.'

He squeezes her wrists. 'Yes, you will.'

Her eyes narrow. 'Make me.'

Dante releases her and steps back, breathing hard.

'Go on, hit me,' Janice says, smiling.

He shakes his head. 'You'd probably get a kick out of it.'

She swings her hand at the side of his face. Dante catches the thin wrist, making the gold bracelets clatter, before seizing her narrow chin with his free hand. He squeezes her mouth until her eyes water and then stops, disgusted with himself.

He looks at the trembling woman, about to fall apart, and suddenly wants to apologise. They stare at each other, both seeming to realise in an instant exactly what Eliot has reduced them to. 'We're going upstairs to your office, Janice. You're going to make a phone call to one of your poncy friends who took a special interest in me at the Orientation. You can tell them I'm coming over and I mean business. After that, you are going to give me Eliot's address.'

Janice straightens her clothes, the emotion seeping out of her in quick breaths. She teeters up the remaining stairs, and steadies herself with both hands as she climbs. Dante follows her back to the office in silence, shivering as the rain steams off him. The sudden change in temperature and his outburst at Janice make him feel lightheaded and sick.

Janice phones the Proctor first. His secretary tells Janice the Proctor is out. Dante clenches his fists with frustration. Janice misreads it as anger and quickly punches out the Hebdomidar's number. 'Hello, Marcia,' she says, fighting to keep her voice under control. 'Is Arthur in? Oh, I see.' She then looks up at Dante. 'He's busy. You'll have to make an appointment.'

'It's an emergency. Tell her,' Dante instructs.

Janice obeys. She repeats his line, frowns, and then hangs up. 'He can't see anyone before ten tomorrow morning,' she says in a thin voice that suggests tears are not far away. 'You can go and bully him for the information then.'

Dante points a finger at Janice. 'You people are crazy. None of your qualifications and Greek salad mean shit. People are dying in this town and you know it. If I get stalled again by any of you, I'll get the truth with my fists. That's warning number one; there won't be another.' Dante storms out of the office and runs into the rain. Ten o'clock the following morning may be too late; Arthur Spencer can cancel the rest of his appointments for the day.

THIRTY-ONE

Huddled into himself against the rain, his head bowed beneath the angry skies of the afternoon, Arthur Spencer walks back to his office. His pace is brisk. During his lunch break he only pecked at a sandwich, but managed to drink three cups of coffee he now regrets. Wheezy from the effort of moving faster than is comfortable, he is propelled by the urgency of his thoughts. Hurrying through the wet Quad, he wonders if things will change for the better with Eliot removed from his post: if this is at all possible after so long under the burden of what they know.

Eliot has been fired – the Chancellor endorsed the termination of contract, and the Principal was also adamant that he go after reviewing Eliot's slipshod contribution to the last academic year. There is no longer room for eccentrics to shelter beneath the antique roofs of an old university. Things have changed; results are monitored. Everyone is assessed. Edinburgh has beaten St Andrews in the national polls for excellence. The university must function as a business to survive. And, without the lecturing post, Eliot is required to vacate the cottage in Strathkinness. There will be nothing for him to do but leave the area. With Beth in tow?

A success? An end to the anxiety that curdles his insides and never gives him a moment's peace? Especially at night, when all the day's distractions cease, and he is left alone with his thoughts. With so many thoughts and with so many memories he tries to erase and then rebuild anew in better terms. It has always been his aim to add a light of reason to what Eliot has done. And when he fails, he tries again, and then again, until he no longer trusts any of his recollections of Eliot from the previous six months. But the feeling, the sense, the instinct that something is wrong, never goes away. Something in his conscience occasionally begs him to make a confession to the authorities, no matter the damage to his reputation. And when the impulse to come clean subsides, in weakness he is prepared to wait and hope it will all end, naturally and discreetly. Harry made the final decision about Eliot. He made all the other decisions too. But how long has he, along with Harry and Janice, concealed what they know about Eliot? How can the other two stand another day of it?

And today marks the time he most looks forward to – the week before the first Monday of term, starting a new academic year, when he gets his first sighting of the students. But his attempt at finding any of his customary enthusiasm fails. The sky is black with rain. Breakfast with his wife was tense. And again, like every other morning since Dante arrived, she asked him what was wrong and he refused to tell her, to explain why he slept poorly, gazed listlessly at the glowing television in the evenings, drank more than usual, and stayed up late to pace the carpet in the living room after she retired. How can he explain? Where does a civilised and educated man begin with this matter? It defies reason and taste and decorum. 'A few problems at work. Always hard seeing the budgets cut when your friends head the departments,' was all he offered his wife, and any of the others that ask after him.

It is a waiting game and Arthur doesn't like it. They have heard nothing from Eliot since his contract was officially cancelled, and he knows he can only relax if the action succeeds in forcing Eliot to leave town. Janice claims he has been living in his office for a week. Wearing the same clothes and drinking himself stupid. He accepted the news of his termination in silence; his face, she said, betrayed nothing. But the early-morning cleaners claim to have heard him ranting to himself, and sometimes he even breaks down. He is a suicide risk: Janice is convinced.

Confiding his fears in no one but Harry – who is impatient with the continual speculations Arthur indulges in to make sense of the situation – offers no relief. He no longer knows what world Eliot inhabits, or what exactly he has done. And at such a tense moment that will cancel their friendship forever, Arthur cannot rule out a reprisal.

He approaches College Gate. Housing his office on North Street, down from St Salvator's and the Quad, the building is the most solid symbol of the familiar and secure left to him. He nods at the security guard on his way into the foyer. His shoes squeak on the polished floor. The security guard smiles and then returns to his paper. It is a local and the headline reads CATTLE DISEASE CREATES CRISIS IN FIFE FARMING COMMUNITIES. Turning left along the ground-floor corridor, he approaches the General Administration area to collect his mail before beginning the afternoon's work in his office. It won't be long before some of the students begin applications for the hardship fund, he has a speech to prepare for the new postgraduate body, and he is in the middle of mediating three disputes between students and their landlords.

With a deep breath and a considerable mental effort,

Arthur pushes Eliot from his mind and enters a large, open-plan office. It is shared by Personnel Services and his secretary, Marcia. When he enters the room, the secretaries and administrators fall silent over their coffees. Talking about me again, he thinks. He smiles and feels playful, eager for the distraction. 'Thank you for the flowers,' Marcia says from behind her desk, blushing.

One of the office girls titters. 'Did I make Jeff jealous?' he asks. His voice sounds too loud.

'You made him sweat. Your bouquet was bigger than his.'

'Well, everyone knows you're my other woman.' Arthur pauses to watch the grins appear on the four young female faces in the office. He winks in the general direction of the Personnel girls.

Marcia smiles and raises an eyebrow.

'If we had our time again,' he whispers, and allows the remark to hang in the air. He raises his mail from the in-tray.

'Oh,' Marcia says. 'That blue envelope on the top. The strangest young girl delivered it about an hour ago. She just waltzed in and dropped it in front of me. "It's for Arthur," she said. And can't say I cared for her tone.'

'Do I sense a little competition?'

'Is there something you're not telling me?' Marcia says, angling her face to one side, her eyes smiling.

'I should be so lucky,' Arthur says, distractedly, as he drifts back to the door, frowning at the elegant linen envelope.

Seated in his orderly office, Arthur opens the envelope slowly, half-listening to the sounds outside – the increased traffic, the slamming car doors, and the chorus of young voices refusing to be silenced by the weather. He smiles, thinking of the youngsters exploring the town for the first time: the mixture of surprise and dread at the tradition of wearing the red undergraduate gowns; the hesitant attempts at making friends; being intimidated by the ambience of the town, which one never becomes completely accustomed to. He withdraws the note from the envelope, reads the message, and then drops the paper, as if the merest touch of it scalded his fingertips.

One hour later Arthur still sits in the same position, with the piece of notepaper on the desk where it has fallen. Since May, any contact with Eliot has agitated him. The infrequent and chance meetings between them have been tense and fleeting, resulting in Arthur's mystification or unease. Today, it has only taken three words to stop time and motion in his office: *Manes exite paterni*. 'Ghosts of my fathers go forth.' Five months have passed since he heard those words, on a night when the very fundamentals of his reason and perception were challenged. The strange girl Marcia spoke of, who delivered the note, must have been Beth.

The phone's sudden trill gives Arthur a start. He opens his eyes and takes a moment to compose himself before lifting the receiver. It is Harry. 'Arthur, we need to talk. Right now.'

'You as well,' Arthur mutters. Something has reached out to touch them both.

'I can't get through to Janice,' Harry says. 'Can you pick her up on the way over?'

'Yes,' he says, vague. Harry hangs up.

The phone rings again. Arthur picks it up in a daze. It is Marcia. 'Arthur, a young man has just been in here asking for you. The same one that was harassing Janice, I think. I tried to get him to make an appointment, but he just walked straight past me.' Arthur hears the sound of heavy boots pounding down the corridor to his office. Marcia continues talking. 'What's with young people these days? Shall I call the front desk?'

There is no knock. The door is flung wide. It strikes the wall with a bang. A picture frame shakes. Arthur's skin seems to contract a full inch all over. 'It's all right, Marcia. He's here now.' Arthur replaces the receiver.

Rising from his seat, Arthur then leans against his desk, as if he needs the support. 'Dante. This really isn't a good time. I'm just off to a meeting.'

Softly, Dante closes the door behind him. But the action seems more threatening than his entrance. 'There's never a good time in this town.'

'I can see you tomorrow, but not right now.'

'No. Right now, you and I are going to talk.'

Arthur sweeps a piece of paper off his desk and tucks it into his jacket pocket. 'If it's about Eliot, it's not a matter for discussion. His dismissal is out of my hands.'

'I don't have a problem with that. Maybe you should have booted him out a long time ago. The man's a lunatic.'

Arthur looks at Dante with surprise and, slowly, slides back into his chair. He wipes his forehead and points at a seat before his desk. Dante refuses by shaking his head. 'This won't take long. When was the last time you saw Eliot?'

Arthur eyes the cuts on Dante's face. 'Is there a problem with the research?'

'There is no bloody research. That'll put a smile on everyone's face.'

Arthur fidgets. He stops staring at Dante's broken lips and looks him in the eye. 'What makes you say that?'

'Do you think I'm incapable of reading between the lines? I've got long hair, mate, but I'm no dummy. You did your best to put me off in College Hall. Remember?'

'I was merely outlining the problems you could face.'

'Cut the crap. I want to see Eliot, and I'm not going out to that cottage alone. It's not safe to be near him.'

Arthur swallows. 'No, I wouldn't advise going. Eliot must be having a pretty tough time at the moment.'

'I don't give a monkey's. My friend has gone missing, and I know Eliot's behind it. If you don't fetch him for me, I'm going to take a walk across the road to the cop shop and get them to do it.'

Arthur raises both hands. 'You're angry. I understand.'

'What do you understand?'

'A lot more about Eliot than you.'

'Now we're talking.'

'Let me know where I can get hold of you. Do you have a phone number?'

'Don't stall. I want Eliot today.'

'Please!' Arthur shouts.

Dante flinches, surprised, finding it hard to equate the aggressive tone with Arthur. He suddenly seems unbalanced.

'Please, Dante,' he adds, in a softer voice. 'I must go immediately. I'm not stalling you, and we will talk. I give you my word. I will be in touch. Today. I promise.'

'When?'

'This evening.'

Dante scribbles his address on Arthur's desk pad. 'If you're not here by seven, I'm coming back with the police. I have a feeling you wouldn't like that. I want the answers tonight.' Dante turns on his heel and leaves the office.

Arthur pounds across town. The storm that has blown in from the sea and raged all day passes further north, allowing the town an opportunity to dry out for a short spell: a brief respite to facilitate the student invasion. And they are desperate to fully explore their new home. He can see it in the faces that watch the sky from doorways. They have been arriving all day like a victorious army, eight-thousand strong. Car engines, noisy greetings shrieked in a variety of accents, and the occasional stereo, create a triumphant fanfare. On every kerb and doorstep, young friends welcome each other back with dramatic gestures that involve the flinging of arms around each other. And before them, cyclists tear, two abreast, through the streets, weaving between the Volvos. Ordinarily, it is this motion and sound and colour that seizes his spirits and sends them soaring, but not this year. Arthur is unable to manage so much as a smile. Now, the sudden car-borne explosion of young faces and stuffed rucksacks, of rolled duvets and young blonde girls on mobile phones, fills him with dread. He watches the anxious but proud faces of parents delivering final kisses and the nervous grins of freshers, cautious in their new groups of enforced acquaintance. He can almost smell the excitement and anxiety of leaving home, rising in invisible clouds off the young first years, some of them only sixteen, who begin to line up outside the Quad to matriculate. At the top of North Street, the second, third and fourth-year students, free from Fresher halls, heave cases and boxes as they file into the Victorian houses. But is the town they flock to safe?

Arthur takes a short cut to the School of Divinity, between Salvator's Hall and Ganochy House. Administrators scuttle about with brightly coloured information packs, and bicycles are stacked in gleaming rows alongside the trim lawns. The windows of the halls have been thrown open and voices swoop down and through the courts: 'Helen, can we use hair dryers?'

'Brian, you old scratcher, when did you get back?'

'Have you got a plastic mattress in your room?'

On the Scores, the weak afternoon sunlight still manages to burnish the walls of mediaeval stone with a tinge of gold, and the wide streets seem to suck the new pilgrims up and along their gracious aisles toward the cathedral. 'We're going to the Sands,' a girl cries out from the door of her flat, beside the School of Divinity. Arthur wants to stop and tell her that she must never venture down there. It is dangerous. Someone has lost an arm and the police are clueless.

How could they know? Upon his arrival in St Andrews five years before, only Eliot sensed the unrest beneath every flagstone. It was Eliot who constantly remarked on how he could feel things, how he was able to intuit unsettling vibrations beneath his feet, and often catch the strains of distant voices from distant eras in the streets after they had been deserted by the living at night. The town was built upon land, he claimed, that seethed with unrest. Enough unrest to become power. You only had to let the imagination leap far enough to see *things*.

'So much has happened here, Arthur, and it doesn't sit well, down there, under all this stone. Don't you get a sense of that? Old things. Old beliefs. And you cannot burn old beliefs out of existence, and merely replace one system with another. Every revolution and reformation can be undone. And what of the lives and aspirations cut short here? Can't you sense them? The weight of injustice? Does it just disperse? Or does it linger for the careful eye to see, and the trained ear to hear? I wonder about this town, my friend. Reminds me of Salem. What's that you say? It's all in the past? It's history? History! A mere construct, my friend. Something we've created to make sense of our cruel, absurd and unco-ordinated scrabble through time. What do we actually know about our place amongst the stars? We're blind to anything beyond the material. There is power beneath these flagstones, Arthur. You mark my words.'

They laughed back then – he and Harry – laughed at the old vagabond. A grown man, back from North Africa, still full of the nonsense they all delighted in at Oxford. But today, as Arthur speeds across the gravel drive toward the School of Divinity, light on his feet for a big man, he doubts whether he will ever laugh at anything that Eliot said again.

Inside the School of Divinity, Janice's office is packed with students. A pair of harassed administrative assistants fire answers back at the cluster of young people gathered about the desks. Phones ring out at a continuous and annoying pitch. Arthur pushes to the front of the messy queue and asks after Janice. The assistant rolls her eyes and tells him Janice went home sick after lunch. As there isn't time to phone her at home, Arthur leaves the school alone and continues toward the Proctor's office, not pleased with the gurgling sounds issuing from his heart.

Stopping to catch his breath before the Principal's offices where Harry works, Arthur rests between rows of poplar and birch trees stretched before the grey stone wall surrounding the Principal's Gothic palace. He mops his brow and steadies himself. The brief respite of sunlight, creating so much energy in the town, was a passing thing it seems, and now another black sheet of cloud, sodden with rain, approaches from the sea. The weather turned nasty a few days ago, and now it seems the dark skies of winter are determined to perform a coup until the following spring. He can't remember it being this way before.

Students amble up and down the Scores, or recline on the benches and stone steps before the fifteenth-century halls and faculty offices. A car reverses into the last piece of empty kerb near the School of Economics. A group of girls, swathed in red wool, disembarks and click-clacks confidently in leather boots toward the nearest computer room, on their way to write e-mails.

Arthur shakes his head. What is he thinking? This is a real world of living, breathing, feeling humanity. The young people are back with their joys and woes. They eat badly and sleep late. They write essays on political relations or construct molecules from plastic beads and rods. They have parties and drink until they are sick, and play practical jokes, and fall asleep in the library. They posture and fight and form relationships and friendships and laugh and find themselves while they are doing this. There is no room in this place for Eliot's old shadows. The macabre is the work of the imagination. Eliot is eccentric. Who knows what facility the mind possesses to tilt the world and distort it – to see what is not there?

'Pain is energy, Arthur. Suffering leaves its own fingerprints. Half-seen whorls on the stones we walk. You must have known religious fervour once, Arthur. Didn't you read theology for a while? Use it, man. Revive it. Look through your god and go up your own mountain. Look hard enough and you will see.'

Arthur removes his coat. Harry closes the door and nods toward a chair, both men too distracted for the playful greetings they usually share. 'No Janice?' Harry asks.

'A sudden illness, apparently,' Arthur replies.

Harry shrugs and collapses into his chair. Air rushes from the cushion with a hiss. 'I wanted a word with you, Arthur. By the look on your face, I think you could pre-empt the topic.'

Arthur pushes his hands along the arm of his chair; his dry fingers make a squeaking sound as if they are made of rubber. 'You too have been in receipt of a note.'

Harry nods and tosses an envelope across the desk toward him. The envelope matches his: expensive sky-blue linen paper. Arthur retrieves the note. One of his eyelids starts to twitch as he reads it; he breathes heavily through his nose. Written in the same hand, but a different message: *Dies Irae*.

'Day of wrath,' Harry says, his grey eyes looking toward the window. 'In May, it was the last thing Eliot said to me, as we pulled Beth out of his cellar.'

Arthur is surprised. 'Really? You never –'

Harry raises a hand. 'Kept it to myself. I thought it was just a part of the usual gibberish he is famous for.'

'That night, do you remember what Beth repeated in the back of your car?'

'She was in shock.'

'Yes, but she said something. And I took it home with me. Up here –' Arthur taps his head '– and made a quick translation. A letter arrived at the Gate, today. It appears Beth wasn't completely out of her wits that night. She wants to remind me of it.' Harry nods, as if graciously accepting bad news. Arthur fishes the note from the pocket of his jacket and slides it across the desk to Harry. 'Look.'

Harry picks up the paper. He unfolds it slowly, reads the note and replaces it on the desk. 'From Caesarius, I think. Eliot was fond of that.'

Arthur nods. 'Amongst other things. The inscription reads: ghosts of my fathers go forth.'

Harry nods, and then places his hands together with the index fingers touching his lower lip, as if in prayer.

'What do they want?' Arthur asks.

'Eliot's trying to frighten us through the girl. Nothing more. These cryptic notes are churlish gestures. For not believing in his little miracles. He's playing a game.' Harry finishes with a sly smile.

Arthur mops his brow with a clean handkerchief. 'Maybe it's not Eliot. I've been giving that night a lot of thought. Something about Beth changed. Fundamentally, she changed. Her character, her attitude. And look at her since. Anyone can see she's different. And the same goes for her relationship with Eliot. It's all wrong. He's frightened of her. Don't you sense it? Think about it.' Arthur closes his eyes and sighs. 'Harry, we should've bloody done something when we had the chance. We swept it under the carpet because we didn't want to understand what they'd been doing out there.'

'Arthur, please. Eliot had been filling her head with his nonsense for months. She had a shock in that cellar. We all did.'

Arthur raises his hands from the arms of his chair in

exasperation. 'But she went back to him. Back to that wretched place. Who in their right mind would ever have gone back after what we saw? Not unless they were no longer in control of themselves.'

Harry chuckles. 'Arthur, you have said so yourself: Eliot is a clever mesmer. A trickster. We have to stay rational. It's time to put it all behind us, and not to drop our guard. We don't know what we saw. Beth was a loner. So was Ben. Both perfect for Eliot. Susceptible to him. Whatever he did to their minds, it's on his hands and not ours. And let's not let him do the same to us. Isn't that what we agreed upon?

'With no salary, he will simply have to leave St Andrews. He'll drift away in his own time, and Beth will follow. No more handouts, Arthur. We haven't betrayed Eliot, we've looked out for ourselves. We have acted according to our responsibilities and we have acted correctly.'

Incredulous at Harry's calm, Arthur rises from his chair and begins pacing the floor before Harry's desk. 'He knows where we live. Or he could just turn up at College Gate or right here in your office. There must be something else we can do. To make sure he will go.'

'A contract killer?' the Proctor ventures, before laughing at the quick twitch of shock on Arthur's face.

'How can you joke? I think the students are in danger. What about that arm on the West Sands? What am I to think of that? And it gets worse. The lad Eliot hauled up here from Birmingham to be his assistant – the hairy one – he came to see me today. He said his friend had gone missing. Something happened between them and Eliot. And now his friend . . .' Arthur pauses. 'What is it?'

Harry straightens in his chair. A frown cuts across his

forehead. 'That is why I have called you here, Arthur. There have been inquiries.'

'Inquiries? What kind of inquiries? The police?'

'Not quite. Or should I say, not yet,' Harry replies, spreading his palms in a characteristic appeal for calm. 'Something far worse than the police to be precise. Parents, Arthur. According to Peter in Accommodation, over the last fortnight a number of very concerned parents have been phoning some of the house wardens about their missing children. I expect you people in Welfare will be the next to hear. And as you'd expect, tongues are beginning to wag.'

'Beth's mother? She's here again?' Arthur says, his voice a whisper.

'No. But a lad called Walter Slater did not show up for his flight to Greece, and his mother has heard nothing from him in a week. A Mrs Skidmore wants to know what has happened to her daughter, Maria, and the parents of Rick Leech have asked me if their only son is in trouble again. I'm not so worried about him, he has discipline problems. But the others were all good students, who stayed over the summer to finish their work.'

Arthur's face turns ashen. 'So many,' he murmurs. Then he raises his voice. It becomes shrill. 'Why did you wait to tell me?'

'What could I say? I have no idea where they are. Two of them disappeared overnight and left their doors open. We cannot keep an eye on every student.'

'Eliot. He is responsible.'

'They were not divinity students. To my knowledge he may have had no contact with any of them. And you know what young people are like, Arthur. They just take off. They

358

don't always think. My own sons are the same. I am sure there is an innocent explanation, and that this is nothing more than coincidence. But if they are connected to Beth, or Eliot, we shall have to be prepared, old man.'

Arthur sits down, heavily. His eyes flash to the walls and then the ceiling and his small hands are unable to find a resting place. 'The friends of the missing students. They must have been told something?'

Harry shakes his head. 'Nothing. But, Arthur, listen carefully. We cannot afford a panic. I need you to keep your head over this. We are in the clear.'

'But the arm, Harry.'

'That is a matter for the police. We genuinely know nothing about it. We'd be laughed out of our jobs and this town if we even mentioned Eliot's little ceremony. I brought Eliot to this town, and we decided against any mention of his escapade in May. If news of his midnight shenanigans gets out we're ruined. Think of the university's reputation. Think of the papers too. They'd wallow in it. Witchcraft in St Andrews? So, if questioned, you do not speak of it.'

Arthur closes his eyes and bows his head. Harry gazes out the window behind his chair. 'When term starts it will all blow over. Of that I am sure. Eliot will be gone, and the missing students will show up and everything will return to the way it was. We have no reason to believe otherwise. What I am asking for, what I am insisting upon, is discretion. If you should be questioned, you say nothing about the night in May. Nothing. It's sink or swim time, Arthur. And as our present connection to him is tenuous at best, we'd best observe public relations.' Harry exhales with an air of satisfaction. A little colour returns to his cheeks.

Arthur stands up. 'Sorry, Harry. I can't agree. What if the students don't come back? And if they do, what if they come back like Beth? Brainwashed. We can't ignore this. If that Dante chap wasn't here maybe I'd give it a go, and carry on turning a blind eye. But I can't. It's gone too far.'

Harry turns swiftly, but speaks slowly. 'Have you taken leave of your senses?'

'Harry, no one blames you for bringing Eliot to St Andrews. He was a friend and you helped him. But we both made a terrible error of judgement before the summer. We should have notified the authorities the moment he mixed a student up in his madness. The young man, Dante, has threatened to go to the police unless we provide answers. And quickly.' He pauses, and then raises his chin, defiant. 'I made him a promise. I'm going to see him tonight. He has a right to know about May.'

Harry closes his eyes. 'Jesus wept. Sit down, Arthur.'

'No. His friend has disappeared and he's desperate. You didn't see his face. He means it. What's more, he seems convinced Eliot's behind it. If inquiries are made, he'll point the finger at us. We made the mistake of trying to warn him at the Orientation.'

Arthur sees the telltale signs of strain reappear on his friend's face. He wonders if Harry would dare to threaten him. 'And what precisely will it achieve?' Harry asks. 'You explain to this Dante character that we saw something in Eliot's cottage. Shortly followed by the suicide of one research student while the other began to jabber in Latin. You are the Hebdomidar of this university, for Christ's sake. Do you have any idea how absurd you will sound?'

'Sorry, Harry, my mind's made up. He can help us.'

'How?'

'He wants to find Eliot. I believe he wants to force a confrontation about the whereabouts of his friend. And something Dante said to me at the Orientation, about *Banquet for the Damned*, struck a chord. He's not a sceptic like you and I. This Dante is far more receptive to Eliot's ravings.'

'I still don't follow.'

'He believes, Harry. If he thought it was a murder or kidnapping, he'd have been to the police already. But he hasn't. Why? Because he believes. He believes Eliot has done something incredible. Something so fantastic the authorities would laugh at his story. We both saw something in that cellar in May. We don't know what and decided it best not to speculate. Or maybe, over time, our minds have told us we never saw what we thought we saw. I don't know anymore. But it's time to recruit an ally who doesn't question the situation. Someone young and angry enough to probe. To push Eliot and to find out what really *was* achieved back then. So I say we go to Dante this evening, and we tell him about Eliot's ceremony and what we saw. And we tell him what we know of Eliot's most recent work. Remember the paper he delivered at Cambridge about the psychic energy trapped in this town? He was laughed off the stage. He disgraced himself. But what if he was telling the truth, or at least what he thought was the truth? That he had actually communed with something here. Something that wanted to come back. If Eliot and Beth believe it, who knows what they're capable of? But let Dante do the work. And if there is a connection between Eliot's experiments and the students, he might uncover something about the missing ones.'

After a moment of silence, as Harry looks down at his hands, he says, 'You are sure he will go along with this?'

'Yes. And the information need never have come from us. But it's time to know, Harry. Time to really know what Eliot has done.'

Harry says nothing, but nods his head in reluctant assent.

THIRTY-TWO

'What is it, dear?' Marcia asks, poised by the filing cabinet in Arthur's office; tall, her glamour subtle but not faded. 'You look worried. More than usual.' The handsome face is turned to him, smiling, full of sympathy, the eyebrows raised in concern. Arthur pushes a set of crisp papers to the side of his desk and sighs. 'Few things on my mind,' he says, sulky in the way that always seizes her attention and softens her voice.

'Can I get you a coffee?'

'No thanks. I have to get off. I have someone to see.'

She turns her body around. Whispers escape from inside her tweed suit. His ears are attuned to them. 'You can talk to me, Arthur.' His name is spoken, so softly.

Looking up, his vision blurs, then clears, and focuses on her face, broad enough to carry the lines, to spread the mouth, painted a dark red. Her perfume wells around his desk. 'Are you going somewhere?' he asks.

'No,' she says quickly; her eyes are smiling, surprise in them now.

'You look good. The theatre, I thought,' he stumbles, not at ease, the flirting awkward when they are alone and not before an audience.

'I thought I'd treat myself –' the cabinet drawer shuts with

363

a whirr and then a click '– a little celebration. I've finished the collection.'

'Oh, you have. Good. Good,' Arthur says, relaxing, and feeling a little foolish. Her painting of course. She's dressed for dinner in celebration of finishing the seascapes. Very good from what he's seen. Her oils. One hung behind his desk. A picture of the pier. The perspective is right, the scene captured well; you know where you are, looking across the East Sands to the west with the cathedral on the hill. But there is something mournful about the picture. Are the colours too flat? Too brown and grey. Perhaps the light was poor at the time she painted it. When she presented it to him on his birthday, just after Christmas, the sombre tone surprised him. He never associated her with those colours.

'Jeff's away again, so I'm afraid it'll be dinner for one,' she says.

'Oh?'

'But I'm used to that now.'

The sense of opportunity glows inside him. The easiness of talking to her, of confessing, of using her patience and quiet smiles to ease the burden of his thoughts and thoughts and thoughts, ever circling in his head. He breathes in, dares himself, but looks down as if engaged in something of interest and says, offhand, 'It's a shame you have to celebrate alone.'

She raises an eyebrow, haughty above a green eye. 'And it's a pity you have plans.'

Silence for a moment. He coughs, looks down again, away from that eye and how it glints with suggestion. Does it? 'I doubt whether I'll be there all evening. But who knows how long these things can go on for.'

She turns away and slides the files she has placed on top

of the cabinet into her arms, where she cradles them against the side of her body, pressed to the breast, tight in wine-coloured wool. 'If you finish early, call me. I'll be in all night. Might even have cooked something nice for you.' She smiles, and through the perfume he thinks he can smell her fresh lipstick. Then she is gone, the heels of her court shoes striking a swift rhythm across the dark floorboards, which smell of polish and look dull beneath the shiny black of her heels with the tiny brass tips on the ends.

Never his mistress, as so many speculate, and as they too joke so often when in the safety of numbers, but have they just crossed a line? They have a successful and mutual sharing of woes; exchange gifts for Christmas and birthdays and anniversaries; drive each other home when their cars are in for repairs. But to visit her when Jeff, her sullen husband, is away? That has never been appropriate. But she is exactly what he needs tonight, after seeing Dante and his fierce, desperate face. After being forced to remember every detail from that night in May. He needs to confess, to be blamed and punished by the stranger who has lost his friend in the town as it darkens for winter. And he needs compassion from his secretary, whom he often thinks of when alone with his wife.

It will be a struggle with Harry there. Will he interrupt and ridicule him when he narrates the story to Dante, the one he's tried so hard to forget? 'Such a Cartesian,' Eliot used to say, with his eyes half-closed and his lips working over a cigar whenever Harry contested one of his stories after dinner. Yes, he will go to Marcia after seeing the lad. She'll untie the knots inside him. Has he not been punished enough?

THIRTY-THREE

After pouring three drinks, Dante perches on the end of his chair and faces his two guests, who sit beside each other, awkward and tense, on the couch opposite. Determined to give no sign of weakness away, which he is sure the clever administrators will pounce upon like a pair of hovering salesmen on a car lot, Dante fights against vague feelings of foolishness over his outburst in the Hebdomidar's office earlier that day. Because here they all are, suddenly, like friends.

Arthur offers weak and conciliatory smiles while the Proctor repeatedly clears his throat and ruffles through papers in the briefcase open on his lap. It is as if they have come to break bad news, but will try and avoid the task given any opportunity: neat-suited lawyers about to explain with tepid smiles that he has no case. The Proctor looks like he's changed his mind, as if he is bound to disappoint. And it is the Proctor who speaks first, to break the uncomfortable silence as much as anything: 'You told Arthur your friend is missing. May I ask for how long?'

'Not seen him since early yesterday morning. At first light,' Dante says, maintaining a hard look on his face despite his desire to fold and express his fears in a torrent at this first sign of interest in his problems. But they have to understand he is not to be trifled with anymore. The fact that

366

he's wasted the best part of the afternoon waiting for the two men to arrive sustains his resolve.

'Are you certain he's with Eliot?' the Proctor asks, his face solemn and guarded.

'No doubt about it. Tom and I had a fight. A bad one. An argument about a load of personal stuff. Nothing new there, but Tom only came home afterward to get some cash. I never saw him. Just heard him come in and he went out right after. And then, while I was out looking for him, my Land Rover was returned. It stank of perfume. Tom never drove it back here. Someone else did. Maybe Beth, but it wasn't her perfume. But someone did. They brought it here. And when I went to find Eliot, Janice told me he'd been sacked, and she admitted she saw Tom drinking with Eliot at the School of Divinity, on the day we had the bust-up. The idiot probably went over there to iron out the problems I've been having. Without knowing how dangerous Eliot is. I know he's behind it.'

'He went to Eliot of his own free will then?'

Dante feels his blood rise. 'He was angry. That's all. But Eliot took advantage of the rift between us. I just know it. When I first met Eliot, he hinted that manipulation had never been a problem for him. I think you both know what I'm saying.'

'Did he offer drugs?' the Proctor asks.

'What is this? I asked you two here so I could find out what I'm dealing with. And now you're giving me this school-teacher routine. I don't need a social worker. I need information.'

'Listen, Dante,' Arthur chirps in, smiling. 'We only want to establish the influence Eliot may have had on you. He's very clever at suggesting things and embroiling people in his little schemes. Especially young people.'

'No, no, no,' Dante says, shaking his head in frustration. 'We've gone way beyond that. It's not about starry-eyed youths eating poisoned candy. I was in awe of Eliot when I first got here, but since then I've hardly had anything to do with him. We never even discussed the work I was supposed to be doing. He deliberately avoided me and any mention of what I'd travelled up for. He fobbed me off with all kinds of excuses. He was always pissed. He was only concerned that I meet Beth. He insisted on it, so I met her. And he doesn't need drugs, she does all the work for him.' Dante pauses and watches their startled reaction at his mention of Beth. 'Eliot's probably used her to get Tom. I don't know how well you know her, but she's not to be trusted either. And while we sit here yakking, time is drifting by and my friend is in danger. I know how fast it spreads.'

The Proctor frowns. 'What spreads?' He looks and sounds sincere. Dante reaches for a cigarette. It is frustrating not knowing what the Hebdomidar and Proctor have on Eliot. For all he knows, the story about Beth and the other thing will sound like a crazy, drug-induced hallucination. Dante takes a deep drag on his cigarette. 'It starts with an illness. After you become familiar with Beth, that is, you get a really bad fever with nightmares you just wouldn't believe. Your body weakens and you go delusional. It's like you're being prepared for the other one.'

The Proctor wrestles with a smile. 'The other one? I don't follow.' But Arthur leans forward on the couch and searches Dante's face.

'Yeah, the other one,' Dante says, taken aback by Arthur's

sudden interest. 'The thing that Eliot and Beth have with them. I don't know what it is exactly, but it's deadly. It appeared whenever I met Beth. She calls it somehow. It sounds crazy, I know, but it wanted me. That's the only reason Eliot asked me up here, to use me. To give me away to whatever he and Beth have with them. I think he made a promise to someone and now he's struggling to keep it.'

'Is this a man you're referring to?' the Proctor asks, half-smiling and half-frowning with disbelief.

'It sounds ridiculous . . . But I know what I saw. Or what I experienced, to be more precise. It was like Beth put me in a trance and then this other party, this whatever it is, arrives.' His voice has weakened and he blushes in embarrassment at what he is trying to communicate. These men are strangers and not ordinary strangers; they are educated men with good jobs and positions at a top university. It seems hopeless.

'I'm sorry, Dante,' the Proctor says. 'I'm not really following and it all sounds a little too fantastic to me.'

Desperate, Dante looks to Arthur. 'But your mate knows what I'm talking about. Don't you?'

The Proctor glances at Arthur, his face stern. Arthur clears his throat and then speaks in the practised tone of a man accustomed to giving sympathetic advice. 'Tell me, Dante. Tell me exactly what you saw.'

Dante takes a deep breath and fixes his attention solely on the Hebdomidar. 'First time I knew something was amiss was in St Mary's Court, late at night. I'd been instructed to meet Beth there, at a certain time when no one was around. And then again down on the beach a few days back. She came and made me uncomfortable right from the start. She was . . . She was always so evasive, like Eliot, but in a more dreamy way, like she was never all there. Like her mind was on some other thing, elsewhere. But although I started off being all confused, she made me relax. She would kiss me. Not in a soppy romantic way, but viciously. She'd cut my mouth with her teeth. Don't start looking at me like that. It was never like that. No sex or anything. It was suggested, but that wasn't what she wanted. No, she wanted me half-conscious. She'd break my resolve somehow until I felt faint, or sleepy, and then . . .' Both men are visibly puzzled and uncomfortable with the intimacy of his confession, but Dante struggles on. 'And then I became aware that she was not alone. It was like something would arrive. Someone in the shadows or just out of sight. I could feel it more than see it. Like the shadows were moving, and there was always this wind. Subtle but cold. And sounds too, like something in the distance was being blown toward me.

'In St Mary's Court it chased me onto the street. And I only just made it too. But on the beach it got hold of me. It dragged me down to the sand and I was knocked unconscious. Jesus, it's so quick. You don't have a chance.' Dante drops his head and stares at the floor, desperate to stop the quiver in his voice and the lump in his throat from taking control.

'But you're still here,' the Proctor says.

'Johnny Law . . . I mean, the police, turned up the second time. They were patrolling the beach, because of that arm they found down there, and they saw my Land Rover. They didn't waste any time getting across to it either. That's the only reason I'm here and still alive. Something's got the local fuzz spooked, that's for sure. They must have startled them. Beth and her . . . companion.'

'It could have been a matter of something Beth suggested to you. She made you think someone was there,' the Proctor says quickly. Dante shakes his head from side to side. 'But Beth is very beautiful,' the Proctor continues. 'And you succumbed to that. And Eliot is very clever. You were in awe of him and of what he wrote and said to you. Perhaps they made you imagine it.'

'No way. Something was there with Beth. Both times.'

'Do you realise what you're asking us to believe? That Eliot has managed to somehow summon this, this spectre out of thin air. An evil spirit? Come on, Dante. We're all intelligent men here.'

'I know how it sounds. I've had a hard time accepting it myself. But the more I saw of Beth, the more I became convinced. She's not some kind of innocent and seductive girl either. Don't be fooled. She's either insane or . . .' Dante's voice trails off. He studies the two men before him. Arthur fidgets as if in anticipation of hearing something unpleasant. The Proctor's face stiffens in preparation to slam or deny anything he says. 'It isn't Beth,' Dante says. 'Not anymore. Not the girl she must have been. There's something inside her.'

The Proctor finally titters with relief and eases back on the settee. The playful creases at the sides of his mouth broaden into a smile.

'Eliot used her,' Dante continues. 'Maybe he had to. Maybe he used her as some kind of medium, like the men he used in *Banquet*, to deliver messages from the other side. Eliot spent his whole life believing in it. And for a reason, I reckon now. Why else would someone like Eliot, from Oxford, respected for his studies, who never made a penny from his work, carry on searching for something unless he was sure of finding it somewhere? Like here. There's no way he'd continue chasing something that he knew didn't exist. Eliot cracked a code he spent a lifetime studying, and it all went wrong. There's no doubt in my mind. Not now. Not after what I've been through.'

'Come on, man,' the Proctor says.

Dante's face flushes red. 'Don't knock it, mate. I'm not an intellectual, but you don't need to be. All you need is your instincts. Maybe I am a naive drifter who thought the sun shone out of Eliot's arse. But things have changed. We're talking about people's lives here, so don't laugh at me. My life is on the line. I know it. I'm perfect for him. A dupe, a nobody, the sacrifice. Eliot needs me for something he brought into St Andrews. Maybe he pulled it up by mistake and now it's out of control. I don't know, but you only have to look at him to know he's got little control of the situation. No control of whatever is loose in your university and inside Beth –' Both men shift on the settee and exchange glances as if they've been stopped in the street by a lunatic with a message from the other side. 'I didn't play ball. Don't you understand? It needed me. Beth and this thing are killing people for some reason. To stay around, maybe. To find hosts, or something. I don't know. But what I'm saying is the absolute truth.'

The Proctor closes his briefcase with a snap and raises both hands. 'I'm sorry. This is absurd. I thought we met to discuss Eliot. To determine any foul play. This talk of possession and what-have-you is sheer nonsense.'

In exasperation, Dante looks to Arthur. The Hebdomidar's face is pale and troubled; he knots his chubby fingers in his lap. 'The lad has said enough,' he says in a quiet though serious voice. 'So tell him, Harry. Stop bloody stalling and tell him why we're here. It's not right to mock him.' The Proctor stares at his partner with a mixture of pity and shock. 'Tell him about May, Harry. Or I will.'

The Proctor turns his face away from both of them, looks at the ceiling, and mutters something to himself out of exasperation.

'May?' Dante asks.

Arthur nods. 'We were both witnesses to a rather unfortunate episode in the spring. And despite the fact that neither of us is prone to believing anything that Eliot has claimed to have seen over the years, something went wrong with his work. We may have humoured him as friends, but until that moment we'd never suspected a sinister aspect to his studies of the occult in St Andrews. But in May, our problems with Eliot began in earnest. They have gradually escalated to the present situation of which you speak.'

'So you believe what I'm telling you –' Dante begins, but the Proctor interrupts.

'Now stop, Arthur. Really. Listen to yourself. I'm telling you to think very carefully about what you're saying. Think, man.'

'Let him have his say,' Dante says. 'The time for rational explanations and back-pedalling and covering your tracks is over. Like Eliot always said, it's time to use a little imagination. I'm not going to go running to some newspaper and ruin your reputation. If that's what scares you, I understand. But that's not my game or style. My friend's gone missing and I want him back. That's all. And today, every student

I've watched roll into this town is in danger. You can deny it for as long as you want, but things are going to get worse.'

'We have no choice but to tell him,' Arthur says.

The Proctor straightens his sleeves and stands up. 'It's nonsense. Speculation and superstition. If we can't talk in a sensible manner, then I'm afraid I must leave.'

'Then go, Harry,' Arthur says, and he looks at Dante, who smiles and nods.

The Proctor stiffens, incredulous at his friend's defiance. Arthur finishes his whisky and coughs. 'Could I have a little more?'

'Help yourself,' Dante answers, and relaxes back into the cushions of the chair.

The Proctor removes his tie, and then, reluctantly, resumes his seat. And as the night claims the world outside, Arthur Spencer begins to narrate his story.

THIRTY-FOUR

'Toward the end of the last academic year, Eliot's behaviour was cause for a great deal of concern. He became increasingly distant, was prone to the most dramatic shifts in mood, was neglecting his duties, and, quite frankly, was making a fool of himself. Not just within his department and the university, but in the town also.

'We weren't sure what to make of it all. Our contact with him had been brief and rather tense for some time. We'd made several attempts to offer help but he wasn't interested. Similar to your own experience. Whenever we managed to catch him, he was either drunk or in such a state of excitement it made normal conversation impossible. There were altercations too. It appeared to me at the time, and I think we were in general agreement, that he'd suffered something of a collapse. A breakdown was our first thought. There had been a relationship with Janice, whom you have met, and this had fallen apart, some time before. His doing, not hers. To be candid, the end of their relationship was a result of his becoming involved with one of his students. A second-year student. A girl you know as Beth.

'But from our attempts to reason with Eliot, we did manage to fathom one thing. A single preoccupation. A belief, an unshakeable belief, that his research assistants, Beth and a young man called Ben Carter, had some ability. Second sight, he called it. Some kind of clairvoyance he'd helped them to develop. Something he wanted to test.

'He'd plucked them from the paranormal society he'd established earlier, in the previous year, before this collapse I've mentioned. You see, he'd gathered a small group of students around him. To investigate the paranormal. It was something tempting for young people.

'And the group enjoyed a kind of celebrity for a while, which increased in proportion to the weight of opposition against it. But there was little the academic authority could really do without raising concerns over civil rights in a place of higher learning. We found ourselves in an awkward position. It was an extra-curricular exercise. Eliot worked with his group in his own time, and had always been popular with his students. How could we rival that? And after all it wasn't a witches' coven, he told us. There was nothing ritualistic about the group, he said. At least, not in the beginning. All harmless. Just a small number of students with Eliot as guide. And for a while, it was seen as something quite exciting here. With the exception of Raisin week, the academic year is quite ordinary and I suppose Eliot brightened things up. But we still hoped, those that knew him well, that the interest in his group would fade. That it would disappear.

'But as soon as they caught wind of it, the Christian Fellowship, backed by several local groups, opposed his society with some vigour. So Harry and I stepped in again and asked Eliot, as a friend, to either suspend the group's activities until things blew over, or to at least be more discreet. We thought it politic to remind him of the risk he was taking with his position. But he took it badly. Us speaking to him in that way.

'And then something happened, quite suddenly, which pleased us and, more importantly, the now rather vociferous lobby in opposition to him. The paranormal group disbanded. Almost overnight. Just when both the Principal and even a local politician were being pressed to do something to intervene, Eliot's group fell apart.

'Or so it seemed. We now know he was only using the group of students as a device for drawing out those he believed were in possession of this special ability. This second sight. And once he'd discovered the individuals who would be of use to him – Beth and Ben Carter – to take his investigation one step further, he lost interest in the others and ended the meetings. And between those three, we can only imagine there then followed a series of attempts to make contact with what Eliot called the "great restlessness" in the town.

'When the last term of the year began, he abandoned his duties as a tutor and was rarely seen. Beth dropped out of her studies too. Ben still attended classes, but seemed especially distracted. And at this point we discovered, through Janice's attempts at reconciliation with Eliot, a little more about the affair with Beth. It seems she had moved out of her hall of residence and was cohabiting with Eliot.

'Imagine the outcry when it became known. Eliot was three times the age of this beautiful young girl, whose parents were clueless as to what she was doing. There was talk of coercion, manipulation, of Eliot's taking advantage of an innocent girl. Once again, it was getting out of hand. Apparently, she'd broken contact with her parents. And when a concerned mother came looking for her daughter and found the girl with Eliot, she kicked up something of a fuss around here. Who could blame her?

'But Beth's obsession was now Eliot. He and his unseen world had become her world. There was nothing anyone could do. She was old enough to make her own choices.

'We did not know a great deal about Beth before this time, save the fact that she was generally regarded as something of a loner. Very withdrawn. Maybe shy or perhaps even a little disturbed. The worst kind of girl for Eliot to become entangled with. If she had been more outgoing, more independent perhaps, and sure of her own mind, none of this may have happened. She may not have allowed herself to have been led.

'And again we tried to reason with our friend and again he refused to listen. His work had reached what he called "a significant stage" to which Beth was vital. And she was out there at his cottage, living with him, when one of the student papers got hold of *Banquet for the Damned*. An exposé of his use of drugs in the sixties circulated. Mescaline experimentation may have been nothing more than an affectation of his youth, but no one seemed ready to think so now the girl was in the picture. Things were very tense here.

'He only broke his silence at the end of the semester, to deliver a long-overdue paper at Cambridge. Harry and I travelled down with a coachful of the students, who still thought him "cool". Quite touching really, but the silence on the coach's return journey was absolute.

'His paper was billed as a discussion of Scottish witchcraft as a cultural phenomenon in pre-Reformation belief systems. But instead of delivering the expected paper, Eliot revealed the rather dramatic findings of his paranormal group's work.

'He was laughed off the stage.

'He claimed to have made some manner of direct contact with a notorious coven, and its unwholesome familiar, from the sixteenth century. He suggested the most preposterous ideas about their existing influence in St Andrews. He claimed a tradition of ghostly sightings and unexplained events was the direct result of their continuing manifestations. Tape recordings of Ben and Beth speaking as go-betweens were played during the seminar.

'I'll never understand what tempted him to play those recordings. Did he have no idea as to how people would react? I think Harry and I both realised then just how far removed he'd become from reality. One couldn't help pitying him.

'Still, Eliot was lucky in one respect. Bloody lucky the police never made inquiries. The voices of the students were awful. And as for the other sounds that one could hear in the background . . . Well, they were rather more disturbing.

'Eliot was furious with the reaction. I suppose it took him back to the personal attacks from critics he endured over *Banquet for the Damned*. But who could blame his audience? People had gathered from all over the country to hear him speak about witchcraft in a historical context, and here he was spouting the most ridiculous claptrap about the existence of spirits in St Andrews, before shocking his audience with those recordings.

'He disgraced himself. And the university. On his return to St Andrews, his position was cut right back to a rather tenuous consultancy role. There was only one year left on his contract and it was generally believed he would go once this period had concluded. He was finished. Ruined. And he brought it all upon himself.

'His drinking worsened after Cambridge. He was never the same again. And there was little more we could establish as to what exactly he was doing with Beth and Ben out at the cottage now. All three of them had withdrawn from any outside contact. It was at this point that Harry and I decided to intervene more forcibly than in any of our previous attempts. It was hard to imagine the situation worsening since the time of the paranormal society, but it was. Now, even we came to believe that students were in danger. Grave danger.

'As a last resort, we thought that what remained of our former friendship could be used to make him see reason. As Hebdomidar, I also have a responsibility for student welfare, and had a right to investigate his relationship with Ben while the young man was still matriculated as a student here. So, we visited his home.

'In Harry's car, we drove out past Knoxville and parked on the lane outside of the property he rented. I remember it being an especially cold night, but the sky was beautiful. Very clear and star-bright, with a three-quarter moon over the hills. From the road, we had a good view of the lawn and the front of the cottage. And what we saw, the moment we were out of the car, was reason for immediate concern. The place looked derelict. The state of disrepair we'd observed earlier that winter had worsened. Several tree branches had fallen against the side of the house and damaged the roof. The yard was overgrown, and the front path was completely lost under the weeds and leaf mould.

'As for the house, there wasn't a single light on inside.

Nothing beyond the roof and gables could be seen in any detail. We paused in the lane and began to wonder if Eliot even lived there anymore. It used to be such a beautiful place. The last Rector owned the cottage until his passing, and bequeathed the property to the Divinity faculty. It was the sort of home that asked for log fires, a busy kitchen, and the sound of children's voices. But not anymore. Eliot had done something to it. Harry was always impatient with any talk of the supernatural, but I remember something came over me as I stood looking at the cottage. Maybe it was just an instinct, or a notion created by the dark and these signs of dilapidation. But I can remember thinking this was more than just physical decline. If I'm not mistaken, Harry felt it too. It was the manner in which the building had developed a new character. An atmosphere, if you like. A stillness emanated from the property. It was unnatural. And it was compounded by a sudden drop in temperature when one neared the fence and front gate. You felt it. It actually became colder.

'And after what we discovered inside, neither of us has been out there again.

'This dreadful mess was another symbol of Eliot's ingratitude to us and his utter foolishness with the young, impressionable people in his charge. We were so angry at the time. Mixed with our fear was our anger. This made us shake off the chill and commit ourselves to going inside.

'What was Eliot's excuse? He was well educated. Privileged. His parents had left him a large private income. He could have chosen politics, academia. Anything for his talents. He'd been blessed with a certain kind of genius and had every material facility to support it. And yet he had chosen to drift around the world like some rootless youth, experimenting with opiates and flirting with religious cults. Slowly extinguishing his wits. This terrible building was the result of one man's criminal waste of time and ability. I remember what Harry said to me then. That we had given Eliot the greatest chance a man could have. A second chance. And it was true. In return, he'd made fools of us. We suffered as a direct result of his behaviour. Our association with him was well known, and Harry had lobbied hard to bring him to the university in the first place. And here we were outside the pitiful remains of Eliot's second chance.

'It was then I realised, we had come to say goodbye to him. Once and for all. He had sabotaged everything. It was his choice to sink.

'His phone had been cut off for weeks, so we'd been unable to announce ourselves in the normal manner, and our knocking on the door had gone unanswered. We hardly expected the police to drive by, but it took us some time to gather the courage to break in. Secretly, I braced myself for the worst.

'It seemed unlikely, but if Eliot was inside there would certainly be a dreadful scene. That I could deal with, but it was the notion of finding something much worse that worried me. Something involving Ben and Beth.

'Quite by accident, before we chose a window to break, Harry tried the handle of the front door. And to our utter surprise, we found the door to be unlocked.

'Our relief at not having to smash glass was brief, though. Nothing could have prepared us for what we found inside. Remember, with the front door closed, not a single sound could be heard from the outside of the building. Everything was still. We were in the middle of a late cold snap. There wasn't even a breath of wind in the air.

'But when the door opened, it was as if we had tripped a wire. How can I explain it? I felt that something inside was enraged at our intrusion. Imagine a storm of noise. A violence in the very air. It was as if every wall and floorboard was being pounded with a hammer. There was no light, we couldn't see beyond the doorframe, and all around us every timber and brick seemed ready to crack. The house was alive. The sheer volume of the noise forced us back to the car.

'I still don't know what prompted Harry to turn and then run back to the place. Perhaps it was the thought of a young girl being subjected to this madness. And I followed him, through the door and into the hallway. I covered my ears, but once inside the din grew worse. As if a storm, an electric storm, had crossed the threshold and become trapped inside. I could feel it in my chest – it was so loud the vibrations interfered with my breathing. I am not ashamed to say I was frightened witless. I would not have been able to stand more than a few minutes in there.

'By an empty coat rack we found the light switches, but they were useless. The electricity had been cut off too. But we carried on. With only a glimmer of moonlight coming through the reception, we went further inside. We bumped around, stumbled into one other. We were utterly disoriented by the noise. I remember looking at the ceiling and wondering what could possibly create such hellish sounds. It seemed to be coming from underground and from above us also.

'Harry led the way. We took a quick look around the ground floor. There were papers everywhere, and books. The ceiling leaked in places, and the latches had rusted the windows shut. Damp had soaked into the carpets and the furniture. It was freezing. Colder inside than it was outside.

'After the kitchen, we couldn't face going upstairs, we were ready to bolt. No one could have withstood the cold or the noise. But on our way back down the hallway to the front door, Harry saw something. A sign of life. A light under the door of the coal cellar.

'We opened the door to the cellar and realised the light was candlelight. There were stone steps leading down. They turned a corner into the cellar. We shouted for Eliot from the top of the staircase but there was no reply. Even if he was down there, I doubt he would have heard us above the racket. So we had no choice. We went down.

'Into the cellar, where the air felt dense, as if full of fog, and terribly cold. The coldest part of the house so far. It was as if it were saturated with water droplets that suddenly froze on you. I was there for no more than a few minutes and yet it got into my chest. I suffered a breathing complaint for some time after.

'There was a smell too. A mixture of things. All of it unpleasant. Tallow smoke, and sour sweat. Damp stones, and other things I can't place. Like incense, it seemed to me, but I can't be sure.

'At the bottom of the stairs, the cellar was partially lit in the middle by the candles. You couldn't see the far walls. It was dark around the edges. But I can still see the middle of that cellar. With Eliot and Beth and Ben in it, just as we found them.

'It's hard to say how long they'd been there. Or what exactly they were doing. But it was wrong. Anyone could see that.

'The centre of the floor was marked somehow. Lashed with lines, angles, circles. All criss-crossing. Marked in white chalk. With candles set on plates and saucers here and there. A circular arrangement, I think, around other things.

'They were all on the floor. Eliot and Ben lay on Beth. All of them in the middle of these marks. They were holding her down.

'Ben saw us first. His mouth opened. He said no. Shook his head. He was afraid. We all were. But we went in there. To the circle, you see. Standing still made things worse. You had to move. But we panicked Ben. He fled. Just knocked us out the way. And Eliot called out to him. Called him a fool, but made no attempt to stop him. He just kept Beth down there, on the floor, as she moved. Horrible it was. To see her mouth open like that. And her body, twisting.

'And him so fragile on top of her. No weight on him. All of it had dropped right off. Yellow too. His skin was yellow. Like jaundice. Dehydration. God knows. And on the floor I saw bottles. Medicine bottles.

'I had no strength left. But Harry called out to Eliot, who ignored us. He was busy. Keeping Beth down and watching something. Over on the far side of the room. At the edge of the candlelight. Then I noticed it too. Against the bricks where he stared. It was moving. Coming forward by going up the wall and then across the ceiling. Against the light. Against the way candles make shadows.

'It looked as if there were limbs coming from it and something about the head. Wrapped around it, but coming loose. But I couldn't be sure in the dark.

'But the way it came across to us. I don't know. I flinched. I must have turned away and fallen. I fell, and took Harry over with me. Maybe I heard a voice too. How can I be sure? No one could think straight or trust their ears or eyes in there. I've been over it again. Again and again. And now, well, who can say?

'But I remember crawling over Harry when something brushed against me. Over me. It swept over me. And I tried to get to my feet. And then she started with the worst sound of all. The girl wailing like that. It went right through me. I wanted to run. And then I stood up and I saw something. The last of it. Going up the stairs. Up it went. Like a spider on a wall. Into the dark.

'And suddenly it was silent. Completely silent.

'Beth stopped crying. She made no further sound down there. But rocked back and forth. On her own, just backward and forward. Looking at nothing, at nobody.

'And Eliot began to laugh.

'He stopped when Harry slapped him, hard.

'I wanted out of it. My mind was still full of that thing going up the stairs, into the house. The house we were still inside. But I wrapped Beth in my coat first, and she stopped the rocking. I thought she'd fainted and she was so heavy to carry, but I took her out of the cellar and out of the house. Harry came behind with Eliot.

'"Did you see it?" Eliot asked us, over and over, as if he had trouble believing it too.

'And when we were outside, in the long grass, Harry grabbed Eliot by the throat and, for a moment, I believed he would kill him. "Is this how you repay us? With your clever tricks? You've scared that girl half to death. Was it mescaline in those bottles? Are you insane?" and so on.

'Eliot grinned. "Yes, Harry," he said. "Mad as a hatter. But it came."

'But I wouldn't let him go on. No. Not like that. Pleased with himself. To have pride at a moment like that with the girl so badly off. And after the movements down there, under the house. I was overcome. I shook him. And he begged me to stop, but I kept on. I hurt him. But it meant nothing. Nothing to Eliot. He just wanted to go back inside. "It's not finished," he said. I was a bloody fool. I didn't understand, he kept telling me.

'Harry stopped me. The girl, he said. We have to take care of the girl. So I stopped. And we left Eliot on the lawn, in front of that place with the door open.

'We drove Beth to the Memorial Hospital. She was our concern, now. Eliot could go to hell. But the night would not end. When I reached into the back of the car to check on her, she was cold. I panicked. I shouted for Harry to stop the car. He pulled over. We put her on the road. There was no breath coming from her. No pulse we could feel. She was stiff with death.

'I attempted resuscitation. It did nothing. The girl, with her cold mouth, was gone. There was nothing we could do.

'We put her back in the car. Harry said we would take her to the hospital and the police would be called. I was numb. It was too much to believe. Eliot had killed her.

'And then we heard her voice. From the back seat. What could we think? Beth was alive. But there had been no pulse. No breath. I was certain.

'I turned and saw that her eyes were open. Bright eyes. Bright with life. Her mouth opened and she tried to speak. But it was so noisy with Harry driving like that, like a madman to get her to the hospital, I didn't catch what she said. I held her hand and spoke to her, but I don't think she could hear me either. It was like she was unaware of where she was.

'When she found her voice, she began to jabber. A jumble of words mostly, but in the same voice from the tapes Eliot had played at Cambridge. I didn't understand any of it. Once or twice she repeated some Latin. A chant, taught to her by Eliot, I thought. I couldn't be sure. But she was alive. That was the main thing.'

Arthur passes two pieces of paper to Dante. He has scribbled the translations beneath each inscription. 'Some of it was sent to us today. As a threat, I think.'

'What about Beth?' Dante asks, filling another glass with Jack Daniel's. 'What happened?'

Arthur looks at Harry, who remains quiet. The Proctor continues to sip his whisky and stare into space. Unperturbed, Arthur then offers a third note to Dante. On this one he has written the address of Eliot's cottage in Knoxville. 'We never found out,' Arthur says, with his hand outstretched, the note held between two fingers. 'As soon as we parked at the hospital and got her standing, she ran.'

'Ran?'

'Away from us. Back out of town. Laughing all the way.' Arthur exhales. He rubs his face, the shape of his body sunken. 'She was too quick for us. We spent the rest of the night trawling the lanes for her, all the way back to Eliot's, but we didn't find her, and Eliot had gone from the lawn. We did not go inside. We couldn't.'

'And this guy, Ben. Where did he go?'

The men exchange glances. 'He took his own life within

days. He never spoke of what happened to anyone. But he left a note. And in it, he explained "that he had to get it out of himself". Nothing more. Just that.'

'You never reported it,' Dante says, his face white with shock.

Both of his guests look at the floor.

'So what do we do now?'

Arthur shakes his round head, clueless. Harry looks Dante straight in the eye. 'Nothing.'

'Hang on.'

Harry raises his hands. 'Listen to me. Eliot's contract has been cancelled. It took a little longer than we supposed it would, but he's finished here. He and Beth will have to leave. Their influence here –'

Dante writhes in his chair. 'What's wrong with you? Eliot doesn't give a shit about the job. The job doesn't matter anymore. Forget that. It's gone way beyond that. And Beth isn't Beth. Did you learn nothing from what Arthur's just said? I can't believe you've sat on your hands for so long waiting for all this to just go away of its own free will.'

'Don't be melodramatic, Dante. Before we take any firm action, we need to know more.'

'About what? Eliot has lost the plot. He couldn't do anything if he tried. Don't you see? Beth is running things. Beth and the other thing we've all seen.'

'Think we've seen. What we've actually seen and what we think we've seen are two entirely different matters.'

Dante stands up, turns around and removes his shirt. 'They're fading, but these marks are for real.'

'Good God,' Arthur says.

Harry swallows, unable to break his stare from Dante's

back. 'She's a fanatic now. We told you. They have such strength. Lunatics, you know,' he says, but his lips hardly move.

'And you're a lunatic for wasting time, mate. We have to get out there and get Tom. He's in serious trouble. They've got him out there. This goes way beyond Eliot now. Tonight, we make a move. We go out there.'

'Out of the question,' Harry says, shaking his head.

Arthur smiles weakly in an attempt to calm him down. 'It's late, Dante.'

'I don't care.'

Shuffling forward on the couch, Arthur attempts to touch Dante, who paces up and down, pulling his shirt back on. His face is set. 'Please, Dante. Listen to me,' Arthur implores. 'I'm willing to help. With your friend. I'll come with you. We'll confront them together. And it won't be the first time I've taken someone from Eliot by force. But not tonight. We have the new postgraduate body to meet tomorrow, and my speech still needs work.' His voice starts to drift along with his attention. 'With everything else, I've fallen behind with so many things.'

Dante stops moving. He has to keep this one sweet. He is willing to help. 'All right, Arthur. I appreciate what you've told me. I mean that. I've been going out of my mind trying to cope with all this on my own. It's good to know I have an ally.' He begins to pace again. 'I've got to get out there. Tom's coming back with me. No bother there.' But his attempts at boosting his own morale fail. How far gone is Tom? He's been out there for two days now while he searched, and sat around, and listened to this pair. He should get the police now. Go to them with the incredible story and take them out to the cottage. Don't take no for an answer. Tell them it is a kidnap or something. If it blows the town wide open – what Eliot has been doing, what he's done to Beth – then so be it. These two will have to look out for themselves. If they'd done more in the beginning everything would be all right now. Arthur is a good sort, but he can't trust old long-jaw. He'll sell them out to save his name. Refuse to co-operate. And he has too much influence over Arthur. And what can Arthur do anyway? He is old and going to pieces. He is scared. They are all scared, but someone has to go and get Tom. If he goes now, out to the cottage, tonight, with or without the police, Tom can be saved. He'll get Tom and then they'll split. Leave right away. Their stuff is packed.

But what about the other thing? His fragile plans fall apart when he thinks of the sounds and the movements in the silence and the dark of St Mary's Court. What is it? What makes it come? Will it be there, waiting?

Harry collects his jacket from the arm of the chair. He looks ill. 'Thank you for the drink, Dante. But I must get off now. My wife is expecting me.'

'Sure, just take off. Let's waste another night.'

'I promise to be in touch. Tomorrow. But until then, I'd advise you to do nothing rash. It would be a mistake going to the police. What could you say? They'd laugh at you. When it's light, tomorrow, after our engagement with the postgrads, I suggest we all go out there and confront Beth. Get your friend. It'll be light. Things are different during the day. Let the whisky and emotion wear off first.'

Arthur looks at Harry with surprise and then admiration. Dante scowls. But the thought of going out to the cottage, alone and at night, fills him with dread. 'You'll call here, tomorrow?' he says, his voice heavy with disappointment.

Harry offers his hand. 'I promise. We're all involved, Dante. I know your friend is there, but he's young. He's strong. It's unlikely he'd do anything . . . Let himself . . . There is a lot at stake for all of us.'

'He is right, Dante,' Arthur says. He puts his hand on Dante's shoulder. 'Let's think of the best for all of us, eh? We'll all go tomorrow.'

Dante can't speak. This is the kind of thing his parents said when they worked out a compromise. Harry is out the door without another word.

'Tomorrow, then,' Arthur says, looking pleased with himself after his confession, as if he can think of nothing else now. On the doorstep, he pulls his collar up against the cold. He nods at Dante and then walks, wearily, away from the flat where Ben Carter once lived.

THIRTY-FIVE

'Well, it's done. I feel better for it,' Arthur says. He buttons his coat right up to his chin and folds the lapels over to further protect his fleshy neck. Behind him, Dante closes the front door of that flat, Ben Carter's flat. There was no need to have told him that. He is right on that account; the lad has enough to deal with.

'You do?' Harry says over his shoulder, his body taut with irritation, as he strides to the car: the older brother defied by the younger for the first time. 'We'll see, Arthur. I can't see any good coming from it. He's ready for the police.' Impatiently, Harry swings his long body into the Rover, sweeping his overcoat under his buttocks.

'It'll be fine. Tomorrow. It'll be fine,' Arthur says, at the kerb. The door of Harry's car slams and shakes raindrops onto his shoes. Harry removes the steering lock and, from a guilty afterthought, winds the window down. 'Lift?'

'No. I'll make my own way from here.'

'Sure?' Harry asks, half-heartedly, pleased they will not have to be awkward in the car together.

'Yes, thanks. I'm going back to the office. Something to finish off.'

Harry nods. 'Right you are. Until tomorrow.' His voice has turned sarcastic.

Let him stew, Arthur thinks. Even if it means going back out there to Eliot's cottage, they must take their share of the burden. The missing students and Dante's friend have to be found. No, there won't be a connection between the missing people and the cottage; he cannot allow thoughts like that. Think positively, a tired little voice says inside his head. A voice that once made a good suggestion or two, but now only irritates him, but he can't switch it off. But stepping out of Harry's shadow tonight makes him feel good. Not even the rain can dull that feeling, churlish as it is. The engine of Harry's car starts – a squeak, a rumble, a purr. There is a final glance from Harry's hard eyes, and then he is gone to the end of the Scores, fast and sliding past a black car idling at the kerb, its lights on half-beam. Same model as Marcia's, Arthur thinks, distractedly. It too reverses away from his sight.

Rain is sweeping across the town again, like an intolerant authority trying to clear the streets. At the open mouth of the Scores, before it narrows to a long funnel under the over-hanging limbs of ancient trees, a group of excited students darts in and out of cars and doorways, glancing at the bitter sky, their faces and voices begging for a ceasefire, to be without a care for the weather.

A sense of what tomorrow will bring makes him clench his fists inside his pockets. His fingers crush around coins and Polo mints. How he can assist Dante has yet to be established, and what exactly they are facing is still a mystery. Can their opponent be something not of this world? 'Not again,' he mutters: the endless circling and questioning, the doubts and then the belief, beginning again inside his head, and stomach, where he can feel it writhe. He's performed his part, and he was right to have done so; he's spoken his lines after a good whisky, but now the rain seems too cold, and the pavement too wet and dull, for that kind of thing, for apparitions. The town reassembles around him in real and hard shapes. Cars fill the road, late dinners are being eaten, there is a smell of cooling chip fat from Salvator's dormitory, and against the horizon a ship is seen to be still, although it moves slowly to the west.

He thinks of Marcia, which raises his spirits. He holds a memory of her, lets it grow, and allows it to pull his big body through the night air to his office, and to the bottle he keeps inside his drawer. No more thoughts of tomorrow. There will be time enough for that.

Passing the School of Divinity, Arthur wonders if Janice is really ill, or if Dante has given her a fright. And has Eliot cleared his office yet? Where will he take his books? He checks his watch. Nearly eight-thirty. There isn't time to check on Janice and, if he is quick, he can be in front of the fire at Marcia's by nine. No more delays. The very idea warms his big body. From the Scores, he takes a short cut beside the goods entrance at the rear of the Quad, and hears two girls, on the other side of Butts Wynd, running and laughing up the lane, heading toward the library to seek shelter. The weather has emptied the Quad.

The rain splashes off the top of his uncovered head, and has begun soaking through his woollen overcoat to chill his skin underneath. He follows the path circling the central lawn, past the now dripping halls of Anthropology and International Relations, to reach the cloisters of the church. Nearly there. He'll skip through the arch beside the offices in the western corner of the court to get to North Street.

But Arthur stops walking when someone calls his name

from nearby. From right behind him. A softly spoken word, just audible over the splash of rain and the torrent of distant traffic. He turns, jerky, a hand leaving his pockets, his eyes screwing up against the beat of falling water. 'Hello.'

No one there. Not between him and Salvator's stark and glassy front, where the rain seems to pause as it passes the gigantic windowpanes – the droplets made orange by the light they fall across. Arthur switches direction, cursing himself. His heels crunch on the loose stones underfoot. He faces the church, before its yawning cloisters, dull with shadow. A pale face looks out and catches his eye. There is a laugh; the face vanishes.

His other hand is out of its pocket, wielding a handkerchief. Wiping his gingery eyebrows, he squints into the dark. He walks forward. Was someone trying to get his attention? A door closes nearby, out of sight. A car skids on the other side of the church, on North Street. He walks to the steps which foot the arches, and is just about to lean in and see who has been peering out when there is a sudden flicker of motion above him. Something moving up there, on the clock tower. Beneath the red clock face, so far up the square tower walls, there are giant slits cut into the tower stone. Is there a flag up there, caught by the wind and made to snap against the parapets? He cannot see one. No, there is never a flag up there. Has an arm waved? No, that would be too dangerous, and no one is permitted to go up there anyway. The darkness hangs over the tower, and the illumination from the ground lights never makes roof level. A pigeon, then, home to roost, to escape the rain.

He carries on, eager to leave the empty Quad, and never takes his eyes from the church. He is aware that his heart is thumping. And he is even tempted to jog the short distance to his office. Now he is seeing things. Talking about the night in May must have stirred his imagination up, producing sparks as if he'd jabbed a stick into the base of an open fire. A drink. He needs a drink to put the sparks out before going to Marcia. He can't go to her like this, wet through with shaking hands.

Back in his office, with the door locked, he searches his desk. Third drawer down holds a green bottle amongst the paperclips, an orange hole punch, and a photo of Marcia at a staff fancy-dress party that he never dared take home. The bottle is half full of whisky, which splashes about inside the green glass as he raises it from the drawer and places it on his desk. It has been saved for the good and the bad. When his wife's shooting stomach pains – which she just knew were cancer because of the way her father died so suddenly – turned out to be a case of gallstones, that was the last occasion the bottle of Laphroaig saw the light.

After splashing a generous measure into a clean coffee mug, he turns the heater on full and pulls the blinds down against the rain, to dull its rapping on the glass. He drops his sopping jacket on the back of his chair and strips his shirt off, hurriedly, wanting to rid his body of its clammy tug and squelch. Pink and bulbous, his freckled belly flops over his thin belt and hangs in his lap when he takes a seat and reaches for the mug.

Panting and coughing at the liquid fire he's gulped, Arthur pushes the mug away as if he can't bear to look at it anymore, and slumps against his desk, head down, arms forward, elbows bent. In a moment he will get dressed into the fresh shirt he keeps for meetings. Over that he can wear his waterproof, hanging from the coat stand. But in a minute. For the moment, he has to get things straight inside his head, and let the whisky's warmth crawl through his gut. There it is, a hot coal glowing and spreading through his empty stomach, with rising vapours that leave a fruity taste in his mouth. His head spins.

He reaches for the mug and downs the second half. Some of it escapes from the side of his wet mouth and splashes onto his mouse mat. Now there is a peaty smell of Scotch in the office, mixed with an odour of sour sweat, and the cloying fumes of the rainwater evaporating off his clothes and skin. Arthur reaches for the phone and tries Marcia's home number. It rings four times, and then he hears Jeff's voice. It gives him a start. His head is cleared by a sudden anxiety, until he realises it is only the answering machine. He exhales and replaces the receiver. A clicking sound begins from inside the little heater beside his desk and his eyelids feel heavy. He swallows another draught of whisky, deciding it will be the last, and then turns his desk lamp off. He closes his eyes to rest them, just for a minute.

At the sound of a knock, Arthur opens bleary eyes and stands up quickly. The floor seems to rise like a wave to tip him backward, over his chair. He thrusts his hands out and seizes the top of his desk. He swallows but still can't find his voice.

'Arthur. Arthur, are you all right? The door's locked.' It is Marcia. What is she doing here so late?

The office is dark now, and insufferably hot. The only light creeps from beneath the pale-green square of the blinds covering the windows that look down upon North Street.

From the heater comes a whirring sound, that will soon become the whine of a machine trying to cool down. He checks his watch; the numbers and hands are luminous in the dark. He's slept for no more than ten minutes.

'Are you in there?' Marcia calls, from beyond the door.

'Jussa minute,' he says, and then struggles around the desk, knocking his fumey coffee cup to the floor as he scrabbles for the light switch. 'Jesus Christ,' he whispers, rubbing his forehead and squinting his eyes against the lightning that crackles in his head when the desk light snaps on. She can't see him like this, drunk, sleepy, stinking of rain and an anxious sweat. He stumbles across to the door. A pale-blue shirt hangs from a hook on the top of the door. 'Hang on,' he calls out, his voice sounding deep and unnatural as he fights to control the slur.

With the shirt draped around his shoulders, standing in his damp socks, he unlocks the door and opens it a fraction. 'Marcia. I'm not feeling too great. I phoned you just now.'

The lights are off outside, and from the dark comes the glint of her spectacles. 'You're drunk,' she whispers.

'Been a terrible day,' he says, slurring his words, and blinking his eyes in a feeble attempt to stop the suggestion of Marcia jolting before his eyes.

'Let me in.' Marcia pushes at the door handle. Arthur presses his shoulder against the edge of the door. 'Ummm. I'm not . . . Oh, I'm not decent right now. Let me put a shirt on.'

'Don't be a silly. Let me in. What on earth are you doing?' she says, her voice softening with amusement. He moves away from the door, back toward his desk, frantically trying to button his shirt over his belly. Marcia turns the main lights on with a quick downward sweep of one hand. She blinks once in the light, spots the whisky bottle, looks at his red face, and then closes the door behind her.

'Got caught in the rain like a fool after my appointment,' he says, his voice stronger, his composure returning. 'Just drying out before popping over to you, and I fell asleep.'

'Not surprised after drinking that,' she says, smiling, beside him now. 'Bet you haven't eaten. Come on, let's get you sorted out.'

'But your celebration. The collection,' he says.

'Still early. I did a little shopping first. Bought some wine and a dessert. And I had an inkling you'd end up back here.' She looks upset now. 'I want to help, Arthur. Don't you think I've noticed how strange you've been behaving? If you need help, you know I'm always here. Is it Elaine?' Arthur shakes his head at the mention of his wife. He tries to smile but it dies on his mouth. 'Is it your heart?' she whispers.

'No. Nothing like that. Something else. A professional matter. It's difficult.'

'That young man, isn't it? With all the hair. He's been making a nuisance of himself. Has he been bothering you too?'

'No, no. Look, it's hard to say.'

'He's been threatening you, hasn't he?'

Arthur licks his lips. 'It's not that straightforward.'

'Well, hiding in the dark won't solve a thing. Let's go home.'

'It's better you don't know. It really is.'

'Eliot, then. We all know about him.' She raises her eyebrow. 'You'd be surprised how much we all know.'

'We?' he says, straightening a cuff.

'Oh, you know. People talk.'

The thought of Eliot makes him want to sink back into the warmth and dark where he's been sleeping. 'In a manner of speaking, yes. Yes, he has something to do with it.'

She smiles, knowingly, pleased with her deduction. 'Come on, let's go and eat. You'll feel better. We'll get you dry. We'll get you ready. And no more of this,' she says, capping the Laphroaig. By the time his shirt is buttoned to the top, the mug has been replaced on the tray above his filing cabinet, his drawer shut, the heater switched off, and his damp jacket has been assessed, swatted, pulled back into shape and draped over her arm; he wants to kiss her. She walks to the blinds and raises them. Tilting her head downward, she stares into the street.

'What is it?' he says.

For a moment she stays quiet, as if distracted by something. And then she speaks, quickly. 'Maybe I should air the office now? No. Better not. In the morning, then, when the rain stops.' She turns and walks to the door of his office, the sound of her heels loud and decisive in his ears. They both try to open the door at the same time. Their hands touch. A moment of silence falls between them. Arthur has no idea what to say.

'It's all right, Arthur. When you're sober, you can go home. So don't look so worried.' She giggles. 'I won't pounce. Not my style. I leave that to others. But you need a bath and a hot meal.'

'Are you sure you don't mind?'

'Not at all. But do tuck your shirt in, or people really will have something to talk about.'

He laughs, and slithers into his waterproof. 'You're a treasure.'

THIRTY-SIX

Sipping coffee, Arthur reclines into plump cushions, and stretches his legs to a footstool. He feels regal, lounging on the crushed velvet seat, propped up with his drink, spoiled by a good dinner and open fire. Beneath his clothes, his skin is pink and freshly scrubbed after the hot bath Marcia ran for him before preparing the food. A faint scent of pine needles escapes from the collar of his shirt. Again his eyes grow heavy as the mulch that is chicken, steamed broccoli and roast potato is digested by his stomach. He ate quickly, having neglected lunch and eaten only a small breakfast before leaving for work that morning. And what with all the shocks the day heaped upon him, and the bitter turn in the weather, and all that lies so weighty on his mind, hasn't he the right to such an appetite and the attentions his secretary has lavished on him out of hours? It is a foolish notion, but the small deceit of him idling at the house of a handsome woman, who assists him in his professional life, pleases him. At least this is a secret, in a town full of secrets, that endangers no one. He will rest here while Marcia assembles her collection for him to see – her secret, her mystery – and then he will go home, replenished and strengthened, with a mind ready to cope with Eliot the following day.

Arthur puts the coffee mug down on a silver star-shaped

coaster and looks at the patio doors his seat is angled toward. Perhaps the sofa has been arranged this way to offer Marcia a view of the garden and the hills beyond. Does she look out there for inspiration? He'd rather be closer to the fire, with the rain lashing against the panes of glass and nothing to see out there of the garden now, save for a few branches and fronds that hang wet and limp from the bushes and trees that grow close to the house, occasionally tapping the glass.

And it is an unusual room in which he sits. Not at all what he expected to find in Marcia's home. He's pulled up outside in his car often enough, but never ventured inside. It would have surprised him if he had done so. Dark walls and an indistinct ceiling watch him from all sides. Although the lighting has been intentionally dimmed, traces of ochre and sweeping crimson peek like an ecclesiastic backdrop from among the plethora of plants and waxy creepers she grows from large ceramic and brass pots. There is little in the way of ornamentation, and not a single painting has been hung. What he's seen of the hall and the coppery kitchen is much the same. When he questioned Marcia about the gloom in her home, she confessed to preferring it that way. The change was recent, she said. Something she was trying. 'But what about Jeff?' he asked. 'Does he like it this dark inside? Is it possible to read in this light?'

'Oh, I don't worry about Jeff,' she said, and laughed gaily. 'Jeff left me,' she added, nonchalantly.

'Oh, Marcia, my dear. I'm so sorry.' He tried to think of something to say; it was a shock. Was he the last to know? But she stopped him there, before he could go any further with his stumbling. 'It's been over for a long time, really,' she said. 'I'm not sorry, though he might be.'

'But why?' he asked. He must have been mad to leave you, he wanted to say.

'Someone came between us,' she said, smiling. 'Or rather, I should say, someone found him. Woke him up. Woke us both up, really. And it's for the best.'

And after that revelation, where no tears were shed, he sat, curious about her new life alone in this dark house. She has this entire private life he's often tried to visualise, imagining a farmhouse interior, with her prints displayed on white walls, strung between beams, and a garden dramatic with colour. Everything orderly and charming, a house as elegant and gentle as its mistress. Now he's seen her real home, he feels naive, and wishes he'd not demonstrated so many of his moments of weakness and insecurity and indecisiveness before her. She is a stranger in her other life.

If he is honest, the house is not quite to his taste. It would have been preferable if Marcia had fulfilled his expectations instead of filling him with the mild unease that comes to those who realise they have underestimated someone close, and have done so for a very long time.

And there is that painting in her room. If he could change anything, it would be the oil he glimpsed on the wall behind the elaborate bed, on his way to the bathroom. He only saw it in part, and briefly at that, but it is hardly the kind of thing you would want on a bedroom wall, especially when you now sleep in the bed alone.

Arthur smiles, shaking his head gently; she is a dark horse. He'll ask her when she comes back downstairs with her collection. He'll ask her what it was. That thing, stooped over, against the smudged background that changes from a pitch black at the top of the canvas to a deep brown in the middle, and then a dirty yellow at the bottom. Is this some phase her art is going through? A way of exorcising the end of her marriage? Or is it a print from an artist she admires? He hopes so, because the figure in the picture looks like a beggar, loping along and hunched over from the weight of what it carries – a reddish-coloured sack of its meagre belongings. Quite an appalling thing really.

In the past, Marcia often made presents of her own sea-scapes, and brought at least one in to the office, but he's never seen anything like that before. While he thinks on it, he realises he's not seen one of her pictures for some time. But if that is one of hers, then she really is quite good in the way she's taken to Impressionism. The more he thinks about it, he realises she's become very secretive about her work of late. At dinner, he made a quick enquiry about her painting, as he expected the house to be festooned with pictures of St Andrews Bay and to reek of turpentine, but she smiled and told him she'd moved on, to bigger things. That she'd taken on a model. A woman? he asked. No, no, she answered, defiant. He felt almost jealous at that, the thought of her sketching and painting a naked man with Jeff gone. What would Jeff have made of all this? Arthur makes a whistling sound, and as he shakes his head from side to side, he stares some more about the dark room.

'You'll see soon enough,' she said. 'I think you'll be surprised, dear. Very surprised.'

Closing his eyes, he begins to drift in and out of a doze. The whisky is wearing off, but it has left him soporific. And with the room so still – so silent, dark and warm like sleep

– it is hard to resist resting the eyes. Just a doze and he'll go home. Go home. Elaine will have gone to bed, and by then she won't be able to smell the drink on him. It doesn't go well with his medication and, after the problems he suffered with his heart two winters before, she's become manic about everything that passes his lips. It is better he recovers with Marcia; there will only be another tiff if Elaine suspects he's been drinking.

Behind him, Marcia enters the lounge. She is smiling. He sits up with a start. 'Can't keep my eyes open.'

She smiles. 'Good. It'll be best.'

'But I want to see the pictures. And it's getting late. I really should be off.'

'Nonsense. Just relax. You need to, dear.'

Arthur beams. 'You're an angel. But I mean it, about the pictures. I've grown rather curious, sitting down here in the dark. What have you got hidden away upstairs? You know, I've always suspected you were a genius masquerading as my secretary. And I want to see if it's true.'

'You will,' she says, and winks at him, which she has never done before. 'I have a call to make, and then you'll see the results, dear. I promise you. In the meantime feel free to doze. Won't be long now.'

'Sure you don't mind? I feel terrible imposing like this. I really should be getting home.'

But she goes from the lounge with a swishing sound, and he hears her run up the stairs. Against the patio doors, the wind rushes in.

With the lights turned off, she likes to stand in her room and watch the sky, and the distant lumps of the hills beneath the stars. Sometimes the moon is bright. That is the best time to paint. It is cloudy tonight, but that doesn't matter; she's not up here to paint. Not yet anyway. Not with the rain and wind so pleasingly close, outside, where he is. For now she just wants to wait, exhilarated in the dark. Tingling in every finger and toe; her skin ready to shiver; the expectation of sound, of the doors flung open downstairs, like the last time she saw Jeff alive – it was wonderful. Just to wait in silence, to sense it building up, the power around her home, rushing forward so close to the ground, rearing up at the prospect of her gift to him: her love, her king. And then the crash and the whirl of motion, dulled through the ceiling, but frantic enough for her to picture every last step and movement and blow, until it is quiet again, and safe for her to creep down.

Tonight the elements know he is coming. They whip the heather and flay the grasses on the common land, blurring the definition of field and tree. They make shadows longer and thicker than ever, a fanfare for the king that approaches her house. Her house. It is almost like fear, what she feels now, but more than fear. There is pleasure in it. Ecstasy, able to tighten her way down in belly and womb, while her mind fills with the living darkness that swoops and seethes and rushes forward to hunt. She can't wait to paint him, again, at his work.

Once, in her life, there had been shopping on Saturdays, visits to an elderly mother on Sundays, and books on steam trains in her house, belonging to her husband and the life he imposed. But no longer. Now she has all the time and space to paint. To paint a god. The god the girl brought to her. A god that touched her and made her shiver against the suddenly cold sheets; someone who came across the floor, and up the walls, and across the ceiling and then down to her bed. He doesn't ask her for much, but she gives what she has, what she can, for his touch, and for his favours. He's taught her to stretch beyond her dull life and to come running back clutching things that have always been forbidden to her. Things she can secretly sketch and then colour in burgundy, royal purple, ox-blood and rust. No more tepid water-colours. Like the food she shares from his table, her new oils are rich and thick.

Late at night, with her hair all wild and her skin naked and her spirit free, she works, and recreates that which so few have seen and felt and tasted and smelled and devoted themselves to. Now Jeff is gone for good, she can be free like that, all the time. A promise her new love has kept.

Before the window, Marcia removes her white blouse and cream camisole top, her fingers clumsy, like they are before the dances on the dark stones at his court. Next, she steps out of her formal black skirt and frees herself of underwear. Sitting on the bed, naked and gleaming in the dark, she picks up the phone and taps in a number on the keypad. It rings five times at the other end before the receiver is picked up. Marcia closes her eyes and shivers at the thought of who stands at the other end of the line. Between the crackles and little clicks, she senses them. 'He's here,' she says, in a soft and grateful and loving voice. There is no answer but she knows they are listening. 'Downstairs. He's ready.'

Marcia is adding a little water to the crusting red paste when she hears the scream downstairs. She smiles and, using a fingertip, dabs the crimson across the thin white streaks on her canvas. The colour draws the eyes out, but it will need to be darker inside the wide mouth. She's already used strands of Jeff's hair for the raiment, mixed with dark browns and then a sackcloth yellow for highlights.

The portrait is taking shape nicely. It is the best thing she's ever done. The melancholy colours sweep like clouds across the sun on the light canvas; angles and lines have been smudged away by swoops of black. She has used real bone for the limbs too, and fashioned the ruined thing in the king's hands with a collage of real skin and chicken fat. She's never even considered using such materials with oil paint before – but this is her own private renascence, a time in her life when everything is conceivable, terrible, and free. Marcia peers down at her palette for a dark, river-weed green – the colour of Jeff's eyes. She has to get that part just right – the astonishment, almost childlike, mixed with the bewilderment of a hare before an eager ferret. Just like she did with the boy in the sea.

There is a lot of thumping downstairs now, and someone is making a sound like a baby in distress. Marcia stops painting for a moment and closes her eyes to relish the honour of having it happen, right beneath her feet, in her own home. She places both smeared hands on the easel, and gently allows her head to fall right back between her narrow shoulders, where the bruises still hurt her. She sighs and shivers as the cold air of his arrival clothes her body.

Not long now before he leaves her, as swiftly as he came from out of the air and hills. Stronger than ever, stronger and pleased with her after the gift, the offering she provided. And when he is gone, she will go downstairs, turn the lights on, and see what has been left for her.

THIRTY-SEVEN

There is no wind, no traffic in the empty lane, and little sound beside the patter of rain through the trees and hedges by the road where he crouches, at the edge where the tarmac cambers into a drainage trench. Little can be seen in any detail around him, save the indistinct shapes of lime-green weeds, or pieces of pale rock. And for the moment he can go no further toward the cottage. The fire of anger and the cold suck of anxiety – or is it impatience? or desperation? – in his stomach, that forced him to drive out to the cottage within an hour of Harry and Arthur's departure, are gone, leaving him immobile now, twenty feet from the cottage gate.

In the Land Rover, he crawled at no more than twenty miles an hour through the unlit narrow lanes for the last stretch of the journey to Eliot's home, his courage gradually fading to futility, a sense of weakness before a greater foe. Traffic on the minor roads thinned once he was past the golf course on the outskirts of town, at nine. Cars behind and ahead passed away like the last few familiar faces in a threatening crowd, leaving him alone in the Fife countryside beneath a cloudy night sky, with only the headlights on full-beam to guide him, and they produced nothing but a comfortless glow of yellow before a backdrop of treeless hills. After a final small settlement of grey cottages, whose orange lights peeking from deep casements seemed to plead with him to turn back, Dante found the last turn on the map to take him to Eliot's home, where it all began.

While he laboured with the contagion of Beth, and when he defied her in the court, and then again, a final time, on the beach, were plans being made for a more suitable candidate? For Tom? For what? To join them? And it was all happening so quickly. There had been a haste in Eliot, a desperation for him to meet Beth. And in Beth too, for him to accept her companion. Instinct warns him their haste is for a reason: a point in time not far away, when something beyond everyone's comprehension will occur. And stifling him, making him all blocked and stopped inside, is the sense that Tom is gone. The moment Tom came out here with Eliot, was he lost? And he drove his best friend to this end. Dante dips his head and lets the worst of it pass.

He stands up and looks behind him at the road he has travelled and can now barely see. The Land Rover is parked half a mile back, tucked inside a shallow opening to a field, bordered on either side by a dry stone wall. Near the field was a sign indicating that Knoxville was two miles away, a landmark he chose so he could find the Land Rover again, in a hurry if need be. But if he is chased from the cottage, will he make it that far? Vivid recollections of his night on the West Sands start to leap through his mind. Quick nervous thoughts make him swallow and then take deep breaths.

For what seems like an hour, he is unable to move at all, and twice convinces himself to turn back and run to the War Wagon. Maybe he should wait for the following day and return, as planned, with Arthur and Harry. Then they can search for Tom by daylight, with the confidence of being in numbers, of not having to face uncertainty alone: like his trip to Scotland in the first place, when he took Tom – the sleek head beside him, the banter, the goading, the twitches of anger, the camaraderie, the bond that seemed unbreakable, the interest in one another inexhaustible. 'Jesus, Tom. What have I done?' he says.

But the following day will be too late. Missing for two days, Tom has been out here. Ill perhaps, a captive for sure. One more night is too long a time to wait for your best friend. Tom would do the same for him. He'd be right here too, looking for Dante, waiting for the moment to pounce at the cottage, knife in hand. Inside the inner pocket of Dante's jacket, the plastic handle of the kitchen knife – the only thing resembling a weapon he could find in the flat – pokes into his armpit. It is one of those long knives with a point and a serrated edge and a handle dimpled for grip when slicing vegetables, bread and cheese. It will mean he'll have to use it up close. Briefly, he imagines forcing a knife into a body. It makes him feel sick, and there is no strength in his arms after the thought has passed.

It's no good; he just isn't made that way. In his two fights at school he came away second best, and the one time he was attacked by a biker at a rock club in Nottingham, the whole episode became nothing to him but a blur, painless despite his many bruises, chaotic so no single image or word could stay in his memory. Just a tumble of emotion and a whirl of lights that left him nauseous and trembling when it was all over. He is no fighter.

But he must go in there with the knife and the screwdriver and torch from the War Wagon's tool box. Into the cottage to find Tom and bring him out. His throat closes and a cold sweat moistens under his arms. Fear is winning again, now he is no more than twenty feet from the gate.

Something else will have to do the terrible things for him. When the moment comes he must count on anger, fear and adrenaline to kick in, to remove his finer parts, and provide strength. 'Come on,' he whispers. It is a struggle to breathe steadily, and he's gritted his teeth without noticing, until the sound of them grating together makes him relax his jaw. Unsteadily, he rises to his full height and stretches his back. A long shiver runs over his body. His fingers are too cold to feel much. Before he freezes, or summons the virus back, he has to make a move. Now or never. For Tom and the poor bastard who lost his arm on the beach. They might get him, but he'll do some damage first. Yes, go. Go now. Pumping faster, his heart spreads a welcome heat through his body.

Running bent over, close to the grass verge between the drainage trench and the road surface, Dante makes it as far as the front gate then drops down from sight of the front windows. There it is: the pale stone of the wide front wall; the large square paddock-style garden, unkempt and clotted brown with leaves; the roof indistinct and lost amidst unpruned foliage: the dilapidated hovel Harry and Arthur entered in May and never since. The guttering is half gone, and the skeletons of two large floral arrangements are sunken beside the door.

He clambers over the wooden gate, not wanting to risk the clinking of metal or the squeak of hinge by using the latch, and drops to the path on the other side. He is in. Every nerve sings; his ears seem to hear the snapping of twigs on every side; there is a rush of blood and hormones to his head; panic rises like a wave and tries to swamp him into flight.

He runs to the left side of the front garden and follows the hedge all the way to the corner. Long grass, thick with rain, drenches his jeans to the knee. Branches from the hedge bordering the side of the front garden whip his face. Clouds cover one half of what's left of the moon and stars. But that is good. If someone were to walk out the front door, it would be hard for them to see him crouched down here. But if they do not need to use their eyes to find a trespasser, what then?

Wide-eyed with emotion, he remains still, and watches the property from his corner, looking for the next hiding place like a mountaineer peering up to see a crack or ledge in which to place his chalky fingers. A stone wall protects the cottage from the road, and scruffy hedges grow down both sides where lines of poplars and thorn bushes bend out of the privet, offering shelter from the winds and concealing the two barren fields beyond. The rear of the property is lost to him.

Screwing up his eyes, Dante examines the outside of the cottage. There are two storeys with sightless windows, glazed and set back inside grey brick. From the sides, it is protected completely from an outer view, and any inspection from the front is partially obscured by the wall. Subtly and in a disorderly fashion, it is as if the building has been shaped into a hideout that no one would suspect of foul deeds because no one can see it. But now he is on the inside, he must be certain he is not seen from those blank windows. Looking for a way in will follow.

Through a tiny chink in what may be curtains on the top floor, he thinks there is a slither of reddish light, but beside

that, if indeed it is a light, the building suggests total abandonment. Squinting, he peers across the silhouette of the
gables and chimney breast, and then down the walls. At the
sides of the building, two narrow grass paths, obscured by
the overhang of privet and tree limb, lead away to shadow.
The rear garden?

Clinging to the trench of night at the base of the tree row,
he moves down to the side of the cottage to check the back,
raising his knees high above the wet grass as if wading
through murky water. Then along the length of the cottage,
between the treeline and house, he moves slowly through a
funnel of total dark with one hand placed against the stone
wall of the cottage for support, while his other arm knocks
wet tree branches from his face.

From out of the shadow, he emerges, grateful, his heart
pounding up around his ears, and sees the rear garden: long,
devoid of flowerbed and tree, covered with long grass and a
seemingly impenetrable tangle of weed that concludes in
what appears to be a high, though sagging, wooden fence.
There is little beyond other than a field or rocky meadow
leading to foothills, dotted with sleeping sheep. Long ago,
precautions were taken against the curious.

With his senses keener, Dante drops to a squat and surveys
the back of the house. There is a single large back door in a
solid stone frame and five windows around it: two to the
side, and three on the upper storey, before the steep roof,
made from grey slate, makes its conical ascent into the elements. Is Tom somewhere under that roof? Can anyone live
here? But it is the thought of what else could be in there that
keeps him in the cold shadows of the garden.

Trying to establish entry will be difficult without a crowbar. How do burglars do it? They force windows or break them. Can he risk the noise if someone is inside?

In a renewed effort to focus his courage, he imagines crashing the lock in and booting the front door aside. But what then? Will Beth leap on him and smash him like a toy against a wall? Or will the other one be waiting, like a guardian, to tear an arm off? Every faded bruise and scratch on his body suddenly sings out in a tiny shrill voice of its own. Are keen eyes looking out too, up there right now, behind those dark panels of glass, watching him? Or can they sense him? If they come to him in dreams, are they not able to feel his presence, now he is so close?

The sound of a car and the dim pattern of headlights down one side of the house makes his head turn in one direction, his stomach in another. A car pulls up in the lane at the front of the cottage; a door opens, then closes, and is followed by the sound of tipped heels on a slabstone path.

Edging forward and trying to stifle his ragged breath, Dante moves back into the dark at the side of the cottage, back through the tight tunnel of dankness and tugging sticks, and on toward the front, one careful step at a time. Maybe Tom is with them, the visitors, or owners, or worse.

Someone is knocking the front door now. When he draws level with the corner of the front wall, he crouches down, below eye-level, and steals a quick glimpse around the cold brickwork before pulling his face back into the dark. A woman is out front, crouched down on her knees in the weeds before the door, with her scarfed-head bowed. She is wearing an overcoat, but is too short to be Beth. Mystified, he looks again.

At the front of the house a door is opened, followed by

the clatter of a latch, and then what sounds like a low mutter of awe from the kneeling woman. Then there is silence. A dark arm stretches out from the doorway. It touches the woman's scarfed head, tenderly, as if stroking an obedient pet.

What little edgy strength has been in his body seeps away, draining from his legs like the water of a bath he's suddenly stood up in, to pass from his feet into the cold earth. One of his eyebrows twitches and for an insane moment he thinks of rushing forward, knife drawn, to do his work – the town's work. Reaching inside his jacket, he places the pads of his fingers on the knife handle.

The kneeling woman rises to her feet; a joint cracks, the skirt swishes. The woman then shuffles to the side of the path, and from the doorway steps someone tall and covered in black to their feet. It is Beth. Slowly, Dante pulls his head back from the corner, and presses his body into the wall.

He hears the front door close, followed by the sound of their heels, kicking and scraping down the weed-choked path. Then there is the grind of the garden gate being opened. Peering back to the front of the property, he can also see the headlights of a car shining over the wall and into the corner of the garden where he first crouched. He draws the knife from the inside of his jacket. It takes a second for the pain to register, and he hisses more from shock than from the slice he has cut, carelessly, against the flesh beside his armpit. Down by the gate, Beth immediately pauses. She turns around and looks back to the cottage.

There is a pale suggestion of her face angled in his direction. As if smelling his blood, she has become still, one hand on the gate, the other lost inside the folds of her coat. Dante stiffens; not even the blink of an eye will he allow himself. For a moment the whitish oval of her head seems to be confronting him from afar. The other woman comes back to where Beth stands, but keeps a respectful distance behind her. Then Beth raises her face, slightly, as if to afford the thin nose an opportunity to sniff at the night air. He thinks of her bony fingers becoming vices on his arms and the sound of his lips being torn once her mouth is upon him. Giddy now, convinced she has sensed him, he wonders in a moment of madness if he should scream, or will it be better to run to them and fall down where he can plead for her to make it quick?

Then, at last, when he feels dizzy from holding in his breath, knowing that even a faint exhalation might give him up, Beth turns her head away from the house and walks, out of sight, to the car. The scarfed woman follows Beth in a haste he thinks obsequious.

Dante exhales. Something heavy and cold drops through his body, to leave a hollow which fills with a sudden tumble of emotion. An overwhelming desire to shout for his friend dies to a whimper in his mouth. Tears fill his eyes and something wet drips from the end of his nose. His fingers tighten on the knife handle. Fear is replaced by anger. Bitter tears are close.

The engine of the car starts and the light from the headlamps arcs over the hedge and wall with white light. Dante wipes his eyes. The car drives past the front of the property. Its roar fades to a distant hum. Unable to dissolve the lump in his throat, he steps from the shadows and wanders onto the front lawn. He listens to the sound of the engine diminish into silence. Seeping through his jeans and against his buttocks comes the damp of the air, and he turns his attention to the cottage. Dante walks to the front door and kicks it. Wood booms; the door shudders in its frame. If it opens, he will rush whoever stands in his way.

The hammering of his fist against the door brings no one to answer him. Stepping back, he looks up at the windows of the house, all blacked out and latched shut and too high up. With the screwdriver from the Land Rover's tool box, he attempts to lever the door from the frame. No good; his hands are cold and shaking with nerves and he can't find purchase for the wedged end of the tool. His efforts succeed in a useless scraping against the wood of the door. Thwarted, he runs back down the side of the cottage to the rear, and begins an inspection of the windows on the ground floor.

The frames are old; he can feel the rough and flaky putty with his fingertips, and the glass windowpanes move when he touches them. Concerned about slashing his wrists on a shard of broken glass, he stabs the screwdriver at the bottom of a pane. The screwdriver tip slips. His knuckles bang against cold glass. He swears under his breath.

Sweating under his clothes, which the night air quickly turns to shivers, he examines the back door. Not as sturdy as the one at the front, and there is a gap at the base. With all his strength, he forces the screwdriver blade against the edge nearest the Yale lock. Wood splinters on the fourth attempt and the blade sinks until it meets stone with a grind. With all his might he leans against the screwdriver handle until it digs into the palm of one hand. 'Open, you fuck,' he swears, panting with frustration. The blade bends and then snaps out of his hand. 'Shit,' he cries out, immediately clutching his chin.

His fingers come away from his face wet. The end of the blade has nicked his chin.

Angry at his uselessness, he begins to kick the kitchen door, sole first, again and again. Until something snaps inside the lock. The door swings inward and crashes against a wall in the dark interior. Instinctively he jumps back, and then scrabbles on the grass to find the knife he's dropped there.

Nothing stirs in the unlit house. No one comes out. Silence returns to the hidden place.

Breathing hard from his efforts and nerves, he reaches inside his jacket and removes the penlight torch. The thin beam of light is immediately swallowed up in the darkened doorway. Moved to the sides of the frame, it begins to shine against the edges of wooden cupboards and corners. Approaching the threshold, he makes ready to step inside, but stops.

Quickly, he pulls his scarf up high, over his nose and mouth, coughs, and then blows through his nose to clear his throat and sinuses. Something has gone bad in there. Thick like the stench from a pig farm he once canoed through while exploring the canals in the green belt of Birmingham, a miasma wafts from the doorway: offal-tinged, sawdust-fresh, and incongruously mixed with a spice that has a church smell – like incense. He is reminded of butcher's shops, of old tombs with unreadable inscriptions, and of wet dustbin bags in disused allotments, left for too long with meat scraps inside them.

Feeling nauseous, taking shallow breaths, Dante creeps inside, slowly, with the feeble light from his torch illuminating the places his feet tread. Wiping sweat from off his eyebrows and feeling the sting from the cut on his chin, he

420

stands inside the kitchen. 'Jesus,' he mutters. He is reminded of the paper round he used to plod through before he went to school, when he nosed around the inside of a derelict flat in a tower block. Cupboard doors hang open, crockery has been smashed across the tiled floor, black-spore fungus clouds what was once white paintwork. And a smell hangs in the air as if he is about to trip over something recently dead.

Through the kitchen, he walks to the hallway, and watches the house in Arthur's story open around him under thin strobes of torchlight. Things have not changed, unless they have worsened. Dark paper, the colour of a pope's robes on a faded painting, coats the walls, emitting a velvety sheen under his thin beam. Clouds of damp and the wet fustiness of neglect soak uncarpeted floors and stained ceilings. In what must have once been a dining room, curtains the colour of heavy grapes left too long on the vine hang over the window frames. Judging by the thick cobwebs along the metal rails, they have not been opened in a while.

Beside the long table, which is covered with cardboard boxes, wet to the touch and brimming with paper, folders and books, there is a clutter of dark furniture. Backing out of the dining room, he inches along to one remaining door on the left side of the ground floor. He turns and shines his torch across the hallway, to light the cellar door, set beneath the staircase. At the top of the frame, he can see a latch, to lock the door from the outside. Although the latch is pulled back, leaving the door unsecured, that is the last place he intends to go looking.

Ahead on the left of the hall, he finds the parlour, cramped and crowded with chairs, upholstered but sagging, and there is a deep couch, set low to the floor. Yellowy newspapers spill from another collection of cardboard boxes. Across the side of one box is a supermarket logo reading SOUTH AFRICAN APPLES. Another advertises bleach. Again there is no carpet, and only a wet rug beneath the legs of a cluttered coffee table. The floorboards feel sticky beneath the soles of his boots.

When he raises his eyes to scan the bookshelves, he immediately notices something odd. Above the blocked fireplace and on two other walls, he can see three paintings set in new frames. Murky-looking paintings, with indistinct subjects. He walks around the table and squints at one, shining his torch at the canvas. After a few seconds, he closes his eyes.

He knows he'll be seeing the figures in the picture again, and probably for the rest of his life. It is the work of a madman. A splash of anger from a broken mind, primitive, childlike. But whence came the inspiration? Are the dense and faintly glistening oils telling a story? A story so few know . . .

Something large rises out of the central shadow in the picture. An indistinct face, grinning or moving its mouth, can be seen in the very middle. And if it is a face, then the thing below its sharp jaw, cowering and made shiny with red, is its prey. It looks like a girl, stripped white, and speckled with pinhead-sprays of crimson. Pasty flaps are open on her body, into which the face of the shadow must have been recently dipping.

Catching the kitchen stench in the paint makes Dante stifle a gag. His only thought is to destroy it.

Stronger now, the smell of the paint thickens and becomes almost palpable, clinging to him like a freezing fog. As he spins away from the picture, tripping his way back to the door, a foolish urge makes him shine the torch on another painting. He likes the story this picture tells even less than the first.

Again, it is completed in an impressionistic style, but the subject is made all the worse for it, especially the look on the youth's face as he attempts to pull himself through the black water, knee-deep, that makes his escape so sluggish. There is just a suggestion of the howl of a mouth and the flash of wide eyes about the boy's head, as hope vanishes and the pursuer closes in. There are few bright colours in the frame beyond the stars, the red of the boy's coat, and the white of the water's surface under moonlight, disturbed into froth. The shadow that sweeps behind him is defined only by the way it obscures the dim horizon in the rear of the scene. But what little definition exists hints that this figure, making so sinister a haste to catch its quarry, is too thin and too tall and too quick for any man to escape. A lunatic painted it, and it should never have been hung on a rust-coloured wall.

Clutching his knees outside in the hall, his lungs filling with the poisonous air that seeps through the wool of his scarf, he looks at the stairs, going cold, colder than he's ever been, or wanted to be, or could be again. No man can suffer much more of this. Empty inside, the wear of it all blunting his edges, he staggers to the stairs and begins to climb.

Darkness, unrelenting and impenetrable, presses against him. His stomach sick through, he turns his torch beam upward and calls out for Tom. It is like striking a waterproof match at the bottom of the deepest sea. But this world without light comes alive around him – seething and jostling, as if every molecule is animate with unnatural energy, threatening to douse him and his feeble light at any moment. Seeing no further than a few feet in either direction, he opens a door.

In here, her smell is strong. There is a dresser and some shelves. In the mirror of the dresser, before the cushioned stool she must sit on, he almost expects to see her face, with all its beauty and confusion and cruelty, looking back at him. Something seizes up inside his chest as he looks at the flickering glass. He turns away from it and swallows. Across the floor are strewn the clothes of a missing girl. Unwashed underwear tangled around sweaters and skirts. An odd shoe, dirty with stains, lies against a broken tape recorder. The bed is sunk into the wall, its furthest edges lost in the dark walls. The impression of a resting head indents one of the pillows. By a bedside table, strewn with sheets of sky-blue writing paper and make-up, is a leather jacket. Its red lining faces outward. It is Tom's biker jacket, with 'Sister Morphine' painted carefully above one elbow in silver paint.

Dante falls to his knees and holds it in his hands. His breath comes fast and turns to condensation about his face. Desperate, he looks about the floor and knocks things over, wanting more, hoping to reassemble his friend from fragments so Tom will stand up before his eyes, smiling. But then he finds it, as his clumsy body bangs against the dresser in his desperate search. Stretched across the top of the dark chest-of-drawers, beneath the mirror and between two bowls, and now looking like some rag in an antique shop that was once thought valuable, or a poacher's quarry left in a glass jar above a bar in a public house full of dust and faded paintings of horsemen hunting in red coats. The way it lies, the shine eerily present as if each strand is still attached to the scalp, makes him think of a horse's tail, used to switch flies. But where the long silky plume of hair begins, it is still wet from the head from which it has been torn.

Staggering back, a great sob fills him. He wants to cry and be sick and sit down from the shock all at the same time. His whimpers are strange to his own ears. In the dark, they sound rough and hard, the crying of a man grown and brought down in the world like a boy before a bully. 'Tom!' he calls, at the top of his voice this time, making the violence in his voice cover the panic that wants to stutter from his throat, from deep down where all the screams and the prayers are ready.

He runs from the room and the thin white beam shoots out from his torch and strikes walls that may have faces in them, and it flashes over doors that appear open, and then cornices from another age, and empty light sockets, rotten skirting boards, until finally it shines across the last flight of stairs he knows he must climb.

And he is not alone with his madness. Nothing speaks, nothing touches him, but something moves, behind him, before him, he even walks through it and feels a chill pass over his skin and into his body, slowing him, taking his strength away, suffocating him. And then someone speaks out there, above him perhaps. Words he can't understand. Mutterings from a low voice. And noises from a child or even a small animal, scuffling about up there, crying to itself.

From the stairs, which are short and cramped, he enters the attic, and the sounds are clearer, emerging, finding a centre, ahead of him. The penlight's beam flickers a few feet ahead before being swallowed again. Every hair sticks out from his neck and scalp. And the smell is worse in here than anywhere else he's been in the cottage; it is the stench of an occupant he silently prays is not home, for if it is he is finished.

Now Dante feels ready for death, going beyond terror, beyond flight, ready to deal blows against anything that moves as he falls. 'Who's there?' he hears himself shout. Invisible spittle leaves his mouth. Ahead of him now, the cries cease. 'Who's there?' he says. 'Tom? Mate? Tom?' He says it again and again until something smashes against his nose. Grunting, he falls with the knife held out. There is a sound of splintering wood, and the whimpering begins again. It takes him a moment to realise, as he heaves at the knife, stuck fast, that it is a wall he's just walked straight into, while holding the blade before him.

Something white skitters sideways across the floor, grazing the torch beam that flashes about in his free hand. Dante tugs the bent knife free, and then lets his ears follow the noises of the scrabbling thing until they settle in a corner of the attic, where the roof slopes down and conducts the sound of someone panting.

Somehow he knows the eyes of this man-creature that cowers in the dark are closed, because it expects the worst, and has done day after day in this terrible place. Maybe the light has gone out behind the closed eyes too. Maybe the mind is ready to close also, and the body is about to subside, to offer itself to the intruder. There is fear in the attic, not an enemy. 'Tom,' he says, in a voice thick with phlegm.

He flashes the torch at the corner where he knows the creature is huddled and now waits for its end. There it is: a bundle of pink sticks, gnarled and grey-headed, shrunken on the bare boards, unclean, tethered to a rope that cuts into its leg.

'Eliot,' Dante says to the ruin, the wretch.

Both hands are clutched across eyes that would consider blindness a mercy. The pale body, scarred in places, shivers. A shrivelled penis dangles between pointy hips. Messy grey hair hangs over the cage of hands on face, and through the middle and index fingers is the glint of an eye. 'Eliot,' Dante says, his voice no more than a rasp. Wide eyes retreat from the torch beam into a squint, burned by light. 'It's me, Dante,' he says, approaching the figure.

It is the man who betrayed him and Tom. Watched carefully by Eliot, he unzips his jacket and then offers it to the wretch on the piss-stained planks. 'Put it on. Get up,' he says, surprised at the strength of his voice in the dark room. The battered jacket is taken by a frail hand and pulled around a red neck. 'Get up, damn you,' he says, sawing the leash from Eliot's ankle with the bottom of the knife blade, where it is still straight. 'My friend, Tom?' he asks, without faith, already knowing the answer.

Eliot's eyes dip. His body begins to shake, and he tries to sit down again from the crouch he's risen to.

'No,' Dante says, gripping him under the arm. 'Let's go,' he tells his hero, and drags him through the dark and then down the stairs. Clinging to his arm like an old woman he once helped outside a shopping centre, Eliot shivers, his thin legs absurd beneath the leather jacket. 'You've done this,' Dante says, shaking. 'You brought this here.' His voice starts to tremble. 'You killed my friend.'

THIRTY-EIGHT

It is the middle of the night and Dante still watches him, the figure all hunched up on the couch in the dark, covered with a blanket from his feet to his neck. At least he's stopped shaking. It made Dante uncomfortable watching him in that state. After they climbed out of the Land Rover and went inside the flat it was the only thing that made him realise Eliot was conscious.

Outside, it has stopped raining, and if you listen carefully in the silence of the room you can hear the sea across the road, at the bottom of the cliffs.

Dante pours another two drinks, watching the whisky splash about in the bottom of the glasses. Eliot sucks in his breath. Without moving his head, Dante looks up. A voice comes from the figure under the tartan blanket. It sounds like he says, 'The American'. And then Eliot goes still under the blanket as if he has died. Dante wants him to repeat what he just said, but hasn't the strength to ask. Even the cold of early morning does not affect him. He can feel nothing. It is as if his head is a block of wood and nothing will ever move inside it again.

After a time he stands up and turns on a wall light and then uses the dimmer switch, so they will not have to see each other's eyes. Then he checks the thermostat and turns the dial until he hears a click followed by the distant whoosh, hidden behind walls, as the boiler comes on. It seems ridiculous to turn the heating on now. He should have done it hours ago. Can warmth make a difference to either man after what they've seen?

He sits down again and reaches for his drink. Now, with the wall light barely on, it is as if they are in an unlit room and only see the dim things around them by the light that creeps in from a neighbour's house. He looks at the silhouette of the two guitars by the patio doors and it seems he has only ever played them in another life. A little shiver passes up the back of his neck and his forearms turn to goosebumps. He feels as if he should sneeze and then the shudder is gone and the strange sensation passes as the warm air begins to cover him. He can feel it moving over his skin. He feels grateful for the warmth, but guilty too, as if he does not deserve to be comfortable. Behind the walls, there is a sound like water trickling. Eliot does not move.

Slowly, so as not to make a sound, Dante leans back in the chair and closes his eyes. Everything is warm and red under his eyelids and inside he is empty. It is as if a big knot, that could not be untied, has been cut out. All his thoughts and worries are not there when he closes his eyes. And for a time he does not have to think of the man who murdered his friend. To even have the word 'murder' in your experience . . . For years he thought his life was hard. But when it comes to it, the past wasn't even preparation. He always lived in another world, a world that never had that word in it.

A voice comes from across the room. Eliot is mumbling.

Dante listens but never moves. Eliot stares into his lap and is holding his glass of whisky with both hands. The glass is nearly full. But Eliot is talking to someone else in the room, so it is like sitting on public transport opposite an old man whose mind has gone. 'Agrippa was followed by two black dogs for the rest of his life,' Eliot says. Through the darkness, Dante suspects the old man is smiling to himself. 'They saw something at Boleskin too, that they would never talk about. Ever. Not even Aleister. That's not far away. It's on the shore of the loch. I think it was the Dark Man too. And it followed him also. You always have it.'

It is a jumble of things that he speaks of, but in it, Dante is hearing things that make him feel cold again. He lights a cigarette, forgetting when it was he last smoked. He hopes it will make everything normal again. It doesn't.

Even though it is dark, Dante can tell that some colour has returned to Eliot's face. It seems to have become animated as he stares at the wall above Dante. He wants to look up too, but is afraid to move in case Eliot stops talking. It is like waiting in a zoo for a rare bird to come outside of its secret nest to peck near the glass.

'Fasting,' Eliot says to the wall. Dante strains his ears and holds his breath. 'A greater period of fasting and the calling of the right names. Maybe I did nothing more. The ceremony is foolish. It happens in spite of it. They were here all along. And when you invite a guest inside, by being in the right state, and believing they could come, and by saying the right name, who is to say they will ever leave?'

Eliot goes quiet and for a while the only noise he makes is a slurping sound at the whisky before a nasty coughing erupts from him – followed by a rattle inside his parchment chest. 'They were here,' Eliot says. 'Before I knew who they were. They were in him and the girl before I knew it. Yes, the boy lived here. I think it was always too late for them. She saw her dead father in her dreams. That's how he came to her. And Ben dreamed of a woman.'

Dante pulls his shoulders in and holds his hands together. He takes his feet off the floor. This is something Eliot has said to himself over and over again, like a man who is unable to apologise, but who will mumble and then vanish into the deepest silences to look for a way of forgiving himself. It doesn't feel as if Eliot is making a confession, but rather that Dante is being paid back a debt, grudgingly, by the old and broken thing under the blanket. Then Eliot makes a wheezing sound and coughs again. Something gathers in his mouth and Dante hears him swallow it. It sounds like he is dying.

'In the meetings it went through the group and touched them. It marked them for later. I never knew.'

Dante closes his eyes.

Eliot's voice softens. 'The boy knew. And he knew I could do nothing to stop it. That it could get into any circle. He knew what was coming. So he put himself away. Did himself in.' Eliot exhales for what seems like a long time, as if he is being punctured by just a thought. 'And with the Brown Man come others, from the time before when the nights here were just the same as they are now. The speaking of the tongues comes from the last ones who served him. The last hunters. But there are things worse than the hunt. The eating . . .' Eliot pauses and swallows more of the whisky from the glass trembling in his hand. 'I used to laugh at the men who wrote about the eating of horrible meats. But who can say how old it all is? Older than the Greeks. Gods are only renamed. They can still be called by the old names.' And then Eliot starts to sniff. He raises a hand that looks too big for his thin arm and puts it against his forehead, as if shielding his eyes from the sun. Inside his eye sockets he places a finger and thumb, and as he stoppers the tears, it looks like he is pushing his eyes into his head.

When Dante clears his throat of a bubble, the sound seems to fill the room. 'Stop,' he says, but feels he cannot direct the word at Eliot. It is lost in the stillness. It has all come rushing back to him, and he recalls the paintings, exhibited in his memory, and he remembers the dresser made from dark wood in her room, with the mirror that seemed to be alive. And on the dresser he saw the hair of his brother, and knows one end of it would have been wet had he touched it. 'No,' he says, and squeezes his eyes shut, and puts his head down until all of these things have gone away for a while so he can feel numb again.

And then Eliot takes his hand away from his face and looks down from the wall. He looks right at Dante and seems to have straightened whatever inside him is twisted. 'She'll come here for me. And you are marked also. You have only delayed things. And when the right number have been taken, things will change here. This place is already damned.'

'What can I do? Tell me,' Dante says. He sits forward, more tired than he has ever been, drained until he is empty, but aware he won't sleep this night. 'You must know what can be done.'

'Nothing,' Eliot says, automatically and so decisively Dante feels something shrivel inside himself.

'They shouldn't be here. They can't stay here. There are laws that keep things apart, and that keep time going, so the past can't come back –'

'But they are here, and they walk. And it spread so fast.

And others came to her and joined her. They were all tainted with what should never have been able to do more than break a glass, or tilt a painting, or predict a death rightly, if asked. But they are here. And not just in dreams, they took shape right in this time, in this here and now, in this plane, and have begun to occupy their old places. I've seen them everywhere.' Eliot pauses and sighs. His voice falls to barely a whisper. 'Once I tried to smother her in sleep. In case it was the bond between them that was used to bring the dark through. But I could not do it. She is protected. He came alive in the very air.'

Now Eliot looks agitated; he moves his thin legs from under the blanket and places his feet on the floor. His face is grey, as if his despair is so great he is already dead. 'Can I have your belt?' Eliot then asks, the way a child asks for comfort. For a moment Dante's vision dissolves into little spots of light and then the room judders slightly at the periphery of his vision. He can't move. He feels trapped, and then, idiotically, a yawn comes over him. He shakes his head. 'But we have to,' Eliot says, his face almost smiling because it cannot react appropriately to the enormity of what he is actually suggesting: that they should put an end to themselves.

'There is another way,' Dante says, feeling reckless and not even believing what he says too quickly, as he thinks of driving very fast and putting up with anything in any other place so long as he isn't here. And then he thinks that if he hears much more, his mind will stop working and will never be able to respond to anything again. But he knows that would be a luxury, because those hunted can suffer forever. He is short of breath and pushes his heels down hard on the floor. He tries to stand up twice but can't. There is a huge pressure inside him again. 'When will it come?' he blurts out, in a strained voice, as if it's escaping from under a heavy lid.

'There is business tonight,' Eliot says, in a matter-of-fact way. Then he stops talking and looks at the floor. 'Oh God, oh God, oh God,' he says, not to Dante. 'I can't even warn them. Who would listen now?'

'Tomorrow,' Dante whispers, but the last syllable is squashed flat inside his throat. He swallows. 'It'll come for me tomorrow then?'

'For certain,' Eliot says, still staring into space. Dante stands up and moves so that he can feel his legs again.

'Could I get out of the town?' he asks, and then hates himself for thinking of running.

Eliot looks at him, and seems to be weighing him up. When he speaks his voice is deep. It has a kind of dignity, the way it was the first time they met. 'And one day, a stranger will walk past you and look you in the eye and say something to you. They could be smiling, but it will be a promise. And when you hear the words and see their eyes you will know it could be the end of you at any time. The end of you that you choose with your fears: a knife, a glass in your throat, a burning at the side of a road in a car, a drowning in a sea you can't swim out of. If you have no preferences for the way you die, they can take a child you love –'

'No,' Dante says aloud. He stops moving and sits down. He knows his face is white because his whole head has gone cold. It feels frozen.

'You are marked. Now, your belt,' Eliot asks, in a soft but insistent voice. 'I won't do it in front of you. I want to be back with my books. Please. I can't ask again. It has to be now.'

Too stiff inside to think about what he is doing, Dante unbuckles his belt. Eliot looks away, as if made uncomfortable by a vulgar act. Dante stretches his arm out, holding the belt loosely, feeling the warmth on the inside of the leather from where it has been around his waist. It is taken quickly from Dante's hand. Their fingers never touch.

'I won't do it,' Dante then says, and backs away from Eliot as if the man is holding a dangerous snake.

'I understand,' Eliot says, impatient. 'Maybe you haven't seen it all yet, but I have.' Eliot stands up, holding the blanket across himself. 'I was locked in with it, and . . .' He stops talking and starts to shake. He closes his eyes and Dante can see the concentration on his haggard face as he tries to control himself. Then he opens his eyes and is restless, eager to get his business over with. 'Do you have a coat? I know where I can get clothes.'

'Tom,' Dante says. A thought of his friend comes to him suddenly, as they talk so reasonably about the way for a man to die. But that is all he can say. He is unable to think of or attach a sentence to the name.

Eliot points at Dante and appears angry. 'Promises were made that I couldn't keep. Offerings were the only things that counted once they were here. I've given enough, friends and strangers. At first to keep it in check and finally because they made me. Now I have to go.'

'You led my friend to his death,' Dante says, still not able to believe that the idea of Tom can be associated with anything so final. An end. And why is he not angry? Why can he only feel pity and revulsion for this man, but no rage? Is it grief, or confusion from the most impossible things having occurred so quickly in his life, that gets in the way of his anger?

Eliot whispers, 'He was to be shared. To be here for those that came up. You too. And who can tell who is right for them and who is not? Whom they will take? And who can use reason with such a god?'

'You're a bastard,' Dante hears himself say.

Eliot looks up with an expression on his face that Dante has never seen before. It looks like surprise. 'If it would help, you can finish this business between us. I would let you.'

It is as if a close friend has made an awkward and un-expected pass. Dante feels an overpowering aversion and stares at Eliot, hard. 'Be grateful I'm not like that. Because it would be my right to make it uncomfortable for you.'

Eliot looks down. 'I know,' he says.

But Dante's fire has not waned. 'Before you do it, Eliot, think of what you've done. So even when you're gone you'll have no peace.' Eliot's face blanches and he looks ready to sit down again, already beginning to shake. But he has enough presence of mind to look to the lounge door and know he will have to leave, wrapped in a blanket, utterly reduced and impoverished in the world he has used and then corrupted.

'There was an American here,' he says, after taking a deep breath. 'He came to see me a few days ago. He knew about things. He lives on Market Street. In an upstairs room. Right across the road from Grey Friars Street. His name is Miller something. That's all I remember. And it might not be enough because I heard talking down the stairs the other day. They went for him. But she came back angry, so maybe he escaped, or maybe he was just no good.' In the dark, Dante can see he's screwed up his face as if in anticipation of a blow. 'Both of you are marked,' he adds, almost under his breath. 'If he's not gone yet, you will have each other. I can tell you nothing else. There are no answers. It just comes down to you finishing me, or for me to do it myself. I'm sorry.' And then he is gone. He walks swiftly from the lounge, through the hallway, and out the door of the flat.

THIRTY-NINE

Looking up from street level, Dante can see the lights are out in the building directly across from Grey Friars Street. If Eliot was telling the truth, this is Miller's flat. Up on the top floor, above the solicitor's office, he can see what appears to be a residential property with curtains behind the windows. Maybe Miller is asleep.

He approaches the front door and depresses the bell. There is no answer. He thumbs the bell again and leaves the buzzer pushed in. Pressing his ear to the cold glass of one of the little windows at the top of the door, he hears the far-off ring of the bell, reduced to a distant trill, up the stairs and inside the flat. Standing on his toes, he peers through one of the windowpanes in the door. Aided by the light of a street lamp behind him, he can see the outline of a wooden staircase leading upward between white walls, and something else. At the bottom of the stairs, in the small reception, is something long, black and rectangular. Dante squints and tries to make sense of the large, immobile, shadowy thing. It looks like a large box has been pressed against the door.

Turning around, he glances up and down the desolate street which glows under the streetlights. No one is watching him, but the empty street itself strikes him as being in a state of expectation. It is almost as if the wide boulevard of

Market Street, with its old buildings and the narrow alleys that lead from it, is waiting, anticipating something. The townsfolk, and the growing student population, are oblivious to what they are walking across or standing upon; but the town itself knows: it has a long memory.

Shrugging off a shiver, Dante peers back through the window. Still no sign of life summoned by the bell. He pulls his penlight torch from the inside pocket of his jacket and shines it into the reception, to get a closer look at the box-thing blocking the stairs. The thin yellow beam hits a padded surface. Moving the beam of light around, Dante begins to see the outline of cushions and the armrests of a couch. Someone has slipped a sofa down the stairs.

Stepping back from the door, Dante stands in the street again, thwarted and confused. Distractedly, he looks back up at the street-facing windows of the flat and sees a movement. It comes to him then: the sofa is a barrier. Miller must have barricaded himself into the flat. Dante starts to grin, his face tense. 'Hey!' he shouts up at the window, but there is no further movement. 'Miller! It's all right!' Dante glances around again and makes sure no one is about. The street is still clear. If his St Andrews experience has been anything like Dante's, the man must be terrified. 'Miller! Eliot sent me! It's OK. I'm one of the good guys!'

The curtains twitch and Dante's hopes rise. He can see the outline of a mushroom-shaped head with a white face in the middle, and the glint of round spectacles in it. Dante waves his hands backward and forward, like ground crew landing a plane, and shouts, 'Open the window! I just want to talk!'

There is a long moment of inactivity up in the flat, but the pallid face remains, peering out. Shrugging his shoulders in frustration, Dante shouts, 'Come on man, please. Just let me talk to you! I'm not going until you open the window!' There is the sound of a latch being clicked back, followed by the squeak of a hinge. The end of a long red-brown beard pokes through first.

'Jesus,' Dante says, never having seen such a long protuberance of facial hair.

'No,' a mellow American voice responds, 'and I ain't Moses either.'

After the silence and the dark and the strain of the night and what he's come to realise were Eliot's last moments, he is glad of the opportunity to let go for a moment. He finds himself laughing. It comes on him quickly and his laugh has a wild ring to it. 'How long have you been shut in there? You're starting to look like Ben Gunn.'

There is a flicker of a smile on the small mouth but it quickly straightens. 'Who are you?'

'My name is Dante. I've been Eliot's dupe. It's a long story.' But the edgy moment soon vanishes, and he loses the strength to continue talking. Instead he finds himself confused. He looks at his boots and holds one hand uselessly in the air.

'How do I know I can trust you?' the voice says from above.

Dante can think of nothing to say. Despite the jocular first impression, Hart Miller is frightened. Even in the dark from a distance, his voice sounds strained and slurred and his hair and beard are matted from neglect. Dante drops his hand and forces himself to speak. 'Look, Mr Miller. I've had a terrible . . . night, week, whatever. In fact my life turned into a nightmare the minute I crossed the county line. Too many shocks for one lifetime, let alone . . .' He can't finish. It is too hard to keep it all back.

'Amen to that,' Hart says, the voice sympathetic.

He looks up again. 'Eliot said you knew something. So do I, and I need help. I can't stand out here forever.'

'I got time,' Hart says, quietly.

Frustration makes him wave his hands about again. 'I had a friend with me, but he's gone.' Dante's voice starts to break, but he squints as if looking at the sun and swallows. 'He's gone because of Eliot. Because of what he brought here. I don't know how much you know, but we could be all this town's got left.' Dante looks over his shoulder at the dim shopfronts, caged within brown Presbyterian stones. 'And they don't even know it,' he adds, softly, to himself.

When he looks up, the face has disappeared from the window. There is a new sound, of feet running down the stairs and something heavy being hauled upward.

'Thank you, God,' Dante says. He takes weary steps to the flat door. Through the glass, he can see a shadowy figure, hunched over and tugging the couch to the top of the stairs. Then the chunky figure disappears indoors before reappearing on the stairs. Miller trots down the staircase, but only opens the door a fraction, leaving the latch chain on. 'Stick your hand through,' he says.

'What?'

'Just do it.'

Dante slips his right hand through the aperture. Tentative fingertips press his skin. 'Well you ain't one of the living dead,' Miller says. 'But how do I know you're not in cahoots with the others?'

'Come on. Do I look like one of those . . . those –' the word still sounds ridiculous even after all he's seen '– witches?'

'Listen, buddy. I've been shut in since midnight yesterday. Before that I was in Edinburgh, trying to get a passport after they turned my pad over. I was going to get on the first plane that'd take me away from this evil place. But I didn't. I'm an idiot. I came back. And I've slept for four hours tops right through, and now I'm forcing myself to stay awake another night. They stole all my stuff. My evidence. Some girl I just don't like the look of, did it. She knows I live here and she's been hanging around. And when I forced Eliot to talk to me, he never mentioned you. For all I know, the whole town's in on this. So what makes you someone I can suddenly trust?'

Dante looks at the sky with exasperation. 'I can't prove shit. I'm tired and my body hurts.'

'You'll have to do better than that. I've half made up my mind to open this door. But whoever is in on this thing, they're worse than Jehovah's Witnesses. They just break in –' there is a pause, and Miller can't support his instinctive attempt at humour '– and I started to see things.'

Dante looks at Hart's blanched face. Suddenly he has an idea. He unzips his jacket, untucks his shirts and shows Hart the bruises and welts across his torso, poking out from beneath the white strappings over his ribs. 'The girl you saw. Her name is Beth. She did this. Beth and the thing that comes with her. Twice they nearly had me. Twice. And I just rescued Eliot from his own home. He told me you were the only one who knew about this. Maybe, I thought, you could help. I understand your caution. Believe me I do. But with or without you, I'm going back to the place it all started, tomorrow.

To bring that shit-heap to the ground. I've set my mind on making preparations, and I don't have time to wait. Risks have to be taken. If you're genuine, take one, right now.' Hart Miller continues to scrutinise him closely through the gap in the door. Dante exhales; he bends over and puts his hands on his knees. 'I'm just too fuckin' worn out to cry, sleep, scream or beg. There's nothing else I can say.'

The latch is unhooked.

When he sees the inside of Hart's flat, he can't prevent himself from gawping. 'Jesus, they put the wind up you.' Every wall in the living room has been daubed with chalk markings. There are primitive-looking scratches and runes around the windows, strange geometric shapes with tiny Latin inscriptions in their borders on the kitchen walls, and massive white chalk circles scratched on the floor, where the rugs have been raised and rolled back to the skirting boards.

'Glad you're impressed,' Hart says. 'Been thinking about a second career in decor. The present one's too risky. You should check out the bedroom.' Dante does.

The bed is raised against the window and held in place by a ponderous brown wardrobe. A single green sleeping bag has been laid out with some candles and a bottle of Scotch in the middle of a huge chalk circle. Another smaller circle has been drawn inside the outer one, and then a fine white powder has been sprinkled over the chalk lines of each circle. Dante walks around the outer circle reading the words inside it aloud. 'Agla, Dominus, Adjutor, Meus.'

'Had a problem getting the circumference points equidistant from the centre without a slide rule,' Hart chips in, his hands on his hips now as he admires his own handiwork.

His voice has grown more confident. It pleases Dante to see Miller feeling the undisguised relief his company provides. He gets the impression the strange bearded American doesn't get much company.

'This shit work?' Dante says.

'Still breathing, ain't I?'

Dante bends over. 'Looks kind of familiar.'

'Careful, dude!' Hart shrieks, and catches his arm.

'What?' Dante says, and jumps back.

'Don't break the seal. Don't even scuff the lines, man. It's been hell trying to keep that flour together.'

'Flour?'

'Yeah. Babylonian trick, and I got the circle from Eliot's *Banquet for the Damned*. Read it the other day. He pinched it from the Lemegeton. I went back to the library this morning, when there were loads of people around, to get some information on protection. His book was still about the best, though. Funny, that.'

'Done your homework.'

'What else has a crazy paranoid shut-in got to do, except read freaky books? I got the *Banquet* second-hand. And this cat over at the library called Rhodes – the only friend I've got left in town – helped me with the rest. Couldn't get any holy water, though, and I wanted to use the Solomon version of the protective circle, but there wasn't room to draw the triangle.'

Dante stares at the enthusing bearded figure and smiles. 'You're fuckin' nuts. But I like your style.'

Blushing, Hart nods. Dante extends his hand. 'Dante Shaw,' he says. Hart shakes it vigorously with a hairy paw.

'Here, help me with the drawbridge,' Hart mutters, and

then scurries off to seize the couch. Dante follows and, in minutes, he's been tutored in Hart Miller's carefully practised art of barricading. 'Should be safe till morning,' Hart says, wiping his hands on his greasy combat trousers before padding back up the stairs.

'Hope so,' Dante says. 'I stirred things up tonight.'

Hart turns at the top of the stairs, his face pallid again. 'Think they could crash the party?'

'Fuck!' Dante says.

'What! Don't start shittin' me, buddy, now I locked you in and all.'

'It's all right. Left my knife in the Land Rover. It's useless. But it gives me some peace of mind.' Hart relaxes, and Dante nods at him. 'We still got the circle, though. Right?'

Hart chuckles. 'Time for a drink.'

'Good call,' Dante replies, his voice tired. He thinks of Tom by just saying it. He clears his throat. It all has to be held back until his business with the town is finished. Closing his eyes, he takes a moment.

'You all right?' Hart asks.

Dante nods. 'I have some smoke too.'

Hart smiles. 'Oh man, I could get down on one knee.'

Through his fatigue, which makes him feel oddly warm, Dante entertains a curious vision of the bearded man in a wedding gown. He starts to laugh, and the two scruffy men go and sit on the bare floorboards in the lounge, inside the circle. They trade slugs from a bottle of Scotch, in between handing around the cones that Dante rolls in his lap. Hart makes some peanut butter sandwiches too, which they eat with a hunk of cheese and bacon-flavoured crisps. After wolfing the food down, like convicts suddenly released from a chain gang to a soup tent, they swap their stories.

Afterward, they sit in silence for a long time. Hart looks at a candle flame and Dante at the end of his smoking cigarette. The holes in each other's mysteries have been filled, but enlightenment brings no comfort; each man is left with a growing sense of insignificance before the power of the truth they have uncovered, unwittingly or otherwise, and now oppose, unarmed.

Hart is the first to speak. He sits back and rubs his stomach. 'Don't know what I can say about your friend. And I guess you don't want to be reminded of it either. Maybe he's not . . .' Dante shakes his head from side to side and Hart lowers his eyes. 'Then I'm sorry for your loss,' Hart says.

'But, dude,' Hart adds, after a short silence they are too tired to feel uncomfortable in. 'We've both been in this town all this time, chasing the same thing, and our paths never crossed. Seems like an injustice.'

'Better late than never,' Dante adds. 'I'm going to sound foolish even saying this, but hooking up with you has given me hope. And that's dangerous.'

'Why?'

'I planned a kind of suicide mission. Arthur and Harry are in danger. I reckon that's what Eliot just said to me. Maybe they've run for it, but I don't think so. I believe they'll go to the same place my friend and your students ended up.' He looks at the floor and stubs out his cigarette in a saucer. 'So I guessed I was on my own. And I've just let the hate and guilt grow with my fear. And I've frightened myself by just giving up on everything. The past, the future. I started to think I could die here. Like the others. And if I did, what would it matter?'

'But now you don't want to die?' Hart says. Dante exhales, noisily. 'Same with me,' Hart says. 'Walked past the bus station twice this morning and watched those lifeboats pull away to Edinburgh airport. Kicked myself for coming back. I should be in Chicago now. And I still think about blowing out of this town like I stole something every five minutes. Something stopped me running, though, and sent me back to the library to learn more.' Hart looks Dante in the eye. 'Until now, I thought there was no one who could help me either, let alone believe what I've read, been told, or plain figured out myself. It means a hell of a lot to have someone here.' Hart sighs and looks around him at the bits of devastation from the break-in, that he never wasted time clearing up. 'My tapes are gone and so are the witnesses. So in the end, I've just sat here, getting liquored, and drawing these stupid-ass diagrams on the walls, wondering what the hell I could do next.' Hart pauses. 'So what do we do? And don't give me any of that *A-Team* shit.'

Dante smiles, and rubs his back, which has begun to ache again.

'We are going to light a fire, Mr Miller. A big fire.'

FORTY

Behind stacks of Doritos and screenwash in the kiosk, the inquisitive and suspicious face of a uniformed attendant watches the grubby, bruised youth with long hair filling his Land Rover with explosive fuel on the forecourt of the garage opposite the West Port arch.

The smell of petrol is beginning to make Dante dizzy. When he began his preparations he enjoyed the first whiff of 'four star', but now, as the pale liquid sloshes from the nozzle of the pump into the eighth gallon drum he's filled, it makes him feel faint. All of the containers are made from red plastic, and he's collected four of them over the years he's been driving the War Wagon, which often runs dry, and bought an additional four from the garage shop. After filling the last one to the brim, he stacks the containers in the Land Rover to one side of the cabin's dusty floor. As he arranges the gallon cans to minimise their movement in the metal cabin, he thinks of the flat leased to him through Eliot. Ben Carter lived there. Why didn't Arthur tell him? He and Harry must have known. And that is the reason the police officers were uncomfortable when they took his address. No penny of rent has been paid since he's been there, he is clueless about the owner and, if Eliot has taken his own life, will inquiries be made about its present occupant? What does he do with the key? The two bedrooms are still filled with guitars, amplifiers and black bin bags containing clothes. If he doesn't make it through the night, where will it all end up? Will the remnants of his and Tom's lives be stored in a police lock-up while Johnny Law scratch their heads looking for next of kin? Perhaps Imogen's baby will inherit it, and wonder for the rest of its life what the mysterious father and his best friend were doing up in Scotland when they both disappeared.

His thoughts mingle with the petrol fumes. He leans against the Land Rover, weak in the legs. Anything suggesting finality makes him unsteady on his feet. It won't be a good end. Not at the hands of that thing. It is enough to make a man turn and run for the hills. 'Fuck it,' Dante says, his pale face unrecognisable when he sees it reflected back at him in the Land Rover's windscreen. He has to stay strong. Things were decided the night before; there is no room for doubt now. Hesitation will be their undoing. And who knows, he has to remind himself, there is a chance, slim, but a chance all the same, that he and Hart can make a difference tonight. Maybe after it all there will be time to grieve for Tom and to think of what Eliot has done, and to consider all that has happened to him and around him in the town: maybe every minute for the rest of his life if he manages to leave St Andrews alive. But until that time, if indeed he ever lives to see it, he has to be strong.

As he pays up at the garage, he makes a joke to the assistant about Land Rover fuel economy. 'Got two fuel tanks, you know. Gets real thirsty,' he says in a daze, because he feels he has to say something to the plump woman in a green overall behind the till, who has watched him closely since he pulled on to the forecourt. She says nothing and stares at his scabbed lips and his swollen, unshaven jaw. Even though the worst of the agony is over, his back still hurts and half of his mouth has stayed numb. At least the painkillers given to him at the Memorial Hospital enable him to keep moving; his blessings are few, but that one has to be counted.

'Adios,' he mutters, and then walks back to the Land Rover. After opening the side windows and pulling his scarf over his nose and mouth, he pushes the ignition button and the War Wagon rumbles into life. On the short journey back to a parking space on Grey Friars Street a stream of salty air whistles through the cabin and helps to clear his head of petrol.

St Andrews is enshrouded in gloom. The sky appears lower than ever and it is still grey, the sea choppy, and rain never far away. A blue sky would have been preferable on his last day alive. He closes his eyes. To remind himself of the hope he felt the night before, he thinks of Hart Miller. They drank and laughed in a strange kind of healing process. Both of them were frightened out of their wits and, independently, had nearly gone insane from the thought of facing a gruesome death alone. But in the strange camaraderie shared by the desperate they immediately came together, raising each other's morale and identifying a common goal: the destruction of the coven.

He let Hart talk until dawn, and wished he'd known him for longer. The American was full of good stories and was a veritable encyclopaedia on superstition, psychic phenomena and tribal magic. But most importantly, Hart filled in most of his blanks about what they were about to confront. If, indeed, Beth played host to a spirit, it was very old. Once human and a beautiful woman, over the last five hundred years it had distilled itself into pure and unrepentant evil, managing to claw its way back into the physical world. But the other thing, the Brown Man of legend, as Hart called it, could only be considered with the imagination. 'Throw out your notions about reality,' Hart warned. 'Forget time. It's been existing somewhere else for longer than we can comprehend. Say another place, governed by different laws. Called by different names. Once worshipped as a god. And then forgotten until somebody created a gap, where the walls are thinnest between that place and this. Like right here in this part of the world, where a concentration of someone like Eliot's knowledge will produce results. If the situation is right and the right receptors are in place, of course, like with the students Eliot picked. Maybe it's the weather too, or the alignment of the planets, or a concentration of what we know as psychic energy in this particular locale, I don't honestly know, but it's come back and it's brought others with it. Followers or disciples trapped with it from its last manifestation. Those banished with it, maybe. And this is a kind of judgement day that no one would expect or believe in. This *Dies Irae*. It's revenge and the bloody reinstatement of an old order. An ancient power. It's our sick privilege to be aware of it and to try and stop it.'

Through the long night of planning and replanning, Dante found it easy to empathise with Hart. They'd both scratched around and never found a lucrative role in life. Hart was a loner and a dreamer just like him. Hart chased phantoms and myths through jungles, while he played in bands and developed concept albums. Freaks on the edge of an abyss.

But it is better this way, Dante supposes. It has been easier for them to accept the impossible and do the unthinkable. They have no responsibilities and few ties. Hart's dad is still alive, but he's nursed his son through malaria attacks twice, and probably expects the worst every time his only child loses himself in a steaming forest looking for night terrors. 'We're the chosen ones, buddy,' he told Hart. 'And don't go expecting free drinks if we actually crawl out alive.'

But something about Hart troubles him. His capacity for indecision seems at cross-purposes with what Dante has accepted as an inevitable course of action. Can he count on the stranger? The whisky talk and back-slapping could be bluster. His sudden appearance as an ally has given the American a temporary release from the worst of his fear, but the amount of alcohol Hart drinks worries Dante. Empty whisky bottles line nearly every flat service in the kitchen, and two large bin bags full of empty beer cans are slumped against the cooker. He begins to doubt whether the American anthropologist is ever sober. But after his years in the field, studying night terrors, Dante finds himself unable to be too hard in his judgement. And drunk or sober, Hart is all he has.

It is doubtful whether the couch barricade and chalk circles will serve as even a mild deterrent to something trying to gain access to him, and Hart has surely been added to the list of persons whose existence threatens Beth. Without a doubt, he's been *touched* too. Beth and her companions are stronger now; nightfall is probably preferable to them, but no longer necessary for their movements. Sleep has ceased to be the only medium through which they can travel, and to *it* a locked door is not a problem. 'You're just a mosquito,' he told Hart, before he slept as Dante kept watch that morning, with dawn breaking in a tangerine colour across the sea until its brief optimism was engulfed by cloud. 'Just a nuisance, mate. You got time before they come, I reckon. More than me, but now we're together, who can say?'

Others are now in the service of Beth and her god; a woman collected Beth from the cottage the night he found Eliot, and someone, perhaps the same lady, drove Beth to Hart's flat to ransack it. Perhaps whoever she is hasn't the strength or the psychic power of Beth, but she is another adversary all the same. But it is the epidemic that Hart fears most. With every sacrifice, the weight of energy and corporeality in the Brown Man must have grown. Vanishing students and drifters are just the beginning of something greater; Hart is convinced and Dante doesn't doubt him. If the authorities eventually begin searching for the menace, they'll look for a man, and Eliot will be easy to frame.

Perhaps it is their goal to summon the original coven back, so the town will have new rulers, with seven thousand young impressionable students ripe for an unconventional education. 'It could be the start of something really hideous,' Hart said, and took a big gulp of whisky after the revelation. 'Once the right number of sacrifices has been taken, the influence of their society will spread like a corruption. Eliot realised this too late. He tried to placate them with you and your friend. They deceived him and carried on snatching students.'

Taking the confrontation to the cottage tonight, surprise will be their only advantage. They must make their move the moment the town streets and the local roads clear of cars and witnesses. They have to torch the coven, or at the very least, maybe destroying the cottage will uproot and destabilise it, or force it into the open and serve to scatter it. There is no other course of action they can think of taking. It is too late to try and reverse what has been done through ritual, and Eliot, with his vast store of esoteric knowledge, has already failed in his attempts at both banishment and containment. It has come down to violence, an option both he and Hart feel uncomfortable with, but one that both men acknowledge, historically, as being the only method they know to have worked. At least temporarily.

Just the thought of setting fire to a building in the hope of incinerating its occupants makes Dante sick with nerves. And there seems to be only one thing in his character that he can recognise and call upon. Revenge. Avenging Tom's grotesque end, which he unwittingly facilitated, will be the only impulse enabling him to act in the desperate and murderous manner required. But will rage hold its own against the kind of terror that paralyses a man?

'What's the time?' Hart asks Dante for the third time in an hour.

'Eleven,' he answers. 'Not even lunchtime and we're nearly there.'

By means of a small rubber hose, he and Hart have begun to fill an assortment of empty whisky bottles with petrol from the gallon drums. In the top of each bottle they then stuff strips of shredded bed sheets, patterned with tiny floral prints. After exhausting Hart's supply of empty whisky bottles – ten – Dante decides on one more cocktail to be safe, and begins pouring milk from the bottle he found in Hart's fridge down the sink.

'Whoa. Dude, don't be tipping it away. Dairy produce takes the oxygen out of the rivers and reservoirs. Fish die,'

Hart says, fidgeting behind Dante, having lost interest in making the Molotov cocktails.

'Unless you want to drink it, there's no other place for it.' Dante looks across at Hart's last two sloppy efforts. 'You'll have to redo those. You have to leave air at the top for the fumes to build up.'

After sighing and blowing, Hart flops down on the chair. 'It's freezing in here with the windows open.'

'Is it?' Dante asks quietly, his concentration taken up with the filling of the last bottle.

'I need a joint. You still have some gear, right?'

'Yup, and I'm gasping for a fag, but we can't risk a naked light with the fumes.' Dante glances at Hart, who now sits in the centre of a chalk circle with his hands clamped between his knees. The small bulbous American bites at his beard where it grows at the sides of his mouth, and rocks his body back and forth, gently. A familiar flush passes over Dante. Seeing Hart on edge does him no good. 'Relax, Hart. Take it easy.' Hart looks at him accusingly, as if he is appalled a man can be without compassion in such a situation. 'There'll be time enough for shitting ourselves,' Dante adds, grinning.

Hart swallows. 'I gotta take a dump,' he says, and rushes for the bathroom.

When he returns, mopping his face with a hand towel, Dante says, 'That big, huh?'

Hart wants to laugh but can't make the effort. He begins pacing instead. 'Sure this is gonna work?'

'No.'

'It's this deal with soaking the place in petrol that bothers me most. We have to get in first, right? And if we get that far, you said it was all damp in there.'

455

'Yup.'

'And what do we need the cocktails for? They could just bounce off . . . things, and leave us out in the middle of nowhere with the . . . you know.'

Dante sniggers. The laughter that accompanies hysteria is not far away. His giggle grows to a chuffing and then to an almost silent gasping. Crouching down, he begins wheezing.

'You gonna get me eaten, and you sit there like it's the funniest thing you ever heard,' Hart says, an undeniable smile twinkling in his eyes and crawling through his beard.

'Stop it,' Dante rasps, 'or I'll wet myself.' He wipes tears from his cheeks and from around his dark wet eyes. 'This is crazy. A bearded hippie and a hair-metal singer with the future of the town at stake. They're fucked.'

'We need to call in an air-strike from that airbase,' Hart says, nodding his head. 'Think I could talk them around?'

In his mind, Dante sees a bearded man in a flannel shirt gesticulating to an armed sentry. He starts laughing again. Hart joins him this time.

'Shit, it's good to laugh again. I don't know why I am. It's that or crying, I guess,' Dante says, between his sniffs.

'Or crawling in my bag, assuming the foetal position, and shivering a lot,' Hart chips in, and starts Dante off again.

'Yeah, your friend Adolpho would come back from Brazil and find a bearded skeleton in his bedroom.' Hart begins wheezing and swatting at the air with his hands. But then the phone rings and each man falls immediately silent. Dante straightens up. 'Should we answer it?'

'No,' Hart says, shaking his head to reinforce the instant decision. 'They like to check up on me. I get calls, but stopped answering yesterday. So they think I've gone.'

Dante turns to face his curious ally. 'We have to do it tonight, Hart. You know that?' Hart swallows. 'You'll be fine here on your own for an hour or so?' Dante asks.

'Why? You can't leave. It's too risky.'

'Look mate, we need food. We both have to eat. No food and the smell of petrol is making me sick.' Hart looks at Dante, unconvinced. 'There are plenty of people about. It'll be cool. I'll be out and back in no time. We're all right for now.'

'I don't know, buddy. They could be watching. Fetching the petrol was bad enough. They must know we're together. Get separated, get picked off, and then we're fucked before we get airborne in that crazy jeep. Maybe we should do it now. Just fuckin' do it now, while it's light.'

Dante fishes the Land Rover keys out of his jeans and clips a Marlboro cigarette between his teeth. 'Too much traffic. People would see the smoke. You want to get locked into a cell and have that thing come for you there?' He moves for the door and swings his leather jacket over his shoulders. 'Anyone gets in my way, I'll drive over them. Stay cool.' He winks and leaves the lounge.

FORTY-ONE

Harry looks across a sea of expectant faces. Seated in a semicircle around the dais, in the expansive wood-panelled Parliamentary Hall, five hundred new postgrads are waiting. About to begin Masters degrees and PhDs, they look up at him from below the oil portraits of the old deans with dour faces, each worthy's name etched in bronze at the bottom of his frame. Tired wisdom above the eager, serious faces beneath.

Harry smiles, sending his stare and welcome out and into the smells of antiquity, and the sounds of fidgeters, coughers, and bench scrapers. His head, mercifully, is clearer now. Two aspirin and a pint of orange juice have erased the damage inflicted by Dante's whisky, Arthur's story, and a night of interrupted sleep. He looks down at his notes and straightens the card on the top of a neat pile. In his mind, he straightens his thoughts too; he blinks quickly, inhales, clears his throat and thinks of the first line of his speech. The whole thing timed at twenty minutes. Honed after ten years as Proctor of the university. He says, more or less, the same thing every year to the assembled scholars.

Final fidgets and hushed conversations subside. His lips part and so do the large wooden doors at the rear of the hall. They click open. Heads turn and Harry squints over the rims of his reading glasses in anticipation of watching sheepish late arrivals shuffle through. But no one enters the hall. Instead, a gust of cold air, wet with rain, hisses through the aperture and lifts introductory papers off the empty seats.

'Looks like a restless spirit has come to hear your speech,' someone says, from the chairs behind him on the stage, where the staff sit. Harry turns, curious. It is George Dickell, Head of Careers, draped in his black academic gown. George laughs. Harry smiles, but with difficulty.

Someone from the back row stands up and closes the door, the sound of their heels echoing to the ceiling, so far above. 'I'll start again,' Harry says, a quaver in his voice. Did the staff notice? 'Ladies and gentlemen, I would like to begin this morning by welcoming you to St Andrews University, for the beginning of the Martinmas term. I hope my short introduction isn't as grim as the weather.' A ripple of titters passes through the rows of chairs, but soon falls mute. 'Assembled behind me is a hand-picked regiment of crack troops –' Harry turns to nod at his colleagues '– the Chaplain, Head of Library Services, our Student Union President, and Careers Officer.' But no Hebdomidar. Where is Arthur? No call, no notice of absence. Did he go out to the cottage last night like a damned fool, with that damned fool Dante? 'They'll take a little of your time to introduce the various services of their offices. At St Andrews, I believe we offer the very best in support services to the postgraduate body . . .' He pauses. There appears to be a small commotion in one of the back rows. Someone at the corner of his vision stands up. They are tall, very tall. He takes another glance down at his notes to find the thread, to stop the stutter. But the far-off figure, which blends into the long curtains, fails to sit down. Harry clears his throat and peers out. A long arm stretches upward, as if to wave at him. From the back, now, where the rows are empty, and the grey light is lost in the gathers and folds of the dark curtains, a thin arm beckons.

Harry swallows and says something about academic excellence. Wrong paragraph. There is a joke before that. He missed it. Will they not sit down?

'Yes?' he says, aloud, looking to the back of the hall. Everyone below turns also to look at the interrupter.

Harry squints. Moving his head to the side, he tries to find a ray of weak light in which to see the upright figure. A fetid odour rolls over the podium. He looks away, one hand raised instinctively to his nose to block out the stench. A shuffling begins in the rows of chairs beneath him. Behind him, a flash of white catches his eye. It is the chaplain's arm, rising to smother an offended nose. 'This town is very old,' Harry says aloud. 'I think it's time we replaced the sewers.'

There is an uncomfortable silence below, and then some laughter – confused, nervous – followed by whispers. Alarm at the stench rises through him and tightens his throat. Humiliation sweats across his brow. His eyes dart back and forth to pick out the chaplain at his side, on the left of the stage. The man's usually florid face is ashen. He is perspiring too. The familiar jolly smile is gone. The priest fishes a handkerchief from a tight pocket in his three-piece suit and applies it to his face. 'Are you . . .' Harry begins, looking at the man.

More chatter rises from below the stage. One or two words are said aloud from the audience too, but are soon lost among the dry shuffles of feet and the creak of benches.

The Student Union President places a hand on the

chaplain's arm and whispers something to the sweating man. The chaplain retches. A loud burping sound issues from his round body. His teeth clamp shut and his cheeks fill out as if he is about to play jazz trumpet. A fine milky spray squirts through his teeth and lands on his black trousers. The Union President gasps. Below the dais, chairs scrape backward, and several female voices express concern aloud. The smell in the hall worsens, and now Harry coughs to expel the taste from his mouth and nose.

The chaplain is helped to his feet and guided toward the fire exit at the left of the stage. Students in the back rows leave their seats, their heads bent forward on to their chests so their noses can escape the worst of the stench. Others from the front join the evacuation from Parliamentary Hall, desperate for clean air. 'I have no idea what this could be,' Harry calls from the dais. 'Sewers,' he adds, and thrusts his forearm across his nose, the scent of the chaplain's vomit fresh like vinaigrette about his face.

The chaplain burps again, loudly, and expels the load in his mouth down his vestments, onto his shoes and across the outstretched arm of the President. It makes a splashing sound that won't stop. There seems to be so much of it.

Speechless, Harry turns back to the audience, now thinning so quickly. Should a recess be offered? A medic called for the chaplain? An appeal for calm and an apology? His thinking derails; he is confused, and the stench is truly awful now, impossible to withstand. Amongst the now fleeing, gagging students, who leap from their seats and stumble to the main doors, creating a tumultuous clatter and scraping, Harry sees the tall, standing figure at the back of the hall again. It moves.

'Jesus,' he says, and falls back from the dais. It grins and the arms, too long, sweep out to catch a young woman with short black hair. She is pulled to it and smothered in a grotesque embrace. The smell of corruption intensifies. She screams, her silky bob suddenly animate around the howl of her mouth. Her stocky legs are pulled from the ground. 'No!' Harry calls. He rushes forward and clears the dais of his notes.

On his knees now, he looks up, but sees nothing. His vision has dissolved into a myriad of tiny hexagons, as if he is peering through the eyes of a fly. An excited voice whispers in his head. '*Dies Irae*,' it says.

'No!' Harry cries out, and shakes his head.

'*Sit tibi terra levis*,' it says. Harry knows the line. The meaning returns from his days teaching Classics: 'May the earth rest lightly on you.' Dropping his head, he covers his eyes with his hands. His grey hair flaps across his forehead.

'Harry,' someone says, from nearby.

'No!' Harry shouts.

'Harry! For God's sake. Harry, what is it?' Another voice.

His vision clears. The smell vanishes. His eyes refocus and the tiny pixels disappear from his eyesight. George Dickell is bent over, staring at him, his face shocked white.

'Did you see it?' Harry asks.

'See what?' Dickell asks.

'That,' Harry says, not daring to look up, but pointing at the rear of the hall. 'The smell,' he whimpers.

'Let's get you some help,' the chaplain says, on his other side, his voice kind, his cheeks red, his black suit clean and pressed. But how can this be? Harry looks away from them and back to the hall. It is full of seated, silent students. The doors to the hall are closed. No one stands tall at the back near the curtains.

'You were ill,' he says, in a weak, humiliated voice to the chaplain. 'I saw you being ill.'

'Come on, let's get him out of here,' the chaplain says to George. Harry is helped to his feet. The Student Union President is talking now from behind the dais, his voice thick with embarrassment as he apologises and tries to make light of the Proctor's disgrace.

'I couldn't have imagined it,' Harry says. Embarrassment melts the ice of terror from his face and back.

'You're not well, Harry. Get some air, for God's sake,' George says.

'He's all right, he's all right. It's OK. Harry, my man, you've had a funny turn,' says the chaplain.

Harry breaks from their soft, guiding hands and runs from the stage.

Beside his watch on the bedside cabinet, he places the coins from his trouser pockets. They slide against the metal bracelet of the watch. Harry sighs. Carefully, despite the thick-headedness of sleep and sedation, he restacks every coin on the coaster, where his mugs of morning tea are usually left by Barbara, his wife. Fifty-pence pieces at the bottom of the stack, followed by the chunky one-pound coins, topped by the twenties, the fives, and then the one-penny coins. No two-pence pieces: lucky. Over his vest, he buttons his pyjama top, and then slinks beneath the duvet. He shivers until the sheets around his feet warm.

Gradually the sense of ridiculousness at having to go to

bed in the afternoon subsides. He closes his eyes, and everything swims in the reddish-black sea behind his lids. Voices and scenes from the morning drift through his mind: 'Your blood pressure's a little high, but it's nothing to get worried about,' the doctor had said, his patient face unmoving.

No good. The doctor was no help. Where were the answers to explain what he saw? And the stench; the appalling smell in Parliament Hall. What of that? 'Why did I see things?' he'd asked.

'Stress?' the doctor. offered, with his back to Harry, who had remained, slumped, on the surgery bed once the check-up was over.

'I'm telling you,' Harry had said, far too quickly from where he lay, too preoccupied to jump from the squeaky mattress to dress in the customary haste, after revealing his nakedness to a stranger with hands that smelled of soap. 'It was as if the world changed. All around me, you know. My vision was . . . altered. It went into a hundred little shapes. And I saw the chaplain, quite clearly, get up from his seat and become ill. Stress doesn't do that.'

'No,' the doctor had said. 'It's not likely. No medication, you say?'

Harry remembered looking at the ceiling of the surgery, and raising both hands in exasperation. 'No.'

'And you're absolutely sure you didn't eat anything disagreeable? Flu symptoms? Any of these unpleasant smells before?'

'No,' Harry had said, emphatically. 'Maybe I'm not sleeping too well, but with . . .' He paused. 'With the start of the new year, everyone is up to their eyeballs. But to imagine something like that. A complete scene, a whole moment, and to then find myself standing like an idiot before the entire postgraduate body.' His face had flushed scarlet and he had closed his eyes for the worst of the feeling to pass. 'Doesn't make any sense at all.'

'No, it doesn't,' the doctor had agreed, nodding. 'I'll send your blood tests off and I'd like you to go to the Memorial Hospital for a scan. Just to be sure. If you have a repeat experience, call the surgery immediately.'

'Maybe I need a priest,' Harry had said, softly, while he buttoned his shirt.

Then he'd driven home, with the prescribed pills in a paper bag, rustling in his overcoat pocket. A speckle of rain had blurred the world, in between the swipes of the wiper blades on his windscreen. But he never saw much past the bonnet of his car, with only the vaguest presence of mind to keep the car on the road while making another fruitless phone call to Arthur on his mobile.

'Not in this morning, Harry,' Marcia had said. 'Have you tried Parliament Hall? He's supposed to be there.'

'I've just come from there. Why would I look there if I've just come from there?' Run from there, he wanted to shout.

Her end of the phone stayed silent.

'Sorry,' he'd said, clutching at the bits of himself that still made sense. 'Sorry, Marcia.'

'Is everything all right –' she began, but he cut her off and dropped the phone, only to pick it back up and place it in symmetry with the side of the passenger seat.

Was the episode with the postgrads nothing more than a reaction to the night before? Maybe it made him peculiarly sensitive; Arthur's story has played on his imagination and made him hallucinate. That is all, perhaps, and it is over

465

now. A funny turn. Not surprising. But the face. The face that looked back from the dark at him.

He turns over in bed and presses his head, hard, into the pillow. Don't allow it. Don't allow yourself to dwell on it. 'No,' he'd even said, aloud in the car when he thought of the face. With a free hand, he'd had to straighten the rack of cassettes before the gear stick, and then adjust the folded windscreen cloth on the dashboard, to force it out of his mind and away. Taking the pills to sleep it off is the only option, the only thing that can offer peace.

He'll phone Arthur again in the evening, when he wakes up. Find out where he's been. What more can he do?

Lying in bed, he begins to fall asleep in stages, only to jolt back out of them again, moments later, as he tries to remember the actual journey back from the doctor's. Where did all the familiar turns go, and the traffic islands he drove around, and the landmarks? 'Not like me at all, at all, at all,' he whispers. The sedatives are strong. His mind softens into the pillows. Never needed them before. Never needed tablets. But the face, from the back of the hall – the grinning of it. Oh, Jesus. Don't take it to sleep with you, he tells himself, over and over again. Let the tablets kill it.

He wasted no time gulping them back in the kitchen, after plucking a glass from the draining board beside the sink. Three of the red and white capsules, instead of two after a meal, are inside him now, swallowed with ease where ordinarily he struggles to swallow any medication, and always has done since childhood.

Did he call the office? Yes, on his way up the stairs to bed. He left a message with his secretary too. He remembers wincing all the time he spoke, at the thought of the explanations he will have to make about his performance in Parliamentary Hall. They will think him mad. And Barbara? Still at work at the tourist board, but he's left her a note, pinned under the magnetic strawberry on the fridge door. That is all he can do. Yes, he's done everything he possibly can now.

In the large bed, with sleep so near and his thoughts dimming, he feels better. What little natural light remains outside, he's already closed the thick curtains against. Sleep will heal him. The doctor says so. Harry curls his legs and arms into the foetal position and wraps the duvet tighter around his body. He sleeps.

Barbara reads Harry's note left under the little rubber strawberry on the fridge door. She smiles. He often leaves his excuses there. She remembers all of the late nights he had three years before. Business dinners and negotiations with the people who built New Hall, and there were funding bodies for the new chemistry research investments to meet too. Lunches, conventions, papers, admissions, vivas and hotel functions, dozens of them, a few she attended, most not. Harry wrote about them all, neatly and briefly on yellow notes, night after night, and left them for her on the fridge door. And all the time he'd been seeing Janice.

Pouring herself a large sherry, she knows she should eat something too, because her stomach is playing up. It isn't painful this time; the ulcer is long gone, disappearing as if by a miracle when she made a very special acquaintance. Tonight, she won't need to sit in a chair and sip warm milk and eat the chalky tablets that taste of marzipan. This is a different kind of disturbance making the little splashing and gurgling sounds inside her tummy. Something she experiences more now, now things are changing in her life, in the town, and in the world out there. Hasn't felt this kind of excitement since her teens. She realises that now. Part of her has reawoken, quite suddenly. Changed: like the weather, and the sound on the streets and between the old buildings, and in all the places now in ruin. Something you can taste and smell, that tingles in every joint and digit, that rushes through your veins like flood water – it is all coming back to those who need it most. And those that don't understand, or can't, or refuse to, like Harry, like the people so long ago in Beth's time, well, there is no place for them.

Fresh blood and old magic, Beth says. This is what is needed. So give. Everyone must give.

It is her turn tonight and she's waited long enough for it to arrive. Time her sons had a new father – someone stronger and more attentive. Her own boys are young men now and if she isn't careful they'll turn out like Harry. No, they are to be great men and not tired devious nit-picking fools, obsessed with inter-departmental intrigue, with habits and obsessions that fill the mind up with stale flour.

We were close today, Beth said.

They nearly had him this morning. Harry will never realise how close he came to not making it home. To not seeing his own bed again. Now their lord is stronger, he can brave the daylight, go out beneath the sun if he chooses, and the hunt can be watched by something other than moonlight on distant sands. But Harry was lucky, if only temporarily, to get home and safe to bed.

Barbara finishes her sherry and places it on the coffee table and not on top of a coaster. She sees the wet ring the base of the glass creates on the table top, and laughs to herself. It will go sticky. Pity Harry won't be around to see it when he wakes up.

She checks her watch and stops laughing. There is work to do. Preparations to make. And they still have to be careful. The bigger something becomes, the more people hear about it. Eliot realised that back in the beginning, he who worked so hard to speak to someone who was standing right behind him the whole time. To think, they were here all this time. Never went away. All they needed was a fool.

Walking confidently into the wide lounge, she spots a newspaper from the day before, and thinks of chips wrapped in newsprint, and how the paper soaks up all the grease. Carefully, she separates it, page from page, and tucks the sheets of paper under her arm. As she turns to march back into the kitchen, she pauses, distracted by something on the shelf above the fireplace. Between the photos of her boys in their school uniforms is a photograph, framed in pewter. She and Harry in Tenerife. Barbara and Harry, 1992. She smiles, feeling slightly faint with another rush of excitement up from the stomach, and turns the frame around so their browned and smiling faces look at the wall.

Back in the kitchen, Barbara opens the utility cupboard between the owl calendar and the microwave. Rummaging around amongst indoor brooms, dustpans, and green Wellington boots, she finds what she is looking for. Her hands return to the kitchen light holding the tight roll of black plastic bin bags. On the marble chopping board, using the scissors with white plastic handles that she uses to cut through bacon rind, Barbara slices the bags along each seam at the sides, so they become large rectangular sheets; plastic and waterproof.

Closing her eyes, she tries to imagine the size of the bedroom. Eight or nine bags she will need. No, maybe ten. Twelve to be safe. With the carpet so new, and considering how excited *he* becomes when near the given and the chosen. Not to mention how hard it was to remove the stain from her cream pullover after cutting her finger on the vegetable knife; it is better to lay too much than not enough. She'd better retrieve the old sheets they used for decorating as well, the ones they placed under the ladder and over the floor while they painted the ceiling. Newspaper and linen at the bottom as an underlay, with the plastic sheets on top. Should do the trick if she arranges them all around the bed. The walls can be wiped afterward and most of the liquid will be gone anyway, by the time Harry is dragged down the stairs and taken into the garden.

Now that reminds her of something. She re-enters the lounge and, despite the cold and drizzly rain falling on the garden, she unlocks the patio doors and then lodges them aside. Best precaution to take, considering Marcia has called in the glaziers twice in as many weeks, to repair her sliding doors.

Back in the kitchen while she works – preparing buckets of bleach-enriched water, readying floor cloths, opening a new packet of scouring pads – Barbara listens to the cassette player by the bread bin. Instead of Radio Four – about the only thing Harry can tolerate on even a low volume – she listens to her old Shangri-Las tape. The one with the missing case. It is unlikely the sound of the music will disturb Harry after taking the sleeping pills. She's seen the bottle and, at one time, before she regained her deep and natural sleep, she used the same brand to get through all of those evenings alone, when Harry was out late and her stomach refused to give her a moment's peace.

Humming through the opening bars, she then begins to sing, 'Here comes my guy, walking down the street.' Nearly time to go up the stairs to lay those sheets out. And then, the phone call. So easy, Marcia said. 'And when I see him in the street, my heart takes a leap and skips a beat. Tell him that I love him, tell him that I care, tell him I'll always be there.'

Barbara drops her sponge and rests her back against the kitchen cabinets. It is too much excitement to bear. Will she see him, when he comes into the house? Best to hide, Beth said. 'Sometimes our lord's passions cannot be trusted. They go astray.'

It's the silence before he stirs, deep and cold as a flat lake, that Barbara loves most. How the air settles, as if every busy particle has stopped in awe or in fear. As if even the earth stops spinning when the god comes. She's seen the face of her friend after she gave to him. How fine Marcia looked after acquiring not one, but two for him. To give for honour, for the momentum of what has begun and will rise further until no one, no one at all, can stop it. To offer something for his reward. Our lord.

Harry sleeps but he will wake, she thinks. She smiles. At the sound of his step, he will open his eyes and see a god coming to him. Just for him.

FORTY-TWO

'Oh, Jesus!' Hart cries out.

Crashing out of sleep, Dante sits bolt upright on the couch. Still in a daze, he turns a blinking face to the lounge windows. With his hands spread apart on the windowsill, Hart leans forward, staring into the street below. In the distance the long and furious wail of a fire-engine siren rips the air. Unsteady on his bare feet, Dante staggers across to Hart, who sticks his head and shoulders from the open window to see better. 'Look at that!' Hart says, pointing up the street, his face white with shock.

Small crowds of students and shoppers gather in excited huddles on the pavement. They look at each other with worried faces before turning their eyes back toward the clouds of black smoke blowing over the roofs and down Market Street. In a flash of panic that feels cold down to his ankles, Dante thinks of the Land Rover loaded with Molotov cocktails and gallon drums of petrol. He peers across the road to the corner of Grey Friars Street, where the War Wagon is parked. It stands alone before a stone wall: a sand-coloured sentinel with plastic sheets pressed against the windows, covering its explosive entrails. 'Thank fuck for that,' Dante says. 'I thought the War Wagon had gone off.'

'It will do soon, if the wind keeps blowing this way. Something's on fire. Maybe on North Street.'

Another fire engine hurtles past the flat. The street is engulfed by its screams and flashes. The wake hits the windows with a whump of air and Dante's hair blows across his face. Below, cars parked at the kerb shake on their tyres, and buildings shudder the length and breadth of Market Street. Across the jagged roofs, pointed attics, and between distant spires, Dante watches the thick hurricane of black smoke rise in a plume before the wind smashes the top off it and blows smoky tendrils across town to the south. The air seems to reek of a thousand winter bonfires, lit all at once and abandoned to the elements. Darkness rushes in from the sea, carried by thick grey clouds, to eclipse the early glow of the moon-expectant sky. Pale-grey light is sandwiched between the street and the ominous blanket of nightfall, through which people run with a safe haven in mind, or simply stand about looking confused. Somewhere down there, a woman begins to cry.

'And another over there!' Hart shrieks, pointing down Grey Friars towards the Tudor Inn. Behind the white plaster and black timbers of the pub, another tornado of swirling black smoke raises itself. This one is closer, and streaked with orange sparks they can almost hear, cracking and spitting.

'Must be something on the Scores, maybe. Or closer at the end of North Street,' Dante says. His stomach flops over.

'The cathedral too,' Hart shouts. By leaning out of the window, Dante can see a third and more distant smudge of smoke. It flows across the far-off skeleton of the fallen church and obscures its spiky silhouette. 'The whole place is ablaze.'

Dante turns to Hart. 'Why?'

Hart seizes the lapels of Dante's jacket and shakes the last vestiges of dreamless sleep from his companion's head. 'Don't you see! *Dies Irae*. It's gonna happen tonight. This is a diversion!'

'Burn the town?' Dante jabbers. 'Can't be right.'

'Better believe it, buddy!' Hart shrieks. His face is ashen and his hands tremble through Dante's jacket. 'The town burned them alive, way back, after the trials. They've been waiting for this. Now's their time. It's why we're still alive. They keep an eye on us, but they've been busy with something else. They've been busy with this. The whole place is gonna go up.'

Dante knocks Hart's hands off his jacket and peers out at the street again. A group of police cars, parked in a cordon at the top of Market Street by the monument, turns bystanders back toward their end of the street. 'We gotta move, Hart. The police are doing a sweep away from the fires. If they evacuate the town, the War Wagon will be stranded.'

Hart stares right into Dante's eyes. His little bullet eyes blink rapidly behind his glasses. With the overspill from the lights outside, Dante can see the tiny thumbprints embedded on the lenses. 'What say you and me just blow out right now. We don't look back. Get down to Edinburgh and have ourselves a time.'

Dante shakes his head. 'Come on, man. It's started. We need to move now. To the cottage. If this is a diversion, the place might be empty. We can set a trap.'

'Oh man,' Hart says. He walks into the lounge, his head in

his hands, and slumps across the couch. Reaching out, he grasps at a bottle of whisky.

Dante looks up at the evening sky and then checks his watch. 'It's nearly eight! You shouldn't have let me sleep so long! I told you to wake me before six. Hart, have you lost your bottle? You know I can't sleep tonight. It's my last night, for fuck's sake. What were you thinking?'

Hart's face is white with emotion. 'I fell asleep! You said we wouldn't roll out till it got dark. Man, you needed rest. Your back is still fucked up.'

'Shit, shit, shit,' Dante says. He claws his face and walks in a circle. He looks at Hart. 'Sorry, man. I'm not with it. I'm freaked. I'm sorry.'

Hart nods with his face in his hands. 'I'm all wired. Just be kindly.'

Dante fills his Zippo lighter with fuel, until the white spirit overflows and trickles across his fingers. Slapping his pocket, he checks for the four disposable lighters he bought from the petrol station earlier in the day. 'Got your lighters?' he shouts across to Hart, over the noise of running feet, screaming sirens and speeding cars down below. Hart lowers the Scotch bottle and nods, before swallowing and then wincing through the afterburn.

'Let's go,' Dante says. He runs down the stairs to the barricade, hardly able to feel his legs or think straight from the adrenaline. On the way down, he loses his balance and hits a wall. The ribs on his back fire off a salvo of short, breath-stopping spasms of white-hot pain. It is so bad he has to sit down on the stairs. Doubling over, he waits for the little explosions to subside. Hart joins him. 'You all right, dude?'

Dante flops back on the stairs, and rests on his elbows. He swears to himself. The sweat on his face turns cold. All the running around and driving since he checked out of hospital is taking its toll. 'Painkillers,' he says to Hart, who is now tugging the couch, singlehanded, over Dante's head. Hart and the couch disappear and Hart says, 'Wait a minute,' over his shoulder. He returns, the small brown jar of tablets rattling in one hand and the bottle of whisky to wash them down in the other.

'Get your jacket,' Dante tells Hart, and stands up on the creaking stairs. He bites down on the last wave of pain, swallows four tablets, and then takes a quick slurp of whisky. Cigarettes are next. Dante dips his Marlboro into a big orange Zippo flame. He opens the front door. 'I knew I'd die with one of these in my mouth,' he says, and waits on the busy street for Hart to catch him up.

Pandemonium is breaking loose on Market Street. Although the high-street shops are long closed, the Metro supermarket stays open until ten. Shoppers and uniformed staff are gathering on the pavement, herded down toward the Union building by two police officers. Hundreds of students, out drinking in Freshers' week, file out of pubs, their faces full of smiles and laughter. When the heavy presence of police, and a fresh wave of thundering fire engines, registers on the young and tipsy minds, they begin running in a large, bemused and muttering horde down Market Street toward Hart's flat.

Dante and Hart trot across the road to the War Wagon. Wasting no time, Dante fires the engine up and swings the Land Rover around, hitting the horn hard to disperse the people who stand open-mouthed on the road. A pretty girl in a green uniform looks at the windscreen, not really seeing either of them before she moves to the side of the road. An older woman in slippers, who keeps her fingers spread wide on both of her cheeks, follows the dazed supermarket worker.

'The top of Market Street is closed,' he yells across to Hart. 'I'll have to turn it around here. Watch out for people bolting in front of me.'

Hart nods. 'How long will it take to get there?' he asks, his bottom lip trembling.

'Fifteen minutes,' Dante says, peering left and right as he moves the vehicle through the bystanders.

Whisky sloshes in the bottle Hart removes from his mouth. 'What we gonna do when we get there? My mind's gone. I can't remember the plan.'

'We didn't have much of one. Make it up as you go along.'

'Fuck.'

'Settle in, mate. And don't get loaded. Got to keep your head straight. Come on, Hart, I need you,' Dante is pleading. His loss of cool seems to rattle Hart even further, who takes another desperate swig from the bottle. 'Look, Hart. We get there and case the place first. I'm not going to go charging in. Don't worry, we'll pick our moment.' The War Wagon roars up North Street and only pauses at the top to let two RAF fire trucks, from Leuchars airbase, pass. Within a few minutes the Land Rover is gliding past the coast, and away from the thickening plumes of black smoke in the town.

As they swing into Knoxville, the sound of rain batters on the roof of the Land Rover cabin. With this drowning out the noise of the clanking engine, it is as if they have driven right into a monsoon. 'Can you see shit?' Hart shouts.

Dante says nothing but slows down, wondering if the night can possibly get any worse. The headlights throw a pathetic yellow glow at the black sheets of vertical rain. It gathers in huge whorls on the windscreen and smudges away the outside world. The two little windscreen wipers swipe hopelessly back and forth, making little squeaks, only offering quick moments of partial visibility along the bonnet, but not much further. He's never seen rain like it, and the deluge began the moment they reached Knoxville. They amble through the village, and for at least two hundred yards they never advance from first gear. He guides himself cautiously, keeping his eyes fixed on the white line painted on the road.

'Ain't no fire going to burn tonight,' Hart says loud enough for Dante to hear. 'And we must be nearly on top of the place.'

No sooner has he voiced another significant flaw in their plans than the rain suddenly stops. For several tense minutes the storm has been threatening to wash the tiny stone village away and the War Wagon with it, but now the sky seems to suddenly light up above them. Dante glances at Hart, speechless with wonder. Hart slides the dripping side window across and looks at the road behind them. 'Stop!' he yells.

'Why?' Dante shouts back, angry now and tired of Hart's delaying tactics. He doesn't know what's keeping him going, and if the American continues to plug away about giving up, Dante is afraid his own resolve will founder too.

'Just stop. You got to see this,' Hart insists.

Dante pulls up. Hart is out of the cabin before the handbrake is cranked on. Dante follows Hart, until they stand side by side, behind the Land Rover, with their backs lit up by the red tail lights. Both of their mouths open in stupefaction. Above Knoxville, the dark sky boils in on itself. A large circular patch of the heaviest and blackest cloud obliterates any vestige of light from above. Around the area of apocalyptic cumulus, the dusky sky is clear of cloud and bright with early stars. It is as if a filthy skylight window has been cleaned save for a small central smudge of soot. Walking slowly, Hart begins moving toward the rainfall.

'Hang on,' Dante says. 'Where you going?'

Without turning around, Hart beckons him to follow. Beneath their boots, the road is bone dry. But after a short distance the sound of rain, splattering off the tarmac, is deafening. Slowly and silently, they approach the vertical torrent of angry water. It now looks like a huge waterfall, dropping straight from the heavens on top of Knoxville. Hart walks through the skirts of spray and plunges a hand into the almost perfectly flat face of rain. He withdraws a dark, sopping sleeve. 'See,' he says to Dante, his voice hoarse. 'The rain stops right here. It's unbelievable. They did this. Even changed the weather to stop the village people going down that lane.' Hart is rambling, but his little eyes are alight with astonishment. 'Torch the town to occupy the authorities, and drown the nearest settlement. The elements, Dante. They control the elements too.'

'How? This is crazy.' His voice is weak and barely audible over the rush and crash of water on tarmac.

'Witchcraft. I took it all with a pinch of salt. But here's the truth. They used to control droughts and deluges here to destroy the crops. The witches can do this shit with a psychic attack. A concentration of their powers as a coven. Same way they leave the body and hunt.' He turns to Dante and seizes his arm. The grip is tight. 'This is where it's been leading. Their god is so strong. Fattened on sacrifice. I see it all now.'

Dante pulls his arm free. 'Come on. It could mean they're all together. They have to make their connection somewhere. It could be perfect for us.' Without turning to Hart, he catches the white of the American's face studying him. 'Told you I'd lost it,' he adds, with a smile. They jog, side by side, back to the Land Rover. Dante releases the brake, dips the clutch, and they drive away from Knoxville. 'Not far now,' he says. When the road rises up a gentle incline, Dante kills the headlights.

'What you doing?' Hart says. 'You gonna derail this crazy train.'

'I know where I am. These headlights will go right through that hedgerow. They'll see us coming from a mile away. Don't worry, I've only crashed this thing twice. Both times I never felt a thing. This is the War Wagon.'

Hart stares at him as if he is mad. Dante smiles, feeling a welcome heat rise through his body. Taking deep breaths to steady himself, he slides his side window open and motions for Hart to do the same. 'Let the fumes out, Hart. We need to get our heads straight. Round the next bend is the field where we park.' Hart goes still and quiet. Dante can feel his stomach churning.

After slowing down to second gear, they reach the small concealed inlet by the field where Dante parked the night before. He pulls up, right against the metal fence, and then noses the bonnet through the hedge. 'Can you drive a stick shift?' he asks Hart, who nods. 'I'm leaving the keys in the ignition and the gear in reverse. If you have to take off without me, depress the clutch, just turn the key clockwise, hit the ignition button, here, and you're off. OK?'

He can see the immobile silhouette of Hart's head staring at him through the unlit cabin. 'Don't start with that shit.'

'If you make it back, get in touch with this girl and tell her about things the best way you can. I've put a note in too. She'll be cool.' Dante hands Hart an envelope addressed to Imogen. Hart takes it from Dante's fingers, stares at it, and slowly tucks it away, inside his khaki jacket. Dante gives Hart his broadest smile and slips his hand on to the cold metal door-lock.

Hart clears his throat with a big swallow. 'Wait.' He leans over the gearstick and handbrake and gently cups the back of Dante's head with one small hand. He pulls him forward so their foreheads touch. 'Listen, kid.' Dante can smell the whisky on his breath. 'We both gonna be old men, with the longest and craziest beards since ZZ Top, telling our pups about the night we saved St Andrews. You hear me?' Dante smiles. 'Two go in, buddy,' Hart adds. 'And two come out. No other way to do it. Now let's get some.' They clasp hands and stare at each other for a while, before disembarking from the War Wagon in unison.

FORTY-THREE

Outside the Land Rover, the air is cool and windless, the night sky clear. A bright moon turns the fields to frosted glass and the trees into jagged shapes, the spaces between them quenched by the dark. Stars seem closer to the earth, twinkling in a purple-black immensity above the hills and glens, patched with snow at their summits and older than the frailest ruin by the sea. The night's icy beauty, and the sense that a ghastly confrontation awaits, overwhelms Dante with the most powerful feeling of insignificance he can remember. For a while, he just stands at the entrance to the field, and holds the top of the gate for support. Watched by Hart, he is allowed to take a moment. Probably the last moment of reflection he will allow himself tonight.

Eventually, he eases himself up one side of the gate and down the next, using the horizontal metal slats as rungs. Hart passes the cardboard box of Molotov cocktails over the fence. Dante places them on the ground by his feet. 'And the canisters. All of them.' He speaks with urgency now. 'We'll break through the trees at the side of the cottage and try the back door. Might still be busted.'

'We'll never carry them all,' Hart groans, hoisting another loaded box with RIBENA printed on the side.

Looking around nervously, Dante zips his jacket up to his

throat. 'Stay here for a bit while I check the place over. Count to thirty or something and then follow me. And be real quiet.'

Hart nods.

'Now pass me the axe. You take the crowbar.' Price tags are still tied with tiny loops of white string around the smooth handles. The arsenal rattled around on the aluminium floor behind the front seats as they drove out to the cottage. He strove to ignore the sound of them as they trembled and juddered against the cold metal of the Land Rover, seemingly aware of their impending role in a violent conspiracy. Crowbar for the door, and the axe for . . . He doesn't want to think about it. That was the plan that afternoon, as he groaned and wheezed his way between lawnmowers, garden chairs and pots of enamel paint in the hardware store.

The heavy fire axe, with the shining red paint on the blade, is handed over the gate. Dante turns to leave, and Hart begins muttering. 'Don't go tear-arsing in there without me. Stay cool.'

'Don't worry. Wouldn't dream of taking the glory without you.' Dante winks at the pale face in the bushy beard, and then turns to look at the distant spectre of the cottage, a black clump on the other side of an open field. For reassurance, he peers over his shoulder at the American and says, 'We're fine on the outside of the property. They can't see us. The trees are too thick and there's a fence at the back.'

Hart appears unconvinced. Dante walks across the hard clay of the field. It is furrowed in long curving rows, but the topsoil is dried hard and crumbly. His boots crunch up toward the distant row of poplars, chestnuts and baby ferns, planted like a natural corral down the side of the cottage. Above the top of the highest branches he can see the solid black outline of the roof.

Stooped over but running, with the axe clutched across his chest, he covers the last twenty feet. His throat dries out and a single greasy strand of his fringe whips across his eyes, threatening to dislodge a contact lens. Engulfed by the cool and piny smell of the trees, Dante pauses and rearranges his hair. After pulling the collar of his biker's leather up to his chin, and drawing his red scarf over his mouth, he pushes himself through the trees.

Branches and sharp twigs crackle and stick into his hair and jacket, preventing him from moving more than a foot. Crouching down at the base of the barrier, he quickly rethinks his entry. By crawling sideways, he finds a small opening at the bottom of the trunks of two trees. Peering between them, he can see the cottage wall and the weedy path leading to the rear garden on the other side of the trees. Carefully, he assumes a press-up position and smuggles his head and shoulders through the hole. The smell of dark soil and peaty leaf mould fills his sinuses, and the cold presses through his jeans. It seems to take an age to struggle through the gap, his back so delicate, and he is forced to roll onto his side to complete the manoeuvre. Reaching out with both hands he drags his body, up to the waist, into the grounds. He looks left and right, tingling from the sense that he is most vulnerable on the ground. To the front of the cottage he can just see where the lawn begins, but the rear is a wall of darkness, made from the shadows cast down by the trees and fence. He pulls his legs through.

Slowly, Dante stands up. The cottage is silent. As before, it appears deserted. He begins to wonder if it is and hopes that the occupants are out, lighting fires back in the town, or wreaking havoc elsewhere. Behind him, on the field side, he hears Hart's boots scrabble across the clay. Dante drops to his knees and peers through the hole he's just widened.

'Hey now,' Hart whispers from the other side. 'I carried both boxes together. But I fell twice.'

'Cool,' Dante says, only half listening. 'There's no one around. Would they be inside directing their energies, or whatever they are? Or would they have to go out someplace to do it?'

Hart sighs. 'They gotta be in there, man. The whole coven. Only way to raise hell elsewhere.'

Dante nods, and then spits at the earth.

'What we do now?' Hart asks.

'Pass the stuff through. Then crawl after it, real slow.'

With his back to the hedge, Dante smokes half a Marlboro inside cupped hands that shake about the Zippo flame, while his mind does loops and circles, trying to think of fresh strategies and double-guess any potential for disaster. Now they are out in the cold, under the stars and moon, the entire venture begins to reek of the absurd. He wants to rely on his wits, but finds himself belittled by the thought of their cardboard boxes stacked up against a hedge. Too much planning only creates a mire of obstacles and indecision in his mind.

But regardless of whether the place is occupied or not, they will have to get inside and burn the cottage from there. And if anything is waiting in the dark for them, they will have to get in close with it and use the axe. The shakes take hold of Dante's legs and arms. Being so near the cottage makes him remember his last visit. He can almost smell the kitchen with its damp and rot stink. But his thoughts of the paintings are the worst.

If the witches can start fires and storms with their minds, what can he and Hart do with a supermarket box of whisky and milk bottles filled with leaded petrol? He thinks of running. It feels like his clothes are soaking. He touches his thigh. His jeans are damp from the grass, that's all. Then he swallows and stands up at the sound of Hart wriggling the boxes through the hedge. Between the wheezes he makes to regain his breath, Dante hears Hart's anxious voice set at a whisper as he comes through. 'Any sign of life?' He bends down so Hart can see his face, and shakes his head, too afraid now to even whisper. When Hart's bulbous shape squeezes itself noisily through the tunnel, pushing the cardboard boxes through before his body, Dante cringes at the noise and reaches into the hedge to pull the boxes free. Sticks snap and leaves scratch Hart's khaki jacket as he follows. In his mind he begins to recite, *Come on, come on, come on*, until Hart is clear of the hedge and crouching beside him, out of breath.

Dante stays silent, and motions to Hart to follow him to the back door of the cottage. Carrying a box each, with the axe and crowbar hanging over the crook of their elbows, they creep to the back door. Dante drops to his knees under the kitchen window. Hart kneels and stiffens against him. Flashing his torch over the lock reveals it to be broken. Splintered wood erupts from the frame after his previous visit with the screwdriver. Tentatively, Dante reaches out and presses the door. It moves an inch, and then becomes stuck against something inside the kitchen. He guesses the occupants have lodged something against the door from the inside.

Standing up, but bidding Hart stay put with a down stroke of his hand, Dante edges his face around the window frame and shines a torch beam through the bottom pane of glass. In the murk, the torch reveals part of a messy table-top, littered with something he cannot see clearly due to the grime on both sides of the windowpane. But the table itself looks solid and heavy, and he remembers seeing the type of table he associates with farmhouses on his last visit to the cottage. 'Hart, we'll have to put our shoulders against the door and push it in. There's a table or something holding it closed. That's all.'

'What then?' Hart's voice is a whisper, followed by an audible swallow.

Wide-eyed, Dante wipes his mouth. 'We go in quiet. Real quiet, and we soak the place. All through the ground floor. Do as much as we can until they hear us. I reckon they're in the basement. That's where everything starts out here. Then we light it up. They'll be scared of fire. Beth is. I remember her face in St Mary's Court when I lit a fag. And there's loads of newspaper and wood inside. It'll all go up.' Hart nods. His eyes are fixed on the boxes while his lips move, in the way mouths move when someone repeats the same thing to re-assure themselves. 'But we got to be quiet. Really quiet,' Dante whispers. Hart nods.

They move the boxes clear of the weed-covered garden path, place the tools on the ground near the boxes, and then put their shoulders to the door. It bends in the middle with a woody groan, but the table doesn't budge. They change posi-tions, with Hart pressing the lower half and middle of the door with his shoulder and Dante pushing the top half with his outspread hands. Slowly, and with a scraping sound they cringe at, the door moves inward with a jerk. A thin black space appears as the portal widens. For a moment, they stop pushing, each reluctant to be too close to the space they have created.

'Can you feel it?' Hart mutters. Dante nods, and remembers the story told to him by Harry and Arthur. A perceptible iciness slips through the gap they have created, as if unnatural currents and draughts are at work inside the building.

'Come on,' Dante says through clenched teeth, and they double their efforts to widen the gap until it is big enough for one man to squeeze through sideways. Outside in the dark, shivering from the drop in temperature that suddenly engulfs them, they pause again, as if by the side of cold water they must plunge into.

'I'll go first,' Dante says. Quickly, he picks up the axe and his torch and then squeezes his body between the door and the frame, leaving Hart on the outside, standing with the crowbar clutched across his chest.

For a few seconds that pass quickly on account of an overwhelming attack of nerves, a feeling that he will jump through the ceiling at the first creak of a floorboard nearby, Dante's torch beam flicks the ceiling and walls, looking for the door that leads from the kitchen to the rest of the property. It is shut. His presence of mind stretches far enough to make sure he is alone in the kitchen, and that it is still sealed from the rest of the house, but it reaches no further, and he is capable of no other thought when the light from his torch shines upon the table they have partially shoved to one side. Something has recently eaten.

'Oh God,' is all he says, before lurching backward and hitting the sink unit. He squeezes the axe handle until his hand is tight and completely white. He points the torch down and away from the table top, but on the floor are scraps, fallen from the table, on which a man lies flayed. Indelibly imprinted on his mind, even once his eyes are squeezed shut and covered by a hand, is the streaky white and red mess that was once the university Hebdomidar. When Dante imagines raking hands and dipping mouths, made wet by their food, he says, 'No,' and shakes his head from side to side. But the image of the exposed ribs and, above them, the eyes still open in agony and shock, he cannot banish. It is as if the bulky remains of Arthur Spencer have been left as a message to intruders.

'Dante, Dante,' Hart whispers through the door. 'Say something.'

Feeling the air cloud in a freezing vapour around his face, Dante is unable to answer. A second torch beam is clicked on and shines through the gap against the side of his face. Dante turns and looks into the light Hart has shone on him. He cannot see Hart through the brightness, but the shock on his face must register instantly with the American. 'Jesus,' Hart says. 'What is it? What is it? What is it?' Uselessly, Dante shakes his head. 'I'm coming in,' Hart says. Holding his torch and crowbar, Hart squeezes through the gap. As he is thicker than Dante, the table moves again from the force of his roundness against the door, and for a moment the Hebdomidar trembles on the table, as if stirring in his sleep.

As it comes into the kitchen, Hart's struggling body bangs against Dante and sends him sprawling against the sink. The risk of falling down snaps him alert and he regains his balance by seizing the cold metal of the draining board. As he stands up and swings his torch around to light Hart's progress, he sees that the American's entrance to the house is complete, and his introduction to the cottage sufficient. Down beside the dripping table, something yellow and runny drops through Hart's beard and splashes onto the floor tiles, adding a new scent to the putrescence already evident in the kitchen.

When he finishes puking, Hart turns and rushes noisily back to the kitchen door. Dante moves in his way and holds Hart's shoulders, his grip useless while he still clutches the torch and axe. 'Let me through, Goddammit,' Hart says, his voice low.

Dante clears his throat of a lump. 'No.'

Hart renews his efforts to escape, and pushes Dante hard against the back door so it slams shut, sealing them inside the kitchen. They wrestle in the dark, their feet skittering on the tiles where they are dry, and occasionally sliding where they are moist. Coughing, Dante turns his head to the side to avoid the gusts of vomit-breath that gush through Hart's beard.

'I gotta get out,' Hart says, panting from exertion, his strength peaking through his panic. Then he gets one hand under Dante's chin, pushing hard so his head cracks against the door behind. But the pain from the blow refreshes Dante. He drops the torch and axe, which clatter on the floor, and then knocks Hart's arms away from around his neck and face. 'Cut it out. Hart, ease off. Just stop, you fuck –' he says through gritted teeth. But Hart continues to fight to get back through the door. With what mobility he can summon with one arm, Dante strikes out at his shadowy opponent. His fist stops short of his arm lengthening, but connects with a crispy beard, and he hears a muffled grunt across the narrow space between them. Then Hart's glasses hit the floor with a tinny clatter.

Suddenly, the struggle stops. All they can hear is their own breathing, hard and trembling with emotion. 'Sorry,' Dante whispers. 'We have to . . .' he tries to say, but never has the air to finish. Hart falls against him, clutching handfuls of his leather jacket and sniffing into the lapels. Dante seizes the back of Hart's matted head and wants to cry to relieve the pressure inside him, the terrifying tension from seeing what has been done to Arthur Spencer, and so many others too. This is Tom; so quickly he has the realisation. So recently, Tom found the same end in this stinking cottage where foulness is worshipped and fed with innocence. 'Burn it. We got to burn it. We got to kill it,' is all he can say, quickly and repeatedly to his friend. Hart raises his head slowly, but it is too dark in the kitchen to see his face.

'Get the fuel,' the American whispers.

Behind him, as he fumbles to reopen the door, Hart shoves the table aside, no longer worried by the noise he makes by scraping the thick wooden legs across the old floor tiles. Outside, Dante greedily sucks at the fresh air and then rearranges his scarf over his mouth. He drags the cardboard boxes, which make a glassy jingle as they are moved, inside the kitchen. We're still thinking too much, he says to himself as he does this. We need to just stop thinking and do this. If we don't, we'll die out here. God, we could die out here.

As soon as the boxes are on the floor of the kitchen, Hart's small hands are busy inside them. The shock of seeing Arthur and the emotion of the fight seem to have given the American a new and decisive approach to his work. Using the torch by holding it between his teeth, he recovers his glasses from the floor and now pulls the rags from the top of some bottles. Staggering about backward, without a pause, Hart then splashes the fuel across the table and the thing upon it, over the kitchen surfaces, up and against the cabinets, down his own clothes, and across the floor, so the petrol runs across the uneven tiles like olive oil in red wine.

'Careful,' Dante says, gripping his axe in one hand, while lighting Hart's clumsy progress with his torch in the other. 'We should light this room last. On our way out. We could get trapped.' He is unsure if Hart hears him, or even if he does, whether he's taking any notice of the precautions they must take with so much fuel now sloshing around beneath their feet and evaporating into the already close air. He is about to repeat the warning when he hears something that stops him. Hart carries on wetting the kitchen, but Dante angles his head toward the inner reaches of the house, beyond the kitchen door. There it is again. A voice. No, more than one. Voices. 'Hart,' he whispers. 'Hart, stop!' he says in a desperate, hissy voice.

'Nearly there,' Hart says.

'Hart . . .'

But Hart only stops, and takes a step back from the kitchen door, when he hears it too. Far away, outside of the cottage or inside it, for they cannot be sure of the direction of the voices, or the distance from which they issue, they hear what sounds like an approaching crowd. Not a chorus, but a clamour of whispers and far-off shouts, coming closer. No individual words can be deciphered in the growing but still distant babble, so they stand in the kitchen, looking about them, at the dirty ceiling and the stained walls, dizzy from the suffocating reek of petrol, not moving or speaking, each straining his ears to get a fix on the sound.

Until something strikes the kitchen door with incredible force. The crash of a charging weight on wood fills the kitchen to the foundations. Dante gasps, and Hart drops to a crouch. 'It's here,' Hart says, his voice louder, but somehow empty of the strength required for shouting.

A tremor begins inside the kitchen, shaking the glass in the cabinets and rattling the loose cutlery on the table. The walls vibrate in the dark, and the light from their torches flickers against anything it touches. A sudden drop in temperature follows. 'Jesus, the cold,' Hart whispers. 'It's so cold.'

Too frightened to move, Dante feels his eyes well up with water and his mouth freeze into a grimace he cannot relax. Fumbling in his pocket, he pulls his Zippo free and is ready to end it all right then, to save himself from what he remembers in the painting, and that which swooped and seized his body on the beach. He cannot see it again and survive. It is too much. What are they even doing here? Everything suddenly falls apart inside him: his resolve, his reason, his sense of himself. He begins to fidget on the spot, his movements fast and animal, as instinct takes over. Hart's face is wild in the torchlight and his small arms are moving the crowbar in small circles out in front of him. 'Now, Dante. They're here now!'

Again a tremendous force strikes the door. Both torches flash across the wood. It shakes in its frame and then swings wide open and crashes against the kitchen wall. Hart shrieks, and Dante immediately feels himself afloat in the chaos that rushes through the door and into the room with them.

Around his face, up near the ceiling, across the walls, things are swirling and screaming through the torchlight. Hart clutches himself and shrinks further into the ground. Shadows leap upward from the floor in long and thin shapes. Here he sees an arm, there a long-fingered hand, and over there by the table is the sound of many feet coming at him in haste. And with these footsteps comes a cold wind that ruffles his hair and makes him squint, as if he is walking facefirst into a snow blizzard. It pushes him back a few steps, until he is trapped against the sink. And there he waits for a blow to fall, for the end to come at him, to stop his heart with fright, or for a face to tear at his throat from the dark.

But at the point where he can run no more, or flinch, or beg, he flings the axe up above his head and runs at the bellowing, hammering, scratching things all over the walls. Three times he swings the axe. Glass breaks. Wood splinters. Refuse is swept up and into the angry air.

With a triumphant and insane bellow that echoes off the walls, he drops the torch and runs for the boxful of cocktails. Something dives into his face. He feels its energy rush through the electric blackness as he stands up, holding a sloshing bottle. Fleeting airborne screams break across his face with a force of air so thick and cold, he is blinded by frostbite. But he keeps his feet, and swats the lid off his Zippo with a crossways stroke against his thigh, before running the flint back down the same leg to spark up a huge yellow flame. In the violence of the whirlpooling air, he dips the rag into the fire of the lighter, which is weakening, too full of gas and hit by moving air. Shielded by his body, first blue and then yellow at the edges, the rag becomes fire. He holds the bottle aloft and then throws it hard against a wall, where things are crawling and then spilling across the ceiling as if it were the floor.

Glass and fluid explode high in the corner, and throw droplets of orange through the undefined room. Half-glimpsed limbs, and stretching faces with open maws, race back across the walls, some of them carrying flames with them. Long ribbons of purple, their spines etched with orange, dash quickly across the floor in every direction and scurry up the table legs. Around the soles of his boots, a lake of liquid fire pools and ripples and stretches to the skirting boards, empty wall sockets, and the littered corners of the kitchen.

Unseen hands bang the walls of the kitchen as if they are trying to break through from the outside or out from the inside. Dante jumps across the kitchen, flames falling from his heels, with another bottle in his hand. His torch is gone and he runs into a wall and then into the side of the open door. His insane leaping progress, lit by the floor-level splash and flicker of a growing fire, takes him out of the kitchen and into the long hall. Something sticky runs down his face from where he's banged his forehead, and one of his hands is numb from where it collided with a wall.

And it is from here, in the hallway, that Dante hears the new sound, the new chorus, the low mutter of more tangible voices, rising as if from alarm, and coming up the brick stairs into the house where the shadows and the cold fight a battle against the new light and heat of fire. 'Hart! Quick, Hart,' he screams, and then runs to the cellar door, to hold it shut. As Hart emerges from the kitchen, struggling with a box, he hears it too. A set of female voices, their pitch growing higher from the passion of their searching and calling. It is a wail from some forgotten corner of Jerusalem, a song from a dim street in Cairo as the sun sets, a chant from around smoky fires on dark nights in wet Scottish woods.

'*Aquerra Goity, Aquerra Beyty, Aquerra Goity, Aquerra Beyty.*' It comes up the stairs of the cellar and through the floorboards of the hall. Behind it, they can hear the scrabble of naked feet on brick, made fast in their ascent by the taint of the smoke that is here to destroy them. At the top of the cellar door is the thick bolt, and Dante's fingers scrabble to work it loose from the rusty mounting. It is a lock he's seen before, and guesses was once employed to keep captives down there – inside the brickwork of the basement where it all started, until the god arrived to banquet with its devotees. Maybe they kept Tom down there.

Twice his clumsy hands slip off the latch, ripping his knuckles. They are so close now. Feet patter up the last few stairs, and the chatter of their frantic voices resonates through the thin shield of wood. But still he pulls, moaning as he tugs at the metal, because this is something Beth never expected: for them to crawl this far on their bellies, after all they know, and to continue after what they have seen propped up on the kitchen table, and still to light a fire after braving the rush and wind of the spirit guardians.

When the door handle turns against his stomach, the latch finally moves, and the heavy bolt slides through its rusty fixture to hold the wood of the door firm at the top.

'*Aquerra Goity, Aquerra Beyty* . . .' The chant diminishes from three voices to one, and then none. The handle is turned again, frantically, from the other side, clockwise and then anti-clockwise. Then they hear the slap of ineffectual hands on the door, and the mutters of a rising panic.

Dante crosses the hallway. With all his might, he kicks

open the door opposite the cellar, sole-first, and watches it swing inward with a bang to reveal a void from which he expects something to come grinning out. Not waiting for it, he leaps through into total dark, shouting to maintain the oblivion in his head, where no thoughts must jostle and make him hesitate in the red and lunatic world he's chosen to reside in until he falls.

And he does fall, across a couch, which strikes both his knees, to send him flying headfirst, arms outstretched, through the air, and then onto a suddenly animate mass of sliding things. At first, he thinks the surface beneath him alive, and retrieves his axe to attack it, cutting into it with long blows that begin above his head and then whizz through the umbra until the blade strikes bales of damp newspaper.

By the time he realises his mistake, the walls of the room are lit up. Hart staggers through the doorway after him, holding his torch and dragging a box of petrol bottles. 'Hold off,' he yells to Dante, shining his torch right into the white and insane face shown to him.

'Don't let them get out! Watch the cellar door!' Dante lights a bottle and sends it smashing into the bookshelves near the fireplace.

'You'll burn us too,' Hart yells, his face wild, his hair whipping around his face in the louring air.

But suddenly, from all around them, the wind and its voices, the sparse and fleeting and half-glimpsed guardians that chased them in a rout from the kitchen, coil into a slip-stream and then flee the ground floor and the fire in it. In what was once a parlour, the air thins and becomes hot as the oxygen is greedily sucked into the growing fire. For good measure, Dante picks up another bottle and, without lighting it, hurls it at the corner of the room now ablaze. Glass explodes. Up go the curtains with a rip of fire to the brass rail. From the ancient furniture, thick grey smoke wearily sniffs at the air it will soon claim for its own. Old timbers and the loose sleeves of forgotten papers give themselves to the inferno. Dusty upholstery crackles and spits from the shock of its sudden ignition. A dark-brown cabinet seems to have backed into a shadowy corner, its lower drawer bubbling and seared as the varnish evaporates and the wood blisters.

Hart grabs Dante's elbow and drags him from the parlour and back into the hallway, their shadows gigantic on the murky ceiling as they stumble out. The hall runs the length of the house, from the closed front door to the oven of the kitchen, now flickering orange and spewing white, caustic smoke across the hall and under the cellar door. A door ready to break open from the efforts thrown against the other side. Wood begins to splinter around the deadlock.

But just as they watch the door with a growing horror, both fumbling for the axe, the box of gallon canisters they have left in the kitchen is overcome by the fire on the floor, walls and ceiling. Exploding upward, the box shatters glass, and fires a hot bolus of air down the hallway to sear each man's lungs. They turn away with their faces covered, coughing in convulsions, struggling to clear their pipes of burning fuel and cindered wood.

A woman screams. The word 'fire' is shouted by another panic-stricken voice. 'They're burning us!' it shrieks again, and then the handle of the cellar door is yanked until its mechanism snaps free from the wooden fixture. Squinting at the smoke, and sucking air in thin slivers through the drenched wool of his scarf, Dante runs back through the heat and smoke to the cellar door and throws all of his weight against it. 'Do the stairs, Hart! And the other room. Now!'

Dante hears Hart throw two bottles into the front room, one lit, another unlit. There is a pause, and then the American flees from the room, chased by a ripple of fire – blue at its heart, gold on its skin – before slamming the door behind him. There is a whump from inside the room and a sudden glow of orange light from beneath the door, as something flammable goes up like a truck full of straw. With the last bottle – the milk bottle – he raises his arm, preparing to hurl it over the banisters at the stairwell. But he pauses and then flinches when he sees Dante's body thrown from the cellar door he has tried to hold shut.

The force of the door, blasted outward, knocks Dante across the hall and into the wall opposite. Winded, he barely keeps his feet, but staggers a short distance down the flickering hallway. He falls to all fours before he can reach Hart. Over his shoulder he sees a stained hand with dark lacquer on its nails reach through and spread its fingers on the hot wall, preparing to pull the body after it.

'They were in a trance,' Hart shouts, reaching for Dante. 'But they ain't now. We gotta get out.'

There is so much smoke in there now, pouring from the kitchen as the fire burns and splutters far quicker than either of them could have imagined, through rotted timbers and peeling paints, over pine cabinets and up neglected doorframes. And from the cellar a white body and contorted face come through the doorway. With arms still stained dark to the elbows, as if she's been pressing grapes in a wooden vat, the wild and beautiful thing they know as Beth comes coughing into the hallway. She looks at them and screams something unintelligible. It is a call, a summoning, a cry for help that Dante has heard before on a dark beach. Recoiling inside, he says, 'No,' and his voice sounds distant, and it breaks around the single syllable.

From between Beth's legs crawls another woman, grey-haired, and yelling like a hysterical mother, her mouth still smeared dark from what she has recently been feeding on. But the rapture of the trance is gone from her face; the words of the chant vanish and she is nothing but a terrified creature, on all fours, trying to escape the smoke and the sound of crackling flames. Another follows, tall, handsome, hideous and crimson-toothed, bellowing in fear.

Beth staggers into the hallway ahead of her accomplices, no more than ten feet from them now, lit up from behind by the backdrop of flames in the kitchen, which lick around the doorframe as if reaching after her. A moment of disbelief passes across her face, which is now wet with tears from the black fumes. But when she sees them, huddled before the front door, cornered by fire and smoke and unable to unlatch the door, another sound issues from her open mouth. Deep and animal, it is nothing that any woman should be able to utter.

'It's fuckin' locked. Oh God, I can't open it,' Hart yells, taking quick glances over his shoulder at the parody of a young woman that runs to meet them.

'Up!' Dante yells, snatching the last bottle of petrol from Hart's hand. Seizing the American by the collar of his jacket, Dante forces a strangled sound from his comrade, and then yanks him away from the door. He lurches up the staircase, through the smoke, dragging Hart behind him, who twists and turns and loses his footing.

Beth is upon them quickly. The animal sound warbles inside her. Her feet slap the floor. As she rounds the banister and comes up at them, her mouth is howling and black and her eyes are wide, like the face of a berserk thing pressed against the window of an asylum. Both of her fists fall against Hart's back. It sounds as if an empty barrel has been struck so hard all the air is forced from it. He collapses face down on the bottom stairs. Her pale arms rise again and drum down against his back a second time, hammering Hart flat against the stairs. Her clenched fists rebound off his body with sickening thumps. In the split second in which Dante sees the pain pass from his friend's eyes, to be replaced with a white and dreamy confusion, as if he no longer knows where he is, Dante ignites the last bottle with his Zippo and then punches his fist over Hart and into Beth's wild head.

Glass explodes, her head snaps backward. She stares at him, numb with surprise. But then the liquid that covers his arm, and her face, and her hair, runs with the red streaks seeping thinly from the tears on her skin – slits cut into the wet pastry of her face. She steps backward down two stairs, blinking, and clutches the railing for support. She sits down. Her hands go to her face. She screams.

Sickened by the sight of the streaky and now howling face below him – cold with nausea at what he has just done – Dante wants to slump there, smoke-choked, his limbs spent, but his jacket bursts into flame. The fuel from the last bottle is splashed all over him, and Beth, and Hart. Mixed in with the stench of burning timber and furniture is the reek of singed hair and blackening leather. Rolling on the stairs, Dante begins to swat and bat at his sleeve, up which creep caterpillars of yellow fire on speeding blue legs. Blood flicks and drops between his fingers from where the broken glass has cut deep, to sizzle in the fire on his jacket.

Rising to his knees, Hart looks about groggily, feels the fire on his exposed neck, and then leaps to his feet. He howls in pain and panic, slapping at the flames on his body.

Beneath them, at the foot of the staircase, Beth rises and smashes about between the banisters and wall, trying to knock the fire from her body. Her voice is deep, inhuman, incoherent. With what feels like the last of his strength, Dante whips his jacket from his body and smothers Hart's, dousing the large-tongued flame on the American's back, neck and head that his own small arms cannot reach. With his friend coated in stinking leather, he drags himself and Hart up the remaining stairs to the first floor, where the smoke has yet to steal all of the oxygen from the air.

On all fours, as if now appealing for help, Beth follows them. With most of the fire gone from her skin, once milky but now dark, her body steams. And when she speaks again, her voice has changed. It is the voice of a confused and frightened child that now comes up at them through the smoke.

As the light from downstairs flicks upward and across parts of her, Dante sees the blackened silhouette of something that looks like a mannequin caught in the blaze of a department store, and found the day after amongst the ashes. The hair is gone, the head is now skull-like and smoking and made all the worse by the whites of the eyes in the middle of it all. She is calling for her mother. Behind her, her two disciples slap and hammer their palms and fists against the locked front door, frantic in the smoke and reaching flames.

To escape the voice, and the sight of crawling Beth, Dante falls against and then through the first door he can find amidst the smoke of the landing, hauling Hart's smoking bulk on top of him. And there, on the rough carpet in the darkness, he rolls his friend around the floor, only stopping to swat at the last few flames that rear up from his jeans, burning the hair and skin off one shin bone. From his hand, the blood continues to pour, but at a faster rate now the gash has widened. Choking for air, his breath wheezing horribly as if he's been gassed, Hart struggles to his hands and knees. Dante runs to the door and slams it fast on the slowly moving thing that crawls after them, looking for a sanctuary from the smoke. Her hands scrape pitifully against the door. In between the sobs passing through a body traumatised by agony, from which it seems evil has at last been driven, he can hear her trying to speak. Dante tears his scarf away from his mouth and retches down his shirt, the terror of suffocation greater than it has ever been.

'God, we did that to a girl,' Hart says, when he finds his voice. 'Jesus, Dante. We did that to a girl.'

Dante can only look about himself, bewildered, his head feeling like the aftermath of an explosion, dazed and strangely vacant and unable to pull all of the bits together to form a reaction, a word, an emotion. And perhaps it is better that his mind remains fractured and that he never comprehends the full horror of what lies smouldering and whimpering on the landing beyond the door, because the night has still not found its end.

Despite the roaring pyre in the foundations of the house, and the swaying light it reflects up the stairs and through the thin curtains of the room in which their seared and hot lungs splutter and taste winter fire, its smoke thick from damp kindling, each man feels a darkness descend over the cottage and then creep through the very air. The night comes alive again, but not with the wind or the babble of voices from unseen mouths. It comes alive with the presence of a god.

Below in the house, something cracks and then falls, and seems to go on falling for a long time. Smoke pours under the door of their room. Beth has fallen silent; the scratching sounds have ceased. 'We got to get out,' Hart says from where he crouches on the floor in the murk of smoke and no light. Dante runs from the door, aware of the thinning of their air, alert to the only means of escape. He moves to the solitary window frame, where a band of silvery light parts the curtains. He yanks them off the rail and, without looking out, immediately steps back from the window as if he is afraid of being seen. In the traces of light from the moon and stars, he can see the smoke pooling in the top half of the room. Soon it will fill every space and then pour from the window. Their eyes smart and water. All over their patched and sore skin is a film of soot and grease and sweat.

On the floor before him, he can see the shape of Hart's head in the thin, cloudy light; it has a misshapen outline from where the fire has burned into his hair. His glasses glint for a moment and then the head bows. 'We got to get out, Dante. I need help. Too much smoke.' His voice is dry and hoarse.

But how can he tell Hart about what is waiting for them down there?

A woman screams from outside the cottage. The sound splits their ears. The shriek rockets skyward and then suddenly stops. They look at each other with blackened faces. 'It's down there,' Dante says, quietly. Hart remains perfectly still. Dante looks through the window at the front of the property. 'It's here, Hart,' he says in a whisper, and then looks away, but what he sees remains deeply imprinted in his thoughts.

One of the witches who escaped from the cellar did finally manage to break open the front door of the cottage, bathing the front lawn and garden path with orange light, around which thick shadows now spring forward and then retreat to the rhythm of the flames beating inside the cottage. In the movement of light outside, Dante has caught a glimpse of what became of her, down in the long grass. Her pale body lies still now, and it is mostly dark where her head once was.

And something impossibly tall but wasted has now risen onto its hind legs on the grass, in the middle of the garden, to sway about as if bemused by the fire in the place it came out of and returned to when called. It lopes about the grass, an appalling thing in rags, its long shadow cast across the road and into the fields. It seems to know no allegiance now to those who summoned it forth and directed its activities with their ceremony and trance. One lies dead, and the second witch, partially burned, crawls through the front door and, despite the smash of things downstairs and the collapse of wood turning to charcoal, Dante can hear her coughing and pleading with it for mercy.

Hart can too. 'I can't look, Dante. I can't see it. Not yet.' Dante stays quiet. Unable to stop himself from looking again, his eyes fix on the grim events occurring on the lawn.

And what he sees makes the skin shrink all over his head, even under his hair, and something goes pop and then sizzles in his ears. 'God,' he says, when the thing rushes for her as she tries to crawl away, slow in the long grass, her naked body stiff with the pain from so many burns. It swats at her. There is a 'thocking' sound and her body leaves the earth only to land soundlessly over twenty feet away. She lies on her back, not moving, only moaning. Her eyes are still open and she watches the dark thing traverse the ground to her. Spare in limb but graceful in motion, it covers her up and becomes immediately active.

Dante turns away and leans against the wall. His body, curiously, feels weightless. Her cries out there are faint and brief, stifled perhaps by the breaking and cutting of her parts as it goes about her like a big crow on bread cast out on a lawn. Dante looks at Hart, somehow shutting out the sounds of its business down there. Hart has covered his mouth with the stretched neck of his jumper and has begun to cough again, with a muffled sound, as if he is coughing to himself in the way people talk to themselves. 'It's time, Hart. We can't stay in the smoke any longer.' Hart nods. He never even looks at Dante, or speaks, perhaps understanding but made silent by what he has not seen but can hear down on the lawn. 'It doesn't care now, Hart. Without Beth, it's gone wild.'

Hart stands up, delicately balanced on his feet like an invalid rising from a wheelchair. Without looking out at what they will have to face, they briefly put their arms around each other's shoulders, and then move apart. Dante pulls at the window, and it squeals upward through the runners in the frame, until there is a gap wide enough for them to jump through. He hasn't realised how much smoke is in the room until it begins to drift under the raised window and into the cold air, where it disperses. Dante raises a leg to swing over the sill, when Hart puts a firm hand on his chest. 'I've taken in too much smoke,' he says, his voice hoarse and whispery. 'I won't get far. Let me go first. When you hit the ground, run.'

Dante shakes his head, feeling cold all over and sick inside that it has come to this, that there is no mercy or justice in the world, no well-earned escape. But before he can react, Hart drops both of his hands to the sill, swings a leg through the window, and then lazily rolls his body out. There is a hand on the ledge, the gingery hairs singed down to stubs, and then it vanishes, dropping away with the rest of him.

With the axe, crowbar and torches lost somewhere below in the burning house, Dante follows unarmed, taking in another mouthful of smoke through the scarf, which stings his gums. Feet first, his eyes streaming with tears, he falls for a long time before his boots hit the earth. Immediately he rolls sideways to break his fall.

When he opens his eyes, his ears alert to every sound, the world is a blur. He wipes at his eyes, and the glowing garden comes into partial focus, its edges and lines still hazy from his tears. 'Hart!' he cries out, and then, coughing, struggles to his hands and knees. He feels the grass cold in his palms, until the shooting pain of a thousand pins in his feet consumes him. He falls to his elbows. 'Hart!' he shouts again, staying still because the agony in him will not let him move. There is no answer.

'Jesus, no,' he says, suddenly aware of something crawling so fast in front of him that no man could outrun it, even with it so close to the ground like that. Straight across the indistinct and glowering grasses it goes, moving spidery and bare-boned on the soft ground, with something hanging from its jaws. 'You bastard,' Dante cries out, getting to his feet, more grief than anger in his words. 'You son of a bitch.' He takes two steps toward where it now pauses and trembles on the garden path, the vague impression of sockets and forehead turned to him. It rises. In the flapping of its surround, the shanks tense.

There is an explosion from within the house. A wave of heat hits Dante's back and pushes him tumbling forward. Fire snaps from the upstairs windows. At the back of the cottage a window shatters. Orange sparks fall through the obsidian air and are doused in the long grass by his boots. The Brown Man retreats from the glare and the heat.

But only for a moment. When the fire ebbs behind Dante, and the shadows in the garden lengthen once again, and the lash of the flames pauses, it moves forward, discarding the reddish bits that swing from its wet mouth. For the third time in his recent life, the Brown Man comes to claim Dante, and very quickly too. And it could be either a leg or an arm wrapped in winding that moves first with a feline tread, but then more of these steps follow, as if it is an animal that walks on four legs, until, suddenly, it is close enough for him to smell it. He flinches away with one hand held out, as if to fend it off.

The sweep of brown rags, with the black and yellow ivory in it, and a pocked forehead emerging, turns the world to wind. Everything slows down in those final moments and Dante thinks, this is me dying. It rears up before him, making him feel so light and so small, and then it falls at him. An arm swings fast, with longish finger-things cupped, quicker than a boom across the deck of a racing yacht, to smash him like a box of eggs. There is a clack of bone; air is punched from his body; the sight in his eyes remains in the place his body departs. Sky, earth, sky, earth, rolling around him in an upside-down world; and then a scream louder than amplified feedback pops his hearing and leaves a whine behind in his head. Everything goes black.

FORTY-FOUR

It is a hand on his shoulder that shakes him awake. Gently at first, but then the touch becomes vigorous. Although the impression of the fingers cupping his arm, and the softness of the palm of the hand, register in his concussed mind, he wants to stay in the warm and reddish peace that pulls like a deep sleep. But a sharp pain makes him recover – a severe stab of heat through his ribs on the left side, making his body suddenly feel as fragile as the thinnest glass. He takes a series of hurried but shallow breaths and opens his eyes. At first he thinks he is blind, but realises the dark and the damp all about is only flattened grass where he lies face-down in the turf.

Then he remembers how he came to be here. He gasps. Grass slips into his mouth. And all about him is the glow of heat from a big fire, keeping him warm and strangely comfortable on the ground. Flames rush upward and whoop through the cottage, close to him. The sound is loud and angry, and he smells smoke. It makes him cough, which hurts his ribs even more. The hand shakes him again. 'Dante, Dante, Dante,' someone says. Urgently spoken, with an American accent, the tone of voice makes it immediately clear to him that he is not out of danger. 'Dante, Dante, you're breathing. You gotta wake up.' It is Hart, and he is wheezing as he speaks. He sounds asthmatic.

Wanting to cry out with elation that his friend is still alive, but too scared to move quickly in case his entire body erupts in agony, Dante moves his head very slowly. His face drags through the damp grass. His head feels heavy, and he moans because his whole neck hurts too. Imagining his body is contorted, for a few seconds he is unable to feel his legs and is sure his feet are somewhere up above his head. Pulling his fingers into the palms of his hands makes him aware of where his arms are, and the sense of where the rest of his body is quickly follows. Carefully, he rolls onto his right side.

Hart smiles, his small face reddish in the firelight. Half of his beard has been trimmed away by flames, and the frames of his glasses look orange, as if they are molten. It is only the reflection of light, he realises. But then Hart turns his face, quickly, and looks away from the house, at the front garden.

Dante hears another voice too. It is raised and desperate and the words are slurred. What little he can hear shocks him. He recognises the voice.

'Eliot,' Dante says, and tries to shuffle around to look in the same direction as Hart. He groans, and has to close his eyes for a moment. Ribs again. Other parts of him fill with sensation too. One of his hands is numb save for a throb. A shinbone smarts and makes him think of cold water. And he has a severe headache. It starts behind the skin of his entire face, like a thin layer of gum pain, and then stretches to the back of his skull, where there is a pain so great he has to squint to see straight.

The wizened shape of a man is moving around the lawn. He staggers in circles and almost falls. His clothes are dark.

The creased trousers and grey overcoat look as if they are wet with something. 'He showed up,' Hart whispers, his voice tense. 'After it knocked you across the yard. I reckon he followed us out here.'

'Where is it?' Dante says quickly, but sees it before Hart says, 'Over there,' nodding toward the far corner of the paddock garden. 'What's happening?' he mutters, with one eye closed on the pain.

Hart coughs into the back of his hand. 'Eliot just came through the gate after we dropped out the window. He called it off you. It moved when he called it. Look, it's confused. It's not that smart, Dante. It's like an animal. Like a child even.'

Dante can see no more of it than what appears as a large shadow as it moves against the front wall of the garden. It is as if it can blend into the dark and become invisible when it chooses, and it seems anxious to be away from the house now. Not so quick or savage anymore, it appears to be baffled.

Tensing the muscles in his thighs and mercifully feeling no pain in his legs, Dante moves them behind his body and sits up, supported by his right arm. Every rib down his left side feels as if it is broken and poking into his organs. He thinks of a sausage on a wooden toothpick and moans.

'You can't stay here,' Eliot roars. In one hand he holds a bottle. Bowing his head to cough after his outburst, he looks exhausted, like a man all bent up and breathless after running a marathon. The shadow watches Eliot, but draws closer to him. It seems as if Eliot is unaware of its crafty swaying, which gradually moves it along the wall toward him. 'She's gone now. There's no one to speak to you. You're lost. She's gone back . . .' Eliot's voice becomes gruff, and there is a loud crackle inside the cottage. Dante strains his ears, trying to catch Eliot's words, but he can only hear fragments. 'I'm the last,' Eliot shouts, and then laughs like a hysteric. 'I couldn't do it with a belt, but I'll go in there.' Eliot jabs a hand at the house.

And then everything seems to speed up around Hart and Dante. Eliot dips his head and, with a burst of concentration, which they can see on his face when he passes them, he runs at a speed neither thinks him still capable of, straight at the burning wreck of the cottage. Recoiling in horror and shock, Hart says, 'Jesus, no.' Dante stays quiet.

It is as if his own shadow chases him when the thing by the wall leaps up and then pursues Eliot through the grass. But he must have soaked himself in something flammable. At the point where he is still three feet from the front door – from which a plume of black smoke funnels out, lit with orange sparks – he stops to allow his clothes to catch alight. Then, suddenly, his head is masked with a yellow and blue fire that runs up his face and streams from the back of his scalp. Headfirst, he launches himself across the threshold of the burning doorway, without even putting out his hands to break the fall. And when he falls inside, Dante and Hart hear nothing, as if he's landed on something soft.

The shadow scuttles in after him. It never slows down, until it too vanishes inside the great oven of stone and cinders. And before Hart and Dante can comprehend what they have seen, the brown thing runs back out of the burning cottage, dragging a limp shape behind it. Chased by flames and smoking white inside its folds and wraps, it moves at an incredible speed across the grass and then up and over the garden wall, until it is gone from sight. They hear nothing more and, with a sense of relief that in itself exhausts each of them, they see no more of it either, nor the blackened and twitching thing it carries, held by a foot.

Still too scared to move in case his spine is injured, Dante lies on the grass and looks at Hart, who sits cross-legged beside him, wiping at his mouth and wheezing. Neither speaks for a long time. Part of them expects a return of the horror, for the night never to end until their hearts cease to beat. In the unreality of the night, in the intensity of its every second, they just stay huddled together, beside the burning cottage. Plumes of black smoke pour from the windows of the upper storey, and in the roof black timbers can now be seen peeking through the smoking tiles that cling to and then occasionally drop from them. From inside the building crackles, snaps and gusts of fire can be heard, and now the trees on the boundary of the property, closest to the house, are beginning to smoulder also. It is the sight of burning hedgerow that makes Hart speak. Wincing, the grease and soot stretching wide across his small mouth and incomplete beard, he says, 'It's gone now. We should move.'

Dante nods, still squinting his eyes. 'My ribs. I think they're broken.'

'Just take it easy then.' Hart looks about the lawn and begins licking his lips. 'I got to think. My lungs are all fucked and I got burned on my neck. Feels bad too.' He looks down at Dante. 'Can you stand up?'

'Maybe,' Dante says, but feels his face go white under the smudges at just the thought of it.

Hart stands over Dante. 'Come on, we got to blow, like we started a fire and people died in it. Give me your arms.'

'Painkillers,' Dante mutters. 'In my jacket pocket. Give me some first. I'll swallow them dry.'

Gently, Hart removes the bottle from Dante's jacket pocket. He unscrews the lid, takes two himself, and then slips the last three between Dante's cracked lips. 'Thing hit you so hard, buddy, I was sure you were dead. Man, you flew right across the yard.'

Dante grins through his discomfort. 'Thought it had you in its mouth.'

Hart closes his eyes and shudders. He points at something white in the grass near the path. 'No, that was her. We were next. Eliot saved us. He was still a link to it. He . . .' Hart pauses. 'He knew it. It was him and Ben Carter. And the thing in that girl.' Hart looks away and blows out a mouthful of air. 'That girl.'

Dante swallows. 'We had no choice.'

'I know, I know, I know,' Hart says, softly, keeping his eyes shut for a moment. 'Shit. Let's get you walking,' he then adds, his voice more urgent from his need to be active and not to dwell on what has been done.

'It's just my head and ribs, I think,' Dante says, as Hart reaches for his arms. 'And some burns.' Hart lifts him slowly from the grass. 'Stop! No, slowly, slowly. Hart, go slow. Jesus, it hurts.' But then he is on his feet, with his right arm held across his ribs and the numb hand hanging loose at his side.

Hart has a limp from when he dropped from the window. 'We got to go to the hospital.'

'We need to, but . . .'

'What?'

'Maybe we should hold off a while. If we go in stinking of

515

smoke, we could get blamed for the fires in town. There might be nothing left back there. Jesus, it could be really bad. And they know I bought all that fuel from the garage. Should we go to Dundee or something? Say we crashed the car, maybe.'

Hart looks at the tottering figure before him. 'We'd never make it. We got to go to town. Think I'll need grafts on my neck?' Dante looks at the swollen skin on the back of Hart's neck. There are some blisters too. From the light of the fire it looks like bad sunburn. Dante shakes his head, having no idea. 'No, it's just sore.'

Hart looks up slowly. He grins. 'We're alive, buddy. Don't you know it. We're here.'

Dante smiles, but suddenly feels a grief so profound, his throat clots and he can't swallow. Hart leaves him standing there, and begins the grisly business of throwing Beth's servants through the front door of the burning cottage. 'They have to go in the house,' Hart says, with a dreamy expression on his face, as he drags something through the grass toward the snap and pop of the fire. 'In there. They have to go back in there.' He is in shock, Dante thinks, and then turns away to face the dark road and the hills beyond it.

'Then we better split. They'll see the fire from Knoxville,' Hart mutters in a methodical tone of voice, looking over the tops of his glasses as he huffs by, hauling a long and white thing through the grass by its wrist. But Dante can't think anymore about what happens next. Tears fill his eyes. And then his whole body begins to shake.

FORTY-FIVE

Sitting on a long beach, in a spot where the sand is soft on the barrier of dunes that protects the golf courses, is a young man with the collar of his jacket zipped up to his neck, and a red scarf pulled around his chin and ears. Even though the sun is bright and yellow there is always a cold wind on this shore, but his long ponytail of black hair shines like a thin snake in the morning light and rests, occasionally twitching in a breeze, all the way down the worn leather of his coat. Hunched over, alone, he looks out at the horizon, and tries to find that quiver of excitement at opportunities awaiting, of sights beginning to unfold in the imagination, that are always engendered when one sees a giant body of water on which solitary ships drift across the horizon. But inside he is still, numbed, and only conscious of the gentle rise and fall of his chest from the shallow breaths that go through him.

He lights a cigarette slowly, not even looking at the one unbandaged hand that fumbles with a lighter and the red and white packet of smokes. With the cigarette lit, he bends forward, closer to his knees, and if you happened to be walking past him, you would hear him gasp, and in his eyes you would see a glassiness, as if all of his concentration is suddenly focused inward. He inhales smoke and coughs. The cigarette drops from his hand, and for a long while he is occupied with suppressing these coughs and the pain they cause him. After the spluttering stops, he wheezes to get his breath back, and makes no move to retrieve the still-smoking cigarette that lies in the sand at his feet.

People are dotted about the beach, walking dogs, watching their children, some holding hands. Frequently, they stop and exchange words, and you get a sense that something important has happened here, something significant that makes strangers stop and unite for a moment to discuss a common matter, an affair that has caused surprise and mystery, and horror and grief, in a confusion of equal amounts.

'They say it's the saboteurs,' a woman in a red coat says to a group of young girls who stop to smile at her little dog. She uses a hand to pat down her white hair, which is picked up and flopped about her head by the wind. 'Even in our town. You girls be careful. Don't be fooled. Things have changed here.' The girls smile awkwardly and walk off. One of them giggles, and the old lady looks sad as her little white dog trots back to her feet, holding a red rubber ball in its mouth. It looks up at her and blinks.

'He's disappeared,' another stroller says to his wife, who has her arm hooked around his elbow, resting against him as she walks. 'This Coldwell chap. They can't find him. I didn't even know he was here in the first place. A man like that at the university, and we never knew. And to think of what they pulled out of his house.'

His wife shakes her head and, for a moment, she closes her eyes.

'All those bodies burned to bits,' he says, and then they turn to each other and stagger a little when a strong gust of wind bashes into them. He puts his hand on his head to stop his hat leaving.

Down at the shoreside, three young men look for stones flat enough to skim off the sea surface. Their feet splash about on the dark sand, sodden with water, as they wait for the next small wave. 'No, no,' the tallest one shouts at his two friends. All of their faces are lit up with excitement. 'The cottage was arson. The places in town weren't. They don't know how they started. I heard a copper talking. It was only the lecturer's cottage with the bodies in it that was burned deliberately.'

'Yeah, sorry, that's right. But there's so many versions,' his friend says, and then whips a stone out to sea, which skims in three hops and sinks sideways. 'They're saying it was a cult started by Coldwell. A suicide cult.'

'I heard that too. It was in the *Telegraph*,' the third man says, looking at the silhouette of the town, up the beach by the breakwaters and cliffs, that now seems more interesting to him than it ever did before. 'But that doesn't explain what people reckon they saw in the dorms. Did you read what those second-year girls said in *The Independent*?' Before his friends can answer, he continues. 'After the fires started, they all saw something run down the Scores. And it wasn't a man, they say.'

'But that's crap,' the first speaker says. 'There'll be so many stories about the ghost. Loads of people claim they saw it. I even heard this morning that they called a priest out to the boarding school.'

'Yeah,' the second man says. He nods his head. 'A porter sounded the alarm. After some nun was found with her neck broken, I heard. But they're keeping it quiet because of all the kids that were in there. They saw it happen. It was going for the kids, I heard. I heard that this black thing, or whatever, was trying to get into their rooms.'

And then they all fall silent and, to distract themselves, as if uncomfortable with the thought, they look about on the sand for more stones to throw at the sea.

Back up in the dunes, the long-haired man is coughing again, and his face looks even paler from a distance because of the red scarf he wears. With the bandaged hand, he dabs at his lips and then puts both of his hands under his arms. He left the hospital at first light. He checked himself out, against the wishes of the staff, but left his friend behind. He was too ill to leave. He was still asleep with a plastic mask on his face.

From behind him, he hears feet scuffing through the sand. Alert to steps and sounds in a way he never was before, he turns his head despite the discomfort it causes him. He frowns. He blinks with disbelief. Recognition dawns across his face and he almost smiles. He swallows, and his jaw trembles from the emotion he appears to suffer.

'There you are,' a breathless girl says. Her slender body is wrapped up in a green fleece jacket and blue jeans. 'I've been looking everywhere for you. Oh thank God, you're all right, Dante.' She talks quickly as she skids down the sand dunes. 'I got the train up yesterday, when I heard about the fires, and I went to the address you gave me. At the flat. When I saw it all burned out, I panicked. I saw them cleaning it up, and I saw a bit of guitar. I broke down. And this policeman came over and said there were squatters in the flat, but nobody was hurt there. He said they were still looking for them. Then I came here just by chance to get my head together and I saw the Land Rover.'

In a daze, the young man watches her. She sits down beside him. When she sees the look on his face, the bandaged hand, and the way his body is cramped up, she goes quiet. His clothes are filthy and he smells of smoke. 'The fire?' she asks.

He nods, but doesn't speak.

'Where's Tom?' she asks. Her voice is quiet, almost a whisper.

He looks at the sand and shakes his head. Then he covers his eyes by putting the unbandaged hand across his eyebrows. The girl puts her arm around his shoulders and rests her head against his temple. He puts his arm around her waist and begins to whisper in her ear. He whispers something that no one else on the beach or in the town will ever hear.

ACKNOWLEDGEMENTS

I would like to acknowledge the advice and support I received at the University of St Andrews on the Creative Writing Masters programme in 1997 and 1998. Professor Douglas Dunn, Brian McCabe, Jenny Itzenson and Brian St John made it a rewarding, stimulating and memorable year for me. Dave Addison and Adam Berger from Anthropology were also instrumental in helping me to create the character of Doctor Hart Miller.

In one respect this novel is as much about the actual town of St Andrews as anything else, a place with a timeless and curious magic all of its own. Throughout, I've tried to do justice to its graces and remain faithful to its topography, though creative licence has been used to alter the locations of some of the schools. And I can assure the reader that neither the cottage of Professor Eliot Coldwell nor the bewitched village of Knoxville exists (at least not at the locations given in the story).

Witchcraft and Sorcery by John A. Rush, *Appearances of the Dead* by Ronald C. Finucane, *Witchcraft and Black Magic* by the Reverend Montague Summers, *The Terror that Comes in the Night* by David Hufford, *Witchcraft and Magic in Sixteenth and Seventeenth-century Europe* by Geoffrey Scarre, *Witchcraft in Europe 1100–1700: A Documentary*

History by Alan C. Kors, *The European Witch-craze of the Sixteenth and Seventeenth-centuries* by H. R. Trevor-Roper, *Transition and Revolution* by Robert M. Kingdon were essential in my research, but I admit taking great liberties with both European and Scottish history and folklore to suit my own malign purposes. The verse quoted in chapter four is from Aleister Crowley's *King Ghost*, the lyrics sung by Barbara in chapter forty-one are from 'Give Him A Great Big Kiss' by the Shangri-Las, and the quotation in chapter twenty-five is from *An Elizabethan Devil-Worshipper's Prayer Book*.

Without the encouragement of the Nevill clan – mother, father, my brother Simon and sister Melissa – I might easily have spent three years doing something else, far less satisfying, than cooking up this *Banquet for the Damned*. And without the interest, the wit and the wisdom of James Marriott, John Coulthart, Ramsey Campbell, Peter Crowther of PS Publishing, and Nick Gevers, this night terror may never have been shared.

Penultimately, I'd like to acknowledge the *Outsider* books and ideas of Colin Wilson not only for the comfort and confirmation they still give me today, but for being the inspiration behind Professor Eliot Coldwell. And, finally, it would be most unwise of me – lest I'm visited by something unpleasant in the night – not to own up to the considerable debt I owe those great masters of terror, Walter de la Mare, M. R. James and Algernon Blackwood.

If you enjoyed *Banquet for the Damned*,
turn over for the prologue and first chapter
of Adam Nevill's

Apartment 16 . . .

PROLOGUE

When he heard the noise Seth stopped and stared, as if trying to see through the front door of apartment sixteen, the teak veneer aglow with a golden sheen. Right after descending the stairs from the ninth floor and crossing the landing the sounds began. Same as the last three nights, on his 2 a.m. patrol of the building.

Snapping out of his torpor, he flinched and took a quick step away from the door. Looming up the opposite wall, the shadow of his lanky body stretched out its arms as if grasping at a support. The sight of it made him start. 'Fuck.'

He'd never liked this part of Barrington House, but couldn't say why with any certainty. Maybe it was just too dark. Perhaps the lights were not set right. The head porter said there was nothing wrong with them, but they often cast shapes down the stairs Seth was walking up. It was as if a person descending was being preceded by their shadow; the impression of spiky limbs flickering ahead of them before they appeared around a bend in the staircase, sometimes even convinced Seth he'd also heard the swish of cloth and the *pumpf, pumpf, pumpf* of determined feet approaching. Only no one ever appeared, and there was never anyone up there when he turned a corner.

But the noise in apartment sixteen was far more alarming than any shadow.

Because during the early hours of the morning in this exclusive niche of London there is little to compete with the silence of night. Outside Barrington House the warren of streets behind the Knightsbridge Road are inclined to remain peaceful. Occasionally, out front, a car will drive around Lowndes Square. Or inside, the nightwatchman becomes aware of the electric lights in the communal areas, humming like insects with their black faces pressed against the recalcitrance of glass. But from the hours of one until five the residents sleep. Indoors, there is nothing but ambient sound.

And number sixteen was unoccupied. The head porter once told him it had been empty for over fifty years. But for the fourth consecutive night Seth's attention had been drawn to it. Because of the bumping behind the door, against the door. Something he'd previously dismissed as a random noise in an old building. One that had stood for a hundred years. Something loose in a draught maybe. Something like that. But tonight it was insistent. It was louder than ever before. It was . . . determined. Had been stepped up a notch. Seemed directed at him and timed to coincide with his usually oblivious passage to the next set of stairs, during the hour when your body temperature drops and when most people die. An hour when he, the nightwatchman, was paid to patrol nine storeys of stairwell and the ancient landings on each floor. And it had never before escalated into a sudden eruption of noise like this.

A clattering of furniture across a marble floor, as if a chair or small table in the reception hall of the flat had been knocked aside. Perhaps toppling over, and even breaking. Not something that should be heard at any hour in a place as respectable as Barrington House.

Nervous, he continued to watch the door, as if anticipating its opening. His stare fixed on the brass number 16, polished so brightly it looked like white gold. He dared not even blink, in case it swung away from his eyes and revealed the source of the commotion. A sight he might not be able to bear. He wondered if his legs possessed the strength to carry him down eight flights of stairs in a hurry. Perhaps with something in pursuit.

He killed the thought. A little shame warmed the aftermath of his sudden fright. He was a thirty-one-year-old man, not a child. Six feet tall, and a paid deterrent. Not that he anticipated doing anything beyond being a reassuring presence when he took the job. But this had to be investigated.

Struggling to hear over the thump of his heart in his ears, Seth leaned towards the front door and placed his left ear an inch from the letter flap to listen. Silence.

His fingers made a move for the letter box. If he knelt down and pushed the brass flap inward, enough light should fall from the landing to illumine some of the hallway on the other side of the front door.

But what if somebody looked back at him?

His hand paused, then withdrew.

No one was permitted to go inside sixteen, a rule pressed upon him by the head porter when he first began the night job six months earlier. Such a strict observance was not unusual for portered apartment buildings in Knightsbridge. Even after a reasonable lottery win an ordinary member of the public would struggle to afford a flat in Barrington House. The three-bedroom apartments never sold for less than one million pounds, and the service charge cost an additional eleven thousand per annum. Many residents filled their apartments with antiques; others guarded their privacy like war criminals and shredded their paperwork for the porters to collect in bin bags. The same instruction forbidding access existed for another five empty flats in the building. But during his patrols Seth had not once heard noises inside any of them.

Maybe someone had been given permission to stay in the apartment and one of the day porters had forgotten to record the information in the desk ledger. Unlikely, as both day porters, Piotr and Jorge, had frowned with incredulity when he first mentioned the disturbances during the morning changeover. Which left one other plausible explanation at such an hour: an intruder had broken in from the outside.

But then an intruder would need to scale the exterior of the building with a ladder. Seth had patrolled the front of the building in the last ten minutes and there had been no ladder. He could always go and wake Stephen, the head porter, and ask him to open the door. But he baulked at the thought of disturbing him at this hour; the head porter's wife was an invalid. She occupied most of his time between duties, leaving him exhausted at the end of each day.

Lowering himself to one knee, Seth pushed open the letter flap and peered into the darkness. A shock of cold air rushed past his face and with it came a smell that was familiar: a woody-camphor scent reminiscent of his grandmother's gigantic wardrobe that had been like a secret cabin to him as a boy, and an aroma not dissimilar to reading rooms in university libraries or museums built by the Victorians. A trace of former residents and antiquity, suggesting vacancy rather than use.

The vague light that fell past his head and shoulders brightened a small section of the reception hall inside the flat. He could make out the murky outline of a telephone table against one wall, an indistinct doorway on the right-hand side, and a few square metres of floor tiled in black and white marble. The rest of the space was in shadow or complete darkness.

He screwed his eyes up against the uncomfortable draught that swelled against the front of his face and tried to see more. And failed. But his scalp prickled on account of what he heard.

Squinting into the umbra, he could hear the suggestion of something heavy being dragged at the far end of the hallway; as if a significant weight wrapped up in sheets, or supported on a large rug, was being moved in short bursts of exertion away from the tiny slot of light he had made in the front door. As the sounds receded further into the far confines of the apartment, they lessened, then ceased.

Seth wondered if he should call out and offer the darkness a challenge, but could not summon the strength to open his mouth. Acutely, he now felt he was being watched from down there. And this sudden sense of scrutiny and vulnerability made him want to close the mail flap, stand up and step away.

He dithered. It was hard to think clearly. He was tired. Weary to the marrow, clumsy and confused, paranoid even. He was thirty-one, but working these shifts made him feel eighty-one. Clear signs of sleep deprivation common to the night worker. But he had never hallucinated in his life. There was someone inside flat sixteen.

'Jesus.'

A door opened. Inside. Down in the dark part he couldn't see. Must have been about halfway down the hallway. It clicked open and swung wide on its trajectory, emitting a slow creak until it banged against a wall.

He did not move or blink. Just stared and anticipated the arrival of something from out of the darkness.

But there was only expectation, and silence.

Though not a total absence of sound for long. Seth began to hear something. It was faint, but closing, as if travelling towards his face.

It grew out of the hushed unlit interior of the flat. A kind of rushing sound not dissimilar to what he'd heard inside large seashells. A suggestion of faraway winds. He had a curious sense of a great distance existing at the other end of the hallway. Down there. Where he couldn't see a damn thing.

The breeze thickened where he crouched and peered. Carrying something with it. Inside it. A suggestion of a voice, far off, but still keen to be heard. A voice that sounded like it was moving in a circle miles away. No, there was more than one, there were voices. But the cries were so distant no words could be understood.

He moved his face further away from the door, his mind clutching for an explanation. Was a window open in there somewhere? Could a radio be muttering, or was it a television with the volume turned low? Impossible, the place was empty.

The wind swept closer and the voices grew louder. They were gaining a precedence in the movement of the air. And though they failed to define themselves, their tone was clear, filling him with a greater unease, and then with horror.

These were the cries of the terrified. Someone was screaming. A woman? No, it couldn't be. Now it was closer it sounded like an animal, and he thought of a baboon he had once seen in a zoo, roaring with scarlet lips peeling back from black gums and long yellow teeth.

It was swept away, the scream replaced by a chorus of

moans, hapless in their despair but competing with each other in the cold wind. A hysterical voice, relentless in its panic, swooped closer, dominating the other voices that suddenly retreated as if pulled back by a swift tide, until he could almost hear what the new voice was saying.

He let the letter flap slam shut and there was an immediate and profound silence.

Standing up and stepping away he tried to gather his wits. Disoriented by the hammering of his pulse, he wiped the moisture from his brow with the sleeve of his pullover and noticed the dryness of his mouth, as if he had been inhaling dust.

He desperately wanted to leave the building. To go home and lie down. To end this strange sensitivity and the rush of impressions that accompanied lack of sleep. That's all it was, surely.

Taking the carpeted stairs two at a time, he fled down through the west wing to the ground-floor reception. He quickly walked past his desk and left the building through the front doors. Outside, he stood on the pavement and looked up, counting the white stone balconies until his eyes reached the eighth floor.

All of the windows were closed, not open, not even ajar, but shut tight and flush within the white frames, and the interior of apartment sixteen was further sealed by thick curtains; drawn day and night against London, and against the world.

But his scalp stiffened beneath his hair, because he could still hear, above him, or even inside his head, ever so faintly, the far-off wind and the clamour of unrecognizable voices, as if he had brought them down here, with him.

ONE

Apryl went straight to her inheritance from the airport. And it was easy to find, direct from Heathrow on the navy blue Piccadilly Line to the station called Knightsbridge.

Swept up the concrete stairs by the bustle and rush of people about her, she emerged with her backpack onto the sidewalk. She'd been on the subway for so long the steely light smarted against the back of her eyes. But if the map was right this was the Knightsbridge Road. She moved into the push of the crowd.

Buffeted from behind, and then knocked to the side by a sharp elbow, she immediately failed to move in step with the strange city. She felt irrelevant and very small. It made her apologetic but angry at the same time.

She shuffled across the narrow sidewalk and took shelter in a shop doorway. Knee joints stiff and her body damp beneath her leather jacket and gingham shirt, she took a few seconds and watched the shunt, race and break of the human traffic before her, with Hyde Park as a backdrop, a landscape painting dissolving into a far-off mist.

It was hard to concentrate on any particular building, determined face, or boutique window around her, because London was constantly moving before and about every static feature. Thousands of people marched up and down the street and darted across it whenever the red buses, white vans, delivery trucks, and cars slowed for a second. She wanted to look at everything at the same time, and to know it, and to understand her place in it all, but the sheer energy sweeping up and down the street started to numb the workings behind her forehead, making her squint, like her mind was already giving up and thinking about sleep instead.

Looking at the map in the guidebook, she peered at the short and simple route to Barrington House that she must have looked at a hundred times since leaving New York eight hours earlier. All she needed to do was walk down Sloane Street, then turn left into Lowndes Square. A cab couldn't have dropped her much closer than the subway. Her great-aunt's building was somewhere on the square. Then it was just a case of following the numbers to the correct door. A good sign and one that infused her with relief; the frustration of trying to read road signs and figure out which direction she was heading on streets like this would have been paralysing.

But she would need to rest soon. The prospect of visiting London, and of seeing whatever it was that Great-aunt Lillian had bequeathed her and her mother had disrupted her sleep for over a week and she'd not managed so much as a micro-nap on the plane. But when could a mind ever rest in this place?

The short walk from the station to Lowndes Square confirmed her suspicions that Great-aunt Lillian had not been poor. On the map, the very fact this neighbourhood was so close to Buckingham Palace, and Belgravia with all those embassies, and Harrods, the store she had heard of back home, made her realize her great-aunt had not spent the last sixty years of her life in a slum. But that knowledge was still no preparation for her first sight of Knightsbridge: the tall white buildings with their long windows and black railings; the plethora of luxury cars gleaming at the kerbs; the thin blonde English girls with clipped accents, teetering about in high heels and clutching designer handbags that made her backpack feel like a sack of shit. With her biker jacket, turn-ups and Converse boots, and with her black hair styled like Bettie Page, she felt the tension of discomfort bend her head forward with the shame and diffidence of the miscast.

At least there weren't many people out in Lowndes Square to see her in this state: a couple of Arab women alighting from a silver Merc, and a tall blonde Russian girl talking angrily into a phone clamped to her ear. And after the melee of the Knightsbridge Road, the elegance of the square was soothing. The apartment buildings and hotels formed an unbroken and graceful rectangle around the long oval park in its centre, where short trees and empty flower beds could be seen through railings. The unlaboured harmony of the mansion blocks stilled the air and deflected the noise elsewhere.

'No way.' She and her mom now owned an apartment here? At least until they sold it for a stack of cash. A thought that immediately rankled. She wanted to live here. It kept her great-aunt here for over sixty years and Apryl could see why. The place was classic, flawless, and effortlessly exuded the sense of a long history. She imagined the polite but indifferent faces of butlers behind every front door. Aristocrats must live here. And diplomats. And billionaires. People unlike her and her mother. 'Shit, Mama, you're just not gonna believe this,' she said out loud.

She'd only ever seen one photo of Great-aunt Lillian, when Lillian was a little girl. Dressed in a curious white gown matching that of her elder sister, Apryl's grandmother, Marilyn. In the picture Lillian held her big sister's hand. They stood next to each other with sulky smiles in the yard of their home in New Jersey. But Lillian and Marilyn were closer at that time than they ever were after. Lillian moved to London during the war to work for the US military as a secretary. Where she met an English guy, a pilot, and married him. She never came home.

Lillian and her granny Marilyn must have exchanged letters or cards because Lillian knew when Apryl had been born. She used to get birthday cards from Lillian when she was little. With beautiful English money inside. Pounds. Really colourful paper with pictures of kings and dukes and battles and god knows what else on them. And watermarks when you held them up against a light that she thought were magical. She wanted to keep them, not cash them for dollars, which looked like toy money in comparison. It always made her want to visit England. And here she was for the first time.

But Lillian went quiet on them a long time ago. They even stopped getting Christmas cards before Apryl was ten. Her mother was too busy raising her alone to find out why. And when Granny Marilyn died, her mother wrote to Lillian at the address in Barrington House, but there was no response. So they just assumed she'd died too, over in England, where she'd lived a life they knew nothing of, the weak connection with that generation of the family finally severed, for ever.

Until two months back, when a probate lawyer sent a letter to inform the last surviving relatives of their inheritance following the 'sad passing of Lillian Archer'. She and her mother were still in a daze. A death, occurring eight weeks previously, and leading to the bequest to them of an apartment in London. Knightsbridge, London, no less. Right here where she was standing, outside Barrington House: the great white building seated solemnly at the foot of the square. Rising up, so many floors dignified in strong white stone, the classicism tempered with slender art-deco flourishes around the window frames. A place so well-proportioned and proud, she could only feel daunted before the grand entrance, with its big, brass-framed glass doors, its flower baskets and ornamental columns either side of the marble stairs. 'No way.'

Beyond her reflection in the pristine glass of the front doors she could see a long, carpeted corridor with a big reception desk at the far end. And behind it she received an impression of two men with neat haircuts, each wearing a silver waistcoat. 'Oh shit.'

She laughed to herself. Feeling ridiculous, as if ordinary life had suddenly transformed into cinematic fantasy, she checked the address on the papers they had received from the lawyer: a letter, with a contract and deeds that would get her the keys. To this.

No doubt about it. This was the place. Their place.